Spellbound

SPELLBOUND

The Changeling Prince
The Conjurer Princess
''Just Another Dragon-Slaying''

VIVIAN VANDE VELDE

FANTASY

Published by arrangement with
HarperCollins*Publishers*
    10 East 53rd Street
    New York, N. Y. 10022-5299
and with the author

Visit the Science Fiction Book Club on the Internet at
www.sfbc.com

ISBN 1-56865-689-0

Contents

Author's Note

I wrote these stories in reverse order.

This means, of course, that I started with the short story, "Just Another Dragon-Slaying." When my critique group read it, their reaction was unanimous. They said, "Yes, well, but . . ." and started asking all sorts of questions: How had two such different people as Lylene and Weiland ended up together? Where had her magic come from? Who was the person "that had been no friend—hers or Weiland's"—who had taught her magic? That sort of thing: background questions.

How was I supposed to know?

So I wrote a novel to find out. The novel—at the time I just called it LYLENE—took place in the time before the short story began and explained Lylene's background. But it didn't sell, at least not right away. (Editors sent "Close, but not close enough," letters.) I waited for new publishing companies to form, or for old editors to retire. In the meantime "Just Another Dragon-Slaying" was published in XANADU 2. Still no luck with LYLENE. But periodically I would dust the manuscript off, work on it, tighten it. And, after nine years, I began to wonder about Weiland: How had he come to be the person he was? Why was he so skittish about magic? What were his regrets? You know—that sort of thing: background questions.

I had just started working on a second novel (cleverly titled WEILAND) that, taking place several years before the action depicted in LYLENE, explored those questions when Jane Yolen, my editor for young adult novels, suggested I send LYLENE to HarperPrism. Editor Caitlin Blasdell said she liked the story, and in fact she wanted to know if I had a sequel.

Not exactly, I told her, but something *like* a sequel could be arranged . . .

So that's the history behind these stories. At the moment I have no plans for another, but who knows? In another nine years or so, I may feel compelled to work my way backwards yet again, perhaps to cover Shile's background.

No plans—but I wouldn't say it couldn't happen.

The
Changeling Prince

*With appreciation to Joanne, who nagged me
into writing this,
and to Toni, who listened to me talk it out
day after day after day*

1

Weiland woke up naked, in the snow, in a part of the forest he didn't recognize, with blood in his mouth. His last clear memory was settling down to sleep by the fire in Daria's hall.

But there were other memories that weren't clear—vague and dark yet familiar memories—which argued with his impression that he had done nothing wrong, that he had given Daria no reason to punish him.

Though that was never a guarantee with Daria.

Still, he tried to convince himself that this could conceivably be a prank by Lon or one of the others, that they might have thought it humorous to pick him up while he slept, to carry him outdoors . . .

It didn't make sense. As near as he'd ever been able to work out, Weiland was sixteen years old, with most of those years spent in Daria's household. Sixteen years had made a light sleeper of him precisely because it was the sort of thing they *would* find humorous.

He could no longer ignore the pain in his right leg, which was more than the cold could account for. He raised himself on his arms, and looked. His ankle was held fast by the teeth of a metal wolf trap, which was certainly beyond what even Lon would dare. And besides, he could see the tracks, padded and four-footed in the snow, which ended at the impression his own body had made. He had apparently already struggled: The trap's teeth had worked their way down to the bone in ragged gouges that went from knee to ankle. Still, bad as the injury looked, it wasn't enough to account for the blood in his mouth, which was what he'd hoped: that the blood was his own—a bad situation, but not as bad as . . .

His stomach clenched in on itself. He managed to get to almost sitting before he began to vomit. The spasms brought up—as he had known they would—raw meat, barely chewed.

A wolf's meal.

There was a time when he'd have examined what his stomach brought up, frantic to find fur or hollow birds' bones, proof that he hadn't preyed on humans while possessed of a wolf's body. But Lon had caught him at it, and gloated that he'd once witnessed Weiland's killing a small child, when Weiland had stayed a wolf long enough to digest what he'd devoured. Of course, anything Lon said was suspect, and particularly this, since everyone knew what Weiland was most afraid of hearing. *Liar*, Weiland called him. *Fool*, Lon retaliated. It had ended, eventually, with Daria punishing both of them, though in some moods she enjoyed seeing her company fight. But this time she had turned Weiland once more into a wolf, and—since Lon enjoyed his true form, a bear—*his* sentence had been to forego his supper. *Liar*, Weiland had said. But since then, he no longer looked for proof that he hadn't killed a human, for fear he might find proof of exactly the opposite.

He continued heaving even after his stomach was empty, first bringing up throat-burning bile, then nothing, until he felt as though each convulsion would bring up his stomach itself.

Finally finished, he rested his face in the crook of his arm, covered with sweat despite the freezing air, which was surely more danger to him than anything he'd eaten—anything he'd done—while in the form of a wolf. There were tears in his eyes, but that was purely from exertion, not from the pain caused by inadvertently jerking his leg so that the trap's metal teeth scraped against bone, and certainly not from emotion.

The fact that Daria wasn't here to see meant nothing: Daria didn't believe in crying, so she had beaten all the crying out of Weiland by the time he was four. That was when she had first told him that the pelt on her bed was his mother. He didn't remember his mother, he didn't remember roaming the woods as a wolf cub or Daria capturing him, or her working that first humanizing transformation on him. In fact, he had spent more of his growing years human than wolf, which might have been why he alone—of all Daria's creatures—preferred his human form. But he'd cried when he learned about his mother, and Daria had beaten him badly enough that she had to work her healing magic on him afterwards, or he would have died.

Now he struggled to remember: What could he have done this time that Daria would wait until he was asleep, then work a transformation on him in her own hall? Surely that had to be inconvenient—dangerous, even—for when he was a wolf he forgot what it was to be human. The sudden thought that what he had just vomited may well have been one of his companions caused his stomach to spasm again.

When the cold was enough to cut through his misery, he sat up—carefully, so as not to drag his leg further through the trap—and he took a handful of snow to clear the taste of blood and vomit from his mouth.

It was so cold, it was akin to burning.

But he'd already waited too long to start worrying about getting loose, if he'd ever had a chance. The blood loss, the vomiting, the shivering that had set in from the cold—all conspired to make him too weak to pry open the jaws of the trap. His fingers stuck to the metal. Skin tore loose, but feeling was already going. Besides, even if he should get free of the trap, what then? Either Daria knew exactly where he was and would fetch him when she estimated he'd learned whatever lesson she thought he needed to learn. Or she didn't know—and that would leave little enough likelihood of his finding shelter within the distance he could travel, even assuming the bone wasn't broken.

Weiland lay back down and trusted to his luck, despite the knowledge that if he were truly lucky, he wouldn't be there. He clenched his fists to hold as much warmth as he could in his fingers, and he pulled his knees up to his chest, as well as he could without dragging against the trap.

Surely, he told himself, the fact that he was in human form proved that Daria was nearby, working her magic on him, for Daria readily admitted that there was a geographic limit beyond which her magic wouldn't reach. Surely, Daria just wanted to make him suffer longer. Even if he lost fingers or toes to the cold, even if he were on the point of dying, her magic would heal him. It had before.

As the cold made him grow sleepy, he wondered if Daria's magic was strong enough to raise the dead.

It was a bad thought to drift off with, for someone who hoped to be lucky enough to die.

2

He wasn't dead.

Daria's voice came from far away—flitting up and down and around corners to reach him. "This is going to be quite painful."

Weiland didn't need Daria's warning. Her healings often hurt worse than the original injuries: burning, ripping, bone-scraping power that skittered and clawed over his entire body, leaving him panting and too weak to rise from his bed for days, even the time he'd only started out with a sprained wrist. But she'd been annoyed, on that occasion, when he'd been unable to serve at dinner, the platters too heavy for his unsteady grip. The fact that her magic made him unfit to serve for two additional days meant nothing to her.

She must have been mightily annoyed this time, too, Weiland realized in the moments of clarity between dizziness and pain: She had obviously healed him enough that he could hear and understand, taking things in stages rather than wasting the pain on someone too far gone to feel it.

Her cool, soft fingers gently brushed his sweat-dampened hair from his forehead. Not that there was that much hair: Swordmaster Kedj made everyone keep their hair cropped short so that an enemy couldn't catch hold of it. Daria was just delaying, making sure he had his wits collected.

Weiland opened his eyes. He was in the hall, on his own sleeping pallet on the floor near the fireplace—the choice spot of Daria's company because—though he was the youngest—he'd been one of the longest in her household, and because since this last year he was strong enough to keep it.

Daria's face hovered a handspan from him; she was practically reclining next to him for the best possible view. She smiled. Daria was a beautiful woman, and she looked younger than she could possibly be, for she had never aged since Weiland had come to be with her. "Welcome back," she said. And let her magic loose on him.

It was always difficult to tell what Daria wanted. She might be watching so closely, so intently, because she was in the mood to see him writhing in agony. But Weiland instinctively bit back his outcry of pain, and Daria continued to caress his face. Apparently she was in the mood for him to be brave. Weiland had long ago learned to always give Daria whatever she wanted; it was just a matter of figuring out *what* she wanted.

By the time the worst of it was over, he was barely able to keep still, and he hadn't managed to be perfectly quiet. Still, Daria leaned forward and kissed him on the forehead before leaving, so she must have been pleased.

His breath still coming in shuddering gasps, Weiland drifted off, too lightheaded to find the blanket to pull up around him, too weak to close his fingers around it even if he had.

It was going to take a lot longer than two days to recover from this.

Days passed. Difficult to tell how many, and it made no difference anyway. One day was much the same as another in Daria's hall. Seasons differed, with the need for warmer or lighter clothing, with the availability of food, and the frequency of travelers to intercept on their way over the hills. But the days did not differ, nor did years.

Gradually, Weiland became aware of being cold and realized the others had pulled him from his place by the fire while he couldn't retaliate. Occasionally someone would surreptitiously kick him, or trod on his fingers as though by accident, but Daria must have been keeping some measure of watch, for his blanket didn't disappear, and he was kept clean and provided with water and—as he became stronger—broth.

Eventually, Weiland opened his eyes and once again found Daria watching him, this time from the full distance of her standing height. "Don't you think this is getting a bit excessive?" she asked. "If you can manage to rouse yourself, I want to speak to you."

Immediately Weiland sat up, but since he was so lightheaded, he couldn't be certain he was upright.

Daria was gone by then. Had he taken only the few moments it had seemed, or had he blacked out? Daria wouldn't take lightly to being ignored. Regardless, Weiland was no sooner sitting up than he had to rest his head against his upraised knee.

Rohmar, passing by, stepped on the hand Weiland was supporting himself with, which may or may not have been due to Rohmar's natural clumsiness.

But the others were watching. Lon among them. Waiting for a sign of weakness. Hungry for a sign of weakness.

Weiland hooked his leg around Rohmar's, causing him to topple, much to the delight of the others, even Lon—who had no doubt assumed the position of leadership within the hour of Weiland's having been brought back to the hall helpless. Lon wouldn't be concerned about who held which of the lower ranks.

Rohmar gave him a look a loathing. But Rohmar was a coward—Weiland thought he was more rabbit than wolf, though he had seen him made—and after a long moment, Rohmar averted his eyes, pretending to be preoccupied with rubbing his foot.

Weiland took a long, slow look around the hall. There was no one conspicuously absent. He had no friends here, no one whose death he would mourn; but there was a difference between that and not caring whether he had eaten one of them. Weiland didn't let this show in his face. His face showed only disdain. His gaze ended with Lon, who grinned at him toothily, probably never suspecting the relief Weiland felt that he had, apparently, not eaten any of them. All Lon would care about was that Weiland was in no condition to challenge him. Weiland felt bruised all over, as though he'd rolled down a mountain slope of rocks. But he grinned back. "After Daria," he said, trying to sound menacing. And confident that he could take on any of them. And at the same time, to remind everyone that Daria seemed to be currently interested in his well-being, and she would probably take it amiss if Lon ripped his head off. Weiland hoped Lon had reasoned things out similarly.

Lon didn't react at all, and Weiland pulled the blanket up around himself since there was no sign of the clothes he'd been wearing before all this had started. When he stood, his legs almost gave out under him, which would have been a clear invitation for the others to jump him. Weakness was provocation in Daria's hall.

But he made it out of the hall without having to lean against walls or tables for support; and if their animal-born senses could hear the hammering of his heart and smell his fear and taste his pain, at least there was no way they could know that black shadows hovered at the edges of his vision.

Once he was out in the corridor, he kept moving because they might be watching. Or was that a human reaction? Sometimes he anticipated things that never occurred, or worried about matters the others never seemed to consider, which may have been a result of being raised, for the most part, as a human. A waste of time, Daria told him. A failed experiment. Since him, she used full-grown animals, who were more dependable and cost less effort.

In any case, Weiland was not aware of any of the others following as he made his way to the storage room where Daria kept articles of clothing they took from travelers who didn't have enough money to pay the toll. Weiland sat on a chest and rested, breathing heavily.

Dressing exhausted him all over again, but he'd taken too long already. Daria wasn't a patient woman. The leg which had been caught in the wolf trap throbbed despite the fact that it looked perfectly fit. Limping painfully, Weiland headed for Daria's rooms.

3

Weiland hesitated in front of Daria's door, weighing Daria's temper against the chance to catch his breath. From inside the room, he could hear a flute playing, which meant he would have to knock hard enough to be heard over the music, which, at this point, he wasn't sure he could manage. He knocked once, and had just convinced himself that he had to regather his strength for a second try when she called out, "Enter."

The first thing he saw was that Swordmaster Kedj was there—always a dangerous situation. He caught the faint whiff of incense from the inner room, but at least the door was closed. Daria and Kedj seemed to be working. All of Daria's clothes chests and jewelry boxes were opened and looked as though they'd been ransacked. Daria was sitting on her bed, surrounded by mounds of dresses, the majority of which apparently didn't meet with her approval, for she had a sour expression on her face as she went through them, and there was a growing pile of silk and linen and velvet on the floor. The second time she mistakenly picked up a trailing end of the damask bed curtain rather than a dress, she yanked the material off its frame and flung that to the floor also.

Kedj was sitting on the lower of the two steps that led up to the bed, his face—as usual—inexpressive as he read out loud from a ledger. Kedj was eldest of Daria's household, looking to be about forty, though it was difficult to judge since he was completely bald.

Llewellur, on the other hand, was both youngest and newest. Still playing the flute, he sat on a stool in the balcony. An incredible risk, Weiland thought. The boy's face was as pale as the gray sky behind him, and he looked even thinner than Weiland remembered. Those who had been born as birds never took well to captivity. Weiland estimated Daria had had at least a score in his lifetime. They always ended up starving themselves to death, or running away and getting themselves killed in the hills or the surrounding forest. And at least four had leapt from the high tower. But Daria claimed no one else could play the flute so sweetly. Since they came and went so quickly, she always gave them the same name, Llewellur. If there was significance to the name, beyond that Daria didn't want to be bothered thinking up a new name every six months or so, Weiland didn't know. Looking at this Llewellur, Weiland didn't think he'd last through the winter, despite the fact that the days were already turning warmer.

Daria didn't look up from her clothes-sorting, and Kedj didn't stop reading.

Weiland hesitated in the doorway, unsure whether to approach or wait for her to acknowledge him. He compromised by stepping all the way into the room, but he didn't shut the door behind him nor did he go up to the platform that held the bed. He waited, standing straight, with his hands behind his back, wearing what he hoped was an alert expression that indicated he was neither daydreaming nor listening in on a conversation that didn't concern him.

The list Kedj was reading was of weaponry, apparently an inventory. And apparently endless. "Swords," Kedj read, "sub-category *broad*." So many in excellent condition, and in good to fair condition, and in repairable condition, and recommended to be melted down and reforged. Then, "Swords, sub-category *long*." And then *two-handed*, and then the wooden training swords, all of which also came in broad, long, and two-handed classes.

A tremor started in Weiland's right leg, but he knew that fidgeting was sure to attract Daria's attention in an unwelcome way.

So would collapsing, of course. Weiland fought to keep his face bland. Mercifully, Kedj appeared to have already gone through knives, pikes, spears, flails, and battle axes. Which only left, after swords were finally categorized, bows: long, short, and cross. At long last Kedj paused.

Daria looked up. At Kedj, not Weiland. "Go on," she told him, while Weiland worked very hard to keep his breathing even.

Kedj listed all their food stores, which Weiland was grateful to hear broke down into only three categories: highly perishable, perishable, and stock.

"Fine," Daria told Kedj. "As you say." Which seemed a fairly good indication that she hadn't been paying attention to what he was saying and that she was going to rely on his judgment anyway. But finally she looked up at Weiland and beckoned him closer.

The chances were about even that his leg would buckle at his first step, but somehow it didn't.

"Have you been paying attention?" Daria asked.

It could be a trick question. The right answer might be, "No, my lady, I certainly was not." He did his best to look attentive, as though eagerly—but never impatiently—awaiting her orders, and hoped he could get by with no answer at all.

She gestured, indicating Kedj's ledger and the disarray of the room. "Speculation?" she asked.

So at the very least she hadn't expected him to be deaf and blind.

Inventory and inspection. That was too obvious to say. "You're planning a trip?" Weiland guessed.

Again a gesture, this one indicating there was more to it than that.

"With"—he hesitated; he didn't look to Kedj for help, because he knew he would get none—"at least some of the household?"

"So very clever," Daria said with exaggerated enthusiasm to indicate she wasn't sincere. But it was still a relief. Another alternative had been that she might be leaving without them—set them all one against the other till they killed each other off, then start anew with a fresh, better, company. She'd threatened that often enough. But now she said, "Sometimes I think you might not be hopeless after all."

And then she just sat there looking at him.

Eventually, she repeated, "Sometimes."

Again the sinking sensation, the realization that she found him lacking. "May I ask,"—he had to clear his throat, fervently hoping it was the right question—*was* it a question she wanted from him?—"when we're going?"

"That's up to you."

At least with the others in the company, he understood what was what. Even the training sessions with Kedj, brutal as they could be—at least there the rules weren't constantly shifting: be watchful, trust no one, fight to the death unless otherwise instructed—those were things one could understand. "My lady?" he said, hoping he sounded alert and eager, not panicked. Alert and eager were qualities Daria usually prized. Usually.

She motioned him closer yet. "Has the thought never once crossed your mind," she asked, brushing her fingers gently against his face, "during your *long* convalescence, to wonder why I let you revert to a wolf this last time?"

He hesitated. Sometimes Daria liked him to apologize profusely, even if they both knew he hadn't done anything wrong; for in some moods she liked to be begged for forgiveness. But other times, groveling would anger her all over again. Her face rarely gave an indication which. She just sat there with her hand still against his cheek, with Kedj at the edge of his sight just watching, and Llewellur playing something sad and lonely on the flute, and finally he had to say something. So he said, again, "My lady?"

She slapped him. He didn't flinch or glance away, which she would almost certainly take as provocation. "A warning," she told him. The slap or the transformation? "Because our situation is about to change." The transformation, then. Probably. "And I want to make sure you behave yourself." She patted his still-stinging cheek, with a force somewhere between the earlier gentleness and the slap. "You *will* behave yourself?" she asked.

"Yes, my lady," he assured her somewhat breathlessly, having no idea what was going on.

"I've decided this,"—she indicated the room—"is too small, too confining." Which probably meant the whole hill fortress then. "I've decided a town house in St. Celia's would probably offer new opportunities."

Their revenue came from possessing access to the best route across the wild and winding hills, from extorting tolls that were not so exorbitant as to attract the attention of surrounding barons—or at least not so exorbitant as to make it worth the barons' effort and expense to routinely try to track them down in this forested hill country that only Daria's company knew well. Weiland couldn't see how any of this would work in a town. He didn't know anything about towns, but he knew not to find fault with anything Daria said.

Daria was still watching him. "I can't very well bring you with me if I have to keep reminding you of your place by letting you return to your true form. The people of St. Celia's wouldn't be happy about that at all. I can no longer afford to be patient with you."

"No, my lady," Weiland agreed. He began to think that it was nothing specific he had done wrong; she had punished him on principle.

"A lady of quality doesn't surround herself with servants who are no more than trained animals. And I intend to try my hand at being a lady of quality. So I want you to be on your best behavior. And I want you to ensure that the others behave themselves as humanly as you like to pretend you are, so that no one suspects what you really are."

"Me?" Weiland saw the glimmer of annoyance. He was being dull-witted again. "I mean,"—he tried not to stammer—"I've . . ." But she knew he'd never been in a town before, that he had no experience dealing with human-born, except to be submissive to her and to demand money from travelers. She didn't need *him* to tell *her* the obvious. At least she seemed to be expecting he would be able to reestablish dominance over the company, regardless of Lon's present position. He was surprised at how pleased he felt that she had that much confidence in him. "Yes, my lady," he said.

"From now on, you are a house servant of the Lady Daria de Gris rather than a brigand, and we are all recently returned from the Holy Land."

"Holy Land?" Weiland repeated, unfamiliar with the term.

Daria turned to Kedj and snapped, "This boy is hopeless."

Unexpected ally, Kedj said, "Ah, but consider his upbringing."

"The Holy Land," Daria explained, "is . . ."—she gestured vaguely—"far away. There's a war that's been going on for . . . at least a hundred years."

Weiland suspected she was making up details she didn't know either. He knew war was like a battle, except bigger. He had fought in battles when groups of travelers had hired soldiers as escort over the hills, trying to get out of paying the toll. All of his training had been to fight battles, and he couldn't see how one could last more than a day or two.

"That way," Daria was saying, "if you should say something incredibly stupid, people will put it down to your being raised by foreigners."

"Yes, my lady," Weiland said.

"If you should embarrass me," Daria said, "do you know what will happen?"

Show no fear. Admit to no repugnance. "Yes, my lady."

"Or if something should happen to me so that I am no longer able to hold you in my spell?"

"Yes, my lady." Weiland found himself breathless again.

Daria raised her hand.

Weiland was expecting only another slap, because he'd been agreeing with everything she said. But the pain was much worse than that and jagged throughout his body. The room spun dizzyingly, the result of falling forward and of the changes in what he was seeing: colors bled out, but everything came into much sharper focus, except that what he saw was no longer familiar, no longer had names. There was the hot, heady smell of prey nearby, and a gnawing emptiness inside that was a clear indication he hadn't eaten in much too long.

And then he was pitching forward, from front feet and back feet, to hands and feet, ending on hands and knees—agony for the right leg which had been the one caught in the trap. He heard wood scraping against stone and even knew what it was: Llewellur on the balcony, scrambling off his stool, trying to get away from him. Kedj had hold of the scruff of Weiland's neck before the gray fur shortened to once again become close-cropped blond hair and Kedj's hand slipped away, so that the sharp spikes of his iron wrist bracer scraped the back of Weiland's neck. Weiland's clothing was all askew, from the wolf's smaller body, and from lunging at Llewellur. He wrapped his arms about himself, as though he might hold what was human inside.

Daria cupped his chin in her hand. "Foolish thing," she said with what passed as gentleness with her. "You'll never get away from me, you know. The best you can wish for, if you're a very, very good boy for a very, very long time, is that I may decide to let you die as a human." She tightened her grip before letting go. "But probably not."

Weiland had no idea what reaction she wanted to that.

Or whether he gave it.

"Go," she snapped. "Make yourself useful." He couldn't tell whether she was annoyed or just finished with him. "Unless you plan to tell me you're unfit for more than lying about, living off my generosity. I have no time for *any* nonsense."

Weiland stood and bowed and took a step backward, trying to sort that out as requiring a "Yes, my lady," or a "No, my lady." He felt the trickle of blood running down the back of his neck into his collar. But Daria was more likely to find fault with him for bleeding than with Kedj for wearing an apparatus whose merest touch had, over the years, scored the flesh of every member of the company at one time or another. Weiland took another step backward lest Daria catch him bleeding on a new shirt.

But Daria had already moved her attention to Llewellur, still standing with his back to the wall, still casting anxious glances from Weiland to the parapet, as though weighing his chances. "Llewellur," Daria snapped. "Stop that immediately."

Still backing out of the room, Weiland had just found the open doorway when Daria called, "Weiland. See about getting another songbird."

He jumped, Weiland thought.

But Llewellur was heading back to the overturned stool, the dropped flute. Apparently he just wasn't moving fast enough, or confidently enough, to suit Daria. Was it a calculated threat? Or was Daria simply making provision for the future, assuming the boy wouldn't survive the move to St. Celia's, and not caring how cruel her words were?

Wondering, Weiland hesitated, and—for a moment, as Llewellur leaned down to retrieve the flute—their eyes met. No discerning, from that look, whether Llewellur understood what Daria had just asked, or if he was only checking to make sure Weiland didn't lunge again, as though—even in human shape—Weiland might make dinner of him.

"Yes, my lady," Weiland murmured, and he closed the door behind him.

4

*H*e dreamt he was in the woods at night, running.

He knew he'd been there this afternoon, hunting for Daria's new songbird. This afternoon the trees had been winter-bared, but now the branches were covered with summer leaves made silver by the moon. It would have been pretty except that, somehow, he seemed to be in the middle of one of Kedj's training exercises. And apparently Kedj had assigned him to be the pursued. Sometimes Kedj had the company give chase in their human shapes, to sharpen their tracking skills; sometimes they were wolves, to sharpen the pursued's ability to evade capture.

Tonight they were wolves.

Weiland could hear the yips and snarls, the breaking of underbrush close behind and off to the sides. The path he followed was lined by trees growing so close together, it was like a tunnel, or a winding hallway deep in Daria's fortress. Except that the wolves, with their more compact bodies, were able to get through where he could not, finding shortcuts, always gaining.

Ahead was a long stretch, before the path angled sharply to the right. He knew not to waste time checking over his shoulder, but he could hear their padded feet on the ground behind him, he could imagine feeling their hot breath, and there was a terrible ache in his side that was, eventually, going to slow him down.

If only he could get around that corner. He convinced himself that this was just the kind of place Kedj was likely to be, waiting to declare the pursued the winner, or to pull the wolves off if the wolves won.

But then Weiland thought maybe Kedj wasn't waiting there—Kedj hated the cold of winter, though he had nothing against sending them out in it. Maybe, instead, Daria was there. He had the impression—

though he had just seen Daria that afternoon—that she had left for St. Celia's already, leaving him behind. It was St. Celia's just around that corner, he suddenly realized, and he had to get there, to beg Daria to let him stay a human.

He heard the click of teeth as one of his pursuers just missed tearing into the back of his leg.

Just a bit farther . . .

Just a bit . . .

Weiland made a wide turn, without slowing.

And Daria wasn't there, nor Kedj. Only more wolves.

Wolves in front, and wolves behind.

With nowhere else to go, Weiland tried to break through the unyielding trees, but the silver leaves had turned to thorns.

He looked down at his bleeding hands and saw his fingers turning to claws. "Daria!" he screamed, though he'd never had mercy of her before. And, anyway, she wasn't there. She was in St. Celia's, where things were going so well she'd forgotten all about him. He felt his humanity dissolving away, and he knew, with his last coherent thought, that this was happening not for something he had done or not done— not through Daria's malevolence—but through her carelessness.

Weiland woke, in the dark hall. He sat up, clapping his hand over his mouth. Which would have been too late to stifle an outcry in any case. But apparently he hadn't cried out, for nobody else was awake, nobody was jeering at him or telling him to shut up. The only sound was his own ragged breathing.

Trying to convince himself that his teeth were chattering solely due to the cold, he lay back down.

Daria was *here*, not in St. Celia's.

And she had indicated, for whatever that was worth, that he was to accompany her. She had told him to bring her a songbird—and he had. Even now it was in a silver cage in one of Daria's rooms, conspicuously ready to replace Llewellur the moment he died, escaped, or failed to please. In any case, Weiland had accomplished the task she had set for him, and it was Llewellur who was in danger, and it was Llewellur's own fault, for not trying harder.

But Weiland still had trouble getting back to sleep.

In the fortress's courtyard these days, there were unfamiliar men constructing wagons and barrels and cases to transport Daria's goods. By the dazed yet not discontented expressions on their faces, they were clearly newly created; by the speed and skill with which they worked,

Weiland guessed them to be beavers and muskrats. Daria had used such temporary workers in previous times of construction and remodeling. Temporary, because—under normal circumstances—she selected for other qualities than diligence.

Of Daria's company, there were twenty-three men—mostly wolf-born, though there were several who had been lynxes and weasels, a couple of rats, and of course Lon had been born a bear. Fierce and ruthless all. In the past Weiland had seen Daria experiment with snakes and hawks; but what she had gained in intelligence, she had lost in ability to control.

Her house servants were chosen to be of a more docile nature: dogs and mice, mostly, though occasionally she would lose patience with precisely the qualities she had created them for, and she had had servants flung from the tower. So far, company and servants alike had been male. Daria liked to be surrounded by attentive and attractive men. Weiland had seen her reject perfectly fit and promising candidates because she hadn't liked their looks. But now she gave orders for traps to be set around the hall and for female mice to be brought to her, and young does—deer or rabbit—from the surrounding forest, a vixen if one could be found. Ladies of quality, she let it be known, had lesser ladies as servants. There was a flurry of new women servants, many not lasting an hour before Daria judged them inadequate, and venison every night.

Meanwhile, the hall was in an uproar, with all Daria's household helping to sort and pack. The only exceptions were Llewellur, who played the flute continually to drown out for Daria the noise everybody else was making, and Kedj, who had been sent ahead to St. Celia's to make arrangements for their arrival.

Kedj, however, had left instructions about which weapons were to be taken, and it was only about half of what they had available.

"She's leaving some of us behind," Lon told Weiland as the two of them rolled and loaded tapestries they'd taken down from the walls of Daria's rooms. No great deduction on Lon's part: Everyone guessed the same.

"Really?" Weiland asked.

Lon often missed sarcasm, but not this time. "Think you'll be one of the ones she brings?" he sneered. "She's said often enough you're not worth the trouble you cause."

Weiland didn't answer, but only shifted where he was holding the roll they carried so that Lon was doing the majority of the work. He sincerely hoped he was going. For three nights now he'd dreamt that he had been left with the fortress group, starting even before it had become obvious there would *be* a fortress group. Still, Weiland thought he *might* be among those going—because of what Daria had told him in her apartments. However, there was never any being sure *why* Daria had told him anything. *I have no time for* any *nonsense*, she had said. And so he had avoided a confrontation with Lon over leadership of the company, precisely to prove that he could follow her instructions. But what if her instructions were a test to see who was the natural leader, and what if he was thus effortlessly ensuring that Lon would go and he would not?

Finally everything that could be packed was.

No food stores remained, Weiland noted with growing anxiety. That might mean Daria expected those left behind to survive solely on the meat they were able to hunt. Or not.

As though things had been timed just this way, Kedj returned from St. Celia's, complaining of the cold and mud and the human-born people of the town. But he must have brought news that all had been arranged to Daria's satisfaction, for she looked pleased as she announced it was time to leave. "Saddle my palfrey," she commanded, though it was almost midday and the best time for traveling was quickly slipping away, "and thirteen of the horses."

Thirteen. That was just over half, assuming the servants would walk beside the wagons. Surely that meant he was going. Surely Daria didn't consider *half* the company to be more valuable than he.

Kedj gave instructions which of the horses were to be saddled, and indicated a dozen more which were to accompany them, and that left a score unaccounted for.

Which was good news if he was to be left behind, Weiland thought. She wouldn't leave valuable horses if she planned to simply abandon the fortress.

Not that Daria's plans couldn't change.

There was still no indication, from the horses selected, who was to go and who was to stay. Kedj believed every rider should be familiar with and able to handle every horse, so there were no permanent assignments.

It was only after the horses were readied that Daria had the company line up. She walked slowly in front of them, pointing at certain men. One was Weiland. Go or stay was still not clear. Weiland watched out of the corners of his eyes, still facing forward as Daria continued down the line. He saw her indicate Lon, also. Surely, he hoped, with the first real expectation, she wouldn't leave both of them behind. Rohmar was not picked, and Weiland's assurance about the situation grew stronger.

But she picked thirteen, and Kedj wasn't one of them, either. Thirteen in one group, eleven in the other, with thirteen horses saddled. Which seemed to indicate . . . But to not take Kedj . . .

Of all the company, Kedj was rumored to be human-born. Never in anyone's memory had Daria—in any of her moods—changed Kedj to animal shape, which—according to the various rumors—might be impossible because he'd never had an animal shape, or unthinkable because he was her lover. Or her father. Or he had some hold over her. Of all the speculations, Weiland most seriously doubted Daria would countenance the continued existence of someone with any power over her. And, while Daria was careful of Kedj, she wasn't that careful to indicate a closer relationship than that of hall lady and trusted swordmaster. But, of them all, Kedj had been with Daria first, and even those of the company who had died over the years had never spoken of a time before Kedj. And she had sent him, on occasion, to human towns: for supplies unavailable from travelers, or for information, or for his own business, whatever that might be.

And she allowed him in her spell room, to witness what she did there.

Weiland was sure, despite the numbers, Kedj had to be in the group going to St. Celia's.

But then Daria waved toward the saddled horses and told Weiland's group, "Mount." And she told the others, "I am entrusting Kedj with this fortress. Obey him as you would me." Then she turned to the new men, those who had constructed the wagons and the barrels and crates. "You are free to go," she said.

Weiland faltered, holding onto the reins of a restive horse—all the company's horses were high-strung—and he thought how much he longed to hear those words from Daria. And yet he felt a chill up his back.

"I give you a gift of one more day and night to spend in human shape," Daria said.

The new servants stood blinking in the sunlight. They had not been men long enough to consider humanity a boon. Either that, or they had been men long enough not to trust Daria's generosity. "Go," she said with a shooing motion.

And even as they began to move, so that they were bound to hear, Daria turned to the ten who would be staying under Kedj's command, and said, "As a parting gift to *you*, I grant you this night—starting at sunset—in your natural shapes."

Wolves and lynxes, for the most part.

The workers began to run. One day, to put as much distance as possible between themselves and hungry predators who would track them. Not nearly enough time to escape the bounds of Daria's magic. And after that, they wouldn't even have the natural resources they had been born with to protect them.

Weiland, still clutching the reins of his horse, was profoundly relieved that he wouldn't be among those who, come about midnight, would be sniffing at the trail of those poor helpless workers.

But which was really worse, a small voice in his mind asked: to spend the rest of his life as a wolf and not know any better, or to keep company with a woman who found such diversions entertaining?

Distracted, he prepared to mount: He tightened his grip on the reins, placed a hand on the saddle's pommel, and shifted his weight. Partway through the motion of swinging up, he caught a dark blur of movement at the edge of his sight. Instantly he realized his mistake, but there was no time to brace himself.

A weight slammed into him, toppling him onto the hard-packed dirt of the courtyard, simultaneously knocking the breath out of him and jarring every bone in his body. His attacker rolled, still holding onto him, so that if the horse flailed, it would be Weiland's body the hooves struck. Then, a moment later—that danger over, and Weiland still unable to see, much less breathe—he was flipped over again, pinned down by Kedj's weight.

"Be watchful," Kedj purred close to his ear. He had his arm across Weiland's throat, the sharp spikes of his iron wrist bracer ready to impale at a wrong move.

Weiland struggled to use one of the holds he had been taught, but Kedj—whose strength at times could seem almost supernatural—jerked him up then down, so that Weiland's head smacked against the ground.

"Trust no one," Kedj continued the litany that was among the first words Weiland had learned. "Fight to the death unless otherwise instructed."

Weiland was ready to, but Kedj held him from budging.

"If I were the enemy," Kedj said, "you'd be dead now." With his face still a handbreadth from Weiland's, he said, "I have serious doubts about the competence,"—he blocked Weiland's attempt to kick—"or strength of this one, Daria. I think you should just cut your losses, and let me have him for lunch."

"Maybe when you come to visit me in St. Celia's," Daria answered in a neutral voice.

Kedj held Weiland down for a moment longer, grinning in the predatory way many in the company had. Then he was up and on his feet, and out of Weiland's range with that uncanny speed he used to best them all in the training sessions.

The company, those staying as well as those already mounted to go, were laughing. Daria looked disgusted with him. Weiland swung into the saddle quickly, before his muscles could protest. He hoped, before Daria could change her mind.

Kedj laced his fingers together to give Daria a lift into her own saddle. Weiland heard him say, "I thought you decided there was only room for twelve."

Daria glanced over the thirteen of the mounted company. Weiland thought he was probably the only one close enough to hear her say, "I need a blood sacrifice to consecrate the new dwelling. For luck."

Weiland felt frozen. The wagons were beginning to move out, and Daria put her heels to the palfrey's sides, passing Weiland with a look that could have meant anything, or nothing.

Had she intended for him to hear? There was no telling.

Nor, in either case, knowing why.

5

As they made their way down from the hills, spring seemed further advanced, which Daria said was the way of things: that winter clung most to high places. Weiland had never been away from the hills, so he had to take her at her word. At night they camped out. One of the wagons had been specially outfitted for Daria to sleep in. There was a tarp that could be raised and secured, tent-fashion, to protect her from the weather and to provide a measure of privacy.

The second night there was rain, and the thirteen men of the company made their beds under the wagons, leaving the servants—including Daria's two new ladies-in-waiting—to fend for themselves. Weiland wondered, in a detached way, whether a real lady of quality wouldn't show more concern for her body servants, but he had no real knowledge by which to judge.

After three days Daria had become mightily cranky by the slow pace forced on them by the wagons and the walking servants. "Kedj calculated two nights on the road," she complained as they stopped for the midday meal. "But the town gates will be barred by the time we get there."

Kedj had calculated based on their sensibly leaving at dawn, not noon, but Weiland knew better than to mention this.

Daria was looking at the low, gray sky, which hinted at another wet night. "I will go ahead."

"My lady?" Weiland said, soft and questioning.

But the look she gave him indicated she could tell he was about to disagree with her.

"Is that safe?" he asked hastily. "If we accompany you, that would leave the wagons easy prey. And if we stay with them, or even divide, and you—"

Daria gave him one of her long, level looks. "Have we encountered that many marauders that look beyond your ability to deal with?"

Lon snorted, for in just over two days they had encountered no one.

There was no answer Weiland could give without sounding an even bigger fool.

"The environs of St. Celia's are not nearly so dangerous as the hill country," Daria assured him. "And I am not totally helpless."

"No, my lady," Weiland murmured. Most obviously not. He felt his face go hot at being derided in front of the company, though he cared nothing for them or their opinion of him.

"But I will take Lon with me, as a protector, since he is eminently sensible."

Sensible. "Yes, my lady." Weiland glanced away, to avoid Lon's self-satisfied smirk, and to hide the thought that might show through on his face, that he should have taken on Lon that first day, that he should have challenged Lon's authority as soon as he was able to stand.

"I'll take my ladies with me," Daria said, "for appearance' sake."

The ladies were two mouse-born women, selected—Weiland suspected—mostly for their appearance, which was more young and wholesome than pretty. While Daria would never subject herself to anything or anyone unattractive, still these two were unlikely competition to Daria's dramatic beauty. Daria called them Bess and Blanche, which she said were human names, but Weiland couldn't keep straight which was which, and wasn't certain Daria was consistent either.

And while Daria's magic transformed creatures so thoroughly that they took on human language as well as human shape, she apparently was unable to give them an innate ability to ride a horse. "Teach them," Daria told Weiland, ignoring equally the anxious looks the women were giving the horses and the fact that none of them had eaten yet. "I'll want to leave as soon as I'm finished eating."

"Yes, my lady," Weiland said, determined to regain stature in Daria's eyes by doing at least this one thing well.

Bess and Blanche seemed just as determined to refuse to learn, as though by shying away and being clumsy they could get Daria to relent and change her mind. Their fidgeting and high voices made the horses even more nervous than usual.

Weiland caught hold of a rein that the younger and chubbier of the women—he strongly *thought* she was Bess—had dropped. He pulled the horse about to where Bess was standing, shaking her head and starting to say, "I can't—"

"Do you remember what happened to the wagon makers?" Weiland hissed at her.

Blanche—he was fairly certain it was Blanche—got all fluttery. But Bess took a deep breath, and the next time the horse tossed its head, she held on.

Fast decisions were necessary. There was no way he could make riders of both women in the time it would take Daria to eat her meal. Weiland's inclination was to teach Bess and to proclaim Blanche hopeless. Daria, of course, had no tolerance for the inept or unfit, and was likely to be furious with Blanche. Still, there was no reason that this should make any difference to Weiland.

Except that Daria's anger might just as easily alight on him.

So, instead, he decided to put both women on one horse: concentrating the lesson on Bess, and counting on Blanche for no more than holding on. It was a risky compromise. Blanche might well end up unseating both herself and the inexperienced Bess. Also, the horse—carrying a double burden—would not be able to travel as long or as fast as Lon's and Daria's mounts. No problem, if they rode the half day's journey to St. Celia's steadily and leisurely. But in case of trouble, of hard riding or pursuit, a double-burdened horse would fall behind, and Daria might lose both her new servants at once.

And blame Weiland's judgment.

But it was the best he could do.

By the time Daria had finished eating, Bess could control the horse, at least while it kept to no more than a fast walk, and Blanche, in back, was holding onto Bess for dear life. The positive aspect of the whole thing was that once the women had settled down, so had the horse.

Despite all Kedj's proclamations about horses responding best to a firm hand, the horse was behaving better for them than it did under normal circumstances. Perhaps it could recognize, Weiland thought, through smell or some other sense, what the company was made up of, despite their human shapes. Perhaps it recognized that the women were harmless and reminiscent of warm stables and food at the end of a day.

Daria mounted and Weiland watched her every move, ready—if she should say—for him to join her. She didn't say.

"Come quickly and quietly," was her only instruction.

For someone who hoped to make himself invaluable to her, this was a set-back.

Don't do anything foolish or malicious, Weiland wished at Lon's back as the four rode away, knowing it wouldn't take much for him to set a pace beyond Bess's ability, or to spook the horse. But surely Daria would recognize such an act for what it was, and she wouldn't hold Weiland accountable.

Foolish thought. More likely, he knew, for Daria to hold him accountable for the rain that was coming.

He turned abruptly, and nearly collided with Llewellur, who quickly darted out of his way, even as Weiland growled, "Move," at him. Unusual for a servant, unordered, to stand that close to one of the company, for everyone knew very well who had been created from predators, and who from prey. Unusual for Weiland, twice in three days now, to be so preoccupied as to let someone get close enough to do harm.

But harm was not likely Llewellur's intent. Weiland estimated the bird-born boy probably felt safer with Daria than with the company—Daria having never demanded more of him than to play the flute. He, too, Weiland realized, had been waiting for Daria to notice him and to order him to accompany her.

"*Everybody* move," Weiland ordered, and the servants scrambled to pack up the remnants of the meal, and the men of the company—to prove they didn't jump to Weiland's orders—yawned and stretched before getting to their feet and heading for their horses.

The rain came mid-afternoon. Weiland doubted Daria's party had reached St. Celia's yet, and he was briefly relieved not to be a part of that group, on whom Daria would take out her frustration.

But out of the hills, not only the air but the ground was warmer, and the thawed road quickly turned to mud that caked the wheels of the wagons and sucked at the feet of horses and walking men alike. The going got much slower. Weiland pressed on. Daria had gone ahead precisely because she knew the wagons wouldn't make it to the town before the gates were locked for the night; but she would anticipate their being there waiting for the doors to open in the morning, and arriving at her doorstep as soon as possible thereafter.

Except one of the wagons rode over a puddle that was really a water-filled hole deep enough to snap the axle.

Weiland dismounted and crouched in the mud, with rain that felt icier by the moment soaking his clothes as he evaluated the damage. It *was* fixable. With time. Daria's company—having no access to shops and trained craftsmen—had by necessity learned to repair those things they needed most. But soon it would be getting dark, which would increase the possibility of another wheel breaking in another puddle that was deeper than it looked. And what if they arrived at Daria's doorstep, muddy and dead tired from Weiland's pushing them through the night, and Daria had instant plans that required them to be fresh and alert?

Of course it would be even worse if Daria had such plans and they weren't there.

It wasn't often Daria or Kedj left Weiland enough room for decisions, but here he was for the second time today trying to anticipate on his own what would please Daria most. Or irritate least.

"We're getting wet, boy, while you're busy thinking," one of the company called out from atop his horse in a tone that indicated he, for one, didn't place overmuch value in Weiland *or* thinking.

Not a good sign, that derisive familiarity, which no doubt hearkened back—again—to not settling things with Lon. But the man—Innas was his name—was speaking into his coat collar to muffle his voice and likely was relying on Weiland's not recognizing who had spoken, which at least wasn't open challenge. Only Lon was a significant risk in open challenge, and Weiland had bested him twice already. Which might or might not say anything for next time. Kedj, of course, could easily defeat any of them, even without the element of surprise. But Kedj, as swordmaster, was really outside of the company, and was not interested in rank or position among them. The danger with the rest of them, Weiland knew, was not in open challenge, but in the possibility that their undisguised dislike of him could spill over into a group effort to teach him his place. Weiland had often enough overheard comments that he needed to learn his place.

Now he wiped his wet hands on his wet pants and stood. "We're going to get wetter no matter what I decide," he said, intentionally looking at the wrong man. Leave it to them to make of that that they were cleverer than he and had pulled one over on him, or that he knew what was what but was afraid of a confrontation. He saw the quick grins as he hastily looked away from the man who had not spoken and added, "We'll make camp, and set out again in the morning."

They were still grinning as he looked beyond them to the bedraggled servants who were waiting to be told what to do. He took a step forward among the still-mounted company. "Set up camp," he called to the servants. And at the same time grabbed hold of Innas who *had* spoken, and yanked, dragging him off his horse to land hard and wetly in the mud. "You," Weiland told him, "can fix the axle and take the first watch."

There was hearty laughter from the others, for—as much as they disliked Weiland—they liked entertainment, and Innas became the brunt of their jokes. For the moment.

6

Dawn broke chill but dry. After a quick cold breakfast, the company mounted and the servants fell in line beside the wagons. With luck, they might arrive at St. Celia's before Daria—often a late riser—had time to lose patience with them.

Weiland did a head count of his companions, because any one of them might consider it a fine joke to go haring off into the surrounding woods and stay missing just long enough for him to have to explain the matter to Daria. But apparently none of them was that inventive this morning. He counted the horses, those saddled and the extra mounts, to make sure none of them had broken loose and wandered away into the night, because—though he had assigned someone to watch out for them, he wanted to make sure nothing went wrong. Next he counted the wagons, which couldn't—reasonably—be missing, but Kedj valued meticulous attention to detail, and then he did a quick count of the servants.

And then he counted the servants again, more conscientiously, so that when he again came up one short, he already had the name.

"Where's Llewellur?" he demanded, expecting "Gone to relieve himself," or "Into the woods for something Cook needed," or . . . Weiland was expecting some errand that would probably be foolish and that he would have to yell at them about, but he was expecting *something*.

But everyone else was glancing around and looking at each other, confused and anxious lest he should take this out on them. Weiland felt his heart begin to beat faster—annoyance at the delay, and fear for Daria's reaction.

"Has anyone seen him this morning?"

No response. And he hadn't really thought it likely. Those born as birds . . .

"Did anyone see him last night?"

"At supper," someone volunteered. There were a few nods of agreement.

Weiland glared at Innas, Adger, and Telek, the three men of the company who had shared the night watch, but there was no knowing when Llewellur had slipped away, so no one of them could reasonably be singled out for blame. Knowing he wasn't Daria, they just shrugged.

Another decision, of the sort he was sure had no right answer.

He could order the servants to resettle camp while the company stayed and looked for the runaway, which—given that Llewellur had the whole night's head start—might take some time. And all the while Daria would be waiting in St. Celia's, growing ever more impatient wondering where they were.

Or they could forget Llewellur and continue on to St. Celia's in the hope that Daria would say, "Never mind." Which she never had before.

Or they could divide, with someone staying behind to search out Llewellur and the rest of the group going on to St. Celia's so that Daria would have her servants available.

But if Weiland was the one to stay behind, that would leave those in the world who wished him worst to explain to her just where he was, and why. And, of course, if they got into any trouble along the way because he wasn't there, Daria would hold him accountable for that.

Yet he didn't dare assign someone else to track Llewellur, for even now they were grumbling that he was a nuisance, and worse than useless, and "Just wait until I get my hands on that little turd."

All of which Weiland could agree with.

But Daria—if she wanted him back—would want him back all in one piece. And there wasn't any way to be sure of that unless Weiland did it himself.

His companions were watching him with that particular hungry look they could get when they sensed trouble: waiting, he was sure, for him to make the wrong decision—at this point all his possible decisions felt to be wrong ones—waiting for him to do something so foolish that Daria would finally throw him to them.

"Stay here," he said—which was greeted by jeers and groans and upflung hands—though he was sure whatever he had decided would have met the same reaction. "Right here. None of you are to cross the perimeter we set up last night. Don't light a fire unless I'm not back by nightfall." He didn't want the camp looking too comfortable to others traveling the same road. "Don't talk to anyone who might happen by. Don't,"—he had a sudden awful premonition of how badly awry things could go—"demand a toll of anybody."

"Hard to do that without talking to them," scoffed Parn—one who never could take anything seriously.

"If I'm not back by next morning," Weiland continued without acknowledging him, "head for St. Celia's without me. Travel through the town as quietly as possible, again without talking to anyone except to get directions. Don't discuss our business with anyone." That would be easy enough—none besides Daria knew her intentions. "Don't talk amongst yourselves once you pass the town gates."

Their looks told him they thought he was being overly wary taking unnecessary precautions. In his estimation, they were lucky he didn't tell them not to eat, since Daria had left assuming they would eat only one more meal—breakfast—on the road, and bring the rest of the food stores with them.

And that was another consideration to trouble him: Was Daria counting on breaking her fast with the food they had in the wagons, so that she would be hungry as well as angry at their delay? He assumed that towns had food supplies; but how that food would be distributed or could be gotten to, he had no idea.

There were no more directions Weiland could think to give: don't cause trouble, don't get into trouble—generally the company needed more specific instructions than that. Daria, in her quest for a company whose members were fierce yet intelligent, and at the same time controllable, often complained that the wolf-born were as close as she had gotten to what she wanted—and that they weren't very close at all. Then, depending on her mood, but frequently, she might look at Weiland and say that raising a wolf as though it were human had combined the worst faults of both. Weiland wasn't sure how, exactly, he failed Daria. He had seen, oftentimes, that he could think better than the others, but he supposed he must habitually think the wrong things. Natural-born humans must be closer to what Daria wanted. Weiland could work out no other reason for this trip to St. Celia's than that she planned to gradually replace the entire company with real humans. He hoped this was yet another case of his thinking the wrong thing.

The company was waiting, since he was still standing there, for further instruction, but there was nothing left to say. Weiland turned his thinking to Llewellur.

Which way was the boy most likely to run?

To continue down the road to St. Celia's would bring him closer to Daria, an unlikely choice. Though Weiland was sure that yesterday Llewellur would have preferred to accompany Daria than to be left with the company, most of all he would prefer his freedom. He would run, Weiland guessed, to escape the reach of Daria's transforming power.

Returning the way they had come, to the mountains, to Daria's old hall, would bring him in the vicinity of Kedj and his men before Daria's magic ran out. And he would have no reason to expect a welcome from them.

Most likely, then, was that Llewellur would leave the road, heading off across country, hoping to keep hidden in the woods until he passed beyond the point where Daria's magic would have effect.

Unless, of course, the boy guessed that was the way his pursuers would reason.

But Llewellur was a flute player, not a member of the company. He had not tracked deer for a meal, nor travelers who tried to escape paying the toll, nor several former flute players intent on regaining the sky. Nor had he had the benefit of ever being the prey in one of Kedj's training sessions, with twenty-some men who wished him no good, all intent on bringing him back before the allotted time was up, and none being overly concerned about doing him no injury in the process.

The camp was a hopeless muddle of tracks, so Weiland walked beyond the people and horses and wagons, beyond the tracks those on guard duty had made last night as they walked the circumference of the camp. Beyond this, he walked in a big circle himself, studying the ground, looking for broken branches, or overturned stones, or leaves where there shouldn't be any leaves.

Weiland began to circle the camp in an ever-increasing spiral, time-consuming excess if he had judged Llewellur's intentions correctly, necessary safeguard just in case he had not.

In man shape, Weiland was neither the best nor the worst tracker of the company. He assumed he was better at tracking while he was in wolf shape; though he had no clear memories, he had seen it in all the others of the company, with animal senses better attuned for surviving in the wild. Still, by mid-morning, he was fairly certain he had picked up Llewellur's trail: Something looking to be man-sized had passed through the woods in the direction he had decided Llewellur was most likely to take. And it wasn't a deer, because there were no droppings and no nibblings of the tender spring shoots that he would expect from deer, which were very easily distracted unless they knew they were being pursued, in which case he would have seen more evidence of flight. And he didn't think it was a bear because a bear, even casually walking, generally left a trail of wreckage similar to a panicked deer in flight.

Then, mid-morning, he saw in the dried mud a clear impression of a human foot.

There was nothing that said it had to be Llewellur. As a wolf,

Weiland knew, he'd be able to differentiate one man from another by scent—though, as a wolf, he wouldn't care. But how likely was it for two men to pass in this vicinity of the woods on a rainy night in early spring?

It wasn't an unbroken path of footprints marking the way. But Weiland was able to make good time: Whoever had passed this way had either been unworried about being followed or had not known how to disguise his passing. Or perhaps both, Weiland thought.

Shortly beyond where Weiland had found the first footprint, he found a nest, of sorts. Someone had gathered a pile of last autumn's leaves and, under the indifferent protection of a bush, had apparently bedded down for part of the night.

Weiland sniffed at the makeshift bed, but in this form couldn't detect any scent beyond the leaves themselves and the rich earth.

It couldn't have been a dry or comfortable bed—no one had taught Llewellur how a human shelters in the wild. Possibly it had been too dark for him to feel he could proceed safely, or he might have been too tired to continue. Weiland was well aware that Kedj's training had made those of the company stronger, faster, more adaptable, and possessed of greater stamina than the people who regularly traveled through the hills. Or than a bird-born boy, who knew only of playing the flute.

By midday, Weiland knew he was closing in on Llewellur. Places where the boy had forced his way through the brush had branches so fresh-broken they were still sticky with sap, and there was a place where he had stopped to urinate, the smell still pungent, even to Weiland's human nose.

But beyond here something had alarmed Llewellur.

Weiland could tell by the footprints that Llewellur was running, regardless of slick leaves. There was a hand print in the mud and what was probably the mark of a knee, where he had just barely kept from sprawling. The near spill had not slowed him down. Though Weiland lost the footprints in the leaves and ground cover, he could see where Llewellur had taken off—veering sharply to the right, where the branches were thickest, rather than working with the land. Trying to confound pursuit, Weiland guessed, and never realizing that he might as well have put up a signpost, for all the snapped branches and trampled underbrush.

Weiland turned to look back, from the point where Llewellur had paused to relieve himself. The ground had been slowly but steadily rising, and the meandering way Llewellur had been taking had caused him to come to a hill with a clear view of where he had passed already, a section Weiland remembered, because the trees had been much thinner there. Thin enough, Weiland estimated, that Llewellur had been able to make out that he was being followed.

Llewellur might, even now, be within hearing range. Weiland considered whether to call out to the boy, but could think of nothing he could say that would encourage him to come back. There were no assurances Weiland could give regarding Daria's reaction to his running away. And Daria *would* be told—everybody knew, and not a one would be willing to accept on Llewellur's behalf Daria's anger for their arriving late.

Silently Weiland followed the trail of broken and bruised branches, confident that Llewellur—by forcing a path—was making no better time than he.

Then suddenly he found himself on a bluff overlooking a gorge cut through the land, far, far below by a river. It was probably the same—or an offshoot of—the one that had formed the way through the hills that Daria's hall guarded and which eventually flowed—so Kedj had described it—through St. Celia's.

The trees went right to the edge, which broke off sharply. From where Weiland had come out, the descent looked too steep for anyone to manage. The whole thing, he thought, looked too steep to manage. There was definitely no one climbing down now, but that didn't mean Llewellur hadn't tried.

It was a long way down.

Surely he hadn't been that desperate.

But how desperate would I be, Weiland thought, *in Llewellur's place?*

Weiland began to look at the ground. No tracks, but he found a way slightly less precipitous than the rest. Still, the slightest wrong move would find him plummeting for a long time before he hit bottom.

If Llewellur had started that way, he had not had time to make it to the bottom except in that one, fatal manner. Unless there was an opening in the rocky wall that Weiland couldn't see from this angle, a crack big enough to hide in.

Weiland tried to picture himself explaining the situation to Daria, describing exactly how steep the way was, and how there was no need for him to go down to ascertain that there were no crevices in the cliff. And he couldn't picture it. Not in any realistic way that didn't end with Daria furious.

With a sigh, Weiland started to ease down the face of the bluff.

And then he remembered who he was looking for.

And he looked, finally, instead of at the ground—up.

With the branches totally bare, he easily found Llewellur, crouched high in the very tree below which he had started to make his descent.

Weiland scrambled back onto level ground, and still Llewellur didn't move.

"Are you going to make me come up to get you?" Weiland demanded from the foot of the tree. Llewellur was slim and birdlike in stature, and could hardly weigh anything. He was probably already higher up than Weiland would dare to trust the branches not to break under him.

Llewellur, looking straight at him, didn't answer.

Of course, Weiland could just wait here until the boy got hungry enough to come down—laying siege to the tree, so to speak—but that would take time, during which the rest of the company would travel on their own to St. Celia's, getting into who-could-guess-how much trouble, with Daria becoming more and more apt to take her anger out on Weiland as well as Llewellur.

"Get down now," Weiland ordered, "before you make worse trouble for yourself." Not that Daria was likely to be made lenient by taking repentance into account. But they both knew Weiland could make things miserable for him long before they even reached Daria.

Weiland expected Llewellur to either refuse or comply. Instead the boy said, "Please don't do this to me."

Weiland found that being in a position of power was no good feeling, at least not now, not in this situation. It was a cold wind blowing across the bluff, though in fact the sun was warm enough to be drawing the moisture out of the ground.

"You don't need to bring me back," Llewellur said.

And Weiland gave the only answer he could: "Of course I do."

"I cannot,"—Llewellur's voice was soft, but his breathing was loud and ragged—"live this way."

Weiland was torn between "I understand" and "People get used to things," and in the end only stood there, feeling wretched but no less determined.

"You're not like the others," Llewellur said. "You could tell her you couldn't find me."

Though Weiland had never felt he *was* like the others, Llewellur's statement was more unsettling than gratifying. And its blatant purpose was to get Weiland to do what Llewellur wanted. "She'd never believe that," Weiland answered resentfully. He didn't add, "And she'd punish me." He thought, without wanting to think about it, of Daria's comment to Kedj upon leaving the hall, that she planned a blood sacrifice for the new dwelling. He would do nothing to make her inclined to use him.

But with that thought came the understanding of which of them she was most likely to be inclined to use, which she had already selected a replacement for.

And that made him feel more like the others than he ever had before as he said, softly, "Come down. Now."

Llewellur bowed his head in acceptance of the situation. Moving slowly and carefully so that he wouldn't fall, he took hold of one of the higher branches to pull himself to his feet. He took one step, cautious or hesitant, then he let go of the branch. He held his arms wide and leapt into the air over the chasm.

For one long, breathless moment, it seemed to Weiland that he would be able to fly, even in human form.

But only for a moment.

7

Having witnessed Llewellur jump, there was no point in climbing down into the gorge. The boy would have been unlikely to survive had he fallen only so far as the surface of the bluff. Weiland didn't need to see the body to assure Daria he was dead. Daria was neither sentimental about such things, nor likely to demand proof of his death—and that fact pricked and nagged at Weiland's mind: Could he have turned back, let Llewellur go, and convinced Daria that the boy was dead? Would agreeing to tell a lie have spared Llewellur's life?

Weiland knew people lied. He'd been lied to often enough by those the company stopped on the mountain road: "No, we have no money"—and there it would be, under the floorboards of the wagon, or hidden amongst the clothes. But Weiland didn't have experience in telling lies and he didn't know if he could carry it off. He knew that some were more likely to get caught at it than others. And he had no reason to lie for Llewellur, he told himself. The boy was nothing to him and had no claim on his conscience.

And yet . . .

Weiland crouched by the edge of the gorge.

And yet he could understand that terrible panic, that sensation of being trapped.

You're not like the others, Llewellur had said. It had been a bald and clumsy attempt to get Weiland to do what Llewellur wanted. Did that make it any less true?

If he continued the way he was, he was doomed. Any other thought was self-deception. There was only one way Daria would let him go, and that was to his death. If she chose the time and manner, it would be—almost assuredly—long and hard. His only real chance at escape, at an easy death, was if she didn't see it coming and had no time to prevent it.

Weiland spread his arms to the wind. He closed his eyes and imagined tipping forward, forward, the air rushing past him, but he was unafraid. He could even imagine hitting the ground.

But he could not imagine being dead.

The danger was Daria getting angry with him. Other than that, he might well live—more often man than wolf—another four, five, six years, even. Daria's household did not generally survive long, and those of her company least of all. Still, there was a difference between not wanting to live life as a wolf and wanting to die as a man. Particularly wanting to die as a man now.

If Daria had planned to use Llewellur for her sacrifice, she may well be very, very angry. He knew this might be his last opportunity to make any choice.

But he could no longer imagine falling and not fighting it.

Weiland opened his eyes and let his arms drop to his sides, choosing, at this time, to live.

He got back to the camp late in the afternoon, about the time they must have just been deciding that he wouldn't make it back, that they could start preparing the evening meal and settle in for the night.

"Couldn't find him?" those of the company asked scornfully. "Bird-boy outwit you?"

The servants made their faces blank, ducked their heads, and tried to move as quickly as they unobtrusively could out of the range of possible trouble.

Daria was the only one to whom he owed an explanation; the others could see for themselves all they were entitled to know—that Llewellur was not with him.

"Strike camp," Weiland ordered.

There was a chorus of jeers and protests.

It was no more than their usual manners, but Weiland began shoving at those who were complaining loudest, knowing it could easily develop into a challenge. Nip and snarl, he would have called it, had he been watching natural-shaped wolves trying to assert dominance.

But they backed off meekly with surprised looks and aggrieved objections: He had misunderstood all. They were just having fun. He shouldn't be so touchy as to take such things amiss.

"Strike camp," he repeated, never raising his voice.

And that time they did, so that they arrived—subdued and somewhat breathless, especially from the last miles—having outraced the onset of evening and the closing of the gates.

The town was nothing like what Weiland had imagined. He would have thought that they had reached St. Celia's when they first came upon the fields and cottages of the outlying farms, except there had been no gates, no walls, beyond those of a height and thickness that seemed more to keep sheep from straying than to protect from humans—or human-shaped creatures.

St. Celia's actual wall was climbable, too, Weiland estimated. It might serve to keep out marauding bands of thieves or barbarians, but he very much doubted it would slow down those whom Kedj had trained. Still, while he was unimpressed with the height or thickness of the wall, he was amazed by the amount of area enclosed. Towns were obviously much bigger than he had pictured.

He rode ahead to speak to the gatekeepers, to assure them that their group of wagons and horsemen was here on lawful, peaceful business.

At Daria's fortress, with a contingent that ranged between twenty and thirty men, there were at any given time at least six guards stationed to watch for approach from any direction—even in the dead of winter, when the mountains were impassable, even given that other men were stationed at other vantages on the lookout for travelers, so that Daria would have ample warning from a variety of sources should anyone come within miles of her hall.

Weiland assumed there must be similar arrangements at St. Celia's, that they had been watched for the last several miles, probably even before they themselves could actually see the town. But nobody challenged him, even when he actually passed through the gateway. There were two large wooden doors—thick and braced by iron bands—but still, Weiland was amazed to see, burnable, breakable, wood. When both were opened there was enough room that a pair of their wagons could pass through at a time; a smaller sally port was cut out of the right-hand door to allow individuals in or out even after the doors had been locked. And no one was standing guard.

Weiland dismounted, to look less intimidating, more peaceful, and because there were no others on horseback that he could see. He tried not to be too obvious about checking out their fortifications, but nobody seemed to be scrutinizing or even noticing him. There was a dizzying jumble of houses crammed together—hard if not impossible to tell where one ended and another started. Three, possibly four, streets met there, at the gate, and wound away up the hill that St. Celia's was built on, providing glimpses at an incredible number of buildings, with no end in sight. More people than he'd ever seen at once milled about, or came from one house and into another, or scurried down one street, around the corner, and up another. And it wasn't even likely, Weiland knew, that the majority of the town's population had selected just this moment to be at this particular spot. Just how many people *were* there?

After a moment, leading his horse, he approached two men who might have been gatekeepers for they were dressed as soldiers, with leather helmets and chain mail tunics, though they were sitting on a stone slab whose entire purpose seemed to be to allow those who watched the gate a place to sit. They were playing dice, which Weiland had seen in caravans the company had raided. Kedj would have ordered the immediate execution of anyone caught sitting while on guard duty, never mind the game of dice.

"I'm with the household of the Lady Daria de Gris," Weiland announced to the soldiers.

He half expected them to say, "So what?" He half expected that something had happened to the real gate guards, and these men just happened to be sitting nearby.

But one of the men glanced up to say, "Yes, the sergeant said a score of men were due in today with about a dozen wagons." He peered beyond Weiland. "No wagons," he observed.

They *weren't* watching, Weiland realized. *Anybody* could come up on them unobserved. "I rode ahead," he said. If they weren't concerned about the kind of people who would come to St. Celia's intent on plunder, he wouldn't raise the subject. "To ask you not to close the gates while the wagons are still crossing the meadow." Daria had warned them all to speak politely in St. Celia's. Not subservient, she had said, but well-mannered. Weiland hoped he had the right balance. The soldiers were looking at him blankly.

"We wouldn't do that," the one who had already spoken said. "We don't have to be that exact about the time."

Weiland nodded, still unsure. He'd wait on this side of the wall, just in case. "Thank you." Daria had said "Thank you" was a polite thing to say.

The two soldiers exchanged a glance, but Weiland had no idea what the significance was. The second man asked, "Anything else?"

Should there be? Or did they just mean, "Go about your business, then, and don't stand there watching us?"

"I . . ." Weiland realized there *was* another question. "Where is the Lady Daria's lodgings?"

"The de Gris compound is the building after the cathedral," the first soldier answered.

Weiland hesitated, not liking to give any more information than he had to, but seeing no other way. "I've never been in this town before," he admitted.

"Cathedral," the man repeated, his impatience beginning to show. "Big building with the tall tower." He glanced over his left shoulder, indicating, Weiland presumed, the tower that was visible from here, as though Weiland should have recognized it as being part of a cathedral. "Located," the man continued, "coincidentally enough, on Cathedral Street."

Which was definitely an indication they thought he'd taken enough of their time.

Weiland stepped away, to a spot where he and his horse didn't seem to be in anybody's way, and where he could watch the men and the doors at the same time.

Cathedral, he repeated to himself. He couldn't recall ever having heard the word before, but if they had named a street after it, it was probably important enough that he shouldn't admit he didn't know what it was.

The men resumed their dice game.

People continued to enter and leave buildings. At this late hour, nobody was leaving the town itself, though several came in—individually and in groups of two or three. The guards did glance up periodically, giving the impression they were aware of what was going on, but Kedj and Daria both would have been furious at such careless defenses.

Knowing the guards considered his questions an imposition, but overwhelmed by amazement at the constant flow of people, he waited until one of the times the guards were already distracted from their game, then called over, "How many people in this town?"

"Over ten thousand, so they say."

The number was incomprehensible, but he was sure he was already making the men suspicious by not knowing anything. *Many*, he thought. So many that he had best try not to think about it at all.

Just then the wagons started in through the gates, and just after the last had passed through, a bell started ringing.

Fire, Weiland thought, which was the significance of the bell at Daria's fortress.

Or the springing of a trap.

Weiland spun around, looking for the soldiers who had been hidden all along, until the wagons were inside and more vulnerable. He dropped the horse's reins and went for the sword at his side. But stopped, just short of drawing it. There were no soldiers coming out of hiding. The two gate guards, though getting to their feet, were not moving hurriedly, and the bell itself was ringing too slowly and deliberately to sound like an alarm.

All around him Daria's company drew their weapons, apparently coming to the same conclusion he had at first, and not to the second realization. *Stop!* he wanted to yell. But it was already too late.

The gatekeepers unsheathed their own swords; the servants dropped to the ground.

"Stand down," Weiland ordered. He placed himself between Daria's company and the gatekeepers, which put him—against all instinct—with his back to naked blades held in the hands of men he didn't know. "Stand down," he repeated. It was an opportunity, should those of Daria's company be looking for it, to get him killed.

But after a long, long moment they obeyed.

Weiland turned to the gatekeepers, holding his hands out from his sides. "A misunderstanding," he said.

Slowly, to indicate they were not entirely convinced and that they would be more watchful from now on, the guards sheathed their swords also. "Nervous," one of them commented.

In the hills, planning an ambush, Weiland would have determined the plan was ruined, the trap sprung prematurely. He would have killed both men before they could spread the alarm.

But this wasn't in the hills. There were people around—over ten thousand, the man had said. Not all people were fighters, Weiland knew that, but some would try to prevent him from leaving if they saw him kill one of their own, and the wagons could only move slowly, and the gigantic public brawl that would ensue would raise just as much alarm as the guards could, and what would Daria have to say about that?

The second guard had gone to the gate and was evidently looking to see if anyone else was in the vicinity. The bell, Weiland realized, had been the signal that it was time to bolt the doors.

It was time to talk calmly and reassuringly. Weiland fell back on the only excuse he had. "I'm from the Holy Land," he said.

"So what?" the first man answered in a tone that indicated Weiland's comment had done nothing to alleviate any suspicions he might have.

Weiland swung back up onto his horse. "Move out," he commanded his group. With relief he noted that they were gazing in amazement at the houses, the people, and they were not saying anything—amongst themselves or to anybody else.

The guards began to pull on the massive wooden doors to shut them, and Weiland rode to the front of the column of Daria's company, servants, and wagons, and set off in the direction of the tower that marked the cathedral and, the next house beyond, Daria's lodging.

Come quickly and quietly, Daria had said.

He was arriving a full day late, having lost Llewellur along the way and having raised the suspicions of the gatekeepers after being there less time than it would take to explain the situation to Daria. It was almost enough to make him hope he couldn't find the cathedral.

8

The number of townspeople decreased as the last of the afternoon light faded, but it was still more of a crowd than those of Daria's hall were used to. Weiland had to fight to keep his hand from his sword. *Be watchful*, the words of his training rang in his ears. *Trust no one. Fight to the death unless otherwise instructed.* It was hard to think of these strangers as "not enemy." And in the end it could prove fatal. They might not be wolf- or bear-born, but that didn't mean they weren't dangerous.

Had he been afoot rather than mounted, it would have been even more difficult—those walking had a tendency to jostle one another as they hurried each in his own direction. *Danger, danger, danger*, every nerve in his body warned. But, *Keep calm. Don't draw attention. Look neither dangerous nor helpless*, his mind told him. A nice, solid wall at his back and his sword in his hand would have helped convince him to trust his mind over his instincts.

St. Celia's seemed a town built for providing cover for traps and attack. The narrow street wound and curved as it climbed upward; twice it crossed over the river that flowed down from the mountains. The houses were crowded together, sometimes—but not always—sharing walls. Sometimes—but not always—the upper stories were built out, overhanging the street in what certainly appeared to be a haphazard fashion. To know the town—its alleys and bolt holes and peepholes and shortcuts—would be to have a distinct advantage over those who did not. Weiland felt closed in upon and very susceptible to ambush.

And attack from the townspeople wasn't the only danger Weiland feared. "Hands away from weapons," he kept murmuring as he rode back and forth along the length of the column of men and wagons.

Those of the company were wearing the kind of looks he probably would have given to someone who offered *him* that inane advice. There was the distinct possibility that a loud noise, a sudden movement, the perhaps innocent approach of a townsperson might set off the already high-strung and distrustful company. He should have had them put their swords, at least, safely away in one of the wagons for they were conspicuously more armed than anybody they'd come across.

"Calm," he kept telling them, despite his own inclination not to trust the apparently peaceful intentions of the inhabitants of St. Celia's. None of them had survived this long by trusting to appearances.

At last they came to the building with the tower, the cathedral. Several streets opened onto this square, and Weiland slowed his horse, wondering if they were meant to go down one of those ways or continue straight. If someone had told him to follow a path in a forest, that might mean to go straight, or it might mean to follow the way that looked most traveled. Were town streets like forest paths?

The cathedral itself was more like Daria's hall than anything they'd passed so far: large and stone and looking to be easily defensible, built at the summit of a series of twelve wide steps, giving the inhabitants the advantage of upper ground should they be attacked. Daria would have picked such a place, Weiland estimated, if she'd had free choice. If the building was already taken, it made sense that Daria would seek lodging nearby.

There was an old man sitting on the lower-most of the cathedral steps, which Weiland guessed was not the place nor the attitude of one likely to be in charge of such a structure. Not a guard, either, judging by the fact that he carried no sword. Perhaps a servant, then, though no servant of Daria's would let himself be seen sitting doing nothing.

On the other hand, maybe sitting on steps doing nothing was what old men did. Those who tried to cross the mountains near Daria's fortress—or those who tried to hunt Daria's company down—had generally been men who looked no older than Lon or Kedj appeared to be. But sometimes, among the larger parties making the crossing, there had been women and children or men with white hair and wrinkled skin, which was what Kedj said happened with age. None of Daria's people had ever reached such an age. Generally, if Weiland saw an old man, he was the rich merchant who owned the caravan. So this old man *could* be the owner of the cathedral.

Just as Weiland was considering whether to ask directions, the man stood. Weiland put his hand to his sword, which was no more than any reasonable person would expect under such circumstances, but he gave a quick glance over his shoulder to those behind and raised his left hand in a gesture meant to indicate they were not to do anything hasty.

"A penny before you pass, Lord?" the old man asked, holding out his hand.

Though Weiland had just surveyed the streets and buildings to ascertain that there was no one within striking distance to take advantage of this distraction, he made another hurried inspection. It was the sort of thing a member of Daria's company might have said, stepping out from among the trees or boulders, to unwary travelers.

But the man had no weapon, and here—where the street opened up so wide—there was no way accomplices could rush them unseen. And why give this warning, if an ambush was set up further along? Which didn't make sense anyway, for how could potential thieves possibly guess which way Weiland and his party were going from here?

"What?" Weiland asked just in case, somehow, he had misheard.

"A penny for a poor blind man," the old man said, still with his hand out.

Blind. That explained the odd, cloudy, gray eyes, and the fact that the man was looking more at Weiland's horse than at Weiland himself. It further confused everything else. "Why?" Weiland asked.

"*Why* what?" the old man countered.

"Why should I give you money?"

"Because I'm blind."

Weiland glanced at those behind to see if this made any better sense to them—giving something to someone helpless to take it. Apparently not. In any case, Weiland had no money. The money they had collected as tolls over the years was in the wagons, but that was Daria's—even if he was inclined to giving it away, which he was not.

"No," Weiland said, ready to go for his sword.

"Lack-wit," the blind man answered. But he backed up out of the way, until his heel touched against the bottom of the steps leading to the cathedral, and then he sat down, with still no sign of violence or sudden appearance by armed accomplices. He seemed to simply be patiently waiting for the next passerby.

Still, Weiland made sure not to have his back to the old man while he evaluated the possible choices. The gatekeepers had said Daria was lodged in the building just beyond the cathedral. The most likely dwelling was on that part of the street that continued straight ahead, for there was one that was set apart from its neighbors, surrounded by a wall, and it was the largest, and it was constructed of stone rather than timber.

Hesitantly, still aware of the possibility of traps, Weiland led the entourage that way. He dismounted and rang the bell that was hanging by the gate, still expecting disaster in some form or another, and so he was profoundly relieved when it was one of Daria's two new maids who came in response to the bell. Bess, he thought, unless it was Blanche.

His relief lasted as long as it took for her to look directly at him and tell him, "The lady Daria wants to see you immediately in the solar." To the others, she said, "One of the other servants will show the rest of you around to the back, where you can unload the wagons and tend to the horses. Lady Daria said to warn you to watch your tongues, for there are house servants who are not of your brotherhood."

Human-born, that meant. And even if she hadn't said it, Weiland would have guessed, for a man came around the corner then who did not at all have the age or sort of looks Daria preferred. Had Daria decided she needed more servants to tend her here in St. Celia's, Weiland wondered, or did human-born servants come with the house?

He didn't ask Bess, for he was concentrating, as she led him through the house, on what he should tell Daria, how he should word the news of what had happened.

The solar turned out to be what in the fortress Weiland would have called the hall.

And Bess had no sooner left him there than Daria came in through another door. "Where have you been?" she demanded. "I expected you hours ago."

Weiland took a deep breath. "Llewellur . . ." Llewellur was in no position to be needing Weiland to cover for him, even if Weiland had been willing. "Llewellur," Weiland started again, "escaped during the night."

Daria made an airy gesture that looked like a dismissal.

Which meant what?

"I had to track him. I wasn't sure whether—"

"Yes, fine," Daria said, which he took to mean she didn't want details.

"He's dead," Weiland said, which was the single most important thing he had to say. "He—"

"It doesn't matter. Come with me."

It doesn't matter? That didn't sound promising at all. Weiland followed as Daria led him deep into the house, hurrying to the point of almost running. *I need a blood sacrifice to consecrate the new dwelling*, Daria had told Kedj. Llewellur had been a logical choice. Llewellur had been a very logical choice.

"He escaped during the night," Weiland repeated as he trailed behind her. Even if she was in a hurry—he didn't dare think of *what* she was in a hurry for—talking while they went wasn't going to slow them.

He was tempted to say, "During Adger's watch," but Daria despised excuses: She would say it was his fault for making an unwise choice; she would say he could have posted two guards, if he wasn't sure of their reliability. He had the queasy feeling she wasn't listening to him anyway. "When I tracked him down, he jumped rather than—"

"*Weiland.*" She turned and looked at him in obvious exasperation. "Enough."

She resumed her hasty pace without waiting for an answer, so that his "Yes, my lady," was addressed to her back.

Llewellur had been the logical choice. Now, who better to take his place than the person responsible for losing him, the person who had already shown he couldn't keep his position as head of the company, who had made one wrong decision after another—and Daria didn't even know yet about the scene at the town gate.

"Get that torch," Daria said, stopping in front of a closed door and taking a key from her belt. In the fortress, there was only one room that was locked.

There are human-born men here, Weiland thought. In the fortress, Daria provided what the company needed, and nobody had individual possessions, and nobody would risk Daria's ire by touching something she had not given them leave to touch. But she couldn't know these human servants of hers yet, not after only one day. Surely she had other things—chests of gold and perhaps recognizable jewelry and finery exacted as toll—that she wouldn't want outsiders seeing until she knew she could trust them.

But the door swung open, and Weiland could smell the same smells as from Daria's spell room—incense, herbs, and blood.

Some of Daria's spells required blood.

Some had required a life.

It took a moment for Weiland—fear numbed—to fumble the torch into the bracket by the door. He turned to face Daria, and saw over her shoulder a table such as the one he'd been relieved they'd left behind at the fortress. It took another moment for him to remember that that table *had* been left behind, to realize that there was only one way— unless the previous occupants of this dwelling had known a magic similar to Daria's, requiring similar spells—for him to be smelling blood.

Finally, finally, he saw that there was a body on the table.

Daria watched his eyes shift beyond her. She said, "At least it isn't you."

And Weiland was ashamed that—even beyond that one didn't contradict Daria—he couldn't deny this.

She lit a candle from the torch and approached the table, and the shape resolved itself into that of a bear. Lon. Lon was the only one of the company who'd been born a bear.

But she wouldn't have killed Lon, Weiland thought, staring at the body, bound at wrists and ankles, lying on its side. He could see where she'd drawn a knife across the throat, and how the blood had run out onto the table and then spilled and puddled on the floor. She hadn't even collected it to draw power from. One never questioned Daria, but Lon was the leader, which made him—besides Kedj—the most valuable member of the company. It *couldn't* be Lon.

Except it was. Weiland recognized the clothes, torn at the seams as they were when he'd transformed from human to the larger form of bear. Obviously a bear would not have permitted itself to be bound—though Weiland couldn't imagine Lon submitting either. At that point, he must have known what was about to happen. At that point, he wouldn't have had anything left to lose.

At the hill fortress, Kedj would have been there. Kedj would go into the spell room with Daria to bind the one whose turn it was, and see to it that the bindings didn't come loose, whether it was a spell requiring blood only, or death itself. But somehow Daria alone had gotten Lon tied, and she would have kept him human till the moment of his death because, she'd said often enough, power came from human blood—even tainted human blood—but not from the blood of animals. Weiland preferred the idea of dying while in human shape—despite the fact that that would mean being more aware of what was happening. He very much doubted that this was what Lon would have chosen.

"You're surprised?" Daria asked.

Weiland wasn't sure what she wanted.

She said, "A sacrifice, by its very nature, calls for something of worth. The sacrifice of something useless or without value is meaningless."

Did she mean him, or Llewellur?

"Yes, my lady," he answered.

"This body has lain here since last night, waiting for you to dispose of it. Were it not for the cold, it would have begun to smell by now, and drawn attention."

"Yes, my lady. I'm sorry."

"Remove the clothes, of course. Under cover of darkness, you can dump the body into the river, which passes no more than a block to the north of here. The body of a bear in the river will excite comment, but not overmuch suspicion. If you hadn't come tonight, I would have had to call in the cook."

That was a thought to set Weiland's teeth on edge, though he felt no sorrow for Lon's death. He didn't ask what Daria's plan would have been had he arrived as scheduled in the morning. He just said, once again, "Yes, my lady."

9

Weiland was relieved to note that while several buildings backed onto the river, none were directly by it. The water moved sluggishly here, probably due at least in part to the grates that were built into the wall to prevent potential enemies from a watery access to the heart of St. Celia's. But the grates, like the boundary between river and banks, were choked with mud and weeds. They were probably lifted and cleaned periodically, although evidently not recently. During the summer, there would be a stench of stagnant water and sewage that was at least one good reason not to build close to the water.

If there had been some way to smuggle the body over the wall, Weiland would have preferred that, for the grates had openings close enough to prevent even large fish from passing through. Yet Weiland was unwilling to butcher the body of someone he had known and worked with, even if that person was Lon. Besides, he reasoned, if he did cut the body apart, some of the pieces were bound to be discovered. After they'd been in the water long enough, they could be mistaken for the remnants of human limbs and organs, which would result in a long and thorough investigation—perhaps thorough enough that someone might remember Daria had entered the town in the company of a man not seen again. As Daria had indicated, the presence of a dead bear in the river would generate curiosity and speculation. That was better than fear and suspicion. So he would put the body in the river, knowing it *must* be discovered, but trusting that it could not be tracked back to Daria.

Telek was with Weiland, helping to carry Lon's body, which was wrapped in burlap bagging. The stiffness of death had passed with the hours, but the body was heavy and unwieldy, and—despite what Daria had said about the cold—had begun to smell.

For several long moments they waited in the dark between two buildings, watching for lights, listening for movement. They weren't wearing swords, which could only get in the way on this particular errand, but naturally they had their daggers at their belts. As well as several others hidden about their persons, because that was the way Kedj had taught them. Still Weiland felt very vulnerable, especially because of his only sketchy knowledge of their surroundings.

There was no sign that anyone else was about in the night.

Without a word, they crossed the open area—uneven ground dotted with winter weeds and offal that had either never made it into the river or had been left behind from a season of higher water. The marshy ground was frozen by the night's cold so that a thin film of ice broke and crackled under their boots.

They set the body down and began to remove the covering. Weiland guessed it unlikely that anyone would believe a bear had somehow—unobserved—entered the town and come to meet a natural death that had—coincidentally—occurred in the river. But there was no use inviting conjecture by leaving the body to be found wrapped and tied.

They rolled the body off the burlap and into the water. The splash was probably no louder than the cracking of the mud had been—which Weiland had *known* was not nearly so loud as his nerves made it seem—but a voice called from across the flats, "Hey!" and he looked up to see a group of men emerging from an alleyway. Five, if they each held a torch, though some of the shadows may have been more men. Town guard, on the search for people such as they.

"Leave those," Weiland hissed at Telek, who made as though to gather up the wrappings. There was nothing there to identify Daria's household—only the two of them threatened to do that.

"Stop!" some of the men called as Weiland and Telek took off at a run along the riverbank. There was no cover here, but neither did they want to run right into their pursuers by heading straight for the town buildings that might—if they didn't run directly into a blind alley—serve to hide them.

The ground was lumpy and pitted, and shadowed weeds caught at toes and ankles, so that nobody made good speed. But they all knew that eventually the river led under the town wall, and eventually Weiland and Telek would have to make a break for the alleys or be stopped by that wall. Their pursuers were able to run up closer to the houses, where the ground was more level.

And there *were* more than five.

"Now!" Weiland called to Telek, with no way of knowing how far that particular alley extended, or if it ended at a household's gate.

It didn't. It connected to a street, and Weiland and Telek turned right, then quickly left down another narrow way, crossed without turning down another street, and *did* end up in someone's yard. They went over the wooden fence that enclosed what—by the smell of curing leather—had to be a tanner's residence and outbuildings, then went over the fence again into another wide street.

Telek and Weiland ran side by side, and Weiland couldn't judge if Telek could have gone faster alone or was just barely keeping up. They were both breathing heavily, their feet slapping alternately against packed dirt or stone—as they moved between side streets and thoroughfares. Dogs were barking, people began opening shutters demanding to know what was going on, so that light streamed out into the streets, and pursuit was close at their heels, with more and more men joining the original group of town guard. They could never outrun the disturbance they were causing, which had been Weiland's intent: suddenly reverse direction and—coming face-to-face with their pursuers—point beyond and say, "They went that way."

Suddenly Telek chose a direction, where previously he had left Weiland to lead.

"No," Weiland gasped, not having enough extra breath for a full argument.

Neither did Telek. "Home," he managed.

Which Weiland already knew: The cathedral tower loomed ahead and slightly off to the left. But the last thing Daria would want was them bringing trouble to her very doorstep. He knew he'd never get all that out; instead he grabbed hold of Telek's sleeve and said, more emphatically, "No."

Telek shook him off and continued the way he was already going.

There was no time to do anything but veer off in another direction, dividing pursuit, hoping that with fewer men following each of them, they might be easier to shake off.

He came to a street that was even bigger than the one he was on. He recognized, after he passed it by, the street he and Telek and the others had taken from the town gate to Daria's: Cathedral Street. A quick glance over his shoulder showed that those following had, indeed, divided. Weiland dodged into a dark, narrow alleyway to his right.

And ran smack into someone.

He'd seen no one, and there was no warning he needed to swerve or slow. He fell, and the person he'd run into fell, both sprawling together.

Light came from around the corner—the torches from those who'd been chasing. The pursuers gave cries of satisfaction at the imminent capture. Weiland tried to scramble to his feet—unlikely as escape seemed at this point—but the one he'd collided with rose also, and they ended up toppling each other again.

Hands gripped Weiland's shoulders. He was pulled loose of the other man's encumbering limbs only to be thrown to the ground clear of him. The town guard had followed for several blocks now; they'd seen that he and Telek both had light-colored hair, and the other man who'd been in the alley was dark: they could readily see who was who. Someone kicked him, or several did, the blows landing on his side more than his stomach, but hard enough and often enough so that once again he couldn't catch his breath. They didn't stop until he gave up trying to move and the edges of his sight were bordered by looming shadows that had nothing to do with the night.

Someone pulled his arms behind his back and tied his wrists together, while Weiland tried to ignore the buzzing in his ears and the thought of just how angry with him Daria was going to be. He felt someone remove the dagger from its sheath on his belt. The foolish human-born man didn't know enough to search for hidden weapons, but those would be of no use now. Maybe later. Kedj would be furious about how badly he'd handled everything so far. He must start thinking smartly.

The men were congratulating he whom Weiland had run into for capturing him.

Capturing, Weiland thought bitterly. *He was as startled as I was.*

The man admitted as much. "I heard all the commotion and came out to see what was going on, and he ran right into me." The others continued to pound him good-naturedly on the back. "What'd he do?" his captor asked.

"Murder," they answered. "We happened upon him at the river's edge just as he was dumping a body."

"Did he?" the man said appraisingly, just as a babble of voices preceded the flood of more light as additional men came from around the corner.

Weiland raised his head from the street to see, and somebody put his foot on his back to prevent him.

But it was more than just those that had been after Telek; there must have been some who had divided from the group earlier. For just as one voice announced, to Weiland's relief, "Lost him," another said, "Better come back to the river. You're not going to believe this unless you see it."

Weiland was pulled to his feet and given a hard shake in case he needed reminding to behave.

"Any more trouble from you, and you can be dragged back," someone told him.

Resistance now could gain nothing.

Weiland was too groggy from the kicks and the voices talking behind him in the darkness to have any idea which was the leader. Kedj's advice was to always give precedence to learning who was the leader, to know who to go after.

They gave him a shove in the direction of the mouth of the alley, but there were too many for him to try to make a break.

The man who had inadvertently prevented his escape was walking ahead. That one started off in the other direction, but someone called after him, "Aren't you curious?"

Either the man hesitated, or time stretched itself out as Weiland swayed on his feet. Then the man said, "Certainly I am," and rejoined the group.

Since they went straight to the river rather than backtracking the serpentine route of before, it took only a short while to get to where Weiland and Telek had rolled Lon's body into the water. A crowd was beginning to form, and the way they were all bunched together on the bank told Weiland that they had already fished the body out of the water.

"Who is it?" asked the man who had warned Weiland not to give them any more trouble. Twice now he'd seemed to take charge. For want of a more obvious choice, Weiland would think of him as the leader, unless someone else more likely turned up. He would kill him first.

"Not *who*," said one from the riverside group, "*what*. It's a bear."

The word rippled through the crowd, spoken in turns in amazement, or amusement, or disbelief.

With a short grunt of impatience, the leader pushed his way through for a closer look, and someone with his hand on Weiland's back shoved him closer, also.

The body was lying face up, eyes wide, muzzle open, the fur sparkling with river water.

The leader crouched beside. His hand touched the gash at the neck, as though he suspected to find that it was only a bear skin, with the real murdered man hidden beneath.

Which, Weiland thought with irony, was the exact opposite of the way things really were with Daria's company.

The leader sought out Weiland's face from those around him. "What's the meaning of this?"

Weiland couldn't think of any answer that would make them let him go, so he said nothing.

"Who are you?" the man asked next, as though perhaps Weiland simply hadn't understood the first question. "Who was that with you that got away, and what were the two of you doing with this bear?"

And when Weiland still did not answer, the person behind him smacked him on the back of the head and said, "What's the matter, boy, can't you talk?" He cuffed Weiland a second time, harder. "Are you dumb, boy?" And again. "Can't speak?" And again. "Brains addled?"

Silence was getting him nowhere. "No," Weiland said, firmly but quietly.

Yet another hit, this one catching his ear, so that his head was full of ringing, over which he heard the man say, "Then answer the questions that are put to you."

Kedj was right about going after the leader first—the loss of a leader often led to at least temporary disarray—but if there was any chance at all, Weiland knew who was going to be a quick second.

"How did this bear come to be here?" the leader demanded.

Nothing he said could make the situation better, but he could potentially make it worse.

Before the man behind him could hit him again, another voice said, "Maybe he doesn't know."

Everyone turned to look at the man Weiland had run into in the alley. The man shrugged. "Maybe," he repeated, sounding less convinced himself.

"You know this boy?" the leader asked.

"Never saw him before he practically ran over me when I came out to hear what all the fuss was." The man shrugged again. "I don't know anything about any of this. I'm just saying maybe you've knocked all the sense out of him, or maybe he's a half-wit to begin with, or maybe in either case he doesn't know anything."

Weiland didn't care if they thought he was a simpleton if that could get him out of this. He'd seen a simpleton once: a boy in one of the caravans they'd stopped—a boy close to his own age, who sucked on his fingers and didn't speak, and didn't move when they had ordered everyone out of the wagon. "He doesn't have all his wits," a woman with him had cried. "He doesn't understand." Now Weiland considered whether he should try to act more like that boy, if that was a good excuse, but he hadn't seen enough to feel he could do so convincingly. Still, not answering seemed to be working for the moment.

The man from the alley turned to look over the crowd, for there was no telling by now which were with the original town guard and who were simply onlookers. He asked, "Did anyone see this boy accost and murder this bear?"

It was so absurdly worded, a few in the crowd tittered.

By his expression, the leader did not approve of this levity. "We didn't see him *kill* the bear. We saw him push the body into the water."

"What, all by himself?" the man scoffed. He kicked at the burlap that had been used to wrap Lon. "He waylaid the bear—I can only assume to steal his money—*did* the bear have any money left on him?— then this boy carried the body here so that nobody would become suspicious, and threw it into the water all by himself?"

Most in the crowd were laughing openly.

Someone from the original group of town guard said, somewhat sulkily, "He had an accomplice."

"An accomplice?" repeated the man who suddenly seemed to be defending Weiland.

What was going on? Weiland knew this had to be a trick. This man was pretending to be trying to help him but Weiland couldn't figure out what he could possibly hope to gain.

Someone was describing Telek. "Another youth. Maybe a year or two younger."

Actually Telek was older, just shorter. Weiland didn't correct them, and the man from the alley said, with scorn in his voice, "Younger than *this?*" Sixteen was a man, and probably no more than four or five years younger than the man speaking, but if they thought he looked younger— though he was as tall as any of them—Weiland wasn't going to correct that, either. The man from the alley looked at Weiland appraisingly. "A brother?" he asked.

Did he see some profit in helping Weiland—was that what he was up to? In the meantime, he was making fools of the town guard. The men were red-faced and squirming, and those who had joined in the chase later were no longer looking ready to hold Weiland down and kick him till he answered their questions. They were waiting for this other man to entertain them.

Was he, for some unknown reason, really trying to help?

Weiland couldn't imagine how admitting to a brother would possibly help.

Nor could he imagine how it might hurt.

Which of course didn't mean there wasn't a way. But if he didn't do something, his might-be rescuer could readily lose patience. Hesitantly he echoed, "Brother," in a tone he hoped could be taken as simple or not, depending on how he decided to answer further questions.

The man from the alley opened his arms out in an expansive gesture. "See. There you have it. Obviously this boy was trying to protect his brother. That's why he wouldn't answer your questions. The two boys obviously sneaked out a window after their parents or master sent them to bed and were out on some innocent mischief—as boys will do— when they discovered the bear's body."

Weiland was aware that people were looking at him, so he nodded.

"All they're guilty of is pushing it into the water—probably to see if it would float."

"Float," Weiland agreed in the same rather vacant voice he had used before.

"How many of you, when you were younger, never took something you found at the water's edge and threw it in to see what would happen? Obviously,"—the man certainly had a fondness for the word "obviously"—"*obviously* this boy couldn't have wrestled that full-grown bear down to the ground and knifed him: For one thing, there are no bites or scratches on him. How do you knife a bear to death and not get clawed? And for another thing, there's no blood on him. How do you knife anything to death and not get blood on you?"

If his hands hadn't been tied behind his back, Weiland would have held his arms out to demonstrate more clearly that he was scratchless and unbloodied, but the leader of the town guard was already talking anyway.

"That's just the point," he objected. "Nobody *knifes* a bear at all. You'd use nets and spears, or arrows. You don't get that close."

"It does no good to say nobody does it. Somebody did. I'm just saying the culprit obviously isn't this fellow. Maybe the bear came up on somebody suddenly. Somebody who didn't have a bow or spear handy. I couldn't begin to guess that."

"And how did the bear get in town anyway? There's something suspect going on here."

For someone who couldn't begin to guess, the man was fast. "Maybe it climbed over the wall." People were making doubtful faces. "Or maybe it was a bear smuggled in for unauthorized gambling— fighting or baiting. It just doesn't seem fair to hold this boy responsible for something he obviously knows nothing about. There's no law that I've ever heard against finding a dead bear and rolling it into the river."

The leader of the town guard looked disgruntled. He had questions to which he was probably beginning to suspect he'd never get the answers, he had a report to give to his superiors—a report that would probably contain multiple repetitions of the phrase "I don't know." He had a wet, beginning-to-stink bear carcass to dispose of, and he had nobody to blame.

Weiland tried to look innocent and harmless, neither of which were looks Daria generally favored.

Impatiently the leader gestured for one of his men to release Weiland.

The man who'd been shoving and striking Weiland cut the ropes from around his wrists with what turned out to be Weiland's own blade.

Weiland accepted the dagger back and returned it to its sheath, unwilling to risk the freedom he had so unexpectedly won for the temporary satisfaction of taking off a few of the man's fingers.

"Go on back to your master," the leader said to him, "and be thankful we don't report you were truant."

"Yes," Weiland said in as meek a voice as he could manage.

Apparently it wasn't meek enough. Or the man simply hadn't had all his say. "And next time, don't run when a duly appointed officer of the law orders you to halt."

Weiland inclined his head and lowered his eyes, which Daria sometimes liked.

"Go on then," the man shouted. He included everybody with a disgusted look and a wave of his hand. "Go home. All of you go home."

10

Weiland didn't wait to see if the crowd would disperse. Truant apprentice or straying son, he would be expected to be anxious to get back where he belonged before his absence was noted. No one could suspect his lady knew exactly where he was—or had, until Telek returned, bearing who-could-guess-exactly-what story. Which meant, in a roundabout way, that Weiland *was* anxious to get back: The situation could only get more complicated by the appearance of an armed and reckless rescue party or by some impetuous action on Daria's part— such as assuming that his best chances would be as a wolf.

Unlikely, he told himself. He forced a calmer pace lest his haste aroused the suspicion that he was running away. Unlikely that Daria would do anything. In the end, Daria could be counted on to do whatever was necessary to best protect Daria. And Weiland could think of no safer action for her than to abandon him. She didn't know, unless Telek or one of the others in the company had said something, that he had all unwittingly seen to it that the gate guards would remember him, and connect him to her. She would assume, incorrectly, that there was no way anyone in St. Celia's could associate the two of them. But she would be right in assuming that he would go to his death rather than betray her, because betraying her would still result in his death, except that then she would be the one to choose the manner of it. One of Daria's sayings was: "I can make your final moments last a long, long time."

Of course, granted that Daria would look out for herself, that didn't necessarily mean she would reason out the rest of it the same way Weiland had.

He tried to analyze the situation, to come at it from different directions in an attempt to see things as Daria might. And realized that, by doing what seemed sensible at the moment, he'd put himself between Daria and those who had been questioning him, those who—if they were interested—had only to take note of where he went to see for themselves what he would have been willing to die to keep from them.

By chance or design, some had set out in the same direction he had on leaving the riverside. Now, without having to look over his shoulder, he could make out three sets of footsteps that had made the turn with him onto Cathedral Street.

He walked past the cathedral, past Daria's lodgings. He had no idea how far beyond that this street went, or where. Should he take off down one of the side streets? How long would it take for those behind to realize he wasn't taking a straight route anywhere? He pretended that something had gotten into his boot: he slowed, looked down at his foot repeatedly, shook it, tapped it against the street as though to work a small irritant down to the toe. Finally, as though he could take it no longer, he sat at the side of the street and removed the boot. He took a lot of time at it, getting the boot off, examining it, shaking it, examining it again, putting it back on, standing, shaking his head as though in frustration, then sitting back down to start all over.

A pair of men passed him. They had to, or pretend to stop for another reason, which—this time of night, with nobody else about, and most shops and dwellings shut and darkened—would have given them away.

"Good night," one of them wished him, and the other said, "God speed," which might have meant they had simply been going to destinations that lay on the same route as his, or it might mean they intended to circle around behind and follow him more secretly.

Weiland was just getting his boot back on for the second time when the last of the footsteps that had trailed him since the river approached. And stopped.

The man he'd run into in the alley crouched beside him. "Isn't that the way of things?" the man commented. "If it isn't one problem, it's another."

To which there was no sensible reply, so Weiland said nothing.

The man watched him adjust his boot. Weiland wondered how often he could put on and take off the same boot before his audience got bored and moved on, but he mistrusted his own staying power.

So he stood, abruptly. And he headed back the way he had just come. *Declare yourself*, he thought. *Give up the chase or drop all pretense of not following me.*

The man dropped all pretense of not following him.

He caught up in a moment; but he had not drawn a weapon, and Weiland—despite years of Kedj and Daria proclaiming him hopeless—knew that he had matched up well against those who came over the mountains. He felt confident enough in his abilities, and unsure enough of the ways of townfolk that he did not spin around and attack, but continued to walk, warily, waiting.

"Do you have a name," the man asked, "or should I just call you 'boy'?"

"Boy" was really beginning to grate on Weiland's nerves. "Weiland," he said.

The man clearly was waiting for more. Daria, Weiland remembered, who had always just been Daria, had added "de Gris" to come to St. Celia's. It must be something to do with having so many people in one place, and needing to keep straight who was who. He thought of the various Llewellurs Daria had made, and how there was no way—even if he wanted—to differentiate one from another.

But Weiland had no idea how additional names worked and suspected he might give away much by revealing this.

"Just Weiland?" the man finally asked, plainly suspecting that maybe he had been right in calling Weiland simple, as though Weiland didn't know enough to give his full name without being coaxed.

"Just Weiland," Weiland agreed.

"Indeed. Well then, I'm just Shile."

Weiland hoped that now, with that settled, the man would go home and leave him alone. They had come to the cathedral yet again, and Weiland picked at random one of the streets radiating from the square, so that they were getting farther away all the time from where Weiland needed to be. He didn't want to do anything to call unnecessary attention to himself, as he had done that afternoon at the town gate, but he was beginning to suspect he might have to hit this Shile on the back of the head to be rid of him.

Shile said, "Well, Weiland, I wanted to thank you."

Weiland read irony into the tone, and decided that, after all, the man expected payment for defending him before the town guard.

It wasn't one of Kedj's official lessons—it didn't need to be—but those of Daria's company knew better than to perform a service first, with the expectation of being repaid later—especially if service and payment had not been worked out beforehand with exacting detail. Weiland glanced at Shile to indicate he had heard, and kept on walking.

Not put off—apparently nothing could put the man off—Shile said, "For not telling them what I was doing in the alley."

This time Weiland stopped, and finally looked fully at him. Apparently he wasn't being sarcastic. "What *were* you doing?" he asked.

The other realized his mistake and gave a wide-eyed look of stunning innocence. "Nothing," he said.

Weiland thought back to the dark alley, and how he had not seen anyone, though he should have, despite Shile's dark hair and—now that Weiland noticed—his dark clothes. He remembered the feel of colliding with him, and realized Shile had been bent over in a doorway.

And with that, everything fell into place. "You're a burglar," he said, amazed that it had taken so long to piece together. "You were trying to break into the place."

"Never," Shile said with such total assurance that nobody could possibly believe him.

"I thought," Weiland explained, "that you were just inordinately fond of your own voice." He had intentionally avoided saying, "I assumed you were hoping for some sort of reward," but guessed, by the man's startled expression, that he probably shouldn't have said anything.

"No, really,"—this time there was definitely sarcasm in Shile's voice—"it was my pleasure to go out of my way to help you. Think nothing of the fact that I jeopardized my own freedom and well-being rather than leave you in the lurch—as, I might point out, your own associate had no problem doing."

"You *do* like the sound of your own voice," Weiland said.

Shile opened, then shut his mouth twice before getting out, "I'm really beginning to regret ever stepping out of that alley."

"Thank you," Weiland said, remembering his manners.

Shile hesitated, as though suspecting a cutting remark was hidden in that. Then he gave a slight inclination of his head and answered, "You're welcome."

Weiland resumed walking, still in that unknown direction. Thief or authority made no difference—he couldn't lead Shile to Daria.

Shile was still by his side. "What *was* going on with that bear?"

"My brother and I were walking along the riverside when we happened upon this bear carcass. . . ."

Shile sighed. "Is your brother as strange as you, or are you one of a kind?"

Weiland hesitated, unsure what Shile was asking. He fell back once more on the excuse Daria had provided for him. "We're from the Holy Land," he said, "my brother and I."

"Indeed?" Shile asked in a tone that Weiland could not identify as mockery, disbelief, or lack of interest. "What part?"

"What part?" Weiland repeated dully. Shile was definitely interested now, and enjoying this, he could tell. He took a wild guess. "North."

"The north part of the Holy Land?" Shile repeated so pleasantly that Weiland knew the answer had been a stupid one.

But he had no idea how to correct it. The only choice was to be brazen. "Yes," he said.

Shile grinned, and said, again, "Indeed."

No North Holy Land, Weiland noted mentally.

Shile said, "You could at least offer to buy me a drink to thank me for helping you out of a potentially unpleasant situation."

Buy a drink. It was a strange concept. At Daria's hall everything was provided—or withheld—by Daria. But Weiland understood the purpose of towns was to buy and sell goods. "No," he said. Then, because he had a grudging respect for this man who seemed as expert with words as Kedj was with weapons, he added, "I have no money."

"Well, then," Shile said, "I'll buy *you* a drink to thank *you* for helping *me* out of a potentially unpleasant situation." He grinned brightly. "And, maybe, get you drunk enough to tell me about that bear."

"No," Weiland repeated. The word hung between them for a long moment, sounding even to Weiland's ears more abrupt and unfriendly than he had intended. He explained, "I must return"—He couldn't say "to Daria"—"to where I belong."

Shile raised his eyebrows. "For someone in a hurry to be somewhere, you're certainly traveling in a roundabout way, making long loops, taking a great deal of time to go a short distance."

Weiland could think of no reasonable reply.

"Unless," Shile speculated, "you're trying to prevent me from seeing where you're going."

Weiland thought that Shile was quick enough that—if their situations had been reversed—he could have come up with some believable excuse. Weiland could not. "Yes," he admitted.

Shile pointed to a cross street ahead of them. "Then I will tell you that the fastest way for me to get to where I'm going is to turn left here, then another left to skirt around the fish market, which always stinks, even at night, cross the bridge, and proceed up West River Street back to where we met. I won't follow you, so if you avoid that route, we won't run into each other again."

Which was no assurance. Weiland would still need to be on the lookout, but he nodded.

"Thank you again for not turning me in," Shile said, "even if you didn't *know* to turn me in."

Weiland said, "Thank you for helping me, even if your reasoning was wrong." And with that he turned back to retrace the way to the last cross street, and Shile—whistling loudly, no doubt so Weiland could hear that he wasn't following—continued on his way.

11

When Weiland was satisfied that neither Shile nor anyone else was following him, he returned to Daria's lodgings. It was Daria herself who instantly answered his soft knock on the door—not a good sign, for Daria believed beauty required regular habits and vigilant pampering, which included not only rising late but going to bed early.

She led Weiland to her apartments with never a word—a reminder, should Weiland have needed it, that they were no longer in the fortress, surrounded only by their own. This was also the direction of Daria's spell room, and Weiland wondered just how angry with him she was. Or if she was more angry with Telek: for deserting his partner, for risking her safety by running straight to her, for being the one to bring her bad news. Weiland pictured her killing Telek—which, all in all, was not an unpleasant thought—except that it would mean having to go back out into the night to dispose of another body.

But she didn't bring him into the spell room. She went no farther than her dressing room before turning on him and demanding, "What happened?"

Weiland would have given a great deal to have known how, exactly, Telek had already described the situation. "The town guard—"

She interrupted with up flung hands and a growl of exasperation.

Weiland hesitated, assuming she was about to speak, but she snapped, "Go on. This isn't going to get any better by your making me drag it out of you."

"Telek and I ran, in case they hadn't seen the body, to draw them away from it." Not that that had been likely, but it had been a distant possibility, and he was desperate for anything to make the two of them sound the slightest bit less incompetent.

"Apparently Telek is a better runner," Daria said, "seeing he made it home in a timely manner, and you took half the night."

"We separated—"

"I could guess that."

Weiland was reluctant to accuse Telek, for Daria's punishments for those who informed were sometimes more severe than for the ones who made a mistake or performed badly. Weiland didn't know if this was due to her dislike of excuses, or if some long-ago time she might have had someone reveal something she had done wrong, or if she simply liked to keep everyone unbalanced, never knowing what to expect. He said, "I was concerned not to have anyone follow us back here."

"Verily," she said. She brushed her fingers against his cheek—which must have been scraped when the crowd had overpowered him in the alley; he hadn't even been aware of the sting until she touched it, and suddenly he realized how bruised and rumpled he must look. Her hand drifted gently down to his sleeve, that was dirty and ripped. "Had a long, hard run, did you," she asked in a very dangerous voice, "leading pursuit away from me?"

"I was about to say—"

He hadn't been, hoping she need never know, and she slapped him on the already raw cheek.

"—that I was captured—"

She slapped him again.

"—but I got away."

She didn't hit him after that one. "How?"

He hesitated too long, and she slapped him yet again.

"I convinced them,"—he certainly wasn't going to mention Shile, which would send her into a real fury, knowing that he had talked to someone without her permission, especially a human-born person, especially because she would suspect that he had stupidly given away more about her than he had intended, which he may well have done—"I convinced them we didn't know anything about the bear's body, that we had just found it when the town guard came upon us."

"Unusually glib tonight," Daria said, "apparently." She patted his cheek gently as though to say all was fine, then, when he wasn't expecting it so much, slapped him again. "Don't you ever try to keep things from me," she whispered. "Don't you dare lie."

"My lady—"

She made a gesture, too small and too quick to see, but Weiland felt the rush of magic. It was not the transforming power that turned him into a wolf that she unleashed on him, but something more akin to her healings: a burning, tearing rearranging of something inside that brought him doubled over to his knees, crying out in pain and unable to breathe.

"My lady, it's true," he managed to gasp. *Don't let the human-born servants hear,* he thought. If he caused a disturbance that brought unwanted attention to Daria, she would lose her temper.

"They just let you go?" she asked in a tone that indicated she didn't believe so for a moment.

"Yes." He could taste blood and felt as though something was alive inside him, clawing to get out. "That's why it took me so long to get back." He coughed, bringing up blood, and tried to stifle a second, bigger cough that was building up in his chest. If she became disgusted, she would turn away and leave him here to die, for one of the others to clean up afterwards. "I didn't come straight home because I wanted to make sure no one was following me."

"And no one was?"

He shook his head emphatically. That he hadn't been followed was the one thing of which he *was* certain. He clenched his teeth against the cough, shivering, unable to speak to offer assurances.

He became aware, after long moments of being blinded by pain, of Daria's knees as she stood before him. The need to cough was dissolving, the pain becoming controllable.

"I should have brought Kedj instead of any of you," she said.

"Yes, my lady," he managed to whisper.

"I should have locked you all in the hall, and taken my magic away, and let you rip each other apart like the mindless beasts you are."

"Yes, my lady," he repeated, because it was what she wanted to hear.

"*Think* of what you are without me."

Weiland nodded.

"Get out of my sight."

Luckily she turned from him even as she said it, and strode into her inner room, because Weiland needed the help of her dressing table to pull himself up, and she hated gracelessness.

He staggered from the room thinking that it would be worth spending the rest of his life as a wolf to kill her.

It would.

But he wouldn't succeed, he knew it—she was so much smarter than he was. She would catch him at it. He heard her voice in his mind: *I can make your final moments last a long, long time.*

Better, if less satisfying, to sneak off during the night, as Llewellur had tried, to escape the range of her magic.

But he wouldn't be able to do that tonight. He knew, from the times she had used healing spells on him, he wouldn't be able to move for a week. And he knew what would happen after that: He would convince himself, as he always did, that things weren't that bad when Daria wasn't angry with him, that living trying to dodge Daria's moods was better than living as a wolf with no sense of awareness, that maybe something would happen to take her attention off him, so that she took no particular notice of him.

Coward, he chided himself. But it didn't help. Whatever happened to him after this was his own fault.

He made it to the hall, where those of the company had their sleeping pallets spread out before the fireplace. When Daria had taken Lon to accompany her to St. Celia's, she had left Weiland in charge for the remainder of the journey. That authority wouldn't last, he knew, especially not if he was crippled for days by the effects of Daria's spell. He needed to reestablish dominance now, before his muscles stiffened and his body gave out—before they saw his weakness—with enough unrelenting force and ruthlessness to carry him through till next week. *A single stunning act of violence*, Kedj would say. It wouldn't have worked with Lon, who had always been hot for challenge, but the whole point, of course, was that Lon was no longer here.

With this group, all he had to do was make them acknowledge him tonight; that, coupled with the fact that they were in the habit of looking to him as leader, would protect him from their taking advantage of the fact that he was helpless—at least for the first few days.

He looked over the sleeping bodies and noted Adger had the choicest position. He made straight for him, ignoring the startled cries of protest of those he stepped on along the way, and keeping off his face the fact that his body protested every step.

12

That night, or one of the nights he spent in a haze of pain and confusion, he dreamt that he was running yet again through the streets of St. Celia's. This time, however, it wasn't a crowd of townsmen who chased him, but Lon himself, and Lon was highly irritated with Weiland for having rolled his dead body into the river.

Through the alleys and yards Weiland ran, and never a sign of Telek or any familiar landmark.

I'll never find my way back, *he thought, but then he ran into one particularly dark alley and tripped over someone.* It's that man I met, *he thought, except that he couldn't remember the name,* the fast-talking burglar who helped me before.

Weiland would have to keep Daria from knowing he was getting help, but maybe the man would help him a second time, by showing him the way home.

But the man wouldn't get up—Weiland suspected he was angry that Weiland couldn't remember his name—and he just lay face down in the alley, with Lon's footsteps getting closer and closer.

Weiland crouched beside the man and the name finally returned to him. "Shile," *he said, and rolled him over to force him to see what was happening. But it wasn't the burglar after all; it was Llewellur, dead, his eyes open and staring.*

The footsteps entered the alley, with Weiland in that awkward and unprepared crouch that put him on a level with Lon's knees. He remembered being at knee-level with Daria and hoped Lon wouldn't turn into Daria. Slowly he looked up. It wasn't Lon, but it wasn't Daria, either; it was Llewellur again, and he was still dead even though he was standing, and he said, "This is all your own fault, you know. . . ."

                                    *   *   *

"Weiland."

A voice reached through the layers of sleep to prod him.

"Weiland."

Before he could find his way back to consciousness, someone touched his shoulder, and he was instantly awake. He struck out to protect himself and simultaneously swept his leg to topple the person hovering over him and lunged, throwing himself on top of the fallen . . .

. . . the fallen Bess, who was trying to huddle herself into a ball to shield herself.

The hall was deserted except for the two of them, the level of light indicating it was probably late morning. By the residual aches and stiffness, Weiland guessed five or six days had passed since the night he had disposed of Lon's body and incurred Daria's anger.

Surely mouse-born Bess had not intended to attack him, especially not with only her bare hands—which the members of Daria's company might do, but probably not her household staff. Still, Kedj's lessons came hard: *Trust no one.* Weiland didn't relax his hold on Bess's shoulders, but only said, by way of explanation, "I didn't realize it was you."

Bess remained with her eyes squeezed shut, as though waiting for him to snap her neck.

Finally Weiland asked, "What were you doing?"

Still with her eyes closed, Bess said, "There's a visitor to see you."

"*What?*" Bess looked about to repeat what she had just said, so Weiland asked, instead, "Who?" He would get no sense out of her while she was held in the paralysis of fear, and he estimated he could easily overpower her if she *should* attempt an attack, so he let go of her and sat on the floor next to her.

Bess finally seemed to accept that he wasn't going to kill her, at least not for the moment. She sat up also, wrapping her arms about her. "He said his name is Father Hadden Heallstede. So I asked whose father he was, and he laughed and said he hoped he was father or brother to all God's children." Bess, like her mouse-sister Blanche, could not sit still long. The nervous energy bubbled over from her voice to her quick little hands, and she started fluffing and rearranging Weiland's sleeping pallet, never slowing down in her talking. "I wanted to ask who God's children were, but before I had a chance he said he'd heard from one of the house servants that one of the lady's men-at-arms was sick, which had to be you, and that you had been laid up in the solar for most of a week. So he must think he's your father and brother. I didn't tell him you're one of Daria's wolf-born, because Daria says not to talk to the human-born any more than we have to." Then she added, "He had a nice laugh."

Weiland tried to think of why anyone would want to see someone who was sick, and didn't like the answers he came up with. "Daria didn't send him?"

"The mistress is out," Bess said. Finished tidying the sleeping pallet, she tugged at Weiland's shirt to get it to lay smoother across his shoulders; then she tried to poke him into sitting up straighter. "She and Blanche went to dine with Lord Geoffrey d'Akil and his lady, who are her new friends." Apparently Bess could tell the names meant nothing to him, and she added, "She knows nothing of this visit."

Weiland lay back on his pallet, feeling weak and sore now that the threat of imminent attack had passed. "Then send him away."

Bess stood and went after a ball of dust she spotted on the floor even though she was supposed to be Daria's personal maid, and there were others assigned to keep the rooms clean. "Father Hadden Heallstede says it's his job to minister to the sick," she said. "I don't believe he'll leave until he's seen you."

What would make Daria angrier: to find him in the hall talking to a townsman, or to find a stranger lingering about her front door, attracting the attention of passersby? "Where are the others?" he asked.

"In the inner yard . . . practicing . . ."—not trained as a warrior, or distracted by the way one of the banners hung crookedly on the wall, she hesitated over the word—"maneuvers?" She pulled at one corner of the banner to make it fall properly. "The mistress told Innas that they shouldn't grow soft from town living, and they should drill in sword work and archery and hand-to-hand combat the same as if they were back at the fortress." She must have guessed what he was thinking. "They don't know Father Hadden Heallstede is here, and I won't tell anyone."

Not unless Daria asks, Weiland thought—whatever Bess's intent, and there was no telling what that might be. "Send him in," he said. Better to go to the door himself, he knew, to give the man less opportunity to look around, should his purpose be to study Daria's lodgings for weaknesses, but he didn't think he had the strength.

Ministering to the sick, Weiland thought. It must be another of those strange town concepts, and he remembered the blind man who had been standing in front of the cathedral that first day, expecting people to pay him for being helpless. Weiland wondered if blindness was the same as sickness, and whether this Father Hadden Heallstede knew about the blind man. Maybe Weiland could talk him into leaving, and ministering to the blind man instead.

He sat up when he heard their footsteps approaching, and tried to look less sickly as Bess came to the doorway and announced, "Father Hadden Heallstede."

The man who entered the hall was older than those of Daria's company, but by no means the oldest-looking person Weiland had seen. He gave a huge smile as though delighted to see Weiland, and he said, "Father Hadden is absolutely sufficient. Good morrow, my son. God be with you."

Son. Weiland saw Bess, in the doorway behind the man, mouth the words, "God's children," before she closed the door so they couldn't hear her laugh. Weiland had heard people from the caravans use the word *God*, but there were a whole collection of words Weiland didn't understand that people had for when the company fell on them. *Oaths*, Kedj had said. *People use them when they're upset.* Weiland had never been curious enough to ask what the individual words meant. Now he wished he had. He couldn't see why this man would want to believe himself Weiland's father, or why he would utter oaths about it if he did. Probably the safest course, he decided, was not to answer at all.

And, in fact, Father Hadden didn't seem to need a response. He said, "I'm glad to see you improved from Royce's report of you."

Royce, Weiland presumed, was the house servant who had summoned Father Hadden. Hoping this might be an opportunity to rid himself of the man, Weiland agreed, "Yes, I'm much better."

But no. Father Hadden sat down on the floor next to him. "You're Weiland, I'm told. I'm glad to finally meet one of our new neighbors."

"Neighbors," Weiland repeated hollowly. Then he realized what that meant. "Oh," he said with increased respect for the slightly old, slightly fat man. "The cathedral. That's your house?"

Father Hadden laughed, and Bess was right: It *was* a nice laugh, more sincerely amused than mocking. "Well, hardly. The bishop presides there; I'm just a poor parish priest. And, of course, if we're talking about whose house it is, naturally it's God's house."

He said this as if the two of them shared a joke and understood it together. Weiland said, "Naturally."

Father Hadden frowned. "Have you been fevered, Weiland?" He put his hand to Weiland's brow, and Weiland fought the instinct to knock it away.

But the man—*priest*, he'd called himself—must have read some of Weiland's thought from his face for he raised his brows and immediately took the hand away, saying, "I'm sorry. I didn't mean to distress you. Shall I say a blessing for you, and then be on my way?"

Be on my way sounded good, though Weiland wasn't sure about the rest of it.

"Bow your head, my son," Father Hadden said, and—though Weiland knew that bowing was a sign of subservience—the man's voice was so gentle, Weiland did as he was told. Father Hadden raised his hands but did not put them on Weiland. He said, in the kind of voice Daria used for some of her rituals, "May the blessings of almighty God the Father, the Son, and the Holy Ghost be with you."

The voice alarmed Weiland, but he didn't feel the telltale tingle of magic.

"There," Father Hadden said back in his normal tone, "now that didn't hurt much, did it?"

But he was smiling, and Weiland suspected it wasn't meant to hurt at all, that the man was joking. So he just shook his head.

Father Hadden stood. "I hope you're entirely recovered soon, Weiland," he said. "Feel free to visit me whenever you care to. And please extend the invitation to your mistress, too, and all of this household."

"Yes," Weiland said, because the man seemed to be waiting for an answer.

And then, just when the danger seemed passed, Daria walked in.

"My Lady Daria de Gris,"—Father Hadden got to his feet hurriedly and bowed—"it is a great honor to finally meet you."

"Indeed," Daria said in one of those tones that gave no hint to her mood.

Weiland could see Bess fluttering nervously in the doorway behind her, unsure whether to come in or flee.

"I am Father Hadden Heallstede," the priest said. "I bring warmest greetings and a heartfelt welcome to St. Celia's from His Excellency the Bishop."

Daria gave a slight inclination of her head, indicating, Weiland hoped, that she was not entirely displeased.

Father Hadden continued, "May I offer my deepest condolences on the death of your grandfather this past winter. Lord Robert's loss will be deeply felt by the entire community."

Daria's grandfather? Weiland hadn't known that Daria had any connection with the town before coming. He'd assumed she had picked St. Celia's at random, or because it was close. She had never spoken of her life before the hill fortress. Even those of the company who'd been oldest when Weiland had first learned to understand speech were not the first men she'd made. If anyone knew of her life before coming to the hill fortress, it would be Kedj, and Kedj never spoke of her past. When he glanced at Bess, she looked as surprised as he felt, so the news was not something he had missed by being on the road when Daria arrived or by being bedridden for the better part of a week.

Daria was inclining her head again, and she told Father Hadden, "You're very kind."

"I saw your mother," Father Hadden continued, "it must be,"— he paused to calculate—"well, it would have been twenty-five years ago, when I first came to St. Celia's, when I was first studying for the priesthood. A beautiful young woman—absolutely beautiful—she could have been no older than you are now, eighteen, nineteen years old?" Daria didn't answer. "You bear a truly remarkable resemblance to her."

"You're too kind," Daria murmured, her eyes downcast. But she was loving this unsolicited praise, Weiland could tell.

"Her name was Daria, also, wasn't it? I remember she left St. Celia's suddenly . . ."

"She had been betrothed to a prince in the Holy Land," Daria said. "Yes. Both my parents were killed in a Saracen raid when I was so young, I sadly have no memory of them. I was raised by an aunt, my father's sister."

"How very sad."

But starting from the knowledge that Daria was not from the Holy Land, Weiland's mind skittered to the thought that Daria had been settled in the fortress stronghold several years before he had been born, regardless of how young she looked: The young woman Father Hadden had seen twenty-five years ago must have been Daria herself.

With no way to suspect that close to everything Daria had said had been lies, Father Hadden was saying, "The Lord moves in mysterious ways which are sometimes hard to comprehend. But now you are here. And St. Celia's is richer for it."

"Thank you." Again the smile, the lowered eyes.

"I was just talking to these delightful young people from your household."

Daria looked at Weiland to see if he had done anything to spoil things for her.

"Delightful," Father Hadden repeated, and the hard edge of suspicion around Daria's eyes softened. He took Daria's hand and raised it to his lips, but Daria didn't seem alarmed, so Weiland didn't try to stop him. "I hope the bishop and I shall have the pleasure of your company soon," he said. And after he said this to Daria, he glanced at Bess and Weiland to include them also.

"I *have* been concerned about my householders' rough country manners," Daria started. "I rushed here with the people available as soon as I heard the news of my grandfather—"

"Not at all," Father Hadden interrupted. "They are charming and unaffected."

This seemed to please Daria. "Then perhaps it is time to give them a little more freedom in St. Celia's."

Weiland wasn't sure if that was good news or bad.

13

There was a new Llewellur to play the flute, a thin-faced youth slightly older than the last one. For the most part, he wandered pale and listless in the upper halls, for Daria frequently was away from home, and none of the company was interested in music.

That wasn't all that had changed while Weiland had lain, more or less senseless, on the floor of the great hall for nearly a week.

Daria had been quick to make many friends among the highborn of St. Celia's, and now she went from house to house to be with them constantly. She was happiest when she was with the most highborn, the family of Baron Geoffrey d'Akil, who—Blanche informed Weiland—not only held the town of St. Celia's and most of the surrounding lands, but was not-so-distantly related to the king. Apparently this was something much to be admired in a man. Blanche told Weiland that Daria had fallen in love with the Baron's three charming young children and she'd become instant and inseparable friends with the Baron's wife, Lady Johanna. All this had happened from the moment Daria had presented herself on her first day after arriving in St. Celia's.

It was hard for Weiland to picture. Especially the part with the children. And especially because that would have been the day while Daria was still waiting for the rest of the company to join her, while Lon's blood-drained body was lying on the table in her spell room.

But Blanche and Bess insisted that they saw more of Daria these days than anyone else did—for one or the other of them was always waiting on her—and that she had changed by being among gentler human-born folk.

Perhaps it was true. The company—which Daria took to calling men-at-arms—she needed only to escort her through the streets, and she took different men at different times. Weiland guessed this was to see and judge how each of them reacted amongst the human-born townsfolk, to begin the process of selecting which she'd keep, but when he mentioned this to the others, they laughed and said more likely she just got bored or upset with each of them in turn.

Those of the company who were not at any given time accompanying Daria or running errands for her were mostly in the exercise yard, doing the same kind of training exercises Kedj would have had them at.

But then one of her new friends questioned her—about how she seemed to be training a dozen fierce warriors, and didn't she realize she was not in the Holy Land preparing for war but in peaceful St. Celia's where one or two men-at-arms were all that were needed, and that only to clear the streets of peasant crowds so a lady could pass?

After that, Daria instructed them they were no longer to practice more than three times a week, and only in the mornings. Instead they could go out, in groups of no more than two or three so that they were less likely to get in trouble. "Get to know the town," she told them. She even gave them a little bit of money each, because this was what highborn people did with their men-at-arms.

But how long, Weiland worried—wondering if he was the only one to worry—would Daria continue to pay and feed and house a dozen wolf- and rat- and wolverine-born men who were no longer of use to her?

As he tried to get to know the town, Weiland would frequently see the blind man on the cathedral steps, calling to passersby, "A penny for a poor blind man?"

Finally Weiland went to him and asked, "Are you searching for your father or brother to minister to you?"

The man clapped his hand to his forehead. "Oh, no, it's not you again, is it? The dimwit boy without any money? Go away."

"I have money," Weiland said. To see what would happen, he gave him one of the silver pennies Daria had passed out.

"God bless you, sir," the blind man said. And that was all. The man turned his face with the clouded eyes to someone else then and repeated, "A penny for a poor blind man?"

Weiland walked away, unable to see the point of it at all.

But in the meantime, the house servants taught those of the company about gambling, which made even less sense to Weiland than giving money to a blind man just because he asked for it. He had no interest in what face would show when dice were thrown, or how far someone could spit or send a stream of piss, or whether someone could walk backwards from one place to another without stumbling, or any of the other things men spent money to find out.

Nor did he care to drink huge quantities of beer or mead, which was another of the ways men spent money. Both drinks smelled better than they tasted, and either could make a man light-headed and silly, or heedlessly belligerent, or could even cause him to pass out. Kedj would not approve of a man losing his edge in such a way, and Weiland had spent too much of his life trying to please Kedj.

Melor, who had always been one who tried to get out of hard work, called him a fool, and pointed out that Kedj wasn't there.

But Weiland remembered Daria saying, "I should have brought Kedj instead of any of you."

Still, he would go to the taverns because this was where men gathered and it was his best opportunity to observe them: how they acted, what they said, the kinds of things that interested them.

And that was how he came, one day after they'd been in St. Celia's for over a month, to hear a familiar voice at the Hog and Bone Tavern.

There was a group of men at a table, and some of them had been drinking only, some had eaten as well, and they were trying to settle the bill. It was Shile, the burglar from the alley, who had put himself in charge. Weiland watched in fascination as he put down some money himself, took differing amounts from each of the men, took some money back from the pile, traded coins repeatedly with this man or that one or the pile in the center. It went on for a long time, and at each exchange Shile ended up with more than he had at the previous.

Finally satisfied, or afraid to push any farther no matter how much his companions had drunk, Shile declared everyone properly paid up. Then, for the first time, he glanced around the room and noticed Weiland. "I see a long-lost friend," he announced to those he was with, "and I owe him a drink."

Weiland waited till Shile had sat down at his table to say, softly, only for Shile, "I don't think I can afford to have you buy me a drink."

"Well, in that case," Shile said, "I'll let you buy me one." He gestured to one of the women who worked at the place. "So, Weiland,"—he leaned forward with arms crossed on the table as though ready to share secrets—"you promised to explain about that bear."

"No, I didn't."

Shile waited expectantly, as though hoping for an explanation anyway. "Ah, well," he said, leaning back only as the serving woman came to set his drink on the table. Perhaps that was an invitation, for without any further sign that Weiland could see, the woman sat on Shile's lap, holding on with an arm around his shoulders. "It's hardly fair," Shile continued as though he and Weiland were still alone. "And here I've been trying so hard not to intrude, steadfastly refusing to inquire into who you work for or what you could possibly be up to."

"Introduce me to your handsome friend, Shile," the woman said. "If you tell me his name, I can tell you something else about him." Despite the fact that she was sitting on Shile's lap, she leaned forward to blow a kiss toward Weiland.

She can know nothing about me, Weiland thought, for he had never spoken to her unless it had been to order a drink, and he wasn't even sure of that. But Shile was having a good time with this, Weiland could tell. Apparently he enjoyed intrigue as well as he enjoyed talking.

"His name is Weiland," Shile said. And, although Weiland had not asked, he added, "Weiland, this is Evangeline."

Evangeline moved from Shile's lap to Weiland's. It was too unforeseen for him to be able to prevent her. She smelled clean and soapy, which he found unexpectedly pleasant. "He's quite shy, isn't he?" she asked Shile.

"I hope that isn't the extent of the information you're trading me," Shile said, but he sounded amused rather than anything else.

"He's friends with some men named Adger and Parn and Telek. There's some others in that group, too. They all work for the Lady Daria de Gris, so I imagine he does, as well, even though he never says anything."

Shile grinned wickedly at having gained this information so effortlessly.

"Usually they come in two or three together, but Weiland,"— Evangeline ran her hand over his short-cropped hair—"is the quietest of them as well as the best looking, very polite and well-behaved, even though he never gives a tip, and a lot of times he leaves before they do, or they decide to follow a game of dice that's moving and he doesn't go with them. *What*," she asked, switching to speak directly to Weiland, "do you do to your hair? Do you cut it yourself, in the dark, when you're drunk?"

Weiland tried to unobtrusively slide her off his lap, without attracting any more attention than they were already getting, but Evangeline used this as an excuse to tighten her arms around his neck. "I don't get drunk," Weiland told her.

"No, I didn't honestly suppose you ever do," she answered, but she was laughing, and Shile was trying to hide behind his drink cup, as though he'd said something foolish.

"Oh, don't frown so at me," Evangeline said, pouting prettily. "I *do* like your hair. But you should try letting it grow out, so that there would be enough for a girl to take hold of.''

Or an enemy, Kedj would have said. Weiland stood, before she could try. She stood also—she had to or risk falling—but she left her arms around his neck, which meant they were standing very close together, which he found very distracting, especially since he was so much taller and got a good look—before he quickly glanced away—down her dress.

She stepped up onto the tips of her toes and kissed him, this time actually touching her lips to his rather than kissing the air as she had done before.

And that was even more distracting than the dress.

''I don't think your friend has very much experience,'' Evangeline told Shile.

''I think you may be right,'' Shile said. ''You better go easy with him.''

At which point, Weiland was sure they were laughing at him.

He turned and left, determined never to go in the Hog and Bone again. But that thought didn't improve his mood, so he said to himself, *Well, why not?* Except that didn't help either.

It wasn't until he was halfway home that he realized he had never given money for his drink but had left Shile to pay, and that, somehow, did make him feel considerably better.

14

The days—at least some of them—were beginning to grow warm when Daria announced she had brought too many men with her. "Six is more than sufficient," she said. "Lord Geoffrey maintains a high degree of order and efficiency, so I will be sending half of you back to Kedj."

Go or stay, Weiland didn't know which to hope for. Not that hoping ever accomplished anything.

"Weiland," she said, and then five other names, "you will stay. The rest of you, I will speak to later. For today, continue as usual, except those returning to Kedj are not to leave the house or eat today. I will explain later."

Weiland could make no sense of her choices. He would have assumed that she would choose for staying those who had done best at fitting in with the human-born. But she included Parn, who had been brought up before the town magistrate for public drunkenness, and Melor, who had nearly killed a merchant because of an argument over whether the merchant had offered for sale—or simply offered—a meat pie Melor had eaten.

And of those sent away, *all* were wolf-born. Weiland had no friends in the company, but any kinship he felt was with those born, as he had been, wolves. Despite that, he tried to look at things with as clear an eye as he could; but still it came down to her sending away some who were better men than some she kept.

And he could make nothing of the order not to eat.

But things had not changed so drastically since their move to St. Celia's that one questioned Daria.

The following morning, she called the six who were to leave into her apartments.

"What do you want to bet they never come out again?" Melor asked.

The comment bordered on insolence, which, as leader, Weiland could not permit, so he struck Melor on the back of the head.

But he wouldn't have been surprised if they *hadn't* come out.

They did, however. And they left immediately, on foot, not even stopping to break their fast. Surely—after more than twenty-four hours—that could only be because Daria had directly forbidden it, though *why* he couldn't begin to guess, unless it was not to waste food on those she had already dismissed.

Daria saw him standing near her door and motioned him to come closer, which could presage a reprimand for loitering. "Weiland."

He approached diffidently. "My lady?"

"Sir Geoffrey and Lady Johanna have invited me out for a day of falconry with them, and it is expected for a lady to bring a man-at-arms with her. Make yourself presentable."

"Yes, my lady."

The baron's home was probably originally a fortress, Weiland had estimated the first time he'd seen it, and the town had built up around it. It was exactly the kind of place Daria *would* be impressed with, much finer than the fortress they had left behind in the hills, and bigger, even, than the cathedral.

He thought that perhaps he had misjudged the people, whom he had seen only twice, both times early after first recovering from the effects of the spell Daria had used to punish him after the botched disposal of Lon's body, before he had seen much of human-born people.

But his opinion did not change at this latest meeting. Lord Geoffrey was a large, boisterous, self-confident man—possibly overly self-confident, in Weiland's estimation—but obviously used to power. Weiland would have expected Daria to want that power, to think herself better suited to it, or to be angry that he had it and she didn't. But Daria didn't react in any of the ways Weiland might have expected. Instead she flattered and laughed and laid her hand on the baron's arm. The first times Weiland had seen this, he hadn't known what to make of it. Now, after more experience in the town, he was reminded of the way the women who served in the taverns acted with the men who had the most money to spend.

Lady Johanna was even more of a puzzle to Weiland than her husband. She was a pale, wispy creature, not the kind of person whose company Weiland would have imagined Daria seeking. More than anything else, she reminded him of mouse-born Bess and Blanche.

And then there were the children. They were very young—Bess and Blanche said the girls were two and three years old, and the boy was five. Weiland was amazed that they could be so small, like perfectly shaped miniature adults that could actually walk and talk, except that the talk was like nothing Weiland had ever heard. One moment they would be bowing and curtsying and greeting the guests in small but otherwise normal voices, and then they would be chattering loudly and insistently, or squealing with laughter, or crying.

"Please excuse them," their mother said, "they're overtired," even though it was not quite mid-morning yet.

Weiland watched Daria fuss and coo over the children. "They're so sweet," he heard her say. And "How precious," and "Come sit on my lap," and "Aren't they adorable?"

Weiland found them noisy and demanding and exhausting, and he was amazed at Daria's extreme gentleness and continuing patience. But then it was time to leave—they would go to the woods a short ride beyond the town gates—and Johanna gathered her children into a cluster to hug them all good-bye. Everybody was saying how lovely the family was, but Weiland's responsibility was to keep Daria safe, and so he was watching her. And despite all Daria's kind words and smiles and the fact that she had said to Geoffrey, "I'm devoted to your little angels, simply devoted," Weiland saw a familiar look deep in her eyes when she didn't think anyone was observing her. And no matter how annoying the children were, he was relieved—not for himself, but for them—that they were to be left safely behind.

The hunting party consisted of Lord Geoffrey and seven or eight of his friends and their servants. Daria and Johanna were the only women. Geoffrey was letting Daria use a peregrine he himself had raised and trained—"A mostly docile creature," Geoffrey called it.

Weiland had of course seen falcons when he'd lived at Daria's hall up in the hills, and he had known them to be efficient hunters. He hadn't known they could be trained to hunt to serve humans.

By mid-afternoon, when they stopped for a picnic lunch, Weiland still admired the fierce wild beauty of the birds, but he'd decided they were more trouble than they were worth. They were very skittish and needed constant coddling and reassuring. *Surely they're not that delicate in the wild*, he thought, but nobody asked for his opinion. And all the special equipment: leather gauntlets to protect the handlers from talons, thin straps called jesses that had one end tied to a bird's leg and the other to a metal ring where a leash could be attached, tiny hoods to be fastened over the birds' eyes to prevent them from being startled while being transported—the handlers were very worried about the birds being startled and ruined, as though no wild falcon had ever been startled and survived.

After the meal, the group sprawled lazily under the trees and the men began to share stories of previous falcons they had owned—always much bigger, faster, and fiercer than the ones taken out today; from there they went on to recount past hunting trips and encounters with boars, and wolves, and—in the case of one man—a dragon, although he did admit it was a small one.

"A *dragon*?" Daria echoed with a laugh in her voice.

"A small one," the man repeated.

The men started debating whether dragons—who were, after all, cold-blooded, being related to snakes and lizards—ever really traveled this far north. Another man backed the first, claiming he'd hunted not only dragon, but basilisk.

Daria turned to Johanna and said, "Shall we leave the men to reminisce at their own leisure on these past glories? I fear these adventures are too strong for my faint-hearted blood."

She was calling the men liars, Weiland saw, but they didn't take offense. Instead they only laughed, which Daria did also—so it must have been joke, not insult—another of those difficult town concepts.

"Johanna." Daria leaned on her elbow to get closer. "When my ladies and I were first approaching St. Celia's, we passed through these woods, just near here—I recognize that lightning-struck linden. There's the most charming pond just the other side of this clearing, surrounded by willows, so peaceful, and the prettiest swans. The wagons were half a day behind, and we weren't even sure we'd reach the town gate before curfew, but they were so precious, we simply had to stop to watch." Daria flung her hair over her shoulder and turned to Weiland. "Do you remember, Weiland?" she asked.

For a moment his wits left him. She might have gotten confused regarding who was with her on almost any other day, but surely not that one. But then he gave the answer she clearly desired: "Yes, my lady."

"Shall the two of us go see if they're still there? We could throw some bread to them if they are." Daria stood and reached down a hand to pull her new friend to her feet.

With a longing look to the company of his friends, Baron Geoffrey asked, as though hoping the answer would be *no,* "Shall I accompany you, my love?"

Johanna patted his hand reassuringly and said, gently, "It's your company we're trying to get away from, dear," to which her husband and his friends laughed good-naturedly.

"My man can keep any . . . say, *dragons*, away from us," Daria said with a smile that asked what danger there could be in such pleasant surroundings, and Weiland—feeling a sudden and great weariness—got to his feet.

He walked, several paces behind the women, watching, all the while watching, trying to keep track of what was going on in all directions at once.

Nothing wrong stirred.

Don't let it be me, he thought. Johanna had spoken kindly to him. She had spoken kindly to everyone, even the clumsy servant who had dropped one of the baskets containing food for their lunch, and she had never lost her temper. He hoped Daria's plan didn't involve him harming Johanna.

They were just out of sight of the hunting party when they sighted the pond, calm and peaceful, just where Daria had said, just as she had described it.

Weiland was certain, despite any evidence, that they were being watched. But there was nothing out of place that he saw or heard, no reason he could give for insisting they must go back, for surely Daria knew what was ahead, surely she had planned things in exactly this way because she must remember which of the company had been with her on that first approach to St. Celia's. And the image in Weiland's mind of Lon's dead body lying on that table was a reminder that Daria was not to be crossed. Still, if only he could just see something wrong and give warning, he would worry later about trying to convince Daria that if she had just shared her plan with him, he wouldn't have inadvertently ruined it.

But *nothing* wrong stirred.

"No swans," Johanna observed, disappointment in her voice.

"Maybe they're in the shallows," Daria suggested, "hidden by the weeds. You circle around that way, I'll go here." She glanced at Weiland to make sure he knew to follow her.

Weiland turned his back on Johanna, trying desperately not to think of anything but that he needed to act instantly on Daria's orders, and only on her orders.

Then he heard Johanna gasp, and he couldn't help but whirl around to see what was wrong.

Six men had stepped out from where the trees crowded closest to the pond, just where Daria had sent Johanna.

Weiland felt Daria's fingers dig into his arm as she hissed, "Stay."

Stay—it was that single word, and not the touch of her fingers that held him, trembling and powerless, back.

Only then did he note two things he would never have willingly admitted to Kedj that he could possibly have missed: The men were naked, and they were Daria's people—Innas, Adger, Telek, and the other three she had dismissed that morning.

Why naked?

In the instant he took to try to fit the facts together, Daria made a gesture with her free hand. Weiland felt the telltale ripple of magic set loose.

The six men took on the forms of wolves.

And where Johanna had been standing, now there was a deer. It still wore Johanna's long gown, its front legs encased by the sleeves, its back legs tangled in the fabric of the skirt—panicked, unable to understand what was going on, with the scent of wolves all around.

Weiland had never seen Daria turn a natural-born human into an animal; those of the company had assumed it couldn't be done. Now he watched helplessly, Daria's fingers not so much holding him back as reminding him of her presence, as the deer tried to leap away from the wolves and—caught by the dress—stumbled.

Then the wolves were on it.

Daria screamed, a wild wordless shriek of terror. Then, "Johanna! Johanna!" Finally she released Weiland's arm. "Weiland!" she sobbed. She shoved him in the direction where the wolves were savaging the deer. "Do something!"

Weiland couldn't imagine what had gone wrong, what Daria had intended that could have gone so badly awry as to end in this instead, but he took off at a run, skirting the edge of the pond, pulling his sword from its sheath.

"Kill them!" Daria screamed. "Kill them! Save Johanna!"

And he took her at her word, and didn't try to use the flat of his blade against the snarling, snapping wolves—which wouldn't have done any good anyway. He jabbed and slashed. Two were down, though he had to be careful lest he strike Johanna. Whatever Daria had done, Johanna was back to her own true form: Weiland glimpsed human limbs among the swirl of slashing wolf claws and snapping wolf jaws, but he couldn't tell if she was moving or just being tugged at by the surviving wolves.

Why didn't Daria change *them* back to human form?

Weiland heard the approaching shouts of the hunting party, but knew they couldn't possibly arrive in time.

He ran his sword through another wolf, with no idea which of his companions he could be killing and finally the remaining three seemed to take stock of the situation. One reached for a final bite at Johanna, and Weiland slashed off its head. The other two were backing off and—then—turned tail.

Weiland heard the distinctive *thunk* of arrows and one of the wolves gave a pained *yip*, but he was no longer even looking at them. He dropped his bloodied sword to the ground and knelt by Johanna. But he could already see she was dead.

Footsteps came running up behind him. Someone said, "No, my lady," then Daria's voice cried, "Let me go!"

Years-long training was stronger than fascinated horror: Weiland jerked his head up and whipped around to protect Daria.

But she had already broken away from the man who held her. And by that one's face, he intended her no harm but was only trying to spare her the sight of Johanna's maimed body.

Daria threw herself to her knees, covered her face, and sobbed. "It's my fault. It's all my fault. I'm so sorry. Oh, Johanna, I'm so sorry."

And then Geoffrey was there, looking like a man who does not yet realize he's taken a fatal wound. "Hush," he said gently, patting her awkwardly on the back. "It's *not* your fault. You couldn't have known."

"I should have never brought her here," Daria said. "I should have never told her about the swans."

Weiland looked away from her. Someone was tugging on him, one of the other men from the hunting party, trying to get him to sit back. He realized, for the first time, that some of the blood was his own, that his sword arm had been badly bitten.

"She made us walk away and turn our backs because she had to relieve herself," Daria said, and Weiland found himself unaccountably shocked by this, that Daria was unable to let Johanna retain any dignity. As a deer, Johanna had struggled half out of her clothes, which everyone would have thought was from the wolves' attack. He suspected she was more modest than the women in the taverns, and that she would have been willing to face much rather than have them all gathered around looking at her, thinking about her dying as she went to relieve herself. He couldn't remember when he had seen his first dead person, it was so long ago and he himself had been so young. He could barely remember the first man he had killed. But it had never been like this.

Now Daria was saying, "I shouldn't have let her be so shy. I should have sent Weiland away but I should have stayed with her. Maybe they wouldn't have gone after *her* so savagely if there had been two of us, then there would have been time." Daria broke down into more sobs, so clearly distraught and overcome by blaming herself that she demanded comforting, even by the dead woman's husband.

"There, there," Geoffrey said, putting a steadying arm around her shaking shoulders.

She threw her arms around him and buried her face in his chest, and he leaned his face down into her hair and began crying, too.

Someone was wrapping a strip of cloth around Weiland's injured arm. It would hurt considerably more later, whether or not Daria used a healing spell on him. He looked up and saw that all six wolves were dead: the four he had killed with his sword, and the other two with arrows in them.

"Normally wolves don't go after people like that," someone said, only it was not spoken in suspicion, but more in wonder, at Johanna's bad luck. "Especially so determined-like."

Unless they're starving, Weiland thought.

15

Weiland had helped to bury the bodies of many an unlucky member of the company, along with servants who had dissatisfied and those who had fought rather than pay Daria's toll. But that had always been a simple matter, performed because decaying bodies brought smell and scavengers. He had never before been to a funeral.

Daria ordered the servants to drape the front door with black cloth. To her people's puzzled looks, she explained, "It's a sign of mourning."

Since she seemed in a mood for explanations, Weiland asked, "*Why* is black cloth a sign of mourning?"

She slapped him, calling him hopeless, and said, "Not another word out of you today."

Weiland bowed and backed away, missing Kedj for no other reason than that, sometimes, Kedj explained things.

Weiland was aware of someone coming up behind him and whipped around, startling Royce, one of the human-born servants who had come with the house. Royce was one of the oldest men Weiland had ever seen, and he had been with the de Gris family—all the other servants agreed—forever. It had been Royce who had asked Father Hadden Heallstede to come that first week after Weiland had lain in the hall as though dying and none of the servants had been able to tell what was wrong with him. "Sometimes," Royce said now, "grief makes people short with each other," which was not the answer to any question Weiland had. But then Royce added, "Black in times of mourning has been the custom for so long—I doubt if anybody truly remembers why."

It was no comfort to learn that even the human-born didn't know why they did what they did.

Daria put on a black dress, and had Bess and Blanche and all the company dress totally in black. For once she had both women and all of her men-at-arms go with her—all six who were left.

At the baron's house, not only the door, but the windows too, were draped in black. *People must prepare for this*, Weiland thought, seeing the black banners hung in the great hall. He wondered if Daria would be annoyed at being outdone, but she didn't complain, at least not out loud. The place was crowded with people, friends of the dead woman and her husband. Weiland recognized everyone from the hunting party. Shile was there also; Weiland heard him described as Johanna's no-account cousin. Father Hadden came, too, and several other men who were dressed in a similar fashion—priests, Weiland presumed, ministering to Geoffrey d'Akil and his motherless children.

The priest who was dressed in the richest looking clothes was speaking in a language Weiland didn't understand, with only a few of the words sounding familiar enough to tantalize, but not give meaning to the whole. Weiland didn't know if Daria wanted him to try to puzzle out what was being said, but now there was no way to ask her. The man used the formal voice of ritual, and he waved a round censer on a gold chain that released thick, cloying clouds of smoke that made Weiland feel lightheaded—this was the bishop, Weiland overheard someone say.

There was no sign of Johanna, but Weiland presumed she was in the black-draped box over which Geoffrey and his friends, including Daria, wept.

At last the box was placed on a type of litter, and several of the men took hold and carried it out of the house, with the rest of the people following afterwards. They formed a black procession through the streets of St. Celia's; and as they walked, others from the town joined them, so that the procession got longer and longer. Some were dressed entirely in black, many simply had a black cloth tied to their arms. Many of the houses they passed bore bits of black cloth, Weiland presumed to show support to their lord rather than because the people had actually known Lady Johanna. He turned to ask Father Hadden, who was walking nearby, but then remembered that he was not supposed to speak for the rest of the day. If it was important, he thought, he'd probably get a chance to ask later.

He had assumed they were heading to the town gate, to bury the body outside of the walls so as not to draw vermin close to the dwellings, but the procession wound its way back to the cathedral.

Inside, the bishop spoke—again—and there was a ceremony all the priests took part in. Weiland stood with the rest of the people, trying to do what they did and at the same time trying to stay alert in case there was any danger to Daria. Each member of the company, Kedj had drilled into them, was always to act as though he and he alone was responsible for Daria's safety.

She had changed Johanna into a deer.

Weiland tried to wipe away the picture in his mind of the wolves attacking. That was not the important thing, he told himself: Daria had been responsible for many deaths over the years. The important thing was that Daria had changed a human-born into an animal. *That* he had never seen her do before. But he couldn't convince himself that the rest was unimportant—he kept coming back to the scene of the wolves leaping at the deer.

The bishop sprinkled water on the box that held Johanna's body—not enough to do more than put spots on the wood. Weiland stopped trying to guess why. The people around him began to speak, more or less in unison. Even if Weiland had been allowed to speak, he wouldn't have known the words, so he just bowed his head, and watched the area around Daria from the tops of his eyes.

Then the whole group went outside again, this time using a different door that led to a grassy area in the back. The bishop sprinkled some more water on the ground—perhaps it was a ritual cleansing, Weiland thought, or some magic to protect the body—then some men began digging. When the hole was deep enough, Johanna's box was lowered into it, and then it was filled up again. The entire business took a lot longer than it needed to, and people were crying all the while, especially Johanna's children. It probably would have been easier for everyone, Weiland thought, if it had been done quicker.

The group began to disperse. Weiland was watching Daria hug Geoffrey and the children when a voice behind him said, "That's a beautiful woman you work for."

Weiland turned to find Shile standing there.

"I'm told she's just back from the Holy Land." Shile grinned. "Of course most people say she lived in Jerusalem, not,"—he mimed a panicked look and gestured vaguely—*"north?"*

Was I that obvious? Weiland wondered. *I must learn to lie more effectively.* It was not a skill Kedj had deemed they needed in the hills.

Shile's face got a more serious expression as he nodded toward the group that included Daria and Baron Geoffrey. "Sad," he commented. "And unusual. You certainly do seem to have the strangest encounters with animals." Shile's tone shifted abruptly. *"What?"* Shile was obviously reacting to something in his face. "Weiland? What did I say?"

Even if Daria hadn't forbidden him to speak, there was nothing he could have answered. He turned his back on Shile and headed directly to Daria, because surely Shile would have the sense not to follow, and he didn't.

That night Weiland dreamt of Llewellur—not the current one, but the one who had leapt to his death from a tree little more than a month ago.

Weiland was tracking Llewellur once more, but this time he had followed him up into the tree, pursuing him from branch to branch. Weiland would never have guessed a dead man could move so fast.

Until, finally, the young bird-boy stepped on the wrong branch, one that extended over the chasm. With nowhere else to go, he backed away from Weiland and backed away until he was near the end of the branch, where it bent under his slight weight.

"Llewellur," Weiland said. "I'm sorry you're dead."

Llewellur reached forward. "So am I," he said, and shoved Weiland off.

Weiland awoke with a start and a gasp, his heart pounding.

I should have done something, he thought—it made no difference he didn't know what. *I should at least have tried.* He lay quietly in the dark and waited for the rising of the sun, not daring to let himself sleep again lest this time he dream of Johanna.

16

The following day, things returned to normal. The black cloth stayed up on the door, but Daria put away the black dress, choosing instead one of soft gray—subdued, but it showed her figure to good advantage. The only black she retained was a band around her forearm. All the company and servants had to wear similar bands, a public show, Daria explained, that their hearts were with the poor baron and his children. "Go about your daily business," Daria instructed the household. "I will pay a call on Lord Geoffrey, to see if I can be of any consolation to him and his sweet lambs."

Daily business. More often than not that would be Daria's business now, Weiland thought, with the number of those she had brought into town with her dwindling alarmingly. But today it was Parn she chose to see her safely through the streets. Let Parn be the one to witness what she did next, Weiland told himself. And he tried not to think what that might be.

He struggled to fill his mind with the details of morning practice in the courtyard, but without Kedj—or Lon, or even Innas—there was little challenge, certainly not enough to keep his mind quiet.

In the afternoon, he accompanied Melor to a tavern, for the noise that would be there—noise enough, he hoped, to drive out of his head the sounds of snarling wolves, and of crying.

He almost walked out again when he saw Shile was there. But Shile had seen him, too, and Shile was suspicious enough already, without speculating why Weiland might be trying to avoid him.

Shile was playing some sort of game with a coin, with people betting which face would land face up after the coin was thrown into the air. Weiland couldn't understand why this should make any difference to anyone, but people kept laying their money down. Shile lost just often enough to keep the bystanders interested; but the amounts of money he lost were small, and the amounts he won were large. Weiland watched, not interested in the coin, and with no idea how Shile was doing it, but certain that Shile could direct how the coin would land. Melor joined in the gambling, but at least he had the sense to bet for Shile.

After losing two tosses in a row—which represented a small portion of what he'd won—Shile declared he could afford no more. He left the game to others and came to join Weiland.

"So," Shile said in a neutral tone, but with a glance to either side that may well have been to determine whether anyone was within earshot.

"So," Weiland repeated, unwilling to give anything away.

Shile sat down next to, rather than across from, Weiland. His voice low but intense, he asked, "*Was* there something more to it?"

Weiland looked beyond him as though fascinated by the new game starting up. Should he get up, leave? Or would that make Shile become louder with his questions, less discreet, and more likely to draw others to the conversation?

Apparently Shile had suspicions already, and if Weiland fled the room, that would only show clearer yet he had something to hide. At least, by staying, he could learn what Shile thought, and if there was any likelihood that others in the town had similar thoughts, and if that way of thinking posed a danger Daria needed to be warned about.

On the other hand, he knew who held the advantage if they should start playing at words. Shile was much of what Weiland would hope to be, when he wished to be truly human. "What," he asked, never looking at Shile, "specifically, are you asking?"

Irritation came creeping into Shile's voice. "*Was* my cousin killed by wolves?"

"There were more than a dozen witnesses, including the lady's husband and a brother."

"That wasn't what I asked."

"Yes." Weiland turned round to face Shile. "She was killed by wolves."

"What did the bear have to do with it?"

Momentarily he couldn't make the connection. Then he said, "Nothing."

Apparently he looked confused enough to convince Shile. Or Shile would come back to it later. "Did *you* have anything to do with her death?"

"I was there."

Shile flashed a grin that had none of his usual warmth. "Anything beyond that."

"I probably could have stopped it," Weiland admitted. "If I had been standing closer when they attacked. If there had been two or three of me, or fewer of them. If—" *Don't put ideas into his head by talking too much.* Weiland shrugged and took a drink of beer and repeated, "If . . ."

Shile leaned back and looked at him as though evaluating. "What about this Lady Daria de Gris?"

Weiland hoped that he was keeping his face from showing any change of emotion. "She was there, too," he said. "She also wasn't standing close enough, and there weren't two or three of her, either." He took another drink of beer and had the feeling he wasn't carrying this off as well as Shile would have.

"Where does she really come from?" Shile asked.

"The Holy Land," Weiland said. "Jerusalem."

"So I've heard." Shile couldn't have forgotten that he'd been the one to supply Weiland with that name. "And what are her plans here in St. Celia's—what does she want?"

"I work for her," Weiland said. "She doesn't share her plans and desires with me." He took a chance that he wasn't saying something Shile couldn't learn elsewhere. "I'm told her grandfather lived here, but he died recently."

"So she decided to return home," Shile said. His tone was openly skeptical.

Weiland decided he'd probably made a mistake volunteering any information. "I don't know anything about it," he said.

"Don't know anything about the dead bear," Shile said, "don't know anything about the wolves, don't know anything about your lady . . ."

He didn't have any definite suspicions, Weiland guessed. He was just fishing. Weiland shrugged.

"Are you in some sort of trouble?"

Of all the questions Shile could have asked, Weiland hadn't anticipated that one. He hesitated, stammered, had to say it twice: "No," and the second time more confidently, "no."

No reaction from Shile. Just a calm, steady, "Do you need help?"

Weiland no longer trusted his voice and just shook his head.

Shile raised an eyebrow skeptically but only said, "It's none of my affair."

"No," Weiland agreed.

Shile didn't look offended, but at that point there was a loud cheer from the group playing their game in the center of the tavern, which gave Weiland the opportunity to be interested in that. Apparently Melor had lost patience, or enough money, that he was getting ready to pull out. The game was more random without Shile. Unwilling to face Shile and Melor at the same table, Weiland stood abruptly.

Never raising his voice, Shile asked, "Do you think the children need any help?"

Weiland didn't turn back, didn't answer, leaving Melor to scramble to follow or not, as he saw fit.

Do you think the children need any help? The words stayed with Weiland all day. Surely the children could present no danger to Daria, no obstacle to her plans. Could they?

And, if they did, so what? *It's none of my affair*, Shile had said. Neither was it Weiland's. He should not grow sentimental just because they were so helpless. Once again, he wasn't thinking properly: It was always the way of nature to prey on the young, the weak, the helpless.

Yet, he pictured the blind man on the cathedral steps. Incredibly brave or unspeakably foolish to stand there day after day, expecting— and sometimes getting—help, rather than being torn apart for what little he had.

And poor, confused Father Hadden, father and brother to all men, and minister to the sick.

And Shile, helping him in the alley. Reciprocating a favor, he said, because he thought Weiland had refrained from informing on him. But going out of his way for little gain, since he could easily have escaped once the town guard left the alley to bring Weiland back to the river-bank. And after it was over, he had said he wouldn't follow Weiland, and he hadn't. And today: *Are you in some sort of trouble*? he asked.

Looking for weakness, for an opportunity, Weiland told himself. But if so, his timing was drastically off, for a man who obviously was used to surviving by his wits.

Things are not *different in St. Celia's*, Weiland thought. *If they seem to be, it's because you know so little, you're misunderstanding what's happening*.

But he still hoped Daria would decide the children were beneath her interest.

That evening, for the first time in weeks, Daria dined at home. Apparently nobody in Geoffrey and Johanna d'Akil's usual circle of friends was entertaining so soon after Johanna's funeral. But the period of mourning was not to be all that long. After the meal, Daria spoke with the cook—the human-born one, not the one she had brought from the hill fortress, who had been demoted to cook's assistant.

"The baron will be dining here tomorrow," she said. "I thought it might be pleasant for him to get away from his sad surroundings."

With the children having weighed on Weiland's mind all day, he asked, with studied casualness, "Will the baron's children be coming?"

Daria was sitting at her loom, which had been brought in after the meal, and she looked up sharply. Suspicious? Weiland wondered, for small talk was not the norm in Daria's hall.

"No," she said, not sounding very annoyed. "Children do not normally accompany adults in such situations." She turned back to the cook with the names of several others, including Geoffrey's two cousins and Johanna's brother, who *would* be there. She did not give Shile's name. She probably had never been introduced to Shile—who was not wealthy, and was a disgrace.

"Yes, my lady," the cook said, bowing. "Everything will be arranged."

"Arranged *well*," Daria emphasized, for this would be the first time that she was the host.

"Yes, my lady," the cook repeated.

Daria worked quietly on the tapestry she had started the first week she had arrived at St. Celia's. Weiland had never seen her weave at the fortress, though apparently she had learned at some time in her past. By her face, she didn't enjoy doing it, and he could only guess that she worked at it because it was something human-born ladies were expected to do.

Bess and Blanche were carding wool—repetitive work that required no thinking and seemed well-suited to keeping their quick fingers busy.

The new Llewellur was playing the flute, a monotonously sad tune that made Weiland anxious to be doing something. Those of the company worked at repairing or shining arms and armor. They had only brought the good equipment with them, and neither men nor weapons had gotten a solid workout since they arrived, but there was little else to do. Daria permitted drink and games during the day, but she liked quiet evenings.

"Enough," she now told one of the household servants who was scrubbing the floor beneath the tables. "There will be work enough tomorrow. Rest tonight. Out from under foot—you and your fellows go to the kitchen tonight so we don't disturb your sleep. You can clean up after us tomorrow morning."

"Thank you, my lady."

Uncommon consideration.

And it didn't make sense, either. There would be more noise and bustling about in the kitchen, with preparations for tomorrow, than in the hall.

After the last servant left, closing the door behind, Daria worked for several more long, silent moments before saying, quietly, not looking up from her loom, "Why the sudden interest in the baron's children?"

There was a flurry of quick, furtive looks from the company, and silence thick enough to be another presence in the room, despite Llewellur's tune, and the crackling of the fire in the hearth, and the *whir* and *thump* of the loom.

"No especial interest," Weiland said. He was a fool. Daria had said it often enough, and Kedj, and they'd been proven time and again, and this was only the latest. *It is none of your concern*, he told himself.

Whir. Thump.

Whir. Thump.

Daria completed another two rows of weaving. And a third. And a fourth.

He was just beginning to think that his answer may have satisfied, when Daria spoke again. She said: "Good. I would hate to think that town living was making you soft. And worthless."

Whir. Thump.

Whir. Thump.

How would a man with nothing to hide react—with silence or explanation?

He said, "It's just, I'm still trying to understand the customs."

It sounded hollow, even to him.

Silence. Silence had been the correct reaction.

"You think I'm harsh," Daria said. Now what? Admit to complaint, or contradict Daria? But she continued without waiting for a response. "The situation is no different from what it was in the mountains. We took what we wanted there, and killed those who stood in our way. Johanna d'Akil stood in my way, because what I want, at least for the time being, is her husband. The children, for the time being, do not stand in my way."

Weiland tried not to look relieved. He tried not to look anything. So far, at least, Daria was still more interested in looking at the fabric she was making than at him.

"I am not used to, nor do I like, having to explain myself to those who would not even exist were it not for my good wishes."

"My lady—"

She did look up then. "Be still. I have wasted much good time and effort on you. Up to a point I think, 'Well, but, I don't want that to be for naught.' But you are very close to the point where I will think, 'Enough is enough.' ''

Protestations of innocence would not help. He simply answered, "Yes, my lady."

"If I require you to eat those children alive while you are in your human form, *you will not question me*."

"I understand, my lady."

Finally, she had abandoned work on the loom. She looked at him as though evaluating his worth.

And in the silence there came a scraping noise overhead, and the rattle of small pebbles skittering down the incline of the roof and then falling off into the courtyard below, as though—he knew without having to stop to work it out—as though someone was up on the roof and had stepped on a broken tile that crumbled underfoot.

"Quiet!" Daria ordered in a whisper that he felt in his bones like one of her spells.

Weiland and Parn had both started to their feet, Melor leapt up a moment later; but Daria stayed them with an upraised hand. Even Llewellur, untrained as a warrior and new to this life, seemed to be holding his breath.

As was, no doubt, whoever was on the roof.

"Llewellur, another song," Daria said in a jovial voice, louder than was necessary, and as though he had finished the previous tune and not cut it off mid-note. She motioned for him to resume playing, but indicated to do so softly. She leaned forward to whisper to the six of the company, "Answer me straight: Has any of you done anything to arouse suspicion?"

They all shook their heads earnestly, even Bess and Blanche who were almost always with Daria. Even Llewellur who had never yet been out of the house. Daria was looking directly at Weiland.

"So this is more likely to be thievery than spying?"

Thievery was a coldness on Weiland's spine, just as Melor turned to him and said, "Your friend."

"What,"—Daria's voice started louder than it finished—"friend?"

"No." Weiland shook his head for emphasis. Surely Shile had more sense than that. He told Daria, "Just someone I was talking to in a tavern this afternoon."

There was a soft sliding noise overhead, moving toward the back of the house. Whoever was up there had apparently decided he had *not* been heard, and that a stealthy escape was called for, rather than a hasty one.

"His name is Shile Costat," Melor whispered to Daria. "He was asking a lot of questions. And he's a thief."

"It's a possibility," Weiland said. It was also a possibility that Shile had decided to try to find out more on his own than Weiland had been willing to tell him. But to admit that was a certain death sentence for Shile.

Daria stood, but held her hand up again, pointing at Llewellur, Bess, and Blanche, and three of the company to stay. Weiland, Melor, and Parn, she crooked a finger at, and they followed her to the kitchen.

"Go," she ordered both the human-born servants and those servants she had made and brought with her. "Immediately." One tried to move a pot off the fire. "*Leave it,*" she said in a tone new to the human-born servants.

As they scrambled out of the room, Daria flung the back door open. The intruder would have heard, would have realized he *had* been found out. They heard his boots scraping on the tiles almost directly overhead. He would have picked this spot to come down—and probably to have gone up—because it backed onto the garden, private from the street and accessible.

If Daria made a motion, it was either too small or too quick for Weiland to catch, but he felt the air shimmer—and the person on the roof lost his footing and came hurtling down the rest of the slope of the roof. But it was a small, compact body that landed with a soft thud on the ground just to the right of the doorway—pale and smaller than a human, and the wrong shape. The creature squealed in fright then took off on all fours into the darkness. Boots and a man's dark clothing, suddenly empty, slid the rest of the way off the roof.

And then Daria did something else, something Weiland recognized in every bone and muscle of his body. He pitched forward onto hands that were becoming front feet; the courtyard swirled before his eyes then leapt into clear focus, the colors gone but everything clear as daylight under the moon. The last thought he had as a human was that pigs didn't normally fall from above, but a wolf can recognize the scent of a meal when he smells it.

17

The world shifted again.

Somebody had a knee jabbed into the small of Weiland's back, pinning him to the ground; somebody else was sitting on his legs. He'd been a wolf—he remembered the transformation—but now he was back in human form, and he was vaguely aware of that transformation, too. The time in between wriggled and evaded human words, wolf sensations: Perhaps he remembered them from one time of being a wolf to another, but they were beyond his human grasp.

But he had been captured—that much was evident from the hands that had hold of him. He tried to toss the man off his back, but he could neither roll nor buck, and the man on his back had his shoulders pinned, too.

"Weiland!" a voice called, an insistent whisper close to his ear. Not the first time. He was vaguely aware that somebody had repeated his name several times now. Somebody who wanted to get his attention, but without arousing the town.

He went quiet, though he was still alert should his captors relax their guard for a moment.

"Weiland." Parn's voice.

Parn was not one who would wish him well, but Weiland remembered Daria calling Parn and Melor into the kitchen with him, before she made him into a wolf. They'd been sent to retrieve him, he realized, to bring him back to Daria rather than leave him to make his way naked through the streets of St. Celia's.

Weiland also remembered the pig that wasn't really a pig, and he felt the stickiness of his hands, and smelled blood. *Shile*, he thought in horror. *What have I done?* But he knew very well what he had done. Bile rose into his throat, but it wasn't enough to cover the taste of blood.

"Weiland!" Parn—wolverine-born—was not good at patience. He smacked the back of Weiland's head to make sure he had his attention. He hissed, "Let's go. You've made enough noise, the stupid human-born will be on us any moment."

Weiland promptly made more noise, by vomiting.

Parn got up from Weiland's back, and Melor from his legs. The two of them had learned a variety of human curses from their forays into the taverns, and they used them now.

No raw meat. He had obviously ripped at Shile with teeth and claws, but at least . . . He couldn't stop shivering. At least . . .

Shile was *stupid* to have come spying on Daria. It was his own fault. Trying to find out what had happened to his cousin Johanna d'Akil, was it any wonder that much the same thing ended up happening to him?

But that was a coward's reasoning, Weiland thought. Nobody had warned Shile. Nobody had told him just how dangerous Daria could be.

My fault, Weiland thought. *Not his. I could have prevented this.*

Parn and Melor were dragging him to his feet. One of them draped a blanket over his shoulders. Daria, of course, would have had the presence of mind to make them bring it, just in case he was seen, so that he wouldn't stand out quite so obviously.

"Is he dead?" Weiland whispered. He could make out the form of what was probably the body not far from where Parn and Melor had wrestled him to the ground, but his human eyes could make out little in this dark.

"The human?" Parn asked. "Of course he's dead, you fool. Daria said she'd change you back when she felt him die."

She could feel the death of those she had changed, and still she ordered them killed?

"Weiland," Melor said, trying to physically shake sense into him.

Lights were beginning to come on. They could hear doors and shutters being unlatched. But they weren't that far from home.

Parn and Melor got him back into the de Gris compound; they led him into the kitchen courtyard, where they pulled up bucket after bucket of water from the well to throw over him, each so cold he was sure it would be the death of him. Which would be only fitting, he thought, for one who had killed the closest he'd ever had to a friend.

Surely the last several bucketsful were pure spite—blood and vomit alike must have long been washed off him and seeped into the ground. Parn and Melor brought him indoors, dripping and still wrapped in the soaked blanket. Melor picked up the now-sodden clothes that had been left behind when men had been turned into pig and wolf, and bunched them together so that it would look to any they might pass on the way like one set of clothes.

The candles in the hall could not have burned down more than a quarter hour since they first heard that scraping on the roof.

Daria was once more at her loom. She stood when they entered, kicking over her footstool as though in a fury. But Weiland knew Daria's furies, and this was for the benefit of the servants who had to be somewhere close by, listening, wondering what had roused such late-night excitement.

He couldn't stop shivering, for any one of several reasons.

She can change true-born humans into animals. He'd known that since that day by the pond with Johanna, but the thought wouldn't stop running through his head: *She can change true-born humans into animals.*

"Are you quite sober now?" she demanded. "I will not tolerate such insolence with the excuse that ale loosened your tongue. Don't you *dare* ever come in my presence drunk like that again."

"No, my lady," Weiland agreed weakly. It came out as meekness, which did nothing to hurt the pretext Daria was building.

"Sleep it off," Daria ordered. "And stay out of my sight for the next few days."

There was nothing in the world Weiland wanted more than just that.

He was supposed to be out of favor with Daria anyway, and this was one of the mornings without practice, so Weiland didn't get up when the others of the company dressed and left. It was only when Royce came in to check on him that he bothered to sit up.

Royce was the oldest of the servants, and he had worked for the de Gris family all his life, first for Daria's real grandfather, then for Lord Robert who everyone assumed was Daria's grandfather. Old as he was, he was always looking out for the welfare of others: Weiland had seen him make peace between arguing servants, smooth over misunderstandings, catch things that hadn't been done properly before they came to Daria's notice. It had been he who had summoned Father Hadden Heallstede to minister to Weiland that first week. Now he came to Weiland with a drink that was warm and frothing and only slightly noxious, and said that it was a good remedy for a body that had had too much ale the night before.

Since that had been the story Daria had made up, Weiland didn't dare contradict her by refusing the drink. It tasted as foul as it looked and smelled.

"A lot of excitement in the town this morning," Royce told him as he took a steadying breath before the second gulp. "A man was found dead not two streets away from us last night. The thing is, he was torn apart by a wolf, apparently."

It was worse than he had expected, to hear it. Weiland took a long drink, to hide anything that might have shown through in his expression.

Royce must have expected Weiland to be more surprised, for after a moment he added, "There shouldn't be any way for a wolf to get in over the town wall like that." When Weiland still didn't say anything, Royce continued, "And whatever it was—wolf or some other creature— it seems to have disappeared without a trace."

"That *is* strange," Weiland agreed, since that seemed to be the point Royce was making. "Must have been a hard winter for the wolves this year." That was what people had said when Lady Johanna had been killed.

"Very hard," Royce agreed, "for a wolf to take a man's clothes before killing him."

Weiland held the cup as if draining the last of it, though he'd gotten the last drops already. *That* particular complication he hadn't thought to worry about. Surely Daria had considered it—and ignored it, for whatever reason. "Thieves?" he suggested.

Royce shook his head. "It could have been—because they say the man was a known thief himself. He might have crossed the wrong people. But they that should know say the wounds were definitely made by wolves."

"Thieves trying to make it look like wolves?" Weiland asked.

"One woman," Royce said, "claims it was a demon."

"Demon?" Weiland wasn't sure of the word.

"She says she opened her door a crack just as the creature was leaving the dead body—without eating it, by the by, which is also unlike a wolf. This woman says the killer walked upright like a man, but it was bigger, almost as wide as the street itself. It had only two arms, but three heads, and a multitude of legs."

"A multitude," Weiland repeated. Someone must have glimpsed him, as Melor and Parn half-dragged/half-carried him away. But, surely the average citizen of St. Celia's wouldn't credit stories of a three-headed creature.

Royce was shaking his head. "It's been a quarter century since we've had such troubles," he said.

Weiland could make absolutely no sense of that. "Such troubles?" he repeated.

His question seemed to bring Royce back from a far-off thought. "Magic," he said knowingly. "Mark my words, there's magic involved."

"What happened twenty-five years ago?" Weiland asked.

"There was a groom here, in the stables of the Lord de Gris. A young man, but we suspected he knew the old ways."

"Magic?" Weiland guessed.

Royce nodded. "He was a bit too good at what he did. He could bring a mare through the most difficult foaling, cure a beast of the colic, nurse back to health an animal that should have been lame for life. Aye, we suspected he knew magic, but he never seemed to use it for ill, so we let him be. But the Lady Daria's grandmother, the Lady Edwina, grew concerned. Her daughter, the older Lady Daria, showed too great an interest in the young man, both for his knowledge of the healing arts and . . ." Royce laid his finger alongside his nose. ". . . and for his other skills."

Weiland supposed there was significance to that gesture made so deliberately at that time, but he understood neither that nor what Royce was saying. "Skills?" he repeated.

"He was her lover," Royce clarified with some exasperation.

But the people of St. Celia's were one generation off, Weiland thought, supposing Daria to be only as old as she looked. This Edwina would in reality be Daria's mother, and there was only one Lady Daria.

"So the Lady Edwina resolved to have the boy sent away. But the very night she announced this, she was found in her rooms lying in her own blood. She was still alive—it took her all night to die—but when they went to pick her up, she was all limp. Not limp like the sleeping or the just-dead, but—so they said—like she had no bones at all."

She was too late, Weiland supposed. All too obviously Daria had already learned all she needed to know about healing, and about its counterpart, destroying. He wondered why she hadn't used a transforming spell—whether that was something she had learned only later. "What about the groom?" he asked.

"He denied responsibility, of course, but no one believed him." Royce shook his head. "I remember he turned to the Lady Daria—as though she would protect him even with her mother dying in the upstairs room. He said, "I swear by all that is holy, it was not I," and even as the words left his mouth, he clutched at his heart, his eyes turned upward, and he fell to the floor, struck dead,"—Royce made the gesture called the Sign of the Cross—"for blaspheming."

More likely for being about to accuse Daria, Weiland thought.

Had her father suspected? Was that why Daria had left St. Celia's, because he had sent her away—unwilling to accuse his own daughter, but knowing she had killed his wife? Or had Daria herself decided she would be safer away? Now, there was no one left to be suspicious of her, for she appeared too young to have been alive that long ago, and everyone thought she was her own daughter.

And who would ever suspect someone of killing her own mother?

Or a thief she had never even met?

Or three helpless little children?

18

Weiland left the house simply to be doing something, improbably wistful, for once, of the hill fortress where Kedj's training exercises left no time or excess energy for thinking. He wished he could run, or climb a tree, or swim in a brook, or have to find his way back home from some unknown starting point deep in the woods.

Something to drive away the picture of himself with his hands around Daria's throat.

It was a useless fantasy: She would strike back with her magic. He would be a long, long time dying, and in the end she would continue for many years exactly as she was now.

The day was fine, and many of the tavern keepers had moved some of the smaller tables and stools outside, to let people enjoy the brightness of the sun, the warmth of the air. Weiland had no interest in company, but as he was passing the Hog and Bone, a familiar voice at one of the outside tables said, "No, that's mine, because half of the money *you* put in went to Josef, who put in too much, and this pile here—"

"No," another voice cut in, "you're cheating me. You're cheating all of us." But by then Weiland had located the table where the argument was starting.

It's just someone else who sounds like him, Weiland had already tried to convince himself, *someone else who causes so much confusion at the tallying of a tavern bill that the others end up paying his portion and enough for him to bring a profit home.*

But it wasn't someone else. It was Shile.

He was sitting at a small, round table with three other men who looked big and mean and well-armed enough to have been Kedj's brothers. Seeing them was nearly enough to wash away the sense of relief at seeing Shile alive.

"You think we're idiots?" continued the man who had been speaking. He had hold of Shile by the front of his shirt. *He* wasn't wearing a shirt, though it wasn't *that* warm.

"*I* think," one of the others said, placing a long dagger along the side of Shile's neck, "*you're* the idiot." A long, puckered scar on his cheek was evidence that he wasn't new to disagreements.

"Nobody said anything about idiots," Shile protested. "Here, let's count it again. Maybe I—"

"Maybe you should pay for all of us," said the one with the knife. "Is that what you were about to say?"

The man who hadn't yet said anything began sweeping all the money toward himself. "Let's start all over again," he suggested.

Stay out of trouble, Daria reminded them just about every morning. *Keep out of town politics.*

And yet the people at the other tables were making a concentrated effort to avoid noticing any problem, and the tavern keeper—who had started to come out to investigate the raised voices—turned back around when he saw the knife and hurried away into the tavern. The three men were probably aware of Weiland as one of the bystanders hovering close enough to see but with enough room to get out of there in case of serious trouble. Nobody—including Shile—seemed to expect that anybody would come to Shile's aid.

Stay out of trouble, the memory of Daria's voice repeated in his head.

But Shile was, beyond all expectation, alive. At least for the moment.

"See here—" Shile started, proof that he didn't always have just the right words.

"Just hand over all your money," the man with the knife and the scar said.

"That's all I have," Shile protested, "there on the table."

"That *is* too bad," said the one who had hold of Shile's shirt. He used his other hand to force Shile's chin up, exposing more of his neck to his companion's knife.

If you don't want to be fighting every single day to maintain your position as leader, Kedj had told him, *I recommend a single stunning act of violence when you first declare your intentions*. It was similar to Kedj's technique when the company would come sweeping out of the hills on some unsuspecting caravan: convince them immediately they didn't really want to fight.

But still, there was no way he could reconcile *stay out of trouble*, with publicly killing three men.

The worst danger was the man with his knife already out and at Shile's throat. But his left hand was out in the open, flat on the table, careless and inviting. So Weiland came up between him and the man who was already counting the money he'd confiscated. That one started to look up just as Weiland used his left hand to grab a fistful of hair and slammed him face-down into the table, and simultaneously used his right hand to bring his own knife down straight into the left hand of the scarred, knife-holding man, pinning him to the table.

With a cry of surprise, pain, and rage, the man dropped his dagger— which was exactly what Weiland had counted on, so he was ready to catch it. When the man reached to grab at Weiland's knife, Weiland jammed the man's own blade into his right arm just above the wrist, pinning that to the table, too.

The bare-chested one had let go of Shile, kicking away his stool and starting to rise. Shile, a man more used to words than actions, had reeled back but was not yet reacting to help in his own rescue. Weiland spared an instant for a backwards jab of his elbow aimed at the nose of the first man, who had just raised his already bloody face from the table.

Then Weiland lunged across the table to grab at the bare-chested man's hair, dragging him down to the table, slick now with blood and ale and dotted with crumbs of bread. Weiland plucked his own knife from the hand of the man he had pinned—he had cut through tendons, and that one wouldn't be able to close his fingers to free his other arm. Weiland held the tip of the knife a fingerbreadth below the last man's eye. "Do you really want to fight me?" he asked, never raising his voice. "Or do you want to see to your companions?"

The man, his cheek against the table, held his hands up and out to indicate he was through. "I don't want to fight," he assured Weiland.

The safest thing was to kill him, for he could easily ask around if that was his intent, and track Weiland and be trouble later on. But just as surely there were witnesses who could identify Weiland to the authorities if he killed this man. And if Daria had been annoyed by the attention Parn had brought by brawling, what would she say to killing? And in the meanwhile she would find out Shile was involved, and once she learned *he* was still alive . . .

Weiland hesitated, and finally Shile recovered himself. He told the men, "You really might consider leaving St. Celia's. I've met this man's brothers, and I can assure you, this one is not only the runt of the litter, he's the nicest by far. You honestly don't want to get on their wrong side."

"We won't," the man Weiland held assured them. The other two moaned in agreement.

Weiland straightened, mindful of the possibility of treachery as Shile gathered up the money from the table. Even as they moved away from the tavern and the crowd that had gathered, he continued to be watchful, but the men seemed to have truly had enough.

"Better put the knife away," Shile advised as they walked through the streets. "You're attracting attention."

It went against instinct to sheath a blade that hadn't been properly cleaned, but Weiland saw the sense of this, and compromised by tucking it into his belt.

"Thank you," Shile said, with enough feeling to clearly show he wasn't referring to putting away the knife. "That time your help obviously wasn't inadvertent."

"I thought you were dead," Weiland said, so relieved he blurted it out before he realized a statement like that would demand an explanation.

Instead, Shile said, in a tone Weiland didn't know what to make of, "*Did* you?"

Weiland thought, *Maybe he thinks I meant he was close to getting killed.*

But before he could think what answer that supposition might require, Shile said, "I saw. Last night."

Don't give away anything. "What," Weiland asked, "exactly?"

Shile stopped walking for a moment to look at him long and steadily.

Weiland thought, *Everything. He saw everything.*

Shile resumed walking. He said, "I thought: 'There's something wrong with that Lady Daria de Gris and her household.' But I didn't know what. I decided, maybe I would investigate a bit. Hear what I could hear, see what I could see. Decide, if things warranted, whether to break in. I got into the compound, sneaked around to the back. But somebody else had had the same idea ahead of me. Well, the breaking-in part, anyway. I know . . . knew . . . the man. His name was Durward. He wouldn't have been interested in information. Strictly in what he could carry off during the night." Shile shook his head. "Durward always was more confident than competent. He was heading for the wing where the lady's rooms would be, and lost his footing. I saw the back door open, and thought she was going to send the three of you up onto the roof to fetch him."

They fell to silence as a cluster of children chasing each other on the street passed them.

Then, "There was enough light," Shile said.

It had never occurred to Weiland to claim that Shile had misseen. "You assumed it was me?"

Weiland shrugged.

"Before?" Shile was making the transition from scared and thoughtful to angry. "After? During?"

"No," Weiland said. "Not during."

Shile took another long look. He stopped walking again. "Do you have human thoughts when you're in an animal's body?"

Weiland didn't tell him he was looking at everything backwards: that Weiland was a wolf, in a human's body. He just said, "No."

Shile sighed, looking as shaky as Weiland felt. "So you don't know if you killed Johanna?"

"Shile, no." Weiland shook his head for emphasis. "I didn't. Shile, Geoffrey and the rest of the hunting party can vouch for me."

Shile considered, then nodded. "But the wolves that *did* kill her— were they men Daria had changed into wolves?"

"No," Weiland said. "But . . ." Shile was looking at him, talking with him, man to man, never suspecting. Weiland remembered the look that had flickered across Shile's face when they'd talked of Weiland transforming into a wolf that had killed a man, and could picture that look growing solid and permanent if he learned what Weiland really was. He finished, "They *were* her creatures."

"Why?" Shile asked.

Weiland shook his head.

"To get at Geoffrey?"

"I don't understand it," Weiland admitted.

"Geoffrey is a very important man," Shile said. "If Daria married him . . . Johanna . . ." Shile shook his head in exasperation. "Johanna wasn't one to grasp at power." He snorted and revised that to, "She wasn't one to accept power if it was thrust at her. But Daria . . . God, Daria has ambitions." Shile seemed to realize they'd been standing still for too long. He took hold of Weiland's arm to get him walking again, lest anyone overhear. "Weiland," he said, "she's got to be stopped."

"Shile," Weiland countered, "she can't be stopped. Besides, I'm sorry your cousin is dead, but now that Daria has what she wants—"

"Do you think she'll be satisfied with just marrying Geoffrey?" Shile asked. "She strikes me as the kind who always has to have everything exactly her own way. She'll misuse the power she gains by marrying him—"

It was true. Now was not the time to tell him she'd killed her own mother for banishing her lover, then killed the lover to keep from suspicion. Instead he said, "Shile, you don't understand. I've tried to fight her. You can't win."

"Geoffrey has to be warned."

"Warn him," Weiland said. "If you think he'll believe you."

Shile thought about that. At length he said, "She'll go after the children."

Weiland shook his head. "They have nothing she wants."

"Weiland,"—Shile took hold of his shoulders, forced him against a wall so that he had to look straight at him—"if she succeeds in getting Geoffrey to marry her, she will have a certain amount of power. If she has children by him, she will have more power. But *if his only children are hers*, she will have the most power possible."

Weiland shoved Shile away. "There's nothing I can do," he said.

"What hold does she have over you?" Shile demanded.

Weiland started to walk away, certain Shile wouldn't shout their business for the world to hear, but Shile called after him, "So the next time she turns you into a wolf, when she sets you after them, you can take comfort in the fact that you can't remember."

There was no possible answer to that, so Weiland didn't even try.

19

When Weiland got back to the house, he found that Daria had been looking for him.

"Where have you been?" she demanded. Human-born and created servants, and even those of the company were scurrying about in a frenzy of activity that Weiland could only imagine had something to do with the guests that should be arriving soon for Daria's dinner.

"I've been in the town," he said, "listening to what people had to say about the man killed last night." It wasn't exactly truth—linking together two things as though one—but close enough that he thought he could manage without his face giving anything away.

"And?" Daria asked.

"They suspect magic. Some compared it to a death that happened twenty-five years ago, in your mother's time." The last was for the pretense regarding Daria's age, both for the servants' sake and because she had never spoken to him directly about it, perhaps thinking him incapable of simple addition.

Incredibly Daria seemed to have to think before remembering. "That stupid stable boy?" she asked, unmindful of servants everywhere. "They're still talking about that?"

"And your grandmother Edwina," Weiland said, very aware of their voices carrying.

"My *grandmother*," Daria said, lowering her voice but emphasizing the word to indicate she remembered herself, "meddled where she shouldn't have." She changed her tone. "Is anybody accusing you?" she asked airily, a clear indication—in case he had not suspected—of just how much help she would be to him if he *did* come under suspicion.

"No," Weiland said, for the truth was he had offered the information to Shile before Shile had had the chance to ask. Then, because of what she had almost caused him to do last night, he added, "Nobody's accusing you, either."

There was a spark of annoyance in her eyes, but then she gave a smile that was every bit as wolfish as anything he'd ever seen from Telek or any of the others. "Well, that's safest for everyone." She gestured him away, impatient but no longer angry. "Go make yourself presentable. We will be going to the baron's house."

"I thought the baron was coming here."

Again the flash of annoyance. "He was. But apparently his whining little brats do not wish it."

He liked neither the news nor the tone in which Daria gave it, but thought best not to ask for details. He'd probably see for himself sooner than he wanted.

And he did.

The location of the dinner was being changed, but not the dinner itself. It was still Daria—or, rather, Daria's cook—who was providing all the food. This seemed to Weiland an awkward solution, with baskets and barrels to be packed and transported, arriving late, Daria in a frenzy, and everybody flustered lest something had been forgotten, or misplaced, or allowed to grow too cold or warm.

But the baron rose from his seat to greet Daria at the very door, and he hugged her in front of his household and the already-assembled guests, and he declared in a loud voice for all to hear, "Daria, this is exceedingly kind of you. Who could have expected such a generous response, to have you indulge in such lavish graciousness,"—he gestured to indicate the servants rapidly setting up, and smiled warmly at her—"to my children's whims?"

"The gathering would not have been the same without you," Daria said with a smile and a polite inclining of her head that gave little indication of what her reaction was likely to have been should the baron have sent notice *after* the other guests had begun to arrive.

Weiland glanced over the people assembled and saw, for the most part, the same as he usually saw at these gatherings.

But among all those other faces, suddenly Shile's stood out. He was Johanna's cousin after all, even if nobody thought very highly of him, and it only made sense that he could contrive to get himself invited at least sometimes.

Shile grinned, seeing Weiland notice him; but Weiland, after hesitating only for a moment, continued to look, very casually, about the room. At least Daria had left the rest of the company back at the house after they had helped get food and drink and servants packed: Melor wouldn't be here to point Shile out to Daria as the one who had been asking questions, the one she had assumed she had gotten rid of.

Meanwhile, the baron turned to gesture his children to approach. "Peter, Margaret," he had to urge them, "bring Didrika with you. Come thank the Lady Daria for bringing dinner to your father, since you wouldn't allow your father to go to dinner."

He laughed as though this were a fine joke, but the children stood, sullen and pale, clustered together. Weiland could see them practically shrink into themselves at being the sudden center of attention of everyone in the room—all adults, and much, much taller. But the boy, being—at five—the eldest, dragged on the arm of his middle sister, and eventually the youngest realized it was a choice of go-with-them or be left behind.

It took them forever to cross the hall, despite their father's persistent smilings and beckonings to "Come, come." Then he poked at them to stand straight and stop fidgeting, and announced, "These last days have been very difficult for them, you realize, without their mother, and they're afraid to be left alone—well, the girls are." He ruffled his son's hair. "Peter's old enough to know I wouldn't leave and not come back."

Peter looked old enough to resent having his hair ruffled, anyway, Weiland thought. He suspected the boy was also old enough to know his mother hadn't been given the choice whether to come back, and to resent his father's implying she *could* have, had she wanted to.

"The poor dears!" Daria crouched with a swish and swirl of her gown, and tried to hug the three children all at once, though the youngest was able to squirm out through the bottom. "This has all been just too awful for them. Of course they shall have their father with them! I should have suggested it this way to begin with. If there is *anything* I can do to help," she told the children, "you just ask."

None of them asked anything, and Daria smiled and patted them on the heads, even the youngest. Then she stood, using Geoffrey's arm for support, though Weiland had been standing at the ready all along.

Shile chose this moment to approach, which was fortunate, for Daria had all her attention on smiling charmingly up into Geoffrey's face. Weiland nudged Shile with an elbow and gave as much of a warning look as he dared—which Shile couldn't have understood, but apparently he did recognize it as a warning. He must have been willing to trust Weiland, at least for the moment, for he stepped back, letting other people put themselves between him and Daria.

"Come," Geoffrey told the guests, "let us begin this most excellent feast that this most excellent lady has so graciously provided for us."

"She knows your name," Weiland whispered to Shile as they

passed, all there was time to say. It should be enough for Shile to know better than to let himself get introduced to her.

Weiland headed for his place at the second table, where Geoffrey's men-at-arms sat. They were a loud, competitive group, mostly friendly, who had given up only recently on trying to include him in their games and conversation. Now they ignored him, which was what he wanted because his duty was to protect Daria, not socialize.

Daria had told those of her company to assume she was safe at this type of gathering, and not to embarrass her by tasting her food before she ate of it—which was something she had required at the hill fortress, and still did at her own house—nor were they to shove away or cut off the hand of someone *they* judged might be getting too close. "I'll find some way to let you know, should the expectations change," she told them. Which didn't mean she wouldn't take it out on them should they miss something.

Now, Daria and Geoffrey sat at the place of honor—the center of the long main table. Shile had wisely selected a seat almost at the end of that table. The children, Weiland was relieved to see, were sitting safely away at yet another table, with those servants who were not serving the meal.

Children and servants ate quickly and then dispersed, to do whatever children and servants did during the day. For the rest, dinner seemed to be going well: Daria was doing a lot of smiling and laughing and looking up at Geoffrey through her eyelashes. Weiland could hear only occasional snatches of what was being said, disjointed phrases and words, but the people seemed to find each other amusing company.

At his own table, Weiland wished there was some way he could direct the conversation to the subject of the man killed last night, to learn their views, but he wasn't sure how to do this without arousing their suspicions. Nobody mentioned it—perhaps not thinking it important, perhaps having thoroughly discussed it earlier. What he *did* learn was that they couldn't have any idea that Daria was involved, for they spoke approvingly of her: her youth, her beauty, her poise. Weiland was aware that they might be complimenting her for his benefit, specifically to disguise their wariness, but he doubted this. They were already beginning to speculate whether, after the shock and distress of Johanna's terrible death had worn off—and after a decent interval of mourning— Geoffrey might not find consolation in Daria. And, of course, a new mother for his children.

"You may yet end up at this table permanently," one of Geoffrey's men told Weiland with what might have been a good-natured slap on the back.

Weiland had the feeling most of the others didn't care for that idea any more than he did.

There was endless playing of lute and rebec, talking, laughing, dancing. As far as Weiland could see, the interval of mourning certainly seemed to be closing quickly. Glancing continually around the room, he occasionally noticed Shile, and that he looked as bored as Weiland himself felt.

Eventually the talk turned to the manor's gardens, which everyone agreed were exquisite. There was a topiary maze that Geoffrey offered to show to Daria, though he apologized that it would not yet be in full leaf.

"Then you will have to show me a second time, later," Daria said, taking his arm.

None of the men-at-arms rose, though several of the guests did. Weiland followed along behind, unobtrusively, though if any of them began to loiter, he would have to push past them to keep Daria in sight.

Shile casually fell into step beside him, as though deciding only at the last instant to join the group.

Weiland didn't even glance at him, but knew that if he didn't say or do something soon, Shile would begin to take his silence as merely an unwillingness to talk. Once outside, he slowed, so that the distance to Daria grew greater than he was comfortable with, but so the stragglers of the group weren't close enough to hear. Still looking ahead rather than turning to face Shile, Weiland said, softly, "The man who was killed—"

"Durward," Shile interrupted, as though Weiland had forgotten the name rather than dismissed it as unimportant.

"When he was on the roof, Melor speculated to Daria that it might be you. He identified you as a thief, and someone who had been asking questions. He gave Daria your name."

"All right." Shile said it evenly, as though unworried. Weiland did glance at him then, and guessed that Shile did, in fact, understand what he was saying. He looked away without saying anything and shook his head in frustration even before Shile said, "I still intend to take every opportunity to stay close to Geoffrey, to protect him and the children from your lady."

The path divided, encircling several flower beds, so that Weiland could see Daria and Geoffrey, who were lingering to sniff at various blossoms. Weiland stopped where he was, to avoid getting too close; he was aware that some of the other guests had paused at different spots, and some had continued down the path, which doubled back beyond some hedges and might well bring them within a distance where they might hear without Weiland's being able to see them.

Still facing Daria rather than Shile, Weiland asked, as softly as he could, "Did you tell him what you saw?"

Shile was ignoring Weiland just as steadfastly as Weiland was ignoring him. He bent to pluck a leaf from the plant he was standing next to. Crushing the leaf and holding it up to his nose, he said, "No. You were right. He'd never believe me. Without having seen it for himself, the story sounds so ridiculous, he'd be bound to think I was either mad or making it up to serve some purpose of my own." Shile dropped the leaf and wiped his hands against each other. "Your backing me—"

"Would make him think I was a disgruntled employee," Weiland interrupted.

Shile sighed. "Probably. But I'm not just going to let it be. I am not going to assume that she's gotten all she wants and is not going to harm anyone else."

"No," Weiland agreed. He kept thinking back to how he had done nothing to help Llewellur, how he had followed Daria to the pond despite knowing that she intended Johanna harm. But in truth there was nothing he could have done then, and there was nothing he could do now.

There was a squeal of high voices, and the sound of small feet running, and the baron's two older children came around the curve of the path. "Father, Father," they both started at once, each trying to talk over the other, the words jumbling into an impression of something exciting they'd seen. But they skidded to a stop and the smiles faded from their faces when they saw their father wasn't alone.

"What did you find?" Daria asked as though their discovery must be wonderful.

The girl just glowered; the boy dug his toe into the ground and mumbled something Weiland couldn't hear.

"A nest!" Daria exclaimed. "How exciting! What kind?"

Again the boy mumbled his reply.

"How exciting!" Daria repeated. "Can you show it to us? I'd certainly like to see, wouldn't you, Geoffrey?"

Geoffrey assured the children he would, but this time the boy wouldn't say anything, wouldn't even look up from his toes.

Daria crouched down to bring herself to the same level as the children. "Will you show us where the nest is?" she asked as though there was nothing in the world she wanted more.

This time the little girl spoke. Loudly and clearly she said, "No."

"Margaret," her father snapped, no longer looking amused.

But she'd given her brother the courage to speak up, so that now he said, clearly enough for Weiland to understand, "It's a secret." There was defiance in his voice, too. He spoke only to his father, ignoring Daria. "Our mother showed me when the leaves were all gone last year, and she said not to poke at it and not to show anybody but you and Margaret and Didrika. And she said maybe then they'd come back again in spring. And they did."

Young Peter didn't look at Daria, but the little girl did. "She didn't say *you* could come."

"Of course she can come," Geoffrey started, but Daria said, "Poor little precious. I understand perfectly."

Geoffrey said, "Margaret and Peter, you must apologize immediately."

Daria smiled sweetly. "Not at all." She stood. "*You* must go see the nest and then tell me all about it. Maybe the children will choose to show me some other time."

"No," Margaret said.

Her father looked embarrassed, but Daria continued to smile and patted the children on their heads. Geoffrey, standing between them holding onto their arms, kept them from squirming too much.

"I'm sure I'll be able to find something else to amuse myself while you're gone," Daria told him.

Geoffrey led his children away, looking ready to discipline them as soon as they got out of hearing.

Shile had wandered around one of the flower beds so that he could remain in hearing without appearing to be with Weiland, and now he headed, with many pauses to admire the plants, in the same general direction the baron had gone—as though putting himself between Daria and his cousin's family could somehow save them from harm.

Daria turned and walked in the opposite direction from Geoffrey and the children, heading back toward the house, which brought her past Weiland. Despite the pleasant smile still on her face, she muttered, "Spoiled little wretches."

Weiland didn't say anything, but just silently followed her.

20

The evening was beginning to get dark and chilly, many of the guests had left, the servants were packing up and preparing to return to Daria's house. Daria declared her intention not to wait but to set off for home, which probably had much to do with Geoffrey settling in with his men and his closest friends and relatives, his attention beginning to drift from her. Shile was there, always hovering around the fringes, expecting who-knew-what? He'd probably somehow talked himself into an invitation to spend the night, Weiland thought. And how many more nights, before Daria made her move?

Weiland was escorting Daria across the lawn as a shortcut to the street, when young Margaret almost collided with them. The children's nurse had been looking for her—Weiland had heard her calling for both Peter and Margaret as Daria had been saying her good-byes.

But instead of saying that people were looking for her, Daria said, "Why, Margaret, where are you going so fast? Have you come to wish me good-bye?"

"No," Margaret said. "I didn't know you were here."

Unexpectedly, Daria sat down on the grass—Daria, who was always so particular about appearing at best advantage. "Come and sit on my lap, little one."

"My lady," Weiland started, full of dread.

"Hush," Daria said gently, as though he, too, were a child. "Come, Margaret, give me a hug good-bye and kiss my cheek. You know your father would wish it."

Weiland saw that children were used to doing what they were told, just as those of the company were. Hesitating, not wanting to, Margaret approached.

"You'll just be back tomorrow," she said. "You're always here."

Daria motioned her to come the rest of the way and hugged her. "Yes," she said gently. "And you must get used to it."

"You're not my mother," the child said, twisting to get away now that she'd done as she'd been ordered. "You'll never be my mother."

Weiland saw the flicker of annoyance, then the furtive glance all about to make sure no one else was near. Then the girl's clothes seemed to crumple in Daria's hands. But Daria held on tight. "Weiland," she said between clenched teeth.

"My lady," Weiland pleaded.

"Get over here."

Weiland saw that, among all those clothes, she was holding onto a tiny brown rabbit. For the moment, the creature was too frightened to move. Or perhaps it was too young to have the instinct to run. Weiland took the rabbit from Daria's hands.

"Go back to the kitchen," she ordered. "Get a basket or something secure to carry this. I *don't* want it getting away, and I don't want anybody seeing it and wondering what you're doing with it."

"My lady, so soon after her mother's death, there'll be questions if something similar—"

"It won't be similar," Daria snapped. Not: "I won't harm her." Just: "It won't be similar." She tugged at Weiland's shirt, loosening it while he stood—for the moment unable to move, unable to think from fear and bafflement. Then she gathered up the girl's clothing and tucked dress and shoes and all away under Weiland's shirt. When she readjusted the shirt, the clothes were so tiny, they didn't show at all, and he could hardly feel them.

Looking very pleased with herself, Daria said, "I will make my own way home. You can help the servants. But fall behind when you get to the river." Weiland guessed then what was coming. "Drown that thing," she said. "When it reverts back to its own true form, dress the body, so that people will assume the poor child wandered too close to the water, fell, and drowned. See you don't bruise her—I want no suspicions."

"My lady," Weiland said, one last desperate attempt, "it's too soon. It's too dangerous. Turn her back into a little girl. No one will believe her story. Her father is already angry with her for the way she spoke to you earlier and he will see anything she says as her clumsy attempt to turn him against you. It will make him angrier yet with her, and more inclined to you. And at the same time, she will know it's true, and she will be too afraid to cross you again."

Either Daria, knowing humans better, knew they wouldn't really reason the way Weiland conjectured, or she didn't care. She reached out and gently caressed his cheek. "Weiland," she said, soft as the evening breeze, "remember what I said about if I ordered you to eat the children? While you're in human form? Would you prefer that?"

Weiland took a deep breath and shook his head.

"Go get the basket," Daria said. "And do what you're told."

"Yes, my lady," he whispered. The rabbit was small enough to hold in the palm of one hand, but he held it close in the crook of his elbow, careful not to drop it, and he felt the frantic beating of its heart. *Rabbits' hearts always beat fast*, he told himself. In this form the little girl would not be able to understand human speech. She would not know what was planned for her. She would not be afraid.

Weiland watched as Daria continued down the gentle incline of the hill, her arms swinging, the hem of her skirt gliding gracefully across the grass, the picture of youth and beauty.

There's nothing I can do, Weiland thought as he headed for the kitchen. All in all, drowning wasn't that bad a death. And children died all the time by mischance or illness. Who was to say this one would have survived the year even without Daria?

In the kitchen, Geoffrey's servants and Daria's were getting in each other's way, but the work of cleaning up was almost done. Weiland no doubt added to the confusion by peeking into the various baskets and packages, always remaining with his arms folded across his chest, keeping his bent left arm to the wall to prevent being jostled—like a man with an injury, he thought. If he was lucky, that's what they'd imagine, if they truly noticed him at all.

He found a small basket filled with leftover bread. By tossing one of the round loaves under the table, there was more than enough room for the rabbit. Fortunately, the rabbit must be of an age where its instinct told it to hold still if it sensed danger, in the hope that danger would pass it by, so it didn't struggle as Weiland put it into the basket and tucked in a cloth to cover it. He sat on the edge of the table with the basket in his lap—as though overseeing the servants' packing.

The children's nurse came in twice, and one and another of the baron's servants, each time looking more frantic, asking if anyone had seen little Margaret.

No one had.

Weiland, too, shook his head, then closed his eyes and rested his head against the wall as though tired, but in reality so he wouldn't have to see people's reactions to the news that no one had word of the child.

There was more room on the wagon, with so much of the food consumed, but even so several of the servants were carrying loads, so

Weiland did not feel that he stood out especially. Outside, he could hear voices calling, "Margaret! Margaret!" Men were calling too. Apparently she had been gone long enough, and it was getting dark and chill enough, that Geoffrey's men-at-arms and those guests who remained had joined the servants' search.

"Good luck," Daria's human-born servants wished Geoffrey's. Some added they were sure the little one would be found soon, no doubt asleep and unaware of the turmoil she was causing, in some safe corner. Geoffrey's servants agreed this was probably so. Daria's made servants said nothing.

They started down the drive to the street, passing Geoffrey coming the other way. By the look on his face, there was no need for anyone to ask what news. He looked as though he couldn't decide whether to be angry or worried, but was inclining to anger, because that was safer, that meant Margaret was misbehaving, not hurt or sick.

Others followed Geoffrey, and they could afford to look worried. Some carried torches, though most had not prepared that well, as though they had originally assumed the search would be a quick one, that the servants had failed through incompetence. The torches cast ominous looking shadows across the faces of the men and women about them, so that Weiland had already passed before he recognized one.

"Shile!" he hissed.

Shile, too, was taken by surprise. No doubt he had watched Weiland leave with Daria, had assumed they were long gone and the d'Akil household safe from them. Weiland saw the worry replaced by surprise, then suspicion. Then fear chased away everything else as Shile recast the meaning of the missing child in this new light.

Weiland jerked his head to the side, indicating they needed to get away from the others before talking.

Even as they walked, Weiland tried out various lies in his mind. He needed to assure Shile that Daria had left long before, that—whatever had happened to the child, wherever she had wandered off to—Daria had nothing to do with it.

But if that was to be his story, he should never have called out to Shile, and he knew it. In truth, this was exactly what he had refused to admit to himself he had been waiting for.

So he was not surprised to hear himself whisper, "Here," to see himself reach into the basket and scoop up the rabbit and shove it at Shile. It kicked this time, several swift and surprisingly hard pushes with its hind feet that raked its nails against Weiland's wrists. He held on tightly and in a moment the rabbit once more went still. From between clenched teeth he whispered, so no one but Shile could hear, "Take it."

Shile was squinting, unable to make out in the dark this far from the house and torches what Weiland was trying to give him.

This would be the death of him—he knew that. "Hold on tight," he said urgently. All he needed was to picture Daria realizing he had disobeyed her, *and* have the child end up dead anyway, and that was almost enough to make him snatch back the rabbit and say, "Never mind." But he didn't. "Hold on tight," he repeated. And Shile took the rabbit and looked at him with growing horror in his eyes.

"Keep her safe," Weiland told him. "But whatever you do, make sure you keep her where Geoffrey can see her at all times. Do you understand me?"

He could see Shile did. His voice was beginning to shake, but it was too late now to think what a bad decision this was. "If she doesn't change back tonight, you tell Geoffrey the only way he'll ever see his daughter again is to take the rabbit and leave St. Celia's—it doesn't matter what direction, two days' hard ride will do it." Then he asked again, desperately, "Do you understand?"

"God," Shile whispered, by which Weiland took him to mean *yes*.

Weiland turned to go; he had to rejoin the servants so that they could assure Daria, if she got so far as to ask, that he had been with them, carrying a basket, and had parted company with them when they passed near the river.

"Wait," Shile called after him. He was holding the rabbit firmly but gently to his chest. "What about you?" Shile asked.

But there was nothing he could answer to that.

"Weiland!" Shile called when he started to turn away a second time.

Weiland turned back with a glare for all his noise.

"Stay here," Shile suggested, at least having the sense to lower his voice. "We'll both tell Geoffrey what we know. Of course he won't believe us at first, but the longer Margaret's missing, the more desperate he'll be to try anything. And whether she regains her true form tonight or if we have to leave St. Celia's, you'll be safe. Geoffrey will protect you from Daria."

"He can't," Weiland said.

Shile seemed to suddenly realize the sense of that. "When he realizes what Daria has done, he'll order her killed. Surely once she's dead, her magic won't be able to affect you." He was looking very scared again. "Will it?"

"No," Weiland said. And this time he did walk away.

Shile had to either chase after him—which was dangerous, with the rabbit in his care—or raise his voice again—which he did, to call after him, "You need protecting in case she uses something nonmagical against you."

Weiland didn't turn back to explain that she didn't need to.

21

After parting company with the servants by the river's edge, Weiland stayed there as long as he dared. He might survive this night, but he didn't think that likely. At the very least, this was probably his last chance to see things through human eyes.

But Daria could in some way sense her creations—she'd know that Margaret wasn't dead yet, and Daria would be beginning to get frantic wondering why. If she got enraged enough to change him into a wolf while he was on the streets of St. Celia's, there was no telling how much damage he could unwittingly do.

Blanche let him in, pale and uncharacteristically subdued. Nobody was stirring, which—considering the unpacking that would be required after the day's feast, and the putting away of food, and preparing for tomorrow—hinted at one of Daria's violent furies.

There was no use deluding himself. "Her room?" Weiland asked, because Blanche wasn't saying anything.

She nodded, without looking up from the floor.

Daria's door was closed. He knocked and waited for a response. Then, eventually, knocked again.

"Come," Daria's voice called from a distance.

She wasn't in the room, but the far door, the one to her spell room, was open.

Weiland hesitated, wanting anything but to enter there. He wouldn't submit, he told himself. Kedj wasn't here to force him to the table, to tie him so that Daria could draw his blood—to the death or not, at her whim. There were human-born people here, whom Daria did not want knowing her business, so that she might relent, if he started to cause a disturbance.

But Weiland knew Daria had other means besides Kedj to force her will. Too late he regretted returning. He should have gone with Shile, admitted to Geoffrey what would happen to him when Daria died, and asked for a swift death at their hands. All of what he was went into standing still, not turning, not trying to run.

Daria came out of the room, wiping bloody hands on a towel. She said, calmly enough, "Try to remember to breathe with your mouth closed."

Not good, Weiland thought, getting a closer look at her eyes now. Whatever she'd done in that room—and he guessed the company was now down to five—she wasn't through. He knew he should have some concern about which of the others her anger had settled on, since he was the real cause, but he couldn't get beyond the relief that, for the moment anyway, it wasn't him.

She tossed the bloodied towel on the floor and took his chin with a hand that was still stained red around the fingernails. "What have you done?" she asked in a voice almost too soft to hear.

"I lost the rabbit," he said. Her fingers didn't tighten—she just kept looking at him. He still had the basket and he held it up, though now it contained only leftover bread and Margaret's clothes. Neither of them looked at it. "I put it in the basket, and carried it to the river. But when I went to take it out, it suddenly squirmed, after sitting quietly up until then." He turned his wrist for her to see the scratches.

She looked. They both looked. There were welts, and some blood, but they both knew it was nothing.

"I was startled," Weiland explained lamely.

Once again Daria's gaze went back to his eyes.

"I tried to catch it, but it was so dark there by the river . . . I lost track." He didn't think it was a bad story, but after a long moment Daria said, "I should have drowned *you*, when you were that age."

He saw her begin to take a breath, and he said hurriedly, "If you change her back now, before daybreak, while she's likely to still be by the river, there won't be anyone there to see the transformation." Amazingly, Daria was waiting to hear what he had to say. "She'll make her way back home, or to someone who will take her home, and nobody will believe her—because her story will be too incredible. The danger,"—Daria was always alert to danger—"the danger is if you wait too long—if someone captures her and starts to skin her, or if dogs catch her scent during the day and tear her to pieces on the street in front of witnesses, and her death changes her back."

"No one would know I was behind it," Daria said.

"But they would know it was magic. The other way, it would just be a frightened child's story. They would think she was making it up to avoid punishment.''

"Yes," Daria said on a long drawn-out sigh, as though she relished the word *punishment*. Then she said, "I still should have drowned you rather than raised you. Kedj always said you were a mistake.'' She glanced at the spell room and complained, distracted, "There just isn't time.''

He was having real difficulty catching his breath. He could feel his heart pounding—not so fast as the rabbit's had, but the rhythm was off, something was wrong. His chest hurt, as did his left shoulder and arm. *Leave well enough alone*, he thought. *At least it's not the spell room.* Considering how little time she had been home and judging from the silence, whoever that was in there had died uncharacteristically quickly. It wouldn't get better than this.

But he had been trained all his life to fight.

"I'm sorry I dropped the rabbit," he managed to say; apologies were rarely wrong—often ineffective, but rarely wrong. He finished in a rush, from the realization that he might not have time to finish at all: "But how many people can you lose from your household in one night, how many bodies can you dispose of before suspicion falls on you?''

From far, far away he heard Daria admit, "I don't know," but he didn't even feel himself begin to fall.

22

The first thing Weiland was aware of was the floor. He was stiff and sore, which meant he was alive, and he wasn't collapsed in a heap but actually lying down, and the floor wasn't as hard as it should be—which, after thinking about it for a long meandering time, seemed to mean he had been set to rest on a sleeping pallet.

He opened his eyes a crack and saw daylight and the walls of Daria's town house hall. Amazingly he was in his own place close to the hearth. He'd have thought, after all this, that *someone* else would have taken the leader's position. Hushed voices spoke nearby: the rest of the company, he realized, just finishing their breakfast and preparing for the day. He assumed the quiet was for fear of setting Daria off on a rampage, but when a bench leg scraped noisily on the stone floor, someone whispered, "Quiet! He needs to rest."

It had taken all his energy to piece together that he was alive. This new puzzle was beyond him, and he let himself drift back to sleep.

Surely a day had passed, Weiland thought, watching the shadows on the walls. He was fairly certain he'd been aware of darkness coming, and now it was light again. Where were the baron and his men? He would have expected them to come after Daria as soon as the little girl regained her own true shape, yet there were no sounds of disturbance. Had Daria overcome them so effortlessly?

Or maybe she hadn't taken his advice. Maybe she had left the child a rabbit, and Shile had had to convince Geoffrey to travel the distance that would take him beyond Daria's magic—at least two days going, and two more returning.

Or maybe Shile had failed to convince Geoffrey that the rabbit was important; maybe Geoffrey and his men had refused to sit still watching the rabbit, and no one but Shile had been there to see it transform back to Margaret.

Somebody from the company came into the room—Weiland's eyes were too heavy to open, but those of the company moved in an entirely different manner from the servants. Weiland tried to brace himself for a kick, but it was so much easier to just allow himself to drift away.

Maybe, he thought the next time he found himself awake and thinking again—and this was the worst thought yet—maybe Geoffrey's men had reacted the way those of the company probably would have: Maybe they had laughed at Shile's story, forcibly taken the rabbit, and killed it to serve as supper.

Not likely, he tried to assure himself. Dead, Margaret would once again look like Margaret, and even if no one had believed Shile before, there would be proof. Unless they decided to hide what they'd done from Geoffrey. Still, they should have come for Daria. So why was the house so quiet? He could hear servants in other parts of the house, apparently going about their daily tasks, and once in a while someone from the company would come in.

After a while he became aware that, incredibly, they were coming in specifically to poke at the fire or rearrange his blanket—to check on his well-being.

He forced his eyes open and found that it was Melor who had come in this last time. *I'm not ready to fight him*, Weiland thought, but Melor knelt beside him and—not ungently—got an arm behind his shoulders and a cup of some kind of broth to his lips.

Unexpected kindness. *Why?* Weiland wondered. There was no reason for Melor to poison him at this time, and Weiland couldn't figure what else he might be up to. "What are you doing?" he asked, his voice a hoarse whisper.

"Trying to give you a drink," Melor answered.

"Why?" He pushed the cup away. Things *could* have changed. Poison *might* be a possibility. "Daria?"

"No," Melor admitted. "All she told us was to get you out of her room." He saw the suspicious look Weiland was giving the cup and grinned, apparently guessing what Weiland was suspicious of. "*She* didn't give us any orders. *We* figure she hasn't made up her mind if she wants you dead or not. So we're taking care of you just in case she settles on *not*."

"Why?" Weiland repeated.

Melor snorted. "You think any of us wants to be leader and have her attention on us all the time?"

Daria had ordered away most of the other wolf-born she had brought with her so that they could kill Johanna. Only Weiland and Melor remained, among two ferrets, a rat, and a wolverine. Considering what was left, Weiland thought this was one of the most sensible things he'd heard Melor say. He estimated the broth was safe.

He managed to take hold of the cup steadily enough that Melor let go. "Where *is* Daria?" he asked.

"With Parn. She and some of her women friends went to check out a shipment of wool that's new in town." As though nothing had happened.

As though nothing had happened.

Melor stood. "If you're going to survive," he said, "I have better things to do than tend to you."

Unsure how much interest he should show in various questions, Weiland asked the one that wouldn't be suspect. "Who got killed?"

"Llewellur."

That was a surprise. Weiland had assumed it would have been one of the company. But at least with Llewellur, the body that she had to dispose of would have been a small one. Still, there must have been more to it than that. Or maybe not. "Why?"

Melor shrugged. "She got tired of the flute?" he speculated.

It was probably as good an answer as he'd ever get.

Once Melor was gone, Weiland pulled himself unsteadily to his feet. Slowly he set out in search of Royce, sincerely hoping that the old servant would be in the downstairs section of the house, for he honestly didn't think he could manage the stairs. He'd have to be careful how he worded his questions, but at least he was fairly certain they wouldn't get repeated to Daria.

Fortunately, Royce had set out in search of *him*, and found him before he'd had to go far. "Melor said you were up and about," Royce said, looking for all the world as though he were truly delighted by the news. "The other servants will be relieved when I tell them you're doing better again."

Weiland doubted the other servants had even noticed his absence.

But Royce continued without even a pause, "I took the liberty of asking Melor to pass along a message when he left just now. There's been a young woman most anxious about you—Evangeline, she said her name was, from the Hog and Bone. I thought she'd be happy to learn you were doing better."

Evangeline?

Weiland considered, and decided this was probably something to do with Shile. He had warned Shile that Melor had identified him to Daria. And Shile, he suspected, would not let pass the opportunity for conspiracy and intrigue.

"What's happened in town," Weiland asked, intentionally vague, "since,"—and here he got more vague yet—"I've been sick?"

"You heard Baron Geoffrey's young daughter was missing?"

Weiland nodded.

"As near as anyone can put things together, she must have gotten lost, perhaps in the maze they have in the garden, and then she didn't find her way out again till morning. By then she was dazed and confused. I gather she's confined to her bed, raving in her fever. The poor baron is almost sick himself with worry, and he hasn't left her side these two days."

"I see," Weiland said, not seeing at all.

Royce insisted on bringing him to the kitchen while he prepared another of his remedies. But at least this one was more sweet than foul, and it *did* lessen the throbbing in his head, which was what he said it was for. Though Royce always seemed to know everything, Weiland wondered how, exactly, he knew his head ached, until Royce described watching Parn and Melor pull him from Daria's room and start to drag him down the stairs. "I managed to convince them that it would probably be better to carry you," Royce admitted. Weiland didn't doubt that Royce was also behind Melor getting the idea that the position of leader might be more dangerous than he liked.

Weiland had just finished the drink when Bess came in to announce Evangeline had arrived.

Evangeline was following closely enough she had probably stepped on the backs of Bess's shoes. "I have been *so* worried," she cried, bursting into the kitchen before Bess had quite finished speaking. She raced across the room to kneel beside his stool, and threw her arms about his neck, practically toppling him, then she buried her face in his chest, and remained there, motionless.

"Come," Royce told Bess, who looked—for some reason Weiland couldn't guess—disapproving and put out.

Whatever this was about, Weiland was just beginning to decide he liked the feel of Evangeline's arms around him, and the smell of her, and the softness of her hair—when she pulled away. "Are you feeling well enough to walk?" she asked brightly. "Just for a short while?" Which probably meant she was afraid of someone listening, so he nodded.

She took him by the hand, which also felt unaccountably pleasant, and led him, of all places, to the cathedral. Once inside, however, they passed by the big room where everyone had gathered for Johanna's funeral, and stopped instead before a closed door. "They told me I'm to go pray," she said, and gave a pretty pout. Then she smiled and stood on tiptoe to kiss his cheek. "What I'll pray is that next time I get to keep you for myself."

Weiland wasn't sure what she was talking about. Still, it took him a good, long moment of watching her walk back to the large gathering room before he remembered the door, and realized the "they" she had talked about must be waiting for him on the other side.

It was Father Hadden Heallstede who opened the door, and Shile was standing right behind him. Beyond him, was Lord Geoffrey d'Akil.

Shile said, "You look terrible."

Weiland shrugged.

"Come in." Father Hadden was ready to offer him a supporting arm, but Weiland wasn't used to being touched, and Father Hadden must have been warned off by his look. Instead he just said, "Sit. Please." The priest hovered anxiously until Weiland sat on the window ledge, as though afraid Weiland might collapse before getting there.

Geoffrey, as though *he* also thought Weiland might not make it that far, waited until Weiland was sitting before saying, "I understand I owe you my daughter's life."

"Yes," Weiland said.

"Thank you." Geoffrey leaned back in his seat, appearing to evaluate Weiland, wearing much the same look Kedj might if someone from the company came back from a caravan raid with a horse—particularly, Weiland sensed, a horse Kedj had doubts about. Geoffrey said, "You weren't able to do anything for my wife."

"No," Weiland agreed.

To fill the long silence, Father Hadden said, "Perhaps, on that occasion, there wasn't enough warning, no time to react."

At length Weiland realized it had been a question, and Geoffrey was waiting for an answer. "That was part of it," he said, which was an answer that didn't seem to particularly please Geoffrey.

After yet another silence, Shile cleared his throat and said, "I've told Father Hadden everything."

Weiland thought, *You don't* know *everything*, but he waited.

"I went to the house," Shile explained. "The steward, Royce, said you'd been struck by a sudden illness." He hesitated, as though expecting Weiland to say something. When he didn't, Shile continued, "He said this had happened before, and that Father Hadden had visited you." Again the pause, a glance at the baron. "Geoffrey thought it was a good idea, too, to bring in a man of the church.'' He looked at Weiland expectantly.

"What are you asking?'' Weiland said. "Do you want me to say you *should* have included Father Hadden? If I say 'no,' what difference would that make now?''

"I could leave,'' Father Hadden offered.

Weiland shrugged.

The priest finished, "Though I think I should stay. The church has long been an enemy of sorcery. With God's help, we may yet be able to overcome this evil woman.''

This answer touched on a matter that had been unclear for several weeks now. "Does God know magic?'' Weiland asked.

Judging by Geoffrey's startled look, and the way Shile lowered his face and clapped his hand to his forehead, this was not a sensible question, but Father Hadden answered gently, "God performs *miracles*, which are like magic.'' He smiled, looking calm and patient and sad, all at the same time. "But I would add, *rarely* these days. His help is ... perhaps less dramatic, in most cases. One can *hope* for miracles, but it's generally best to back that hope by action.''

Weiland didn't follow this exactly, except that the answer to what had seemed his last chance was *no*.

"This illness of yours,'' Father Hadden said, "it was caused by this woman Daria de Gris?''

Illness, injury—it was all the same. He said, "Yes.''

Geoffrey interrupted, "Because you refused to harm Margaret?''

"Yes.''

Father Hadden gave Geoffrey a look that said *he* was the one asking the questions. "Whom Lady Daria had changed into a rabbit, by means of—?''

"Magic,'' Weiland finished.

"Magic,'' Geoffrey repeated in a tone that could have meant anything.

"Does she pray to the devil?'' Father Hadden asked.

"I don't think so,'' Weiland said, but hesitantly for the words were unfamiliar, and Geoffrey was looking wary. But Weiland's hesitation made him look even more wary.

Shile said, "I don't think he understands.''

Father Hadden clarified: "Have you heard her call on Satan, or the names of pagan gods?''

Weiland thought of how she had killed Lon, to bring luck to the new house, not gathering his blood, but leaving it to drip uselessly to the floor. "I don't think so,'' he said. "Maybe. Not out loud.''

Father Hadden considered. Then he said, "Tell me about her magic."

Weiland had never tried to put it into words before. "She can . . . do things . . . to,"—for lack of a better word, he settled on—"people— their bodies. She can transform animals to humans, humans to animals, she can heal, she can . . . cause injury."

Geoffrey interrupted again, "Can she manipulate the physical world?" To Weiland's blank look, he explained, "Say . . . knock down a castle wall, cause a river to overflow its banks . . ." He stopped trying to think of examples because Weiland was shaking his head.

Weiland was thinking, *Isn't what she does enough?*

Father Hadden asked, "Just people?"

"And animals," Weiland corrected.

"Does she need to prepare in any way—gather herbs or roots, or wait for a particular time, or . . ." Father Hadden hesitated, either unable to think of what he wanted to ask, or afraid to.

"No," Weiland said. "Sometimes she needs blood, but not before any particular transformation."

"What kind of blood?"

"From us," Weiland said. "Those of her company."

The three men exchanged a distressed look.

"Does she drink it?" Father Hadden asked.

"I don't know," Weiland admitted. But he certainly thought so. All the company did. At the hill fortress, they were all afraid to be summoned to her rooms, for there seemed no pattern to when she'd want their blood. But periodically she would summon one of them, and Kedj would be there, in case they fought, which some of them did—some of the times—though this was always useless.

Still, Kedj would bind them to the table, and sometimes she would take a knife and cut them, leaving them to bleed into a gathering bowl until the blackness overtook them. And other times she would do something to them first, causing pain without needing to touch them, so that they would wake up dazed and weakened from the injury or the blood-letting or the healing afterwards, and they would not be able to remember any of it. Nobody—at least nobody who had survived—was ever awake to see what she did with the blood. Only Kedj was allowed to watch.

Sometimes the person died, and sometimes not, and Weiland didn't know if this was decided beforehand, or if it just worked out that way. Those who had not been chosen that particular day could often hear the dying person screaming, even through the thickness of the stone wall. On those occasions the rest of them would be called in afterwards, to wash blood off the walls, and floor, and even the ceiling. Daria had a separate chamber off the spell room, where there was a reservoir of water in what she called "the old Roman style," a fire to heat the water, and a tub for bathing. Apparently, she didn't mind Kedj watching that either, for he'd stay with her till the others came in to remove the body, when she would already be cleaned and wearing fresh clothes. Lon, who had liked to claim that Weiland was as squeamish as any human-born, insisted that one of the bodies he had removed had definite gnaw marks.

Weiland wasn't willing to talk about any of this.

After waiting for further elaboration about the blood, or for Father Hadden to ask another question, Geoffrey finally asked, "How long do these transformations last?"

"As long as she wants them to. Except . . . if the person or animal dies. Then the body goes back to its original form."

"Has she transformed many people to animals?"

"No," Weiland said. "I didn't even know she could, until she came to St. Celia's."

Again the three of them exchanged a look. Shile started to ask something, but Father Hadden interrupted. "Where does she come from? *Is* she the granddaughter of Robert de Gris?"

"I believe she's his daughter," Weiland said. That, he could tell, was another surprise. To Father Hadden he said, "I believe she's the same woman you saw leave St. Celia's twenty-five years ago. I believe her father sent her away, after she killed her mother. Since then, she's lived in a fortress up in the hills. She's lived there—despite how young she looks—for at least most of those twenty-five years." All those words together was enough to leave him breathless.

Geoffrey said, "*She*'s the robber baron who's been plaguing the overland route all these years?"

"Yes."

"And now she's come here to St. Celia's," Geoffrey said. "Why? Why has she chosen to destroy my family—my wife, my children, me next, for all we know?"

Weiland shook his head. Their guesses were probably at least as good as his.

Father Hadden looked at him levelly and asked, gently, "And you, Weiland, tell us about you."

Obviously they knew he was one of her company.

He shook his head helplessly. "I want . . . someone to stop her," he said. "But I'm not sure anyone can."

Father Hadden cleared his throat. "If she dies,"—Weiland closed

his eyes, knowing what was coming, knowing that they all must know
what Father Hadden was about to ask, and to have guessed the answer—
"if she dies, what happens to you?"

"I go back to being a wolf," Weiland admitted.

23

He expected revulsion, or at least contempt, but Father Hadden said, "Tell us."

So Weiland told how Daria changed animals to the appearance of men, to be able to prey on the traffic that passed over the mountains. How she had collected tolls for twenty-five years till boredom brought her to St. Celia's. How she had experimented with different kinds of animals, trying to select for intelligence, and how she had raised him mostly human for the same reason. He didn't tell them that she considered *all* the experiments failures, or that all she had gained by raising him human was a wolf who wasn't satisfied to be a wolf.

"Surely something can be done," Shile said.

Weiland waited to hear what he had to suggest, but apparently that was the extent of his idea.

Father Hadden was sitting with his head bowed, his lips moving silently, which was no more helpful than Shile.

"When she does these transformations," Geoffrey started to ask, but Shile interrupted, "Maybe there's some way to stop her without killing her?"

"We could ask her to stop and please go away," Geoffrey suggested.

Sarcasm, Weiland guessed. Nobody who was that truly dimwitted could have survived so long.

Father Hadden and Shile both looked annoyed, and Geoffrey said, "I'm sorry. I *don't* mean to make light of the situation. It's just the way he's presented it, I don't know what we can do to help him."

Weiland didn't either, and recognized—in Geoffrey's expression and tone of voice and the way he wouldn't look directly at Weiland any more—what he had expected from all of them.

"Don't they say," Shile persisted, "that iron binds magic?"

Father Hadden answered, "Folk legends tell of elves and dwarves and such magical creatures not being able to perform magic in the presence of iron; in fact they can't bear its touch." He shook his head. "But even if that's true,"—he glanced at Weiland—"how would that help if it's only her magic that keeps him in the form we now see him?"

Shile settled down in his seat sulkily, obviously still giving the matter thought. Weiland couldn't see how he could come up with anything when in all these years he himself hadn't, but he didn't say anything, just in case.

The baron said, "I'm trying to decide the best way to come at her. You say she can transform people, or cripple them, with no more preparation or forethought necessary than a look?"

Weiland nodded.

"So collecting an army is useless." Weiland took this as a comment, not a question, until Geoffrey said impatiently, "Well? Or not? *Can* she transform many people at once, or must she do it one person at a time?"

Weiland thought about Johanna being turned into a deer, and the six men who became six wolves. "If only one at a time," he said, "very quickly."

"Is there a limit to how many people or animals she can hold in false shapes at once?"

"I don't know," Weiland admitted. For having lived with Daria all his life, there was quite a bit he was realizing he didn't know. He couldn't think of a time that there had ever been many more than three dozen in the company at any one time. That may have been because that was all she needed. He thought of the household servants, and the temporary workers she had made to help pack for the move to St. Celia's, and how a few more hands then might have made things move more smoothly. Or they might have gotten in each other's way. "Possibly," he said. "It might be no more than three score."

"So if we came at her," Geoffrey speculated, "quickly, and with a big enough group, we might be able to overpower her."

Father Hadden said, "Lord Geoffrey, I'm not a military man, but that sounds like chaos, with those in the front lines suddenly transformed into beasts." He turned to Weiland. "Does she choose what beast, or is there something in the person that determines that?"

"I don't know. She's never changed any of her company into anything besides humans. And of those who are human-born, I only saw her change each of them once.''

"And they wouldn't know their fellows," Father Hadden asked—"those who had been transformed to animals? They wouldn't recognize their friends?''

"No," Weiland said.

"It doesn't make any difference," Geoffrey determined. "If we are forewarned, and those who are neither changed nor harmed act quickly enough, she will be dead before the animals can turn on us, and then everyone will be men once again." He gave a quick look at Weiland and said, as though already absorbed in other thoughts. "Sorry." Then he asked, "Which is she more likely to use: this transforming spell, or the one that causes physical harm?''

"The transforming spell," Weiland replied. "That's done in a moment. The other . . ." He didn't describe how she had stood there, slowly squeezing his heart; or the time before, when he had felt as though she were inside, clawing her way out; or the times in her spell room.

Geoffrey didn't seem interested in details anyway. "Not counting the human servants, how many of you . . .''

"Made people," Weiland supplied. "There are fourteen servants—'' Then, remembering about Llewellur: "Thirteen. But they're mostly mice and voles . . ." He was finding it hard to remember, because the servants came and went so quickly, and had never been important. ". . . a couple of chipmunks. The cook is a raccoon, I believe . . .''

Geoffrey made a dismissive gesture. "How many fighting men?''

"Six.''

"She originally brought a dozen," Geoffrey said, clearly mistrustful of this answer, "then she announced she was sending half away. Are they well and truly gone, or likely to show up at an inconvenient time?''

Weiland had assumed he knew. "They were the six wolves who killed your wife.''

Shile sighed, loudly.

Geoffrey stood, strode to the other window in the room, and remained there for several long moments, before turning back to Weiland. Then he turned away again. Eventually he said, facing outside, "I think the best plan would be to act quickly. Before more harm can come to others. I have sent word, since two nights past, summoning those who owe me fealty. There will be upwards of seventy men. If there are limits to her magic, that will be enough. If not, then we're all doomed. I will invite the Lady Daria to my home in two days' time.''

"In your own home?" Father Hadden asked. He had been leaving the questions of strategy to the baron, but now he spoke in a voice of horror.

"I think that would be safest for the townspeople," Geoffrey said. "My men can be warned what to expect, and that the effect will be temporary, so they will not panic."

Father Hadden didn't look convinced.

"If you delay," Shile said, "we could try to find a wizard with enough power to counteract Daria's magic. Someone who could allow Weiland to retain his human form."

It was hard not to try to hope. But Weiland saw the look on Geoffrey's face.

"Do you know a wizard?" Geoffrey asked.

"We can look for one," Shile insisted.

"We will." Geoffrey turned from Shile to Weiland. "We will," he assured Weiland, too. "But we can't wait for that. We'll keep you safe, and look for a wizard, but in the meantime, we must stop Daria."

"Yes," Weiland agreed, believing in Geoffrey's good intentions, but not in his ability to find someone who had the same power Daria did who would be willing to do this for him.

"Is she suspicious of me?" Geoffrey asked Weiland. "Of the fact that I have not allowed her in my house the past two days? We put about that Margaret was ranting, and that I would not leave her. Does Daria believe this?"

"I don't know."

Shile didn't give Geoffrey time for another question. He asked, "So where, exactly, is Weiland going to stay during all this?"

"For the time being," Geoffrey said, "he will return to Daria's house. Otherwise Daria would become wary."

"Obviously that's not safe," Shile started to object.

Geoffrey asked Weiland, "Are all Daria's men wolves?"

"No, only two of us are left here in St. Celia's."

"So," Geoffrey said, "try to be the one to accompany her that day. If she chooses another, see you follow closely so that you are in the house when we attack. I will order my men *not* to harm the wolves." He ignored Shile, who threw his hands up in the air to show he was disgusted with this plan. "In the meanwhile, I will see to the constructing of some sort of enclosure—"

"It won't work," Shile said loudly to be heard over the baron.

"It won't work," Weiland agreed in a quieter voice.

They all looked at him.

"I would rather," Weiland said, "die as a human. Please don't leave me a wolf."

Once more Shile flung his hands into the air, as though to say he was surrounded by fools.

Geoffrey turned once more to the window. The sun was beginning to set, Weiland noted. If Daria wasn't back at the house yet, she must be arriving soon.

Father Hadden said, "We don't know for certain that killing Lady Daria will negate the magic she has woven. There *is* a chance you might survive this."

Weiland couldn't tell if he really believed this, or if he was only trying to make everybody else feel better, or if he was trying to make himself feel better—until it would be too late to do anything about it.

"St. Paul tells us," Father Hadden continued, "that the only unforgivable sin is to give up hope. With hope in God, anything is possible."

St. Paul, Weiland was willing to bet, had never been a wolf. "I need to go back," he said.

"I will pray for you," Father Hadden told him.

"It's not fair," Shile muttered.

"No," Geoffrey agreed.

But none of that did him any good.

24

As he returned, crossing the large gathering room of the cathedral, Weiland found Evangeline had fallen asleep. Because she had waited for him, he woke her up. "Was the plan for you to walk back with me?" he asked.

She smiled up at him. "Is everything all settled then? Did Shile fix everything?"

Weiland realized they would never have told her what was really happening, so he said, "Yes."

"Good." She took his arm, and held it all the way back to Daria's door.

Weiland thought to kiss her, as she had kissed him, but wasn't sure, and in the end simply watched her leave.

Sighing, he walked into the house. But no sooner had he entered than a shape hurtled out of nowhere to send him sprawling painfully onto the floor.

"Haven't you learned a single lesson in all these years?" a voice hissed into his ear.

Kedj—with one knee digging into the small of Weiland's back, the other pinning his right arm. Weiland felt the studs of Kedj's wrist bracer jabbing into the back of his neck.

"Be watchful," Kedj said, shoving his arm harder for emphasis. "That means all the time. That means everywhere. Yet here you come dancing into the house like a fat, self-satisfied town burgher who's too stupid to even worry about thieves in the night. What has Daria done, letting you all go soft with town life? We're going to have to get you back in shape again."

Weiland stopped struggling, which was getting him nowhere, thinking he might be able to lie still, then unseat Kedj by surprise. Not that that had ever worked before.

"And here comes Daria now," Kedj said.

Weiland hadn't even heard the click of the gate or her steps on the walk, or whatever it was that had alerted Kedj. But Kedj was always better and faster and stronger at everything.

"Smile nicely for her," Kedj said now. "It's been only your pretty looks that have saved you this long."

The door opened, which Weiland hadn't been sure there was enough room for, without hitting his head.

"Hello, Daria," Kedj said.

Blanche looked startled to find them there on the floor. Daria only answered mildly, "Hello, Kedj." She removed her shawl and handed it to Blanche to put away. Still ignoring Weiland, she told Kedj, "I'm glad you understood my message."

"When everyone at the fortress suddenly transformed back to animal shape," he said, "it had to mean either that you wanted to get my attention or you were dead. I decided I'd better come in either case. Are you aware that there are armed men gathered in the shop across the street?"

Geoffrey. Geoffrey must have placed them there to keep a watch on Daria even before they'd spoken. Of course Kedj would be watchful enough to have noticed.

But Daria had not. There was a flicker of fear in her expression. "No," she said.

"Armed men?" Blanche squealed in her high-pitched voice. "Why?"

"Go away," Daria ordered, but Blanche retreated only to the foot of the stairs, fluttering anxiously.

"You *have* surrounded yourself with fools," Kedj said. "I told you this wasn't a good idea. The five dolts in the hall came wandering in over the course of the afternoon, totally oblivious to the fact that we're being watched. I haven't had a chance to ask Weiland here yet." He dug his knee even deeper into Weiland's back. "I'm told the other six are gone."

"Yes," Daria said. Finally she acknowledged Weiland. "*Did* you know about the men across the street?"

"No," Weiland told her.

"Liar," Kedj said. "I also saw the village wench you were with. *I* think you're growing over-fond of human life."

Weiland used bits and pieces of what he'd heard today. "The wool merchant next door—they suspect he's a wizard, that he's the one responsible for everything that's been going wrong. That's what the girl said. If there are men across the street, they must be watching him."

"Possible?" Daria asked Kedj. "That they're watching next door, and not here?"

"Difficult to say," Kedj admitted. "But unlikely."

"There can't be more than six or seven of them in that small shop," Weiland said, risking that Kedj might have seen more and would know he was intentionally underestimating to lull Daria.

But Kedj didn't answer.

"I think,"—Daria made an exasperated noise in her throat—"I think after all my work here, I'm going to have to leave, and start all over again."

Not *now*, Weiland thought in rising panic. Not without Baron Geoffrey's men having a chance.

"*All* over again?" Kedj repeated in an eager tone that, frightened as Weiland already was, sent a chill up his back.

"Yes," Daria said. And then she said, "The room is upstairs."

"I can smell the spilt blood," Kedj told her. He moved his arm, to get hold of Weiland's neck in the crook of his elbow. Only then did he move off Weiland's back, but he pulled his arm tight, immediately cutting off air, so that Weiland had no chance to break loose.

Still, Weiland tried, and for one brief moment as Kedj surged powerfully to his feet, he was slightly off balance, so that the two of them stumbled, crashing into the small table that Daria kept by the door.

The table broke under them, with Weiland in the middle, between Kedj and splintering wood. The weight of Kedj landing on top of him was enough to knock the last of the air out of Weiland's lungs. Kedj, who always had a sense for such things, took the opportunity to spin Weiland around and hit him in the jaw. Weiland's vision disintegrated into bright shards of color in his head, then Kedj had him by the neck again.

But in the interval right before Kedj's fist had struck, Weiland had seen something he'd seen countless times before, except now it took on new meaning. *Iron binds magic*, Shile had said. And a cascade of things began to fall into place: that Kedj wore a pair of iron wrist bracers no one had ever seen him take off. That Kedj had been with Daria for as long as anyone could remember. That he was therefore older by far than any of the company—yet he was stronger, faster, more agile than any of them. That in all that time Daria had never transformed Kedj into any animal—which they had assumed was because she couldn't transform natural-born humans, but now he knew that wasn't so.

And, worst of all, that—with the exception of Lon and the new

Llewellur killed in this house, which had been acts of consecration and frustration—Kedj was always with Daria during the bloodlettings in her spell room.

Daria and Kedj.

Kedj and Daria.

Everyone had gotten it backwards all along.

It was Kedj who took their blood, Daria who assisted.

Kedj stood, pulling Weiland half up with him, and began to drag him backwards over the rubble of the table to the stairs.

Weiland was aware that Blanche was crying and moaning and whimpering in fright.

"Quiet," Daria ordered, but there was the sound of running feet approaching—the human-born house servants, Weiland knew: those of the company and Daria's made-servants would know to stay as far away as possible at the sounds of trouble.

"What's going on?" voices called, and "See here, stop that," for they didn't know Kedj, that he was one of Daria's, or what he was capable of.

And Bess was there, too, who should have had more sense, but then she had been made only days before they had left for St. Celia's. "What are you doing?" she demanded shrilly. "Leave him alone!"

"Everybody, get out!" Daria shouted.

"Move!" Kedj snarled at Blanche who was standing by the stairs. No doubt it was terror and not defiance that kept Blanche rooted in that spot, but Kedj reached around, sweeping his arm, and Blanche tumbled to the floor, screaming now, rather than just crying. And then Bess started screaming, too.

But Kedj had started up the stairs, dragging Weiland with him.

Weiland squirmed, tried to trip him, tried to hold onto stairs and walls with hands and feet, anything to slow their progress, to keep from going to that room where—he was now sure—Kedj would feed on him.

He recognized Royce's voice in the turmoil, calling his name, then shouting, "Somebody get the town guard!"

"No!" Daria screamed, but servants were shouting, too, yelling, "Help!" and "Murder!" and "Guards!"

Then the noise cut off abruptly.

—And restarted, as the neighing of a horse, the bleating of a sheep, the squealing, braying, honking noises of a roomful of animals.

Kedj hoisted him up three more stairs, so that they were more than halfway up.

And then there was a thud at the front door, then another, and the door burst open around a wooden head in the shape of a ram, and then armed soldiers were pouring in.

Finally—finally—Kedj stopped trying to get him up the stairs, though he still held him in a grip that allowed very little breathing.

Geoffrey's men—they had to be. But the plan was for two days from now, at the baron's house. Even if a dozen men had been posted across the street to watch Daria's house, that wasn't enough to stop her. And now she would know they recognized what she was, and she would be able to escape after all.

The soldiers in front began to drop to all fours as Daria's magic washed over them. More pushed in from the back.

"Daria!" Kedj called. He was the only one who would call her by her name rather than "My lady," which Daria preferred or *She*, how most of the company called her most of the time.

Daria scrambled over fallen-away clothing and frightened animals—some snarling and snapping at each other in natural species' hostility. So far, the animals in the doorway were slowing down the men behind, who didn't want to hurt those who—a moment before—had been their own fellows.

But there were more than twelve. There were more than twenty. There couldn't all have fit in that single shop across the street.

Daria tried to hurry past Kedj and Weiland, probably thinking to escape by one of the upper windows.

Kedj caught her wrist, and still managed to hold onto Weiland, one armed.

Now was the time to try to break away, he knew it, but no matter how hard he pulled on Kedj's arm, Kedj didn't even seem to feel it.

"Daria," Kedj said, "there's too many of them. They'll be surrounding the house." He shook her, not nearly as hard as he had shaken Weiland. "*Daria*. You'll be the death of both of us. You're going to have to trust me." He let go of her wrist and held his arm out to her, exposing the wrist bracer. "Unbind me."

She looked over her shoulder to send another cluster of men into the shapes of animals.

"Daria," Kedj repeated. "You found me wounded and dying. Now you have to trust that my gratitude for being alive is greater than my resentment at being bound. What do you have to lose? *Trust me*."

Held immobile in Kedj's grip, Weiland was close enough to see the fear in Daria's eyes. But Kedj was right: She had no choice. She reached out her hand. Her fingertips barely brushed against the iron encasing Kedj's left wrist. Kedj's right arm was still against Weiland's neck, but Weiland saw the metal drop loose from that wrist, too.

Weiland was flung back, thrown against the wall by Kedj or by Kedj's transformation, he wasn't sure which, it happened so fast.

Those men who had just managed to force their way in the doorway, fought to push their way back out.

Kedj's huge wings spanned the entire length of the staircase. His talons were long as daggers, his immense jaws held scores of sharp, foot-long teeth. His dark eyes were just as intelligent as they had ever been, and Weiland was sure—despite his own experience—that in the brain behind them Kedj held every single memory he'd formed as a human.

"Dragon!" voices on the street began screaming. There came the sound of panicked fleeing.

Kedj turned his massive head slowly, first watching the street through the broken doorway, then the remaining animals—that were oblivious now to normal roles of prey and predator in their rush to escape. Then his gaze rested for a long moment on Weiland. And then he turned to Daria. Slowly, gently, as though bowing to her, he lowered his head to a level with hers.

And then he bit off her head.

Her body toppled, spurting blood to which Kedj seemed oblivious. He swallowed, spread his wings, then leapt at the outside wall, which crumbled as he burst through out into the night sky.

Weiland could hear the screams from outside grow more frantic as people dove for cover.

Her blood's still running through her veins, he thought, though a good deal of it was, in fact, on him. Her heart was still giving its last dwindling spasms, her body apparently not yet realizing it was dead. In another instant, when things caught up with themselves, he would revert back to his wolf body.

Except that, on the lower level by the door, men were picking themselves up, confused but disentangling their human limbs, picking up articles of clothing to try to cover themselves.

Shile burst into the house, looked around wildly, swore, then came up the stairs two at a time. "Where are you hurt?" he demanded.

"What?" Weiland asked numbly.

Shile shook him. "Where are you hurt?" he repeated, in what sounded like mounting panic.

Weiland shook his head.

Shile swore again and tried to roll him over before Weiland understood.

"It's her blood."

Shile didn't look convinced, even after glancing over and seeing Daria's body.

"I didn't change," Weiland said, which was more important, more amazing than that he wasn't hurt. He held his hand out for Shile to see the fingers, though obviously Shile could already see all of him. "Was it Father Hadden?" he asked. "Praying? Did God make a miracle after all?"

Shile sat down next to him, heavily, suddenly looking nearly overwhelmed. "Maybe," he said, sounding exhausted. "Or maybe Daria lied to you all along."

25

Weiland tried to gather up into safekeeping the animals that were still animals—the company, and the servants Daria had made. Most of the dogs ran out the broken door or jumped from the gaping hole in the wall while he was chasing the wolverine that had been Parn, and, in the end, the wolverine escaped, too. He managed to catch hold of one of the ferrets, but it bit his hand, cutting clear down to the bone, and he dropped it, then it disappeared into the other part of the house, from where it probably made its way outside. The mice, of course, were gone without a trace.

Weiland sat down heavily, staring at the human blood that welled out of the cut. The skin was gray from a film of stone dust, but it was human skin.

Shile watched him with a worried expression, but he had a goose under one arm and was occupied with holding down what had been Bess's dress over a hare that was trying to squirm its way to freedom.

Nobody had explained anything to Royce; but he had seen how distraught Weiland was to capture the animals, and once he'd pulled on his shirt, he'd joined the chase. But now he abandoned the spitting cat he'd cornered. "That needs binding," he said, and, when Weiland didn't move, "Here." Royce tore a strip from a shirt no one had reclaimed and tied it around the finger.

"Let them go," Weiland said, overwhelmed by the hopelessness of it. There would never be a wizard to give them back their humanity. "They're wild animals. They know how to fend for themselves." He was being unaccountably sentimental. *He* was the only one who had preferred the human state—and now he knew why. *They* had lost nothing they had ever wanted—even Bess who, he suddenly realized, had always been kind to him.

Shile hesitated before letting go of the animals he held, as though afraid Weiland might change his mind yet again.

All those years. He could have run away at any time. She had held onto the others with shelter and food and promises of rewards and threats of punishment, and that was mostly enough for them, but she had held onto him with the gossamer threads of lies.

In the end, Kedj didn't do nearly as much damage as he could have, before disappearing into the southern sky, heading—people could only hope—for warmer climes. With his fiery dragon's breath he incinerated, besides a good two-thirds of Geoffrey's men, two minor lords who had answered his call to arms and eighteen vassals representing other lords who lost no time in making complaint to the king. Of the townsfolk, only the blind beggar was killed, though many were injured, when the dragon knocked down the cathedral tower.

Of Daria herself, the people of St. Celia's took what Kedj had left of her to bury outside the town wall. Once she was dead, her body reverted to its natural state—that of a woman of some forty-odd years.

At the hastily convened town meeting, Geoffrey blamed everything on Weiland, who had not warned them there was a dragon in Daria's house.

"Of course he didn't know there was a dragon," Shile snapped. "Who'd walk in there knowing there was a dragon?"

Weiland didn't argue that it would have made little difference. One could learn more by listening than by speaking.

Some of it was pure speculation. Father Hadden said that Daria must have been drawing power from Kedj, somehow, from having bound him in iron that Kedj, being a magical creature, could not remove himself. It was through Kedj that she had gained her ability to transform.

All of that was possible, but everyone knew that, in truth, they would never know for sure.

There was also speculation about Weiland: who he was, how Daria had come to find him or take him from his parents. But after all this time, there could only be guesses.

Of facts, Weiland learned that Geoffrey had lied to him about the plan to entice Daria to his own house in two days. From the time he had been speaking to Weiland at the cathedral, he had decided it was to be that very night, at Daria's house.

"I determined he was unreliable," Geoffrey testified, "being her creature. Being she killed my wife, and he did nothing to stop her."

Weiland could even understand that. It was Shile who complained bitterly, but then it must have been harder—Weiland supposed—to be mistrusted and lied to by a kinsman. Shile revealed how Geoffrey had ignored his promise to order his men to be careful for the wolves, despite being reminded by both Shile and Father Hadden. Melor, Weiland learned, had been killed by a soldier directly outside of Daria's door. Seeing a dead wolf explained why Shile had looked so frantic when he had first come in.

But in the end, Baron Geoffrey said he'd only done what he'd seen as best for the town. The town, which had had quite enough of bodies in the streets and in the river and under the rubble of the cathedral tower, agreed. Geoffrey added that, since his fortunes had taken such a downward tumble, he would no longer be able to support indigent kinsmen—his own or those of his poor, dead wife.

"I have," Shile announced stiffly to Father Hadden, who expressed his concern after the hearing, "other possibilities."

"I'm sure you do," Father Hadden laughed. "And what about you, Weiland?"

"I . . . don't know," Weiland admitted. He was distracted, watching Evangeline from a safe distance. She had walked directly past Weiland without a word, called out something to Geoffrey, and now stood on tiptoe to kiss the baron's cheek. "All I know . . ." He was going to say, ". . . is being a wolf and a highway man," which was what they had told him he'd been.

But Shile finished, ". . . would fit into a thimble."

Which was appropriate, too.

Shile shook his head and sighed and looked put-upon. "Well, obviously I can't leave you with Father Hadden—he'd be so busy looking after your soul, you'd never learn anything. Do you want to come with me?" he offered. "I could teach you what I know about getting along in the world."

"You mean," Father Hadden asked amiably enough, "lying and cheating and stealing?"

"Well," Shile said, "yes."

So Weiland went with him.

The
Conjurer Princess

*For my writers' group, whose encouragement
keeps me going. And especially for Nancy,
whose kind words lead me to write this,
Mary, who assured me it was worthwhile,
and Jane, who wouldn't let it die in my file drawer.*

1

Beryl had always been *"the pretty one,"* and Lylene *"the sensible one."* There were probably worse things in the world to be called than "sensible," but Lylene was sensible enough to know that even without Beryl as an older sister, nobody would ever call *her* pretty.

It was July, and the wedding ceremony was taking place outside, by the flower gardens behind Delroy Castle's west wing. Beryl wore a lovely pink gown which brought out the goldenness of her hair, the green of her eyes; and Randal had a new soft brown jerkin and matching breeches which were well-cut enough to hide his skinny legs.

Lylene, being sixteen and unsure whether she belonged with the adults who'd taken refuge in the shade of the spreading oak or with the children fidgeting and poking each other in the shadow cast by the castle, stood between the two groups and part of neither. It was a bad compromise, leaving her where the sun beat down on her shoulders. The sun brought out the color of her hair, a color which could most charitably be called copper, though she knew it was really orange. And she had the pale complexion that went along with the hair—a complexion prone to freckle in the sun. She wished Father Tobias would talk faster so they could sit down in the cool pavilions to eat.

Or she wished Aunt Mathilde would beckon her closer, giving her a clear sign that she belonged. Considering that it was Beryl's wedding day, Lylene told herself she was being petty to feel the old familiar pain at not being included as one of Mathilde's children. Not that she was, of course. But, then, neither was Beryl. Still, when their parents had died of the red flux that cold, wet spring when Lylene was about to turn seven and Beryl was eight, their father's lands reverted to Randal, his nephew's son—the closest male relative—and the girls had come under Mathilde's guardianship.

One year older than Beryl, Randal had already proposed to her—on one knee, in the garden, with one of the servants at a discreet distance strumming a lute, all according to Beryl's directions—by the time he was eleven.

And now here they all were.

In the stillness of the moment after Father Tobias finally pronounced Randal and Beryl husband and wife, Lylene thought she heard the whinny of a horse behind her, beyond the garden wall. She glanced in that direction, though she knew all of Randal's knights were here; and besides, there was only forest beyond the wall—the only road ran north and south beyond the front gate.

But as she turned, an arrow sped out of the forest, close enough that she could hear the hiss of its passing—it happened too fast to see—and she heard the thud as it hit.

What the arrow hit was Randal.

Randal, who at the best of times wore an expression of vacant bewilderment, looked more surprised than anything else. He let go of Beryl's hand and slowly, slowly sank between tables set out with cold meats and steaming pies and other feastday treats.

A bowl clattered to the ground after him. Dish and cover hit separately: two distinct sounds in a silence so complete Lylene could tell which was which in the moment before at least two dozen armed men began leaping their horses over the wall.

Beryl screamed.

Someone knocked Lylene aside—one of the knights, Randal's friends—as he ran toward the castle, where their chainmail and weapons were.

But there wouldn't be time before the attackers were on them. Even Lylene could see that.

Wedding guests and servants began to run, knocking over tables, trampling those who moved more slowly. Voices raised in terror and dismay and momentarily blocked the sound of horses' hooves tearing up the garden.

Lylene fought against her own inclination to flee. A clearing formed around Beryl and her fallen husband: There was no telling yet whether the Lord of Delroy Castle had been the first victim by chance or intent. Yet Beryl stood exactly where she'd been standing all along, still screaming: a perfect target in the quickly emptying garden.

With a cry of exasperation, Lylene pushed against the press of the crowd, trying to get to Beryl. The adults were no help at all. Not that it was fair to blame them. Nobody in this secluded corner of Dorstede was used to violence and murder. Delroy Castle stood quiet and in a greater state of disrepair than could have been permitted in almost any other region and few of the knights had ever fought outside a jousting field.

So who were these armed men, and what could they possibly want?

The tone and pitch of the screams heightened as the first of the horsemen began riding down the slowest stragglers.

"Beryl!" Lylene was tall, too tall, Aunt Mathilde had always complained, but at least she could see over the heads of many in the crowd. Still, Beryl was temporarily lost in the swirl of confusion.

Then suddenly the flow of wedding guests had surged past her and she was in the area of calm. She didn't look behind, knowing what she'd see—the horsemen, almost on her heels. "Beryl!" she called, hoping to snap her sister out of her shock and into flight.

But Beryl, seventeen and pretty and used to being fussed over, only stood there in her persimmon pink gown dappled with Randal's blood, perhaps waiting for someone to come and make things right again. Screaming. Drawing attention to herself. Letting the raiders know where she was and—should that be their interest—who she had to be.

"Beryl!" It took all Lylene's resolve, and she barely got the name out when a booted foot struck her high on the back, between her shoulder blades, and sent her sprawling. Blackness edged her vision, threatening to engulf her.

Hooves did not pound the life out of her, and her vision came back as she raised her face.

The man was not interested in her. He had his horse aimed directly at Beryl, Beryl who had finally—finally—stopped screaming and now stared at him with eyes gone wide, waiting for whatever would come.

Stupid, helpless . . . Lylene, flat on her stomach, couldn't get enough air to breathe, much less shout a warning. Where were the Dorstede knights?

The man caught Beryl around the waist, pulled her up in front of him, and she never even struggled.

It was Aunt Mathilde who reacted.

"Beast!" screamed their guardian, Randal's mother, suddenly at the horseman's side. "Murderer!" She beat at the raider's leg with her bare hands. "Murderer!"

He bumped his horse against her so that she staggered backward. But as he raised his arm to gather his men, she came at him again, tears streaming down her wrinkled face, all the while screaming, "Murderer! Murderer!"

Keep back, Lylene wished at her, struggling to get to her feet, but her legs shook and wouldn't support her.

The man kicked Mathilde in the chest. Then he started to ease his horse backward, out of the clutter of fallen tables and broken dishes, back in the direction of the garden wall, toward the forest from which they had ridden.

And still Aunt Mathilde came after him.

"No!" Lylene used up what breath she had been able to catch, then watched helplessly as her aunt, clutching at the top of her gown with one hand, used her other fist to pound against the horse's rump.

The animal, caparisoned in thick brocades, hardly flinched. But the man's face, that visible between his helmet and his thin blond moustache, paled with rage. Lylene saw his blue eyes narrow, and he raised his sword.

Beryl finally found her voice again. "No," she murmured, and—almost as though for her sake—the man let Aunt Mathilde go with another kick in the chest.

As the old woman fell, he put his heels to his horse's sides, and headed back the way they had come. The other men followed, leaping their mounts over the scattered bodies and the debris of the wedding feast.

Leaving. Whatever they had come here for, it was accomplished. Randal dead. Beryl taken. Gingerly, Lylene sat up. She had to close her eyes to keep the horizon from dipping and rising. Only by crawling could she make it to Mathilde's side. Fighting a wave of dizzy nausea, she put her arms around her.

Several of the riders were taking women with them: castle servants and wedding guests indiscriminately. A few of those taken struggled; most, like Beryl, did not. Perhaps they were dazed; perhaps they hoped that if they didn't resist they would be allowed, eventually, to return.

The raiding party stopped at the wall, facing around. Lylene became aware of galloping horses from behind, the direction of the castle's stables: the Dorstede knights.

Finally, the Dorstede knights.

With cool deliberation, the leader of the raiders moved the point of his dagger to Beryl's throat.

Randal's men pulled to a stop.

One by one the raiders had their horses leap over the wall, and then they disappeared into the surrounding forest.

Lylene clenched her fists, recognizing the helplessness of the situation but still hoping *some*body would do *some*thing.

The leader was the last. Smiling sardonically, he sheathed his knife, then wheeled about and urged his mount over the wall, and all that remained was the July sun glinting off the armor of the helpless Dorstede knights.

2

It was probably after the start of the new year, though most likely not yet Twelfth Day. Lylene had begun to lose track.

About six months had passed since her sister's wedding day. "Wait," everyone had told her. "We know who the abductor is," they told her: "Theron of Saldemar is the one who has her. He'll ask for a ransom, and Beryl will be returned safely."

Six months.

And in that time, Aunt Mathilde had died of her injuries and the Church had recognized Theron as Beryl's husband and therefore entitled to all the lands she had inherited as Randal's widow.

Lylene had had enough of waiting.

Now, with the snow swirling around her, she stood in front of the house, the last house on the last street before the town disappeared into the hillside that gave the place its name, Cragsfall. It was large for a town house, and none—remarkable in itself. She had seen the house during the day, before she had gathered enough courage to approach, and she'd seen that it was entirely constructed of white marble, and than any castle or cathedral she had ever heard of. A gust of snow momentarily obliterated the ornately carved door, and she pulled her cloak more tightly around her, aware that with it slapping in the wind she looked like a scarecrow. The bell in the church tower rang the last warning before curfew, the closing of the town gate.

Lylene raised her hand to knock, and silently the door swung inward. She waited for a servant to invite her in, but there was no servant, no invitation. There was, in fact, no hand on the door.

What else should she have expected at a wizard's house?

She stepped inside. The hall flared into brightness as hundreds of candles burst into flame spontaneously. The light glinted off polished gold and brass, off mirrors and almost translucent marble. Lylene squinted against the brightness, temporarily bedazzled and off balance.

A young man stood in the hallway, not near through to the door that he could have been the time to open it, but near enough that she could see him clearly. Which was no doubt exactly his intention. He gave a condescending smile, as though waiting for her to notice how tall and handsome he was, and only then he made a dismissive gesture with his hand, and the door swung shut behind her.

She tried not to jump, but he probably saw that she did. He'd probably arranged everything just so she would.

He approached, his robe of gold and white brocade trailing behind on a floor as smooth and highly polished as the walls. On first seeing him, she had been surprised: blue-eyed, with dark hair and a trim beard, no older than thirty—as though wizards were born wizened and old. But up close he was much more what she had expected. Cruel, she judged by his eyes; vain, spoiled.

"Lady Lylene Delroy of Dorstede," he greeted her.

Oily, she added to her list, before thinking there was no way he should know her name. "Yes."

The smile widened. "Come seeking my help in a matter of rescue and revenge."

"Yes." He was moving too close, and she retreated until she found her back pressed against the closed door.

He placed his hand on the door, almost brushing her shoulder, almost brushing her cheek, and braced his arm in a gesture that could have been casual except that it caged her in. She flinched. She'd had nightmares, since Beryl had been taken, of what Beryl must be going through. "And offering . . . what, exactly, in exchange?"

Her voice betrayed her, coming out an embarrassing mouse's squeak: "The lands and properties of Delroy."

"What, all of them?" She recognized the sarcasm in that tone of amazement. "Very generous terms. Considering they're not yours to offer."

The words came before she had a chance to think: "They will be if you're half as good as you seem to think you are."

There was a jagged flash of lightning, a crash of thunder. The singed air crackled. She had to brace herself, to keep from being swept off her feet as a blast of wind extinguished the candles and hurled racks of them against walls and floor. Lylene's hair whipped about, stinging her eyes. The wizard, his face all bone-white and shadows in the lightning-light, stood with folded arms in the center of the storm, looking much like the picture in Father Tobias's illuminated Bible of a calm Jesus amidst the tempest at sea.

The indoors gale calmed. The thunder lowered to a sulky rumble, then faded away. The candles, those that had survived, re-lit themselves and flickered more brightly to compensate for their decreased numbers.

"Oh, I'm good," the wizard said. "The question is, can you afford me?"

She didn't tell him that she had no money, that she had left Delroy with nothing except the clothes she wore, which was Father Tobias's charity, for she was entitled to nothing. She told him: "I'm not even convinced that I *will* hire you. How do I know you can help me? You don't even know what I want done."

The wizard laughed, sending a chill skittering around the back of her neck and shoulders. "Oh, you will hire me. You have nowhere else to go. The Bishop of Glastonbury refuses to see you. The Archbishop won't let you past his most minor functionaries. The local lords and barons have laughed you out of their halls. You've sent a letter to the Pope, but timeliness is not one of his virtues, and you can probably expect to wait a year or two before you get an answer from him. I'm assuming he won't have much to say, but if you want to wait, that's your business. I'll still be here, though my fee will no doubt have risen." He had taken hold of her arm and was guiding her toward the door.

"Let go of me." Lylene hated being touched by him. She yanked free and glared.

"True or not?" he asked, smirking.

She didn't want to talk about the Church and how they couldn't help. Father Tobias was the only decent one of the lot. Theron of Saldemar obviously had bought friends in high places—and she estimated that this included the Bishop of Glastonbury. Why else would he insist that Beryl had agreed to the wedding of her own free will, and yet not force Theron to allow Lylene to see her? Why else had Theron's penance for killing Randal been no greater than to donate one year's revenues from the property Theron had gained by that killing?

She pressed against the door to put more distance between herself and the wizard. "How do you know so much about me?" she demanded.

He held his hand out, palm up, which meant he didn't know everything.

"I don't want a mere spell or potion," she said. "I want to learn magic. How long will that take?"

"Ooo," he said in mock awe. "The lady would be a conjurer. How much money do you have?"

"Well . . ."

His eyes narrowed suspiciously. "You've wasted my time," he growled, his voice getting louder with each word, "and you have no money?"

"I was hoping I could work for you," she started, "I can—"

He spun her around and flung open the door, manually this time, no spell. "I prefer my women to be women," he said. "You're too young."

Lylene was aghast at what he thought she'd been offering. She planted her feet in the doorway. "I wasn't—"

"Except when I want children. And for that you're too old." He shoved, which loosened her hold on the door frame.

"That's disgust—"

"And in any case, you're not pretty enough." He slammed the door shut.

Who needed him anyway?

Except that she couldn't go anywhere because the door had caught the trailing edge of her cloak. Tugging didn't help. It was too firmly held to work loose without ripping. "You revolting, horrid creature!" She kicked the door, which hurt her more than the door. She stood there, while the snow swirled around her. Already she'd begun to shiver.

"Hey!" called a voice from the street.

Lylene whirled. Two men. One carrying a lantern: town watch. For one instant, she was relieved, thinking that they might help her.

Then the one without the light pointed his finger at her. "Wench! Here!" He indicated directly in front of him.

Lylene felt the door at her back. She could guess what they thought, seeing her beating at the wizard's door, screaming at him.

"Get over here," the man on the street bellowed.

Lylene turned her back to them, leaning her head on the wooden door. She heard the crunch of snow—the guardsmen approaching. From beneath her arm, she could see the lantern swinging wildly as the men waded through the snow, momentarily illuminating sections of the night, briefly outlining the snowflakes caught in its glare. "I'll work for you"—she didn't raise her voice, for if the wizard wasn't listening, all was lost anyway—"I'll cook, I'll clean, I'll chop wood, I'll run errands." She had done all of those since leaving Dorstede, to earn her keep. "I'll work as hard as any two people, for as long as you say. If you'll just teach me magic."

The snow fell on her hair, on her eyelashes. She could hear the annoyed huffing of the approaching men.

The wizard's voice came from the other side of the door. "What's the magic word?"

She raised her head, amazed to hear him when, truth to tell, she had already given up. "What?"

The light from the lantern fell upon her, upon her hand pressed expectantly against the door. "Now look here, you . . ." one of the men said, slightly out of breath.

"The magic word . . ." the wizard insisted.

"Please," Lylene whispered. "Please let me in."

The door swung open, unaided. She spared no glance for the re-action of the townsmen. The handsome wizard stood there smiling, his arms held wide. "Why certainly," he said. "Of course. Come in, my dear."

3

The wizard's name was Harkta. Or at least the name he told her to call him was Harkta. Lylene gathered there were names and there were *Names*.

"You can be my scullery princess," he said.

"I'm not a princess," she told him, but he was too impressed by his own wit to stop.

"A scullery princess in training to become a conjurer princess."

She said: "I want our agreement in writing."

He gave a skeptical look. "Women in Dorstede are taught how to read?"

Of course they weren't. Most men couldn't read. "I want it in writing anyway," she insisted.

Harkta flung his hand open, and a scroll of parchment appeared before her eyes. He held it open against the wall, his finger poised as though it were the writing implement. "What do you wish me to say?"

"I, known as Harkta . . ." she started.

He rolled his eyes, but red symbols and squiggles that certainly looked like letters flowed from the tip of his finger onto the parchment.

She watched over his shoulder. ". . . will teach Lylene Delroy . . . everything there is to know about magic—"

Harkta snorted. "*Everything*. I can't do that."

"You don't know everything about magic?"

He refused to take offense. "Nobody does."

"All right, then, write: . . . everything I know about magic . . ."

Harkta shook his head again. "You're out of your depth, girl. You're getting into things about which you know nothing. Do you think magic is a list of rules and formulae I can teach you to rattle off, like

the books of the Bible—Genesis, Exodus . . . when you get to the Apoc-
alypse you're done . . . congratulations, now you're a wizard? It's a matter of skill, girl, of balances, of inner resolve and strength.''

"Then it's not teachable?"

Harkta made a blasphemous comment that turned Lylene's cheeks
red, even here, this far from home, in this room, for these purposes.
Then he said: "Of course it's *teachable*. I said I'd teach you, didn't I?
I'm just saying conjuring is not as simple as you seem to think.''

A sudden suspicion dawned. "Just how long will this *teaching*
take?''

Harkta stroked his moustache and gazed through her. "One day,
two at the most.''

She glared at him, still suspicious. "Write this: I will teach Lylene
Delroy everything she can learn from me about magic, and I will teach
her as quickly as I can, beginning as soon as I can.''

Harkta evaluated this, bowed his head with exaggerated formality,
and began writing. "There,'' he said, signing with a flourish: "The
Wizard Harkta of Cragsfall.'' He blew on the paper to dry the ink, if
that's what it was, then resumed writing. "And,'' he recited slowly as
he wrote, "in return for these 'magic lessons,' and until such time as
they are completed, I, Lylene Delroy, agree to work for the wizard
known as Harkta at such household tasks as he shall stipulate, including
but not limited to helping him with wizardly pursuits.'' He looked at
her, looked at the parchment, then added, ''. . . with a cooperative attitude and cheerful demeanor. Signed: Lylene Delroy, formerly of Dorstede.'' He grinned, showing a vast quantity of white, even teeth, then
said, "Make your mark here.''

Lylene touched her hand to the contract, leaving behind a smear
that looked like blood. "Read your part out loud. I want you to say it
so it counts even if you didn't really write it.''

He gave a look that said he was shocked and hurt by her suspicions,
and read her words back to her. "Now repeat your part,'' he said
smugly.

A day, she told herself, two at the most.

He handed her the document before she realized that since he had
magically made it appear, he could just as well magically make it disappear. With no place safe to put it, she crumpled the parchment, then
threw it into the fire. "There, now it's in both our hearts.'' She hoped
it didn't sound as foolish to him as it sounded to her.

The wizard laughed at her. "As you please.''

And she certainly didn't like the way he kept on laughing, even as
he walked away from her down the hall.

Her room was cramped and dusty. And cold enough that she could see her breath. There was firewood for tonight behind the kitchen, Harkta told her, but from now on she would have to gather it on her own: for her room, his, the hall, his consultation room, for the cook's room, and for the kitchen. She was surprised and pleased to hear there was a cook.

She scrubbed down the walls and floors of her room, which were simple stone, not marble. She changed the straw in the mattress, laundered the blankets, cleaned out the hearth, all requiring about three hundred trips up and down the stairs to fetch fresh water

The rest of the house wasn't very clean either, she noted on her way through. The cook was quite elderly and apparently didn't see well enough to clean thoroughly. Lylene guessed the woman must have worked for his family for years and so Harkta kept her on despite her failing eyesight, for which she liked him a little better than she would otherwise.

She liked him a little less when he told her that before she went to bed she must clean up the spilled candles in the front hall. She bit her tongue and didn't point out that it was his own bad temper which had caused that particular mess.

At first she thought she'd gotten lost in the house. Hadn't the front hall been much larger than this? And surely there had been glass mirrors on the walls: She'd noticed them particularly and been impressed, glass being so rare. But now, up close, she saw they were only hammered metal. No, it had to be the wrong room—the walls were stone, just as in her room, despite the dozen or so candles strewn about in congealed puddles of dried wax, looking like a lesser version of what she had seen happen when the wizard had caused an indoor gale which had knocked over hundreds of candles.

Shaking her head to clear it, she stepped back out of the room.

And noticed that the stairs she'd been going up and down all evening were no longer marble either. They hadn't been, now that she thought about it, since about the time Harkta had gone up to bed.

So. He could work magical illusions. It was a good thing she had had him declare their contract out loud. She reentered the hall and began to scrape up the wax. With so few candles, her work would be easier.

Two days, she told herself, at the worst.

4

She got up the next morning at dawn, so that Harkta couldn't claim their contract was invalid because she was lazy. She built up the fire in the kitchen hearth, then gave all the pots and dishes a good scrubbing.

"Too much energy," the cook complained, shaking her head.

Once breakfast was ready, Lylene put Harkta's on a tray and brought it up to his room. "It's morning," she greeted him, forcing herself to smile.

"Marvelous," he grunted. "Let me eat in peace." He gestured her out.

After what seemed a reasonable time she returned to his room but found him instead in what he alternately called his "workroom" or his "consultation room." She glanced around at all the books and maps and glass containers. Soon she would know all about them.

She cleared her throat, and Harkta, sitting by the window leafing through one of the books, glanced up.

Then resumed reading.

"It's morning."

Turning a page, he murmured, "So it is."

"Harkta, you promised."

"Promised what?"

"To teach me magic."

"Yes."

"You said you'd teach me as soon as you could."

"Yes."

"It's morning!" Lylene's voice cracked.

"Yes," he said, still never glancing her way. "Wrong morning."

"What?"

With a sigh, Harkta marked his place and closed the book. "I will explain once, then it's up to you to fulfill your part of the bargain. I said, and I quote, 'I, known as Harkta'—that's me—'will teach Lylene Delroy'—that's you—'everything she can learn from me about magic, and I will teach her as quickly as I can, beginning as soon as I can.' Correct?"

Lylene just glared.

"Your . . . shall we say induction? . . . has to take place under certain specific conditions. One of those conditions is that it be an equinox—vernal or autumnal. I presume you're interested in vernal."

She was having trouble breathing. "Spring is two and a half months away!"

"So it is."

"You didn't tell me."

"You, my dear conjurer princess, didn't ask." He opened the book again.

She went and stood in his light and saw his eyes narrow in annoyance. "No, wait, please, just a moment," she begged.

"What is it?"

"This rite, ceremony, whatever . . . You'll do it *this* March?"

"Yes."

"Does it need to be done at a particular time of day?"

"Oh," he said, "midnight. Of course."

"Any special equipment?"

"I'll bring it." He was becoming dreadfully impatient, but she had to make sure there were no more surprises.

"Does any training come with this?"

"Afterwards. A day or so. Depending on how fast you learn."

She licked her lips nervously. "And then I'll be able to . . . you know, do the sort of things you do . . . ?"

Harkta threw his head back and laughed. "I very much doubt it." He grabbed her wrists before she could go for his eyes. "Everyone's different," he said, still laughing. "Some people are inclined to one thing, others to something else. Take healing, for instance. I can't do it at all. Some people take naturally to that, or to shape-changing, or to pyrotechnics. Most can't learn any magic worth a damn. There's no telling before you try, though." He tightened his hold on her wrists— though she hadn't moved, had been too shocked to move—intentionally hurting her. "Don't worry, little conjurer princess, you come through the equinox and I'll teach you magic. But don't even think of trying to

leave. Wizards have ways of getting even with people who try to back
out of contracts.''

He shoved her away and said, ''Clear the snow from the walk so
my clients can get here easily. And when you're through with that, you
can clean the cellar. That should keep you out from underfoot for a day
or two.''

The worst task was the one to which she had been looking forward.
Help him with his magic, he had said.

People would come to him, asking for healing poultices, or love
potions, or something to make an enemy's wife run away with somebody else. Lylene learned that there was nothing more than ground
turnips and chunks of rosemary and laundry water that went into these
mixtures, but if somebody complained that the spell didn't work, Harkta
would tell them it was because they weren't pure of heart.

She would have suspected he didn't have any magic, except that
she washed the front hall every day and sometimes it was rough gray
fieldstones, and sometimes it was all polished marble and glass mirrors
and flickering golden candles. And once in a while, bringing him his
breakfast in the morning, she would catch Harkta still asleep, and she
would find him a middle-aged man with too big a belly and not enough
hair.

She discovered how he could know so much about her during that
first meeting. Harkta paid people to bring him news, to tell him about
what was going on in the town of Cragsfall, who was arguing with his
neighbor, who was suffering from winter fevers, whether any strangers
had come. Someone must have run all the way from the inn where she
had stopped to ask directions, bringing Harkta word of the young
woman seeking a wizard.

Now, when a woman came whose daughter had died, Harkta had
Lylene hide in the next room and talk in a little voice, saying things
that were either vague or common knowledge around Cragsfall. (''Remember when we went picking apples together? I miss you, Momma.'')
Another time she helped Harkta locate a lost breeding sow, an animal
he had enticed out of its pen the night before.

But mostly he told futures. And since it was when he was doing
this that the appearance of the front hall shifted, she suspected that here,
finally, was something he really could do. It was this which kept her to
their agreement, which kept her from leaving. This, and the knowledge
that she had nowhere else to go.

Once a young man came, wringing his cap in his hands and asking

Harkta to read his fortune. He left afterward, his face ashen, his hat forgotten, and Lylene said, "As long as you're going to cheat some poor fool out of his earnings, you could at least have given him good news." The more she knew him, the less she hoped for from the coming of the equinox.

"Lylene," Harkta said, putting his hands behind his neck, stretching, like a man whose muscles have stiffened from hours of hard work. "Lylene, my precious. I never cheat. Well, hardly ever. At least not as far as future-seeing goes."

"You cheat about everything."

Harkta laughed. "Well. But I *can* see into the future, and the future won't let me lie. It's all hard work. I hope you aren't under the misconception that magic will make everything easy for you. Maintaining this house, farseeing: That's hard work, you know."

Maintaining the house. Opening and closing doors. Lighting fires. How was any of this going to help win Beryl back? "If you can tell what's to be," she said, "then you could look to the vernal equinox and let me know what to expect."

Harkta caressed his moustache. "Oh, I would if I could, my dear. And since you've won such a special place in my heart with all your hard work, I'd do it for a bargain rate. But I'm afraid you're a blind spot for me, at least for the time being."

"Excuse me?"

He held up his hand. "How many fingers?"

She pulled back. "Two."

He moved the hand closer to her face. "No, don't back away." He held the fingers together, laying them against the tip of her nose. "How many?"

"Two."

"Stop being stubborn. How many do you *see*?"

The view jumped from one eye to the other until her eyes began to water. It could be anywhere from one to three. "I can't *see*," she said, pushing his hand back. "You're too close."

"Exactly."

"Exactly what?"

"You're too close. For the time being." He touched the side of his brow. "My own future's a blind spot." He grinned. "Which means, of course, you're a part of my future." He raised his eyebrows and his grin became lecherous. "Perhaps you will grow up to be pretty after all. Perhaps you'll consider staying on after the equinox, and be my own little conjurer princess."

"I'm not a princess," she reminded for the twentieth or thirtieth time. "And you're a pig and a liar!"

He shrugged. "I can't lie about the future. It's the verbal equivalent to a blind spot." Again the grin. "Of course, you have no way of knowing if that's true."

5

The vernal equinox finally came.

Tomorrow, Lylene promised herself. She would be satisfied with whatever she could learn by tomorrow, and would not spend another night under Harkta's roof, for she mistrusted the way he'd been looking at her lately, as though he no longer considered her a child.

They needed a crossroads, the wizard said, and they set out after supper, walking in silence down the street, through the town, beyond the outlying farms. They passed several crossroads.

Harkta offered no explanations and Lylene didn't ask. Generally half of what he said could safely be ignored anyway, and after tonight she would know for herself.

The sun had set and a full moon had risen in the cloudless sky before Harkta spoke his first words since they had set out: "This will do."

The road that crossed the one they'd been on—the Cragsfall to Arandell route—was overgrown, as though it hadn't been used in years. Lylene bent to look at the weather-grayed sign that had fallen among the weeds.

"Derrick's Crossing," Harkta said, nodding to the left as he emptied his satchel, "and that way: Fairhaven."

"Popular places." Candles, she saw. Harkta had brought nigh onto three score candles.

"Both gone now." Harkta stood in the center of the road, took five paces in the direction they had come, and plunked an unlit candle down in the road. "But I remember them well." He returned to the center, marked off a distance of five paces in the other direction with another candle. "Derrick's Crossing got plague one summer, probably brought in by the local priest who'd just come back from a pilgrimage. Then they got Vikings. No doubt blown off a course to better pickings. Big blond lack-wits. Come looking for gold, looking for women. In a place like Derrick's Crossing. By the time they caught on that the pit was for burning bodies, not garbage, they must have known it was too late. They burned the whole place down, people and all, then set off in their dragon boat. If they had any sense at all, they sank it under them before they reached the sea.'' The wizard took five paces toward Derrick's Crossing and put a candle down.

Lylene rubbed her arms. Now that they were no longer walking, the night seemed chill.

"This way, here, this was the shortcut to the mill. Can't see the path anymore, but it used to go between those two trees there. Nice family, the people that ran it. Priest I was telling you about, he went to visit right after getting back from the Holy Land so that he could baptize the daughter they'd had while he'd been away.'' He yanked out a handful of grass, set a candle in the indentation that was left. "Now Fairhaven—ah, Fairhaven. That's a different story entirely.''

"I don't want to hear it.''

The wizard shrugged.

"Anyway, there hasn't been plague—or Vikings—around here in at least fifty years.''

Harkta paused, considering. "That's just about right,'' he said.

Lylene looked away skeptically.

"I'm older than I look.''

It was his standard answer whenever she caught him trying to pull something over on her: You're ignorant and know nothing about magic, if the issue was of a supernatural nature; I'm older than I look, to cover anything else. She indicated the moon. "Let's just—''

"These things can't be rushed. You don't know anything about magic, so stop pushing me. Stand here.'' He had set out five candles, one for each of the diverging paths, and now moved her to a spot near the center. Next he pulled his sword from its scabbard and used it to scratch a circle into the ground within the perimeter of the candles.

With the remaining candles, the wizard formed a five-pointed star within the circle, its points aimed at the spaces between the original five candles. He had her stand in the exact center of the star. "Kneel, princess.''

Lylene had forgotten all about being cold.

Harkta knelt in front of her and used the sword to loosen a clump of dirt which he then crumbled and put in a pouch at his belt. He took the last item from his satchel, a clear flask which contained clear liquid, removed the stopper, and put the flask in a second pouch. "It's just water," he told her. "Don't be startled. Once it starts, stand when I stand, speak only when I indicate you're to speak."

She nodded, then finally found her voice: "Once it starts?"

"Now we wait for midnight, exactly."

Lylene glanced at the sky.

"I will know," he answered her unasked question. He knelt with the sword across his knees, his hands upraised at shoulder level, his face tipped upward.

I will know, Lylene thought. *What pretentious nonsense!* She gazed at her hands folded in her lap because it made her uncomfortable to watch the wizard's face, drained of color, of movement, of anything human, staring at the stars. She had just enough time to grow impatient when she felt a touch: the merest brush of a fingernail perhaps, at the base of her neck, under her hair, where no one could possibly get, then up, up, almost past feeling, onto her scalp.

At the same moment, Harkta bowed his head, sketched graceful twin circles in the air with his hands, then let his hands drop to the sword—the left at the jeweled hilt, the right at the tip. He raised the sword over his head and stood, so suddenly that Lylene had to scramble to keep up.

He planted his feet firmly apart, holding the sword as though offering it to the heavens, and spoke in a loud and firm voice. "By the power of air," he said, and as though in response, a breeze came out from the dark stillness, lifting her damp hair from her damp face. The wizard was still speaking: ". . . and earth . . ."—he let go the tip of the sword, reached into the first pouch, then traced a gritty star on her forehead—". . . and water . . ."—he reached into the flask, sprinkled her face, then took hold of the swordtip again—". . . and fire . . ."—the five outermost candles flickered into flame—". . . I summon thee. When the bright hours of day equal the long minutes of night, when the time is neither day nor night, when the place is neither here nor there, from the in-between times, from the in-between places—come to us."

At the first touch of the breeze the crawly sensation spread from Lylene's neck and head to her entire body.

Nothing—nothing—stirred in the night.

Harkta stretched his arms higher, spoke in a louder voice: "By the power of air . . ." Inside their circle, the wind spun last year's leaves around their legs. ". . . and earth . . . and water . . ."—Harkta's hands remained on the upraised sword, but Lylene's face tingled everywhere he had touched her with earth and water—"and fire . . ."—the candles that formed the outline of the star in which they stood blazed upward, preternaturally high—"... I summon thee. By the seven orders of angels, by the six fingers of Satan's left hand, by the five points on this star, by the four primal elements, by our three summonings, by the two of us, by the one Power—come to us."

The wind ... the moonlight on the sword ... Harkta's voice ... Lylene held her breath, waiting.

Harkta nodded at her. "We summon thee..." he intoned, then waited for her.

"We summon thee," she repeated shakily. *I'm coming, Beryl*, she thought.

"... by the power of air ..."

This time, no reaction.

Till she said it: "... by the power of air ..." The blast of wind nearly knocked her down, but she kept her feet firmly in the center of the star, as he had told her to.

"... and earth ...." Harkta was shouting to be heard over the howling gale.

"... and earth ..."

The tingle where he had touched her brow began to burn.

"... and water ..." There was a wild exuberance in his voice. He was in his glory, Lylene could tell: The power, the danger, the drama—he was loving every bit of it.

She repeated, though she knew the burning would spread to wherever the water had touched her face: "... and water ..."

His voice had a final, triumphant ring to it. "... and fire!"

"... and fire!"

The flames burst from within her, exploded down onto her, were her, as she was them. She threw her hands in front of her face to protect her eyes from the shimmering glare. She opened her mouth to scream, sucked in fire that seared her nose, throat, chest. Screaming, fire came from her mouth, then got pulled in again with the next inhaling. And still she breathed: She was alive, not dead, not dying, alive.

Her head spun, sparkles of color like bursting blossoms pricked her closed eyelids, noises crackled and hissed and chittered within her ears. She could still smell the fire, not the scent of something burning but the flames themselves, and she felt the pleasant, unbearable heat on her body, even though she realized her body was no longer there.

Her senses had no words for what she experienced, and she couldn't hold on to it. She felt the memory slipping, already—escaping, irretrievable, like womb-dreams, like water through fingers.

There were voices, and of all things they spoke of what Harkta had

spoken of: names and Names. They spoke of making things, of destroying, of illusion. Some of the voices she almost remembered, from a time
before memory; some almost solidified into shapes. At times they
seemed heartbreakingly clear—pure and beautiful; other times she was
sure it was demons to whom she listened. But: No evil, they whispered
to her just before they faded away the last time, no good, only . . . only
. . . She missed the last word.

Again her body was burning. But this time it was different. It was
the sensation of a leg too long sat upon—all prickles and heat. And the
more she thought about it, the more she thought that now she had a
body again, and it was lying down. Yes, she was sure of it. Face down.
On the ground. She smelled earth and grass, felt dampness that may
have been dew underneath her and warmth that may have been sunshine
on her back.

She was left with one strong memory: seeing herself put her hands
on either side of an object, and that object doubled. It was a simple
matter of concentration. But meanwhile . . .

"Harkta," she said, "get your hands off me."

Her voice creaked, rasped like an old woman's. She opened her
eyes.

Early morning. Harkta was crouched next to her, grinning. He made
a show of lifting his hands away, then stood and backed off.

Her hair was all tangled around her face and arms, suffocating her.
The prickling sensation had gone, but she was all aches and pains. She
blinked to clear the film from her eyes. Everything else looked fine, but
the mass of hair lying across her shoulders and arms was out of focus.
(She remembered the wizard holding two fingers up to her nose.) But
would being too close account for the lack of color? It looked palest
silver, an old woman's hair to go with the old woman's voice. *Something's not right*, she thought, even before she lifted her hand to brush
the hair out of her eyes, even before she saw the distended veins, the
brown spots of age, the cracks and wrinkles.

She tried to jump up, gasped at sharp pains in her back and legs.
Pains not of exposure, but of age.

Harkta leaned over to hold her elbow, to support her.

She beat his hands away. "What did you do to me?" Her accusing
scream came out a petulant whimper.

"I did nothing," the wizard said. "These things take a lot out of
you."

She looked at her hands and couldn't tell if they were shaking from
palsy or agitation. "How long?" she demanded. "How long?"

"How long have you lain here? One night: seven or eight hours.

No extraordinary amount of time has passed, if that's what you mean. Near as I can guess, time between the astral planes passes at a faster rate than it does here—speeds up the body processes. If you mean how long does it look like you've lost . . .'' He shrugged. "I'd say you look . . . seventy.''

"*Seventy?* Why didn't you tell me this would happen?''

"The right moment to approach the subject never came up.''

"Damn you!'' She tried to rise but made it only as far as her hands and knees. Harkta had more than enough time to back out of range. "You beast! You miserable . . . treacherous . . .'' She started to cry because she didn't even have the vocabulary to tell him what she thought of him.

"Oh come now,'' the wizard said. "Stop making such a fuss. You're taking this quite badly, don't you think?'' He fidgeted at the periphery of her arms' reach. "See. You don't listen. It's not as though it's forever.'' He indicated himself.

Lylene gulped. Once. Twice. Whispered: "You mean it'll go away?''

The wizard pursed his lips. "Well. Not exactly 'go away' as such . . .''

"What—exactly?''

"It's part of your new-found magical ability.''

"I . . . *wish* it away?''

Harkta grinned. "There,'' he said expansively. "Yes. Now you've got it.''

"I'm wishing it away now.''

"Well, yes, but . . . Someone's got to be there. With your hands on him.'' He was well back of her now.

"I can get young again by making someone else old?''

The wizard nodded. "All at once, or a little bit at a time. You can divide it how you will.''

By making someone else old?

The wizard sighed at her reaction. "Yes. Well. And it works with natural aging as well. Be careful and you may live forever. Somehow I get the feeling you're not the sort to be careful. But now you know. Any other questions?''

"I hate you.''

"I said: Any other questions?''

Lylene reached into her mind, into the experience she had just been through, for which she had lived the past several weeks, and tried to find something with which to hurt the wizard. She couldn't make fire, she hadn't the ability to weave illusions, and the future was beyond her.

Duplication. That, too, was a matter of wishing, of concentrating. But what a niggardly power for such an awful price! How could that help her with the wizard? How could that help her with Beryl?

"Well, if that's it, then . . ." Harkta said. "I'll be willing to take you back, once you're presentable. . . . You might consider stopping at seventeen or eighteen. That's much nicer than sixteen." He smoothed his moustache, shouldered the satchel, and started walking back the way they had come, toward Cragsfall.

He *knows*, Lylene thought: He had to know. He was aware of what had passed and of the extent of her magic. If he had seen her endowed with an ability that surpassed his own, he would have beat a hasty retreat while she slept. Or killed her. Or killed her, she realized.

She pushed herself up to her feet. "Does it work with animals?" she called after him. "Can I pass my years off onto an animal?"

Harkta stopped, turned. "I have no idea." He resumed walking.

She forced her reedy voice into a shout, asked the question she had never thought to ask before: "How old *are* you?"

Harkta looked over his shoulder. "Lessons are over, little one," he laughed. "Our contract's fulfilled."

Lylene shouted at his retreating back, "How old's your cook?"

The breeze carried his laugh to her, but he didn't turn back again.

6

She headed away from Cragsfall, toward the city of Arandell. If she kept moving, she wouldn't have to think.

By nightfall she had made it only as far as one of the outlying villages. The people there told her that another hour would get her to the city, but that the gates would be closed by then. Lylene knew she couldn't have made it if the city were on the other side of the village common. She sat down heavily on the ground.

The villagers stood off to the side, watching her warily. Here she was, with hair as white as the oldest of them, dressed in good-quality clothes except that her dress hung on her shrunken frame, exposing more of her than would have been seemly but because she was so wrinkled and shriveled she appeared more ludicrous than lewd. In the end, they must have decided she looked too pitiful to be dangerous, for they offered her the use of the village byre to spend the night.

With the wind rattling the daub and wattle walls and starlight showing through the badly mended thatch, Lylene knelt in the fresh-smelling straw and studied the two cows with which she shared shelter. They looked as old as she felt, as they stood there chewing, chewing, and watching her. "Easy," she murmured, "easy. I won't hurt you." Gingerly, knowing that the villagers' livelihood depended on these animals, Lylene wished away a year or two.

She felt nothing.

If the cow felt anything, it didn't indicate so.

Lylene wished away more years. Still she saw no change. She concentrated as hard as she could and wished she were sixteen going on seventeen again.

The cow flicked its tail and kept on chewing, oblivious to her now.

So. It didn't work with animals.

Now to try the other . . . She removed her cloak and held it in her wrinkled hands. Concentrated on that. A shiver started in her chest. A flash of light inside her head. And Lylene held two identical cloaks. It gave her a grim sense of satisfaction: She was old, she was friendless, she was no closer to rescuing Beryl than she had been that afternoon in Castle Delroy's garden—how many lifetimes ago?—but at least she wouldn't be cold.

She wrapped herself in both cloaks and went to sleep.

She woke when the villagers came to let out the cows in the morning. A group of children were gathered around, watching her.

Stiffly, she sat up. When she stood, the children scattered. She shook the straw out of her cloak—and realized there *was* only one.

Lylene went outside, hobbling from a dull pain in her hip. "Where's my cloak?" she demanded of the villagers. "Who stole my cloak?" The idea that someone had been able to sneak in, had watched her while she slept all unaware—this was more upsetting than the loss of something she now knew she could replace with little effort.

"It's on your back," someone muttered.

There was snickering. Because she was a crazy old woman? Or because they knew where it was? "The other one," she said, knowing the innocents in the crowd—if there were any—would have no idea what she was talking about.

They looked at her with blank faces. No telling which. She took the hand of the man who had spoken, holding it in both hers. "Thanks for all your kindness," she said, wishing a year onto him. She felt a slight tingle.

"Yeah, right," the man said, pulling his hand away.

Lylene reached for another hand, the woman who had suggested that she stay in the byre. "You've been so kind," she murmured. Again the tingle.

The woman nodded, saying nothing.

"And you," Lylene grabbed at another hand, no matter which, and another, and another. "So kind. Thank you for your hospitality to an old woman. Thank you." She shook their hands, to distract them from the strange tingling. It must be beginning to show, she thought, after several long moments of it. Not on any of them, but she had just dropped more than a dozen years, and they were beginning to look askance at her.

"Good-bye," she said, backing away from them, edging toward the road to Arandell. They continued to stare at her, nobody saying anything, nobody making a move to stop her. She started down the road but turned, uneasy with them at her back. No one was following. She forced a jaunty wave. Several times more she checked and always found them still gathered at the edge of the village, until a curve took them from her sight.

What had she done? she thought.

And what had she become?

Lylene reached Arandell about mid-morning.

It was a big place, crowded, and with an incredible number of shops and stalls selling everything imaginable. Vendors hailed her, encouraging her to step closer: to try their savory-smelling meat pies, to look, to touch—"Go ahead, touch!"—leather goods, worked metal, satin ribbons, tiny carved wood saints. Black and white shaggy goats bleated in their stalls. The breeze flapped the canvas tents, set to tinkling the glass beads one merchant had hanging on a wooden rack. For the first time in her life she saw slaves being sold.

She had paused before approaching the city gates to make another duplicate cloak, and now she sold this so that she would have money for lodgings. It was a bad bargain—the merchant could see her desperation—and Lylene knew it. She leaned over the counter to shake his hand.

She doubled the money he gave her and put some of it in her belt pouch, used some to buy a steaming mince pie. The woman charged a reasonable amount, and Lylene didn't shake her hand.

Next she found a stall that specialized in blades, old and new: knives, axes, swords. The proprietor was a burly man with a sun-darkened, scarred face that made him look more a soldier than a merchant. *That's what I need*, she thought: *soldiers*. How much, she wondered, to buy an army? When she asked him where she should go to find some men for hire, he looked her up and down and gave a lewd laugh that earned him a hearty handshake. But he gave her a name— the Happy Wench Inn—and told her that come evening she could find a man there for any job.

"Happy Wench?" Lylene repeated, suspecting he was making fun of her, sending her to a whorehouse.

The blade merchant wiggled his eyebrows at her suggestively, which was not promising. But when she stopped and asked someone else, she was assured there really was such a place and it really was an inn.

Lylene hesitated again outside of the place. The painted sign that hung over the door was of a woman with a big bosom and a small dress, but she *was* holding two mugs overflowing with beer.

Truth be told, Lylene knew she wouldn't know a whorehouse if she saw one.

"Is this a tavern?" she asked a woman who was walking past.

The woman gave both Lylene and the place a disapproving glance, but nodded.

As soon as Lylene stepped into the public room of the inn, her head began to whirl—the barrels for tables, the smell of sawdust, the other patrons. Not honest shopkeepers or farmers by the look of them. She doubted that even here in Arandell did honest men have such scowling looks or knives tucked so ostentatiously in their belts. Still, no one was paying any attention to her. Apparently there was an advantage to appearing more than fifty years old, after all.

"I'm interested in a room," she told the surly-looking young man behind the serving counter. She'd rest until evening, then see about hiring some men to rescue Beryl from Theron. She handed the barkeep a gold piece. She had smaller, but she wanted to see the expression on his face when he had to make change.

He led her up a flight of stairs and opened a door for her, where he made a flourish with his hand and bowed. "Anything else, my lady?"

She closed the door without answering. The room was small but surprisingly clean. There was a bed, a stool, and a small table. She moved the table to block the door. Then she sat on the bed, wrapped her cloak around her, and leaned her back into the corner so that she faced the door, lest anybody tried to get in.

7

She woke up confused, unable to remember where this moonlit room was or what she was doing in it, all stiff and sore and cold.

Lylene reached to pull her cloak back up around her shoulders and couldn't find it. She stood up, patted the bed, still couldn't find it.

Unease crawled over her body. The table was still up against the door—nobody could have entered that way. But she hadn't thought to shutter the window.

She thought of it now, seeing the nearby roofs. A thief would have had no trouble getting up here while she slept. *Stupid!* she chided herself at the thought of someone leaning over her, silently deliberating whether to rob her, kill her, or rape her.

Lylene closed her eyes until the shaking went away. Nothing had come of it, she reassured herself, nobody had touched her. And in searching for the cloak she had felt her coins on the bed. They were still there. Fewer than there had been; but as long as she had any she had an unlimited supply.

She ripped a strip from her dress's hem to bind her hair back from her face. With the years she had wished away handshake by handshake, her hair had gone from pure white to grayish red—very unbecoming. Only another three dozen or so touches and she would be back where she started.

If she didn't keep making stupid mistakes.

She took a deep breath, moved the table away from the door, and went to the head of the stairs.

The public room, so nearly deserted this morning, was crowded. The place smelled of many bodies, of ale and roasting mutton. There were many weapons, some armor—metal as well as leather—and a good deal of loud talking. The Happy Wench clientele looked like mercenaries and thieves, every one of them. She made it halfway down the stairs when the barkeep from earlier in the day burst in from the back room. He started for the stairs, then stopped, seeing her. "You," he yelled.

What now?

"Where is it?" the man demanded.

"Where is what?" She had a question of her own for him, about the security of the place and how a cloak could disappear from someone's room, off someone's very back. But before she had a chance to complain, he yanked her the rest of the way down the stairs. "What the hell are you trying to get away with?" he demanded.

"What?" She glanced at the night bartender behind the counter, who watched but said nothing. As did several others. She hoped she appeared calmer than she felt. "What are you talking about? Stop pushing me."

"The money you gave me, woman. What d'ya do with it?"

Someone interrupted—"What are you talking about, Marsh?"—someone who was standing at the bar, involved because the disturbance kept him waiting for his drink.

"She gave me money this afternoon for a room, and now the money's gone."

"Seems to me that's your problem, Marsh," the night man said, "not hers. It's your responsibility to keep track of what you take in."

"But I had it," the man called Marsh said, shoving his face close to Lylene's. "A gold piece. Fancy money for an old hag who don't belong in a place like this to begin with. I kept it in my pocket all afternoon, then I laid it on the table when I was counting up just now. I was looking right at it, and it just faded away."

"Gave it to Lena, more like," someone called, "for what Lena does best."

One of the serving girls tossed her hair. "Not me!" she exclaimed, hand on hip.

"Or lost it," the night man interrupted. "I told you, Marsh, that's your responsibility."

But Lylene felt a cold, hard spot in her stomach. She remembered the cloak that had disappeared last night, and the second one today. She tried to think back and realized the duplicates had always appeared to the right. She *had* sold the original and kept the duplicate, just as she had given the barkeep the duplicate gold piece. The cold spot enveloped her entire body. Her magic didn't have staying power. The things she made wouldn't last out the day.

And hard on that she thought of the villagers—and how she had repaid their hospitality.

"Witchcraft," Marsh said, glaring, knowing that he spoke the truth about the missing money, and knowing that she knew. "This old woman gave me enchanted money."

Somebody gave him a good-natured shove, which he returned with less good nature.

Lylene eased around him. This had been a bad idea all along. She had thought a strong man or two—or twenty or thirty—could take on Theron and his armed fortress at Saldemar. But even if that plan would work—and at this point she was no longer sure it would—certainly this was not the place to find trustworthy employees.

Lylene kept moving but glanced back. A ruddy-faced man with a blond beard was talking earnestly with the two bartenders. Someone from the village of the night before? There was no way to be certain. And even if he were, what could he possibly say against her?

Still, she kept watching them, rather than where she was going, and bumped someone's arm, spilling a drink and getting soundly cursed.

And re-attracted Marsh's attention.

She apologized profusely, but the man with the wet sleeve kept on and on, and in a moment Marsh loomed in front of her. "I want to talk to you," he said, loud enough to attract the attention of anyone who wasn't listening already.

Lylene shrank back. "I've done nothing wrong."

"I want to see your money."

"I already paid you once."

"I want to see your money."

She took another step away and felt the wall at her back. "I'm here with friends," she lied. "You'd better leave me alone."

The man snorted. "Who're you with, witch?"

Lylene glanced around the room. Cutthroats and thieves. Which, of course, was what—until a moment ago—she had been looking for. Several watched her with eager leers and shining eyes at least as dangerous as what she already faced.

"Come on, witch, who you with?"

She dragged her gaze back across the room, searching for someone who might help her and not cut her throat afterward. She stopped at a table with two men: one probably not yet thirty years old and dark haired, the other slightly younger and blond. The one with the fair hair stood out, in this room of knives and swords, as being heavily armed. He was one of the few who was uninterested by the situation in the room and instead faced the door, watching whatever was going on out-

side the ale house. His companion, on the other hand, sat with his elbows on the table, chin resting on his fists, watching her. Once he caught
her eye, he raised his brows, then glanced at the empty stool at their
table.

"You're coming with me." Marsh reached for her.

Lylene dodged. "Them," she said. "I'm with them."

The burly barkeep turned to look, and Lylene slipped past him,
rushing to the table, where she hurriedly sat.

Her benefactor smiled at her—a smile that seemed kind and gentle
yet indicated he would fight like the devil to protect her. Or at least that
was what she hoped the smile told her. He winked—but he seemed to
be shrinking even as she watched. In truth, he was sliding down off his
stool, slowly, slowly, until his knees were on the floor and the edge of
his chin hit the edge of the table.

Lylene grabbed his arm just before he disappeared under the table
and hauled him back into his seat.

He smiled and nodded in acknowledgement, then gradually dropped
forward, with his face in the spilled ale on the table, and began to snore.

Lylene swallowed hard, took a deep breath, and sat back down,
facing the second man, the fair-haired one.

At least she had his attention now. He looked at her coldly. No
telling how sober he was—nor what he was thinking—from that expression.

"She with you?" Marsh called across the room.

Her table companion looked up, perhaps evaluating the speaker as
he had—perhaps—evaluated her.

Lylene stole a glance at the man asleep on the table. Dark, curly
hair and a swarthy complexion. He might have been a Greek—as his
friend, with his long flaxen hair, may have been a Norseman. She
wouldn't put it past her luck to have chosen as rescuers two foreigners
who didn't speak the language.

The possible Viking was watching her again, his blue eyes still cold
and unfathomable, even as Marsh stopped at their table and repeated,
"She with you?"

The steady gaze didn't shift from her. "Yes," the young man said,
no trace of an accent after all. "She's with us."

Marsh considered for a moment, then grabbed Lylene by the arm
anyway.

The blond man caught hold of the barkeep's wrist.

"All right, all right. She's with you." Marsh let go of Lylene and
was released in turn. He readjusted his shirt, glared at Lylene without

looking at either of the men at her table, and headed back to his friends, ignoring the snickers and catcalls from the inn's other occupants.

"Thank you," Lylene said.

The young man—mercenary, she was sure of it—sat back with that appraising look still on his face.

Lylene lowered her gaze to her clasped hands and wondered how one went about hiring mercenaries.

The conversation around the room resumed. When she looked up again, the mercenary still faced her but was obviously focused on a point somewhere beyond her left shoulder. She turned and saw Marsh and his friends gathered near the bar, their heads close together. "If you see me safely out of town," she whispered, "I'll pay you."

"How much?"

Lylene pulled her last silver piece and two coppers out of her money purse and set them on the table.

The mercenary folded his arms across his chest and looked at her skeptically.

Lylene untied the purse so that the entire contents spilled onto the table: two more smaller copper pieces, several tin.

He sighed, as though not used to selling himself so cheap, then swept up the money. And continued to sit.

"Should we leave?" she asked testily.

"Eventually." He finished his drink while she thought she'd die of the strain. Then he ordered another.

Lylene watched the serving girl approach, smiling and swinging her hips. The girl leaned over the blond mercenary to give him his fresh drink, then moved round to the other side of the table to lean way low while mopping up the spilled ale around their sleeping companion's face, living up to the establishment's sign. The third time she ran the cold wet cloth over Lylene's hand because she was too busy showing off her bosom to notice what she was doing, Lylene said, "I really don't think we need you any more."

"Maybe *you* don't," the girl said, blowing a parting kiss to Lylene's mercenary.

Lylene felt her face go red. Here she'd just handed over all her money to this man so that he would protect her, and he was spending that money on beer, flirting with the serving girls, and looking at her frustration in open amusement. "Plan on drinking yourself into a drunken stupor?" she snapped.

"No."

"That's probably what your friend thought, before he fell face first into the table."

"Ah, but it was Shile's turn," he answered, as though that explained anything.

She wondered what he'd say if she demanded her money returned, then wondered what the rest of the room would say if she tried to leave alone. She turned around in her seat. Marsh was still there, as were his friends. Lylene waited.

The man she'd employed had just finished his drink—and he had taken a very long time at it—when three heavily armed men came in wearing unmatched pieces of armor, equipment scavenged from the field. Nothing out of the ordinary, not here. Except that her Viking friend was watching them.

"What—" she started, but he cut her off with a whispered profanity. Lylene whirled around. One of the just-entered men and Marsh were greeting each other like long-lost brothers.

"Turn around!" her companion commanded her between clenched teeth. He nudged his friend under the table with his foot, hissing, "Shile."

The dark-haired man raised his head a handspan off the table. He saw Lylene, and his face softened into a smile. "S'alright, I'll take care of you," he said, then sprawled across the table again.

His associate kicked him more roughly than before. "Shile!"

The older man opened his eyes, his face still on the table. "What?"

"Can you walk?"

"S'e here?"

"Your sure thing never showed."

"Ah, well," Shile said philosophically. Then: "We in trouble, Weiland?"

His friend, looking beyond him, nodded.

"Just give me a moment."

The one called Weiland moved his head slightly, an indication that there wasn't a moment to give.

"Right," Shile said without moving.

Weiland stood up abruptly, knocking his stool out of the way.

Lylene kicked back her stool, stood and turned in the same movement. Six men, including the three newcomers and the barkeep who had started all this, were closing in on them, so that now only one table separated them. But Marsh was bent over double, and one of the others had a very strange expression on his face. Lylene saw that before she saw the knife handle sticking out of his throat, right above where the chain mail started.

Weiland was holding another knife—this one pulled from its hiding place in the leather bracer around his left wrist. His third shot went wide, bouncing harmlessly off chain mail. Marsh lay motionless on the floor, a red puddle forming beneath him.

Swords scraped against scabbards. Chairs and tables scratched across the floor as some, who had found themselves too close, scrambled out of range, while others, who wanted to be a part of the coming melee, moved in.

Shile was still sprawled across their table. Weiland had pulled an incredibly long sword from its place at his back but now grabbed Lylene's arm with his left hand and started for the door, abandoning his own partner. "But . . ." Lylene protested.

Weiland jerked on her arm as he countered a sword thrust from someone blocking the way, then slashed across that man's chest before moving against another whose weapon was still half-sheathed.

There was a shout and a crash from behind. Lylene turned. At the last, Shile hadn't been as drunk as his posture had indicated: He had flung the remains of his drink into the face of one of Marsh's friends, then tipped the table over onto several other men.

Watching him, she stumbled, jerking on Weiland's arm as two swordsmen closed in. Weiland yanked her to her feet, cursing, then let go as the two men separated, coming at him from either side. He lunged at the one on his left, but the man danced back, just out of range. Weiland whipped back in time to parry a blow from the other and had enough power behind the stroke to stagger the man a few paces backward. But he wasn't able to press his advantage; he had to face left again.

This time the man on the left pressed in, battling blow for blow so that Weiland couldn't turn away for an instant. Couldn't defend his back. Couldn't see the right-hand man raise his sword.

Lylene kicked the back of that one's knee.

The man's leg buckled, and he hit the floor.

Weiland thrust into the first man's stomach, then whirled around, killing the second man before he could retrieve his fallen sword.

Lylene's hands flew to cover her mouth, and she took a step away. Someone grabbed her from behind. Steadied her. Then started pushing her forward. "Move!" It was Shile shouting into her ear.

Weiland cleared a way to the door; Shile covered their backs. But by the time they got to the door, there was no more opposition.

At the far end of the common room, some of those who hadn't gotten involved, or who had taken themselves out of the fracas early, had seated themselves at unturned tables, as though nothing out of the ordinary had happened. Others made their way back to that area of calm, hugging to the walls to keep out of harm's way. A few scattered into the darkness outside. The night man peeked out from behind the counter. "All right, all right," he said, trying to sound in control, "break it up now. Excitement's over."

Shile pushed Lylene out through the open door, into the clean outside air.

8

"You killed those men," Lylene protested. "Some of them didn't have their swords out." Even Randal, despite his tendency to be a bully, had believed in chivalry and wouldn't have cut down an unarmed man.

Weiland swore and set off down the street.

Shile took hold of her arm and made to catch up. "Weiland, slow down."

Weiland paused only long enough to wipe his blade clean on his breeches leg before slipping the sword into its sheath. Dark stains on clothing were less likely to draw attention than a naked blade.

"Weiland." Shile let go of Lylene's arm to catch up to his taller friend's long-legged stride.

Weiland turned an instant before Shile reached him. "We have to assume some of those people had friends," he said.

"Aye," Shile agreed tiredly. He sheathed his own unbloodied sword. "Best we left town."

Weiland nodded beyond him. "Someone's coming."

Lylene whipped around, hearing footsteps approach from around the corner they had just passed. "It's only a lone townsman," she hissed, hoping for no more bloodshed.

Weiland and Shile put themselves between her and the corner. Neither had drawn a weapon. Yet.

The townsman gave a startled glance at the three of them blocking his way. He put his hand to his side, where he may have kept his money, or a knife.

Didn't he have eyes to see? Perhaps he too had come from an alehouse and that was where he got the courage to stand up to what her companions obviously were.

And with that thought of alehouses and companions, Lylene began to sing. It was an old drinking round, one that her father had used to sing—much to her mother's chagrin. She couldn't remember half the words, and probably half of what she thought she remembered was wrong, but inaccuracy wouldn't hurt her credibility. Nothing odd, nothing to fear in an old drunken woman.

All three of the men looked at her as though she were mad.

It was Shile who caught on first. Moving backward, he tripped on a cobblestone, and only Weiland's intervention kept him on his feet. "Thank you," Shile said, loudly and tipsily. "Thank you very mush. So kind." He staggered, almost fell, almost brought Weiland down with him. "So nice to have good friends when one is indis . . . indis . . . indisposed." He came close to falling on the townsman, who watched him with growing distaste. "Isen it?" Shile insisted, putting a friendly arm around him. The man leaned as far away from him as he could get. "Isen it nice to have friends?"

"Shile. Come on, Shile." Weiland disentangled the two men. "Sorry," he said to the other, who, seeing they were harmless after all, was beginning to look annoyed. "Shile!"

"S'nice," Shile insisted. "Is."

The man shoved past him but stopped short of pushing Weiland, who was considerably taller and not quite so unsteady on his feet. He scurried around Lylene, as though afraid she, too, might try talking to him.

Shile gave a deep bow, his hand nearly brushing the street.

Weiland whacked Shile on the arm to get him moving. Each grabbed one of Lylene's arms, and they took off in the opposite direction from the townsman.

"Good thinking!" Shile told her.

Before she could ask what the hurry was, they made a quick left turn, then a right; they scrambled over a wooden fence that blocked off an alley, squeezed between two shops closed for the night, made another left, then another, and finally entered an inn, though one with more ordinary-looking folk in it than at the Happy Wench.

But she had time for no more than that quick observation as they crossed the public room at a half-run; then they were in the back wing, where the sleeping accommodations were.

This was all going too fast. Lylene stiffened, ready to dig her feet into the wooden planking, but Shile skidded to a halt, and Weiland let go and pulled out his sword.

Shile moved her against the wall and motioned her to silence.

Weiland raised his foot and kicked in the door. Lylene heard the wood splinter—*crack*—as it slammed against the wall.

Apparently there was nothing amiss.

Weiland sheathed his sword as Shile pulled her into the room, then Weiland kicked what was left of the door shut behind them. While Shile threw open the shutters to give them light to see by, Weiland took a money purse he hadn't had earlier when she had paid him, and he dumped the contents on the bed to count it.

Lylene remembered him separating the townsman from Shile, Shile who had so readily played the drunk—to avoid a confrontation, she had assumed. "You do this often," she asked, "these cut and run tactics?"

"My Lady!" It was Shile who pocketed the money. "Only in desperate times. Under less hectic conditions, Weiland and I are what you might call master locksmiths." Weiland, gathering their belongings, gave a sharp look. Shile shrugged. "Of sorts."

A timid knock sounded on the door—politeness, for the door sagged, a wide gap between it and the frame. "Excuse me . . ." A balding man who had to be the proprietor peeked in, wiping his hands nervously on his apron. "Excuse me, is there some sort of trouble?"

Weiland had pulled a knife from his pack. He slipped it into his wrist bracer to replace one of those lost at the Happy Wench.

The owner nervously wet his lips, as Weiland got another knife and fitted it to the harness which held his sword.

"No trouble," Shile said. He held out several copper pieces. The owner finally tore his gaze from Weiland. "We'll need our horses readied. We're leaving right away."

Which was what the man no doubt wanted to hear. He took the money and fled.

"Now," Shile said, "my Lady . . . ?"

"Lylene."

"That's a pretty name."

She didn't know how to answer that, from a man such as this, in a situation such as this.

"Will you be joining us?"

"The *Lady*,"—Weiland's tone indicated he thought she was no such thing—"has paid us to get her out of town." He got yet another knife and hid it in his boot.

"Which road?"

"Any road."

Shile raised his eyebrows. "That's . . . rather vague."

Lylene cut in. "That was all I had the money to afford."

"That was more," Weiland said, "than you had the money to afford."

"Now, now." Shile smiled at both of them. He had never quite lost his dazed, half-drunk look, but he was gentle as he took Lylene's hand in both of his. "You're in some sort of trouble, I can tell. And that's what Weiland and I do best: We help ladies in trouble."

Weiland leaned against the door, holding it open for them. Lylene looked from one to the other and evaluated them against Harkta. "I have no money."

"Well,"—Shile smiled equably—"that's always a disappointment, but we won't worry about it just now."

Lylene considered the two men and put things together. "You heard the innkeeper talking about that gold piece that disappeared."

Perhaps Shile considered denying it. He took a deep breath, but in the end only said, "Yes."

"Disappearing money," Weiland said to him. "Sounds like just what we need."

"But fascinating. It does sound fascinating. Look,"—he turned to Lylene—"you already paid Weiland for us to escort you out of Arandell. . . ." What he had just said seemed to suddenly catch up with him. He turned to Weiland. "Did she pay you in gold?"

Weiland winced.

She glanced from one to the other. That was all she needed. "The money I gave you was good. Truly it was."

Shile looked more convinced than Weiland. He answered, "Then all that leaves is for you to decide: Will you join us or not? You've already paid us."

Which meant no refunds. Things had been simpler at Castle Delroy, where decisions were made for her. Now here was Shile with his trust-me look and Weiland with his I-hope-she-says-no look, and who was to say they were any different from Harkta or Theron or the men back at the Happy Wench? Yet Shile trusted her, that the money she had paid them to risk their lives was real. And that trust seemed to demand a certain amount of trust in return. "I need to get out of here," she admitted.

Shile took her arm. The three of them went out the back way, then circled round to the stable, avoiding the public room. The heavy set owner was seeing to the horses himself, one chestnut-colored, the other a magnificent bay. Destriers, the two of them: very fine, very expensive. Knight's war horses, though Shile and Weiland were obviously not knights. Weiland went to see to the bay, to check the saddling, to adjust the girth.

"We don't want any trouble," the owner said, back to that again.

And Shile, looking over his own horse, again said, "No trouble," and handed the man more money.

They fastened their kits to the saddles, then set out, Lylene riding with Shile. "Anything you need to go back to the Happy Wench for?" he asked.

She shook her head and tightened her grip around his waist as he kicked the horse into a full gallop.

Although neither man wore armor, destriers were bred big to carry a fully clad knight. The few people they saw scrambled out of the way as Lylene and her two companions tore through the streets.

They left by the north gate—the gate warden convinced to let them through by more of the money Lylene had unwittingly helped them steal from the passerby.

9

They set up camp still short of dawn. The men weighed the chill of the air against the likelihood of pursuit and finally built a fire, albeit a small one. They had strips of smoked venison and loaves of hard bread packed among their provisions. So, Lylene estimated, hasty departures were nothing new to them.

It was Shile who pointed out that there was a quantity of dried blood on the hem of Lylene's dress. Holding out a shirt and a pair of breeches, he said, "If you think you'd be more comfortable in men's clothing than . . . you know . . ."

Shile went to help Weiland rub down the horses while Lylene retreated out of the campfire's glow and with shaking hands pulled the breeches on under her dress. Shile's, she thought; Weiland's would have been much too long.

Once changed, she gingerly folded the dress, dyed with dead men's blood, so that the stiff, dark stains were on the inside, where she wouldn't have to look at them. She stepped back into the circle of light and knelt. She was still shaking, perhaps because the shirt—probably Weiland's—was thinner than her dress had been. More likely it was from all the physical exertion: the running, the extended riding, the constant state of fear. Her heart was beating hard enough to hurt, leaving a metallic taste in her throat. She was too old for this, she reminded herself: She kept thinking like an almost-seventeen-year-old, when her body was more than fifty years old. She was going to kill herself if she wasn't more careful.

Eventually, Shile brought a blanket for her—stiff and scratchy and smelling of horse, but it felt wonderfully warm.

She stole a glance at him while he wasn't looking. He was kind.

He could no doubt be invaluable in rescuing Beryl. She more or less trusted him. But she was afraid. As he clasped her shoulder reassuringly, she put her hand over his and squeezed, wishing one of her extra years onto him. It was not as though, she assured herself, it would ever come to make a difference: With the life he and Weiland led, neither was likely to see forty, and one more year off their old age would never be missed.

He gave her his vacant though amiable smile and began poking at the fire.

Weiland came carrying his sheathed sword and crouched next to her, the sword across his knees.

"I want to thank you for all your help," Lylene said, and momentarily rested her hand on his wrist.

But of all people, she shouldn't have tried it with him. He seized her arm and pulled her down closer to him, closer to the fire. "Whatever the hell you just did," he warned, "don't try it again."

She considered proclaiming her innocence, denying that she'd done anything. Instead, she just whispered, "No."

"Weiland," Shile said, confused and earnest. "*Weiland*."

Slowly he released her arm.

She sat back on her heels, wishing she could move farther away from him without looking like a cringing dog.

Shile sat down, crosslegged, and warmed his hands at the fire. "Now," he said, eager for peace, "tell us what set an obvious lady of quality, such as yourself, into a place like the Happy Wench Inn, desperate enough to seek help from . . . strangers . . . like us."

Lylene was at a loss for words. After her night in the barn, she had picked all the straw she could feel from her hair; but that hair hadn't been combed in two days. Her clothes, before she had changed to men's garb, were filthy. She had been accused—and rightly so—of witchcraft, had engaged in a brawl that had left a half dozen dead, and had run off with two men, strangers, who did this sort of thing for a living. And she was old, more than a half-century old.

Weiland supplied the words she couldn't: "*Obvious* . . . lady of quality?"

Shile didn't take his gaze from her. "Obvious. From the way she carries herself, her walk, her speech, the expression in her eyes: gentrice. Come on hard times, and recently at that." Finally he did look away. "I can understand hard times."

Weiland swore and pulled the long sword from its sheath. Close to her as he was, his arm brushed hers, and this time she shrank back, expecting . . . she wasn't sure what. But he didn't even look at her. To all appearances he had nothing more ominous in mind than to see the weapon properly cleaned after their hasty retreat from Arandell. But she didn't trust the coincidence of the timing nor his apparent lack of attention.

Shile put his hand on her shoulder and said, "Relax. Any time you desire it, you're free to leave."

Hesitantly, Lylene nodded.

"Weiland and I are what you might call free agents . . ."

"Mercenaries." Again her voice wasn't cooperating; it came out a whisper. But she hated the way he danced around words— at least Weiland was honest about what he was.

"Occasionally," Shile admitted. "We do . . . odd jobs. For pay."

"I told you: I have no money."

"Sometimes a situation just gives the impression of being fraught with monetary opportunities."

She had no answer for that.

"This strikes me as just such an occasion. If not, we've wasted a little time, had a little adventure, and tomorrow morning we part amicably, never to see each other again. On the other hand, we may be able to help each other."

Slowly, weighing each word, she nodded.

"So. From the beginning. My name is Shiley— please call me Shile—and this is Weiland."

Weiland looked up from working the edge of the sword and gave a sardonic nod.

"My name is Lylene of Dorstede. My parents were Lord and Lady Delroy."

"Deceased?" Shile asked.

She nodded. "After their deaths, I . . . my sister and I were raised by my aunt. It was her son, Randal, who inherited the Delroy estates. Six months ago Beryl was marrying Randal." It was becoming increasingly difficult to speak.

Shile rested a hand on her arm encouragingly.

"Some men came. Marauders. Lead by a baron named Theron. They took Beryl—forced her to go with them. Nobody was willing to do anything about it: the Church, the neighboring lords . . ."

"What about this cousin," Weiland asked, "this Randal?"

"Dead. He was killed in the raid."

Shile patted her hand gently. "No other cousins? Nobody to redress—"

"Nobody." She gnawed on her lip and tried to compose herself. "The bishop said . . . Theron . . . In the eyes of the Church the two of them are married. After all that: In the eyes of the Church the two of them are married. I'm not telling this well.''

"You're doing fine. This sister of yours, she had been widowed before?''

Lylene shook her head. Then saw the problem. "Beryl's only eighteen years old.'' She saw the looks and knew she strained at their credulity. But she needed to impress on them the urgency of the situation, Beryl's helplessness and innocence. "I'm . . . not as old as I look.'' She winced, realizing what she had just said, the counterpart of Harkta's *I'm older than I look*. She covered her face with her hands, speaking between her fingers. "The law seemed to be on Theron's side. And the Church. So I sought the help of a wizard.''

She felt Weiland shift uncomfortably.

"He's the one who did this to you?'' Shile urged.

She put her hands in her lap and nodded.

Shile glanced at Weiland, who had finally left off with the sword. "You can't trust wizards,'' Weiland observed dryly.

She hoped he meant that merely as a sympathetic response. If he found out *she* was a wizard, would he recommend abandoning her, or slitting her throat?

Shile ran his hand through his dark hair, then he looked at her levelly. "This wizard. Does he have anything to do with that gold piece that caused such a stir tonight?''

She nodded, slowly. She'd never been a good liar and hoped her face wouldn't give her away, for she certainly wasn't going to trust these two with the truth. "The money was Harkta's. He said that he would help me, but I had to work for him for three months.'' Could they hear her swallow? "Then, after my time was through . . . he tricked me. He turned me old and threw me out.''

She saw Shile and Weiland exchange glances. What were they thinking? "I stole the money.'' She bit her lip, unable to look either man in the eye, and hoped they'd put her unease down to guilt over the thievery. "It must have been some kind of magic money. But what I paid you with, that was my own. That won't disappear. I swear it won't.'' Again that look: disbelief? Or chagrin at having misjudged the possibilities of the situation?

Weiland slipped his sword into its sheath and stood, finally giving her space to breathe again.

"Listen.'' Shile was obviously less willing than his partner to give up. "Why don't we rest for the night? There are possibilities here. We'll talk more tomorrow.''

Weiland appeared about to protest. Instead he made a helpless gesture and headed for the horses.

Lylene, hurrying lest Shile change his mind, asked: "You think you can rescue Beryl from Theron?"

"I'm sure of it."

"He lives at Saldemar, and it's highly fortified." She'd heard that often enough from the Dorstede knights. "It's on a hill—"

Shile placed a finger to her lips, silencing her. "We'll rescue her for you. Weiland can get us in. He hired out to Theron a few years back." He raised his voice. "Think Theron will remember you?"

Weiland, checking the horses' tethers, didn't answer.

"We'll rescue her for you," Shile said.

10

*M*orning *was bright and warm. Since they had camped within* walking distance of a pond, Lylene decided to bathe.

It was good to be clean, but the goodness was tempered by the sight of her wrinkled skin and her sagging breasts and forearms. True, there had been some improvement. She had wished close to two dozen years onto various people and was no longer bent over with pain. Her hands, though stiff and swollen at the joints, had loosened from the gnarled claws they had been that first day.

Still, she sat in water deep enough to cover to her shoulders so she wouldn't have to see herself, and she cried, softly, hoping that Shile and Weiland wouldn't hear her. And the next moment hoping that they would. She wanted to be held, to be comforted. To be taken care of.

But she remembered she was naked, and she knew what she looked like, and in any case the camp wasn't so close that they could possibly hear her, whether she hoped it or not. And who was there to hold her? Weiland, who was at least as dangerous as Harkta and Theron? Shile, with all his grand plans? She rinsed her face and waded back to the shore to dress in her borrowed clothes.

Tying her grayish-red hair back out of her way, she was scrubbing the blood stains from her dress when from behind a nearby bush she caught the glint of sun on metal. Two thoughts followed, one on top of the other: that despite any other moral deficiencies, neither Shile nor Weiland seemed the kind to skulk behind bushes peeking at bathing women—especially bathing fifty-year-old women—and that the only armor either man wore was padded leather.

Someone from Arandell, most likely: brother or father or son or friend to someone they had killed last night.

Her hands shook, and she dunked the dress into the water to hide them. She paid attention to the sounds around her: the self-satisfied coo of a dove, the buzz of insects. She thought she heard the creak of metal, an armored man shifting weight. As far as she could tell, there was only the one. There had to be others, but where? Had they found the camp already? Not likely, or this one wouldn't be quietly watching her, waiting for her to lead him to her companions. On the other hand, given enough time, this one's friends would find the camp anyway, and overrun it without warning. Given enough time . . . She had already been gone too long. How much time before Shile or Weiland came looking for her and walked into a trap?

She swished the dress around in the water, grazing her knuckles on a submerged stone. If she returned to the camp, that would give the two young mercenaries at least a few moments' warning. She forced herself to regulate her breathing, sure that her watcher must be growing suspicious by now. She would be between them: between the pursuers from Arandell and their prey.

And there was nothing else she could do.

Once more her hand brushed the underwater stone. It was sharp and slightly bigger than her clenched fist. With no plan in mind, but because a rock seemed a good thing to have at a time like this, she tucked it into a fold of her dress. Sure that she must be acting unnaturally enough to alert even a simpleton, she wrung the dress, never looking in the direction of the bush. With the sodden dress wadded in her arms, she started back the way she had come.

Her back prickled, from sweat, from the knowledge that behind her was someone who wanted to see her dead. She kept walking, her eyes forward.

There was a crunch of underbrush from behind but to the side: Someone—or possibly more than one—had joined the first stalker. The whistle of a warbler sounded from off to her right. She realized she had heard an inordinate number of warblers this morning. That was the fourth or fifth since she left the pond. If each call represented one man, plus the one who had been watching all along, plus the two (she was sure of it now) who had joined . . . And there were horses out there amongst the trees, too: She heard the muffled jangle as one shook its reins.

She recognized the lightning-struck spruce. From this angle of approach, the camp wasn't that obvious until one was practically in it.

Surely the men who followed must smell the smoke from the camp cookfire.

She gauged the distance, how long it would take to traverse it at a run, and screamed, "Shile! Weiland! Ambush!"

Behind her, the woods erupted into sound: men and horses crashing through, no longer intent on secrecy. She stumbled over a root, half-falling into the clearing. Shile was standing, facing her direction, his sword drawn. Weiland was moving in to his side, holding an oversized bow with an arrow already nocked.

Lylene saw her mistake at once: She had led the men of Arandell in at an angle to keep them from seeing the camp until the last moment, but this had brought them in between the campfire and the horses. There would be no chance for flight.

Weiland's arrow whizzed over her head, close enough that she thought he had aimed at her, suspecting betrayal. But from behind she heard a cry and a thud, and a riderless horse crashed through the thicket, narrowly missing her.

Her outstretched hand kept her from falling. Now, as she started to straighten, Weiland called, "Down!" and he loosed another arrow that cut the air just above her head.

She began running in a low crouch, still holding on to her dripping dress, following the perimeter of the clearing to get herself out of the fighters' way.

"My Lady!" Shile was on the move, trying to get to her while Weiland covered them. She headed for him, out of Weiland's range now and able to run upright.

A horseman broke into the clearing, then a second. One of Weiland's arrows hit the first, but by then there were three more. He fit another arrow to the bow but took a step back before releasing.

Shile grabbed Lylene's free arm and yelled Weiland's name. Weiland began to retreat, slowly, toward the trees on the far side of the clearing. Shile directed Lylene in a path designed to intercept him. More and more men poured into the clearing, men on foot as well as those who were mounted, spreading out to cut off escape into the woods.

Shile released her arm, and Lylene saw that three of the horsemen were headed directly at them.

The one in the forefront had developed too great a lead. Shile sidestepped the swing of his sword, then brought his own weapon up into the man's abdomen, and there was no one close enough to take Shile at disadvantage.

But the remaining two came at them together.

Closer.

Closer.

She braced herself.

One toppled from his horse, one of Weiland's arrows in his back, and by then the remaining horseman was level with Shile.

He swung his sword at Shile's head. Shile took the force of the blow on his own upraised sword. He wasn't nearly as good at this as Weiland.

Lylene watched in fascinated horror, twisting the wet dress she still held. Weiland was running toward them, but there was no way he could reach Shile in time. She took a step forward as Shile's opponent raised his blade again. Foolishness. What could she do to help, an old woman brandishing a wet dress? What good would getting killed serve? But they were in this because of her, and she wasn't going to abandon them. She had abandoned Beryl, and she wasn't ever going to abandon anybody again.

She swung her dress at the man. There was an audible *clunk!* as the forgotten river rock put a dent in his helmet. The man dropped.

Lylene was torn between hoping she had killed him and fearing that she hadn't.

"Some dress," Weiland acknowledged, running past as she lingered in guilty numbness. She glimpsed the remaining horsemen, seeing the surprise on their faces before Shile spun her around. They were just fumbling with their bows as she and Shile broke through the edge of the clearing, close on Weiland's heels.

11

T*hey burst into the woods, weaving, always looking for ways that* would tax the pursuing horses yet be clear enough that they themselves could pass rapidly. But they still heard their pursuers behind them. And then to the left. And finally outflanking them to the right.

"This way." Shile pulled her toward a rocky hill.

They scrambled up, and she bent over, resting her hands on her knees, afraid she was going to retch from the exertion. And from the realization of how many men had died back there—and that she might have killed one of them. Still, she managed to look around. Too open. She didn't have enough breath to give voice to the words.

But surely they could see as well as she.

There just wasn't any place better.

Weiland peered into the distance, examining the landscape or checking for pursuers—Lylene couldn't tell.

Out of breath himself, though he was half Lylene's age, Shile asked, "What do you think?"

Weiland shook his head.

"Any more-helpful thoughts?"

Weiland paused, catching his breath also. "If one of us headed off down the south slope, back into the woods, that might draw them off, or at least divide them."

"Divide us, too."

"There is that to consider," Weiland admitted.

Several men appeared, coming through the trees. Then more, in from both sides. They drew their horses in to confer. Thirteen in all.

"Can we defend the hill?" Shile asked.

Weiland held up his nearly empty quiver.

"Let's see. At thirteen of them, three of us, and five arrows . . .
Think you can hit two and a half of them with each shot?"

"Probably not."

"Probably not," Shile agreed. "You stay here with Lady Lylene
and the bow. I'll try to draw them off."

"Or the other way?"

Shile indicated Weiland's bow. "I could never use that thing. Even
if you'd brought your short bow, I'd be more likely to hit my own foot
than any of them. You can do more good here."

"You'll only get lost in the forest, and we'll have to come looking
for you."

"Toss a coin for it?"

"Not with you."

"You know I'm right." Shile grinned at Weiland, then took Lylene's sweaty hand and raised it to his lips.

Lylene, who had thought she'd caught her breath, found she
couldn't breathe again. "Wait." She looked from one to the other. "I
don't understand what's happening."

Shile kissed her hand. "Stay with Weiland. We'll regroup when we
can."

Lylene grabbed his arm. "They'll leave a few men here to guard
us, then the rest will go after you and tear you apart like a pack of
hungry dogs. And then they'll come back and get us."

"Lady Lylene." Shile pulled free of her. His dark eyes were dis-
turbed. He had obviously meant to do this quickly. As though her fear
were catching, his face began to show the strain despite his best intentions.

From below, someone barked an order: The men separated to spread
out around the hill. Shile firmly handed her over to Weiland, who told
her: "You handled yourself well down there. Don't lose control now."

"You'll have the bow," Shile added. "They don't know we're
almost out of arrows."

"*They* have bows, too," Lylene protested.

"They have crossbows," Weiland said.

"So?"

"This is a long bow." That meant nothing to her. It just looked
terribly ungainly, giving Weiland the appearance, despite his height, of
a child playing with an adult's weapon. "A Welsh bow." That didn't
help either. "It has more range."

"More range than a crossbow?" Lylene asked incredulously.

"Yes," Shile and Weiland told her together. Shile made to leave
again, and Lylene, again, grabbed his arm.

This time Weiland swore at her and took her by the shoulders, but she demanded: "So if you had more arrows, you could shoot at them while they couldn't shoot at us?"

"*If* we had more arrows," Weiland said. "Lady, there's at least a chance this way. Let him go or you'll be the sure death of him."

"I can make more arrows," Lylene said.

"So could either of us," Weiland snapped.

"I can make more arrows in the time it'll take those men to get into range for their crossbows."

That got their attention.

"My Lady?" said Shile.

Weiland's hand dropped from her shoulder.

Ignoring Shile's skeptical look, she took the five arrows and set them on the ground before her. Gently she rested her hands on them. She closed her eyes and concentrated. One of the men, Weiland or Shile, inhaled sharply. She spread the ten arrows out and concentrated again. Spread the twenty arrows out and concentrated again. Spread the forty and concentrated again.

"Mother of God," Shile whispered.

Lylene gathered up a handful of the arrows and held them out. "I can make more," she offered. More deaths which would be her doing. But the alternative was dying.

Shile looked ready to hug her. He grinned, took the handful, and turned to hand them to Weiland.

But Weiland took a step back, away from the hand that held the arrows, all the while staring at Lylene.

"Weiland," Shile said. *"Weiland."*

Lylene had to turn from the look on his face. There was a certain element of fear, of horror, but mostly what she read was betrayal.

"Weiland," Shile urged between clenched teeth. "We're almost in their range."

Weiland backed another step from her.

Shile snatched the bow from him, nocked an arrow, and released it into the advancing line. It curved low, hitting the ground near the feet of one of the horses. The horse skittered. The rider maintained control. Shile released another arrow. It came close to hitting one of the men but, mostly spent, bounced harmlessly off his mail sleeve. The men of Arandell were becoming skittish. They could see that the weapon Shile held could outdistance theirs, despite his lack of skill. They were obviously trying to decide whether to retreat or to rush the remaining distance so they could bring their own weapons into play.

"Weiland," Shile said, "you're going to get all of us killed."

Weiland glanced at him, the first he had looked away from Lylene.
Shile shook the bow at him.

Reluctantly, Weiland took it.

"Take the arrows. *Weiland*."

Looking like a man who is knowingly condemning his soul to hell,
Weiland took the arrows. He drew on the bow, and even Lylene, unfamiliar with weaponry, saw that he pulled with much more strength
and decisiveness than Shile. The arrow whistled through the air and hit
the chest of the man who had been shouting the orders. In the time it
took the arrow to make the flight, Weiland had readied and fired another.

At the third arrow, they started to back off. At the fifth, they turned
and ran. They stopped under the branches of the surrounding trees, well
out of any bow's range, and drew together to confer.

By then, Weiland had shot eight arrows, with only the last a clean
miss. Five men lay motionless, another had been hit in the thigh and
was laboriously crawling toward his fellows at the fringe of the forest,
and one more had kept on his horse and was being seen to. Weiland fit
another arrow to the string, sighting on the crawling man. But perhaps
he took pity. Or, at the last, he decided the man had gotten beyond his
range, for he lowered the bow unfired.

Lylene stared at the body-littered ground. It was too much like the
wedding feast. She prayed for all the wasted life, and she prayed for
the survivors, and—since Father Tobias had taught her it was presump-
tuous to dictate one's desires to God—she prayed that His will be done,
with the fervent hope that His will was that she and Shile and Weiland
would remain among the survivors.

Shile paused to give her shoulder a reassuring squeeze, then he went
to join Weiland, who had crouched down and was watching the remnant
of their attackers as though, with enough concentration, he could discern
their plans from here. Shile stooped down next to him. Lylene watched
them with their heads together—Shile's dark and curly hair almost
touching Weiland's long and pale. They spoke too quietly for her to
make out the words. But a look, a set of the back and shoulders, a tone
deciphered without benefit of the actual words: Lylene had just realized
the men were arguing when Shile glanced back at her and motioned for
her to join them.

Hesitantly she approached, crouching also.

Weiland took the excuse of keeping watch on the remaining soldiers
and didn't face her.

He was afraid of her, of her magic. She had been drawn to him,
and simultaneously repelled by him, and all the while—the clearest
feeling—frightened of him. And here he was, afraid of her.

She liked him better for it: this proof that he was human after all. And she liked herself less, that she should feel that way.

"We owe our lives to you," Shile told her.

"And I to you. Several times over."

"If," Shile said, "we are to make full use of this gift you have given us, we must understand it fully. My Lady Lylene, now is not the time for secrets."

Lylene followed Weiland's lead and scrutinized the men at the forest's edge. Leaderless, they appeared unable to settle on a course of action. Various ones would glance in their direction, or point at them, or beyond them, or back toward Arandell, and so far made no decisive move.

"My Lady,"—Shile shifted his weight—"are you a witch?"

"No," she said. "I mean, I don't think so. That is, not really."

Weiland, his face pale and strained, shot her a wary glance.

"I'm not trying to be evasive. It's just I'm new to all this."

"New?" Shile jumped on the word. "You weren't born to this power?" She shook her head, and he made the connection. "This wizard of yours . . ."

"Harkta. Yes. My bargain with Harkta was that he teach me magic. I thought it could help me rescue my sister. But my only power is to duplicate things. That seemed little enough. Last night was the first I learned that what I make doesn't even last."

"*Things?*" Shile repeated. "What? Coins, arrows . . . ?"

"Clothes." She shrugged apologetically, for not being more knowledgeable, more helpful.

Shile waited for her to go on.

"Whatever I touch, I suppose."

Weiland interrupted. "Is now the time—"

"Horses?" Shile asked. "Could you do horses?"

"They'd need to be here, first," she reminded him.

He grabbed her by the shoulders so that she fell back, sitting on her heels. "But you *could* do them, living creatures?"

"I suppose. I never tried."

"And only the duplicate disappears, not the original?"

"Yes, but—"

"And the duplicate doesn't disappear for at least several hours?"

"Yes, but—"

"And it's just like the original, no one can tell the difference?"

"Yes, but—"

"Jesus," Weiland whispered.

Lylene still had her mind so set on horses that she assumed Weiland had seen something in the gathering below. But a glance assured her that the situation hadn't changed, and Weiland wasn't looking there anyway, but—with his face even whiter than before—at Shile. She glanced from Weiland to Shile and felt the color drain from her own face as she realized what Weiland had guessed, what Shile must mean. "You?" She whispered also. "Make a duplicate of you?"

"Can you?"

"Surely you're not serious."

"Why not? There's seven of them, two of us—that trick with the dress was neatly done, my Lady, but you'll not get away with it more than the once. They're not going to try a frontal assault again. They'll circle around and pick us off from the back, where they'll have more cover, or—if they're in no hurry and want to play it safe—they'll dig in and starve us out."

"Shile," Weiland said. "Shile."

"And the fact that the duplicates don't last is all for the best," Shile said. "How would we ever feed all those extra mouths?"

Weiland put his back to them, refusing this madness. But then he whipped around again. "Shile, be sensible—"

Shile reached into a pocket at his belt and pulled out a coin. "Toss you for it?" he volunteered, and sent the coin spinning through the air, then caught it against his arm.

Weiland grabbed his wrist. "Would you—"

"I have no idea what will happen to you," Lylene interrupted, "when I make the magic, or when the . . . second you . . . goes . . . wherever it goes."

Weiland jerked back around to face the men of Arandell.

Shile took her hand. She felt a tremor in his hand, but he covered it by bringing her fingers to his lips. "It's our only chance."

"Shile—"

"You need to stop worrying about everything that could go wrong. You need to learn to make your wager, hope for the best, and just go ahead and throw the dice."

This from someone who no doubt knew how to cheat at dice.

He squeezed her hand. "Standing? Kneeling? What's the best way?"

"I don't know." She placed a hand on his head. The dark hair was fine and surprisingly soft. He twitched a nervous smile as she wondered what to do next. Unbidden came the memory of one of the young scullery maids at home telling in delighted horror how a witch would consecrate herself to Satan: Crouching on her toes, one hand on top of her head, the other under her heels, three times the would-be witch repeated,

All that I hold between my hands, I offer now to you. Lylene shifted her hand to Shile's shoulder, putting her other hand on the opposite shoulder. "I don't know if this will hurt," she said. She almost refused then, faced with that look of trusting apprehension.

Weiland was steadfastly not watching them, resting his head against his knee.

She closed her eyes. She pictured Shile as he had been at the Happy Wench Inn—when he caught her eye across the hostile crowd and motioned for her to join him. She thought of his dark, always bemused eyes, of the soft hair she had just touched. He was in danger because of her. Forced to leave Arandell because of her. Pursued because of her. Risking his life, perhaps his very soul—

She thought he had twisted, balking at the last moment. A heartbeat's worth of relief. But her arms were extended, the left still going forward to rest gently on one shoulder, the right stretched wide and resting—God help her—on another shoulder. She opened her eyes and snatched back her hands with a stifled cry. Two Shiles looked back at her. The only difference was that the one on her right gave a jaunty smile, while the left one looked about to be sick.

"It didn't hurt," the right-hand Shile said, taking her hand, smiling. "Everything is fine."

The left-hand Shile snatched her hand away, forced her to pay attention to him. "Again," he said.

She shook her head, trembling. "I can't."

"You can. You did with the arrows. It doesn't hurt. I didn't feel anything." He glanced up at Weiland. "Are we getting any reaction?"

Weiland, who she wouldn't have thought could get any paler, seemed to be having trouble breathing.

"Hey!" Shile shouted. "Are you jackals paying attention?"

Lylene saw that, indeed, several of the people gathered at the forest edge were pointing and talking excitedly.

"Again," Shile said.

She put her hands around both Shiles. This time her right hand slipped away, unable to contain the four men who crouched before her.

"Again," two of them said simultaneously.

"Enough." Weiland gazed at them with an expression that was hard to look at, that no doubt mirrored her own, and had Shile any sense, she should have found the same on his face. "*Enough*, Shile."

"They're going," Lylene said, seeing that the makeshift army from Arandell suddenly couldn't get under cover of the forest fast enough. "They don't want anything to do with us. Please, Shile, no more." She covered her face with her hands because she couldn't be sure which of the four she should be addressing. She felt him—one of him—get up. Someone patted her shoulder. Someone else said, "My Lady, everything's fine. Don't be upset."

She jumped, found two Shiles kneeling before her, another hovering anxiously nearby, and one standing next to Weiland—watching the scrambled retreat.

The one with his hand on her shoulder smiled, Shile's quirky smile exactly. The other who knelt leaned forward to caress her hair from her face, and gave the same smile.

She cringed away from both of them.

"My Lady . . ." said the one who was standing—not the same who had spoken before: It was the same voice but from a different location.

"Weiland," she begged, but Weiland, still in a low crouch, was staring up at the Shile who stood next to him.

That Shile rested a hand on his shoulder. "It's all right," he said. He smiled at Lylene to include her. "Really. Everything is fine."

Lylene put her hands over her ears. "Shile!" she screamed. She could only complicate matters by getting hysterical, but she was unable to stem the growing waves of panic. "I can't tell the difference! Shile!"

The one who had been standing near her approached. "My Lady, it's me," and all the others nodded agreement. The two who had been kneeling realized the effect they were having on her; and, true to Shile's solicitious nature, they backed off, giving her breathing room.

The real Shile, the first one, knelt before her. He took her hand and squeezed, trying to reassure her with the same anxious smile she had seen on three other faces only moments past.

"They're all gone," said the one who was watching their attackers. "Perhaps we should move quickly—before they talk themselves into believing that they mis-saw and get their courage back." He had distanced himself from Weiland, probably for the identical reason the others had done the same for her. Mindful of Weiland's pride, he stalked the edge of the hill as though merely searching for the best vantage.

Her Shile stood, and Lylene, still clutching his hand, scrambled to her feet also. He went to Weiland, who watched his approach warily. Lylene forced herself to let go of his hand. One of the others smiled shyly, and she did her best to smile back.

Another picked up the quiver and started filling it with the arrows that lay scattered where Weiland had dropped them. Finished, he approached hesitantly. "These are the made ones," he said, handing Weiland the quiver, "and these are the originals."

"Better keep them separate," a second said.

The third nodded. "The made ones will be gone by dusk."

Weiland took both batches of arrows without a word and finally remembered to close his mouth, finally remembered to breathe.

"We better get back to the horses." The original Shile took hold of Weiland's arm and pulled him to his feet.

"If they're still there." All four Shiles said this last part, like a chorus of monks joining in for an antiphon.

Weiland stole a glance at her—he knew who was responsible for this state of affairs—and started down the hill.

"Somebody—" the original Shile started, but the others anticipated him: One was already moving to take the lead, another went down the back way, apparently to scout out possible ambush, and the last fell in behind, to guard their backs.

Shile took a steadying breath, then held out his hand to help Lylene. Lylene tried very hard not to think of anything.

12

They *found their horses much as they had left them, the chestnut* munching at a clump of grass, looking disconsolate at having been ignored so long, the bay stamping restively. The third Shile, who had circled round to check for ambush or stragglers, hadn't caught up yet.

Weiland went to see to his horse, which nipped at him to show that all was not so readily forgiven, but allowed itself to be scratched between the eyes nonetheless. Lylene clung to her Shile's arm as one of the other Shiles fussed over the chestnut, and the second other Shile moved among the dead bodies, occasionally turning one over with his foot for a closer look.

"He's not stealing from the dead, is he?" Lylene asked.

Shile, also watching his double, said, "I don't know."

"No." The one who was tending the horse appeared shocked at her question, and even more so that Shile didn't know the answer. "Of course not."

Shile shook his head as though to clear it. He seemed to remember he was, to all purposes, talking about himself. "No," he said. "Checking for survivors."

The man had stooped down beside one of the bodies and stayed there. Now he looked in their direction, and Shile pulled loose of Lylene's grasp. "I won't be long."

Lylene watched his retreating back. That way she didn't have to look at any of the strangers who bore his face, nor at Weiland.

The Shile nearest her cleared his throat. "We're . . . ahm, going to need more horses."

"Not with my horse you don't," Weiland growled.

"Actually, it'd be better with Whitcomb." The man scratched under the chestnut's cheek. "Wouldn't it, boy? You're more used to us."

And indeed, if the horse was disconcerted about seeing three Shiles, it gave no indication. Lylene couldn't help but consider it a betrayal.

Weiland looked from horse to man, opened his mouth, closed it again, shot her a look of pure loathing, and turned his back on all of them.

"Put the saddle on first," Lylene advised. Same face, that was obvious, same voice, same mannerisms. They must smell the same, feel the same, that the horse couldn't tell the difference. Her head was beginning to hurt. They must think the same, share the memories—for that one had known the horse's name. She glanced at the two Shiles crouched together talking, and she could not tell which was which. The sun glinted off metal—weapon or armor of one of the fallen men. She blinked against the brightness and was left with an afterimage of dark trees looming above her. She brushed her hair from her face and realized her face was hot, her hand was shaking. As from a great distance, she watched Weiland stamp out the campfire, which was almost burned out anyway, breakfast an unrecognizable cinder. Inexplicably, her heart was racing and she was filled with a definite though nameless dread. It was suddenly hard for her to breathe, to swallow. She saw a fleeting image of an overgrown gully, a stream she didn't recognize. A hand touched her arm, and she jumped with a gasp.

That Shile took a step back from her, his hands held out to show no harm was intended. "I'm sorry. I didn't mean to startle you. You look unwell. Do you want me to call Shile?" He must mean the real one.

"No, I just . . . This place . . ." She glanced around, unable to shake the feeling that she had been running, that she was being closed in upon. Her nostrils were filled with the scents of sweat and forest.

She put her hands on Shile's horse and concentrated. Weiland's bay reared, whinnying at the appearance of a new horse. The two chestnuts shied away from each other.

Weiland grabbed hold of his horse's reins, tried to calm it.

"My Lady," the Shile who wasn't Shile said to her, "are you sure you're—"

She put a shaking hand on the forehead of each of the chestnut horses and, ignoring the unreasonable fear which had beset her, concentrated again.

The nearby Shile jerked on her arm, and she fell against him, out of range of the four chestnuts, one of whose skittish hooves had come close to striking her.

Sun glinted on metal, again stabbing at her eyes. "Get away!" She shoved at him, and he took a step back. "Shile." Her voice was little more than a whisper. "Shile!"

But the original Shile was too far away to hear.

"Shile!" The duplicate who stood near her raised his voice, and—from very, very far away—Shile looked up.

And the sword she felt suspended above her plunged.

She screamed, falling backward, though she had the sensation that she was already with her back to the mossy ground of the stream bank—down and with nowhere to go. Her body was afire with pain and twitched convulsively. The scream echoed in her skull, worse pain yet. Fighting, trying to hold on with fingernails and willpower, she felt life slipping away, running out onto the ground like so much spilled water.

Someone was cradling her head, was holding her down to prevent her from doing injury to herself, and was gently rocking her, repeating calm, meaningless reassurances as one might do for a sick child or injured animal.

She opened her eyes, saw that it was Weiland, of all people. A final shudder worked its way through her body, and he held her tighter apparently afraid another fit was starting.

"What happened? My God . . ." One of the Shiles threw himself to his knees beside her, took her hand and started rubbing it. Two of the others stood nearby, looking afraid that they might be the cause of her distress. *The* two others, she corrected herself.

"He's dead."

Weiland and the Shile who held her hand both leaned closer to hear her whisper.

"What?" Shile asked.

"Who?" Weiland asked.

"Shile. The . . . other Shile." She swallowed, her throat raw. "I felt him die."

Shile caressed the hair away from her face.

"Did you," Weiland asked, "*feel* . . . any details?" All three Shiles gave him the same hard look, which he shrugged off. "Was it our pursuers? All of them?"

"I don't know. I think so. I couldn't see that clearly. He was panicked, chased. They were closing in. I saw a sword." She turned her face away from them, felt Weiland rest his hand on her head.

"Any survivors here?" Shile's voice. From one of the ones who wasn't really Shile, to the one who had been checking the bodies.

"No," that one said.

"You took a long time," Lylene said, "for no survivors."

"There was one, my Lady, but he was badly wounded."

"He would have died anyway," Shile added.

"I understand," she said. And she did. But it was a reminder of just what these friends of hers were.

"We should get moving." Shile got to his feet. "My Lady, are you well enough to travel?"

She glanced back at Weiland, suddenly self-conscious about being in his lap. Just as he looked chagrined with himself for having been caught at gentleness. One of the Shiles helped her stand. Weiland pointedly ignored the hand offered him.

Shile swung up onto one of the chestnut horses, unconcerned—or not showing his concern—about which was the original. "It'd probably be safest to avoid the Arandell road, head off to the southeast, then circle round Cragsfall to Saldemar."

The duplicate who had helped her stand now helped her get up behind Shile.

One of the others untethered the bay horse, and Weiland snatched the reins from him, then mounted, looking sullen and stubborn.

The man didn't take offense. He went through his own saddlebag and pulled out a red handkerchief, which he tied at his throat. "Maybe this will help lessen the confusion," he said equably. "You can call me Duncan."

The other, already mounted, had found a strip of leather that he tied around his head, to hold back his hair and make him distinct from the others. "I'll be Jerel."

"We'll say that it was Newlin who died." Duncan looked vaguely toward Arandell. "No one should die without a name."

Weiland went pale again, looked from Shile to Shile to Shile, swore, and headed out of the clearing.

Under the clatter of leaving, Lylene asked Shile, "What's wrong with those particular names?"

"Just that they're ones I've used previously." She thought he sounded more shaken than he would have her know.

"What about Newlin? Shouldn't we try to find—" She remembered and rested her head on Shile's back, dizzy and nauseated. He patted her hand, and neither gave voice to the obvious: Come the next day, burial would make no difference.

13

The large destriers were more than Lylene could manage by herself, so she rode with someone, shifting periodically so as not to over tax any one animal. Now that Duncan and Jerel had names, as well as a means to tell them apart, they were less intimidating. Lylene still found their tendency to finish each other's sentences disconcerting.

At one point while she was riding with Duncan, and he and Jerel were telling her a long, convoluted story about a larcenous monk, Weiland—looking particularly sour—shouldered his horse past them.

Duncan and Jerel took up their story again as though they hadn't noticed. But Lylene, casting an annoyed look at Weiland's back, saw him pull alongside of Shile, and, with the slightest inclination of his head, indicate his empty quiver.

Lylene looked at Jerel, suddenly unable to make sense of his words. Unlikely that he had caught Weiland's gesture, or seen that the arrows she had made had faded away, though it was hard to be certain. She found herself getting angry at the two of them, Duncan and Jerel. Couldn't they understand the seriousness of their situation? How could they remain so unremittingly cheerful? But that wasn't fair. They understood their situation at least as well as she.

Maybe, she thought, maybe the amount of energy she put into making her duplicates counted for something. The things she had created before—cloaks and money and arrows—had meant nothing to her. She had created them almost off-handedly, while with Shile she had been thinking how very fond she was of him. She had been shaking with the emotion of the moment, concentrating so hard her body had ached, and afterward . . . afterward she had felt drained. Surely that counted for something? Would wishing give these duplicates life beyond the short span she had given the arrows that she had known were for immediate use?

Jerel and Duncan's voices had died away. Whether they had finished their story, she had no idea. Shile, from up ahead, announced that they were coming on a village and that they would stop there to eat and rest the horses, and never a mention that they had already had a long stop just a little while back.

Jerel patted her hand, as Shile was wont to do.

The people of the village gathered about them, silent and apprehensive. A moment before, everything had been noisy activity: men and women working in the surrounding fields, or churning butter, or gathering kindling sticks, or—in the case of one young couple—bickering bitterly while rethatching the roof of a cottage. Now the silence was broken only by a baby crying and by one youngster, squealing and clattering his milk pail, who chased after a runaway goat that zigzagged amongst the cottages.

The headman of the village approached, wiping his hands on his tunic.

"I'll handle this," Shile whispered, obviously feeling that the uncanny resemblance among the three of them would be cause enough for unease without Duncan and Jerel complicating things by opening their mouths.

"Welcome," the headman said, sounding as though he meant the opposite. "My Lords. M'Lady." There was no way he could have taken them for members of the nobility. No doubt he hoped his addressing them as such would be flattering and that, flattered, they might leave him and his people alone.

Shile nodded. "My companions and I have been traveling all day, and we have need of food and rest."

The man started to point off to the right, but before he could get a word out, Shile said: "We shall stay here."

The man gave a slight bow. "As you please, my Lord. But as you can see, Tiswold is but a small village, and we have no inn nor any accommodations such as my Lords and Lady—"

"We have traveled far and hard, and one of your cottages turned over to our use until tomorrow morning will suit perfectly."

Again the bow, though if he believed their bedraggled appearance was due to a hard ride, he'd believe anything.

"We will pay for any slight inconvenience we may cause."

The man bowed yet again, looking better pleased about it this time. "One cottage will suffice for my Lords and Lady?"

Shile grinned. "We're all family."

The man's eyes darted nervously amongst them, then he bowed again.

He escorted them to the doorway of one of the larger dwellings, where he introduced himself as Fitch, the village headman, and the owner of the cottage. He invited them to take their evening meal outside, saying it was the villagers' custom, weather permitting.

Long tables were set up, and they sat with Fitch and several others, though each household had its own food. Theirs was a thin, though tasty, vegetable stew.

Shile sat on Lylene's left, and Weiland next to him. Several times the people on that end of the table tried to strike up a conversation, but Weiland would give one-word answers, or none at all, or look at them as though they were fools for whatever they had just said, and eventually they gave up.

On her right, Jerel and Duncan did better. They joked and chatted with their neighbors, seeming totally at ease. Nobody asked them who they were or why they were there. Nobody commented when Duncan referred to Shile and Jerel as his brothers, and moments later Jerel—not having heard—called them his cousins. The conversation paused . . . then resumed.

The air had already gotten chilly before the end of the meal, but Lylene couldn't bring herself to return to the close quarters of their borrowed cottage. Her head had begun to ache and she felt desperate for fresh air. But the villagers quickly stripped the tables and returned them indoors, then disappeared themselves.

In the fading light she strolled along the edge of the cultivated fields. From behind, there was a step, the crack of a twig—scant warning before someone had hold of her. She jerked around, breaking the man's grip, ready to scream and struggle, before she recognized Shile holding out a blanket for her, protection from the evening's damp.

"Sorry," he said. "I seem determined to startle you." He put the blanket around her. "The cottage may not be much, but at least it's warmer than out here." He didn't move but stood looking into her eyes, smiling as though he could see more than the fifty-year-old woman she appeared. She wasn't used to thinking of herself as pretty—even when she'd been her true age, no one had ever called her pretty except the innkeeper at Branford, and she certainly didn't count that. But standing here, looking into Shile's eyes by starlight, exasperating as he could be, she wondered if he found her pretty.

He gave his gentle, quirky smile and brushed a loose strand of her hair out from the blanket. He hesitated a moment, then said: "Better come, before Shile starts worrying about you."

And that was the first she noticed the scarf, all but indistinguishable in the dark: Duncan, and not Shile after all.

She turned, the ache in her head suddenly remembered—and the wrinkles, and the sagging flesh.

Perhaps he didn't notice, for he hooked his arm around hers and headed back toward the cottage.

"Duncan . . ." she started.

But he was looking upward, at the bright stars clear in the crisp air. "I heard somewhere that each falling star represents someone's soul being called to heaven." Duncan stopped walking and gave the sky all his attention. "When I—" he started, then amended it to: "When Shile was very young, he had a dog once . . . which died. Shile's mother told him that even though most animals don't have souls, God makes a special dispensation for pets and allows them into heaven." He suddenly turned on her. "Do you think that's true?"

"I . . . don't know." She didn't know what to make of this mood either, which didn't seem characteristic of Shile. Before she could add to her lame answer, he suddenly started pulling her along again, so fast that she tripped and would have fallen twice except that he held her up. The jostling made her already aching head throb.

"We're late," he told her.

"For what?"

"For Shile wanting to see you."

She was too breathless from their pace to question him. But despite all that, he abandoned her a few feet from the cottage. "Jerel's waiting for me in the barn," he told her, practically pushing her toward the door.

At the doorway she turned back to see him running between two smaller cottages on the way to where the horses were being kept. Shaking her head, she opened the door.

Shile was sitting at the table, surrounded by feathers and newly made arrowshafts. He glanced up and smiled but quickly returned his attention to his fletching.

She moved the candle by whose light he was working, saying, "You're going to set your hair on fire, if you don't watch out." When he still didn't say anything, she added, "Duncan seemed to think you wanted to see me."

Again the smile. "I always like to see you."

Thank goodness the light was bad enough that he probably couldn't see her blush. "Yes, but he seemed anxious to have me in here—"

Inside her head, something shattered. She probably screamed, though she wasn't sure. She felt that she was falling, although the sensation lasted far longer than it would have taken for her to reach the floor, so she couldn't be sure of that either. What she was sure of was that there had been a glass vessel in her head and that it had suddenly burst. It sent jagged shards up through her brain and out her skull, taking with them the lives of Duncan, with his concerns about God and souls, and Jerel, whose concerns she had never learned. She put her hands to her head, trying to hold the sharp pieces in, willing to endure the pain, if that would save the men she had brought into the world. She screamed their names, begging them to come back, offering to go with them in repentance for what she had done, but already reality was rebuilding itself around her—she felt Shile's arms around her, heard him calling her name—and she knew they had gone, like Newlin, leaving her behind.

She opened her eyes. Shile was bent over her, his face gray and damp with sweat.

The door flung open and Weiland burst in, his sword drawn. His eyes went from Lylene and Shile on the floor, around the room, back to Lylene. "Jesus," he whispered.

She began to shake, and didn't stop for a long time.

14

For all the clarity of the evening sky, the next day dawned gray and damp. They broke their fast on the cold remains of stew, hoping to be out of the village of Tiswold as quickly as possible and to cause as little stir as possible. No one had come to investigate Lylene's screams last night, and no one came this morning. What the villagers presumed or feared was anybody's guess.

Lylene sat huddled in one of the blankets while Shile and Weiland gathered together their few belongings. After an endless night of staring at the underside of the cottage's thatching, Lylene suddenly found herself hard pressed to keep her eyes open.

Shile knelt before her, taking her hand, providing warmth at last. "My Lady, we have brought enough attention on ourselves. We should be leaving." She started to rise, but he didn't move, didn't let go of her hand. "My Lady, I hate to ask this of you. . . . I did promise that we would pay for our lodgings, and our funds are rather limited. . . ."

"It won't last," she said, as though he—of all people—needed reminding. "Shile, the money's no good."

"Of course it's good."

"It won't last."

With an oath, Weiland rammed his sword into its sheath and left, slamming the door.

How slow could they be? "Don't you see, anybody that you paid today . . . Oh." How slow could *she* be? "They would have let us stay without," she said.

"I know. But the promise assured us a more favorable welcome."

"It's like stealing." Lylene felt light-headed, as though she were on the brink of falling asleep. Or of awakening. That was a thought. Would she find in another moment that Shile's duplicates were still here, waiting to be lost all over again? Or perhaps that the whole past day had been a dream and they had never existed at all? Cold comfort, that: The ache was just as real.

She jerked upright. She'd closed her eyes and couldn't be sure how much time had passed. Shile still knelt, one hand holding hers, the other a handful of small coins. She had had no dream: Duncan and Jerel were dead.

She took the coins. It needed less energy to duplicate them than it would take to stand afterward. She held the two batches out to Shile. "The one on the left is always the original." But he knew that, too, from personal experience.

"My Lady," he murmured.

The villagers were waiting outside. Some of them made pretense of being busy with their day to day activities, but they were all waiting. Weiland brought the horses, two of them: one bay and one chestnut. The villagers stayed clear of him.

Fitch, the headman, swallowed visibly when he saw her, then forced himself to approach Shile. "If my Lords—"

"We're not lords," Shile corrected wearily.

"If you'll be requiring anything else to set you on your journey—"

"Nothing." Shile held out some coins. "We thank you for your hospitality."

Fitch stared at the money, swallowed again. He looked at the three of them, then, apprehensively, behind them, at the closed door of the cottage. "Your two . . ."—he obviously weighed Duncan's "brothers" against Jerel's "cousins"—". . . kinsmen . . ."

"Gone." Shile kept his voice even. "They left ahead of us, during the night."

Fitch didn't offer his opinion on the likelihood of that.

"Do you want the money or don't you?"

Fitch took it.

He probably assumed he'd find dead bodies in the cottage. Lylene was too drained to wonder how he would sort it out. Desperate people, he probably thought them. Some desperate people. She settled herself behind Shile. No doubt Shile thought she hadn't noticed him slipping some of the real pennies in with the group of made ones he had given Fitch. And Weiland, swinging up onto his bay and scowling at her for watching him: She'd seen him leave one of his knives on the table—a finely honed blade in a village where iron was scant. She, still dressed in borrowed shirt and breeches, had left her dress, the only thing she had of her own.

Desperate people.

They were pathetic. How would they ever stand up to Theron?

15

F*or part of the journey she rode with Shile, who tried to cheer her* with humorous tales and had no way of knowing that the story he started off with, the one about the thieving monk, was the same Jerel and Duncan had told her yesterday.

The rides behind Weiland were a different matter entirely. No idle chatter here: Twice he told her to sit centered, and once, when they passed through a thickly wooded area, he warned her to watch her head. Still, he didn't seem short-tempered, and—considering the consequences if she *hadn't* ducked—he might in fact have been making an effort to be pleasant.

Perhaps, Lylene thought, just as he had gone up in her estimation when she learned there was something he was afraid of, it could be he thought better of her once he saw that she obviously hadn't intended for matters to end the way they had—that she wasn't a totally heartless wizard. She relived finding herself with her head on Weiland's lap after Newlin had been killed by their pursuers, and she was thankful that she was sitting behind Weiland, where he couldn't see her face go red. More likely than being concerned about whether she was heartless, she told herself, Weiland was just relieved that she wasn't as powerful a wizard as he had feared.

They stopped short of Cragsfall, though it was only afternoon. Saldemar was another half day beyond that, and they didn't want to arrive at dusk, when the gate would be most carefully guarded.

"What I think we should do," Shile said, "is rest here overnight. First thing in the morning, we'll go to Cragsfall to pick up the things we'll need, then we'll head off for Saldemar at our best speed. That way, if Theron's got anybody in Cragsfall, they won't be able to send word ahead of us.''

"What," Weiland asked, "things that we'll need?"

"Disguises," Shile said. "Supplies. Accouterments for getting into Saldemar."

Weiland cursed.

"What?"

"Can't you keep it simple for once? Can't you just—"

"Weiland, Weiland—"

"Don't 'Weiland, Weiland' me. You *always* make everything more complicated than it needs to be."

"No, I don't."

"You don't know when to let up. You construct these grandiose schemes which collapse under the sheer weight—"

"Name me once."

Weiland didn't need time to consider. "Five days ago when you tried to talk Humphrey—"

"Besides Humphrey."

"The tournament at Stafford."

"Well, Stafford—"

"London."

"Not—"

"Ridgeshire. Charbonne. Lincoln."

"Maybe a little—"

"How about *Wales*, Shile? Our trip to Wales wasn't 'a little' anything."

"You're upsetting the Lady Lylene."

As though Shile's comment hadn't been totally irrelevant, Weiland purred, "Then she can take the first watch," and turned his back on them.

In the end, it was Shile who took the first watch, saying that was no job for a lady. Lylene suspected that Weiland was secretly relieved, that he wouldn't have slept had she been on guard. Shile watched and Weiland slept, and she lay under a gnarled oak tree with her face to the stars, thinking the ache would keep her awake forever.

And she awoke when someone gave her a hard kick in the ribs.

She curled around the new, physical pain. A pointed weight pressed against her chest, just enough pressure to let her know not to move. It took several hard blinks for her eyes to adjust to the darkness, to follow the length of the sword to the man who held it. "Harkta," she spat.

"Hello, little housekeeper. Not quite the conjurer princess yet, but no longer exactly the conjurer hag. For such a noble and self-righteous creature, you've dropped quite a few years." The wizard turned his face slightly, looking beyond her, and said: "Don't even think of trying anything."

Lylene slid her gaze to what the wizard looked at: Weiland, who appeared to her to be sound asleep. But Harkta said: "Put your hands behind your head and sit up, as slow and easy as you can," and Weiland put his hands behind his head. "Easy," Harkta warned. "*She* will pay for any mistakes *you* make."

Weiland sat up, apparently slow and easy enough to please him.

"On your knees." Then, finally easing up on the sword. "Now you. Stand up."

Lylene brought her legs around. From this new position she could see what would have been visible to Weiland all along: Shile, an untidy sprawl on the ground. *Please, not again*, she thought. Not someone else dead because of her.

"*Stand up.*" Harkta slapped her arm with the flat edge of the sword. She stood.

With his free hand the wizard tossed something at her. She flinched, but it was only a length of rope.

"Pick it up." Harkta spoke as though to a tiresome child. "Tie your friend's hands behind his back. And be advised: For every knot that isn't secure, I'm going to cut off one of your crooked little fingers." He leaned his left arm on a low-slung branch of the oak tree, comfortable and poised.

Lylene knelt behind Weiland.

"No talking," Harkta warned before she could get her mouth open.

She tied Weiland's wrists as loosely as she dared, which wasn't very loose at all, and waited for some sign, some signal to let her know what to do. If Weiland gave one, she missed it.

"Now your other young friend." Harkta tossed another length of rope at her.

At least he wasn't dead, which was what she'd feared. He groaned at her touch but didn't awaken. There was a large bump at the base of his skull, evidence that Harkta had come up behind him with sword hilt or rock. She pulled his limp arms behind his back and tied them there.

When she looked up, the wizard was checking Weiland's bonds. He jerked the sword, motioning her away from Shile and down on her knees between the two mercenaries. He examined Shile's bonds, then went back to his pose by the tree.

"I guess you can keep your fingers after all," he said with that boyish smile she remembered. "You've been busy. I understand you're responsible for killing off enough people to populate a small fishing village.'' His teeth flashed in the moonlight.

His words stung, too close to what she knew as truth.

''Witch, they call you,'' he continued, ''the Demon Woman of Dorstede, who sucks souls from living men and steals children away into the night. They say a man who looks you in the eye is doomed to die within the hour. I alone have known your power and lived. I must say: You've enhanced my reputation enormously, and I *am* grateful.''

''Vile buffoon,'' she said. ''Without your magic you're a pasty-skinned toad.''

His air of urbane aloofness vanished. Nostrils flared, eyes narrowed, and he took a step forward of the tree, his hand raised to slap her.

''Strike me,'' she dared. ''Go ahead, touch me for one instant and see who comes out the worse.''

That sobered him. He backed off. ''You're *old*,'' he taunted instead. ''You're old, and you're soft, and you're very, very stupid. And Lord Theron is waiting to meet you.''

Beside her, Shile stirred and groaned. He'd probably have a headache for the next two days.

Harkta's attention wavered from Lylene to Shile, back to Lylene, then snapped to Weiland, who had leaned backward onto his heels as the wizard glanced away. ''Lord Theron might pay for the famous witch,'' Harkta said. ''You I'm bringing back out of forbearance. Don't try me.''

''Just a cramp,'' Weiland said, wide-eyed and guileless.

Lylene didn't believe that act for an instant, and neither did Harkta. ''Turn around,'' he said shrilly. ''Let me see those bindings again. *Now*.'' He raised the sword but was reluctant to get close enough to use it.

''Easy,'' Weiland urged, the calm voice of reason. Was there the signal for which she had been waiting? She thought of Arandell, the Happy Wench, and the barkeep Marsh, killed by a knife Weiland had pulled from nowhere. Weiland turned on his knees, moving slowly, awkwardly, which was not like him at all, putting his back to her before Harkta. There was no time to make sure in the dim light. She turned to her right, to the still half-conscious Shile and screamed, ''No, Shile, don't!''

Harkta jumped, swung toward Shile for the merest instant, probably realizing his mistake even as he made it.

Lylene heard him cry out. She turned in time to see him drop the sword and clap his left hand to the opposite shoulder, from which blood welled out.

Weiland was on his feet already, strands of cut rope falling loose from his wrists. The wizard's attention was all on the knife in his shoulder, and he made no attempt to defend himself. Weiland collided with him, slamming him into the trunk of the old oak. His left arm jammed against the wizard's windpipe, and his knee jerked up into his groin.

Harkta gave a strangled gurgle, and his eyes rolled upward.

Weiland ripped his knife out of the wizard's shoulder and swung it toward his belly.

Lylene recoiled, stunned by the savagery—no matter that it was directed against the treacherous Harkta but Weiland checked the momentum of the knife just short of the wizard's mid-section, and finally eased up on Harkta's throat.

Harkta sucked in deep rattling breaths. "Damn . . . murderous . . . gutter trash," he wheezed. "Can't you see . . . I'm bleeding to death?" His eyelids fluttered and he started a slow downward slide, but Weiland left the knife where it was. Apparently Harkta wasn't so far gone that he didn't realize he was about to impale himself. He pulled himself back up and pressed against the tree, gasping.

No more than two handspans from Harkta's face, on the branch on which he had earlier been leaning, there was movement. For a moment, Lylene thought it was nothing: night shadows, breeze on loose bark. The movement slithered closer to Weiland's arm and flicked its tongue out to taste the air.

Icy revulsion fingered her back and arms. The snake was big— almost as wide around as her arm, its length lost in the shadows of the branches—and fast. Already it was within striking distance of Weiland. And still he hadn't seen it. She realized that she'd taken an instinctive step away and hated herself for it, for having thought of herself first. Her throat had constricted on itself, squeezing in the warning that she wanted to shout.

In that moment—battered by fear and guilt and self-loathing—it struck her how lucky Harkta was to get such a distraction at such a time.

Her throat relaxed somewhat, and she put her hand on Weiland's arm, the arm close to the snake. If she was wrong, at least she wouldn't live to regret it. "His specialty is illusion," she reminded him.

Weiland followed her gaze to the brown and gold snake. It had reared up and was swaying, its eyes on Weiland. For a moment Weiland just looked, no discernible expression on his face. What if he thought it was a real snake and, startled, let the wizard get away? What if he thought it was just an illusion, and it wasn't? What if—

Weiland slammed the wizard against the tree. "All right. That's it.
I'm going to kill him."

The snake lunged.

Lylene screamed.

Weiland trusted her first inclination. He stayed where he was and
hit the wizard across the face.

The snake disappeared.

"Don't kill me," Harkta begged. "Please. I swear: no more tricks.
On my honor. Don't hurt me. I can help you."

Weiland glanced at her. "What do you think?"

This was a new game, asking her opinion. Did he want her permission to kill Harkta? Or an excuse not to? He and Shile knew each
other, knew what to do and what to say in this sort of situation. She
didn't know what was expected of her. "I . . ."

Next to her, Shile groaned yet again.

"Do you have a knife to cut his rope?" Weiland asked.

"No," she answered.

Without lowering the blade he held against the wizard, Weiland
pulled another from his left boot.

Shile lifted his face out of the grass as she sawed at the rope. "Don't
worry," he mumbled, "I'll rescue you."

"That's all right," she said. The frayed rope snapped, and she
helped him sit up. "Easy now."

He rubbed the back of his head. "What are you doing?" he asked
Weiland. "Are you tormenting that poor fellow for a particular purpose
or just for the fun of it?"

"Yes," Weiland said.

Shile kept rubbing his head, then finally stood up, supporting his
weight on Lylene's arm. "Theron?" he guessed.

"The Lady's wizard."

"Pity. Would have saved a lot of trouble if he was Theron. Is he
likely to bleed to death in the immediate future?"

"Yes," Harkta moaned at the same time Weiland said, "No."

Shile approached, and the wizard backed right up against the tree.
"Now, now," Shile told him, "don't be afraid of me. Just because you
tried to crack my head open like a walnut doesn't mean I'm necessarily
going to retaliate."

But Harkta wasn't even noticing him. All his attention focused on
Lylene, and if he could have pushed himself into the tree, it was obvious
he would have. "Don't," he said. Then to the others: "Don't let her
touch me. I'll do whatever you want, tell you whatever you want. Just
keep her away from me."

"Oh, I like the sound of this." Weiland grabbed the neck of Harkta's shirt and swung him around and down, so that he was kneeling at Lylene's feet.

Harkta had his eyes closed. "Don't touch me!" he begged.

And Lylene, with her hand reaching out, stopped, knowing that if she gave Harkta her extra years, he'd shed them on the first poor unfortunate he could touch. She let her hand drop to her side. He had been partly right: She didn't suck souls or steal children, but she had caused grief enough already.

Whatever Weiland was expecting, he looked bitterly disappointed.

Shile took over. "You work for Theron?" he asked.

"No," Harkta said.

Weiland said nothing, just rested his knife, flat side down, on the wizard's shoulder.

"That is—I mean—not generally."

"Tonight, specifically?" Shile asked.

"I Saw you coming. Word came about what happened in Arandell, so I cast about, Saw the three of you."

"Future-seeing?" Shile asked, looking to Lylene for confirmation. She nodded.

Harkta glanced at her nervously. "I Saw you would go to Saldemar, so I went to Lord Theron. It's not that we're friends"—again the glance at Lylene—"but I thought he'd pay for the warning."

"You saw us going to Saldemar," Weiland said, moving the knife closer to Harkta's neck, so that the wizard had to tip his head back to keep from getting cut, "but you didn't see me disemboweling you and throwing the little pieces to the wolves?"

Harkta closed his eyes, and Shile silently mouthed, *Wolves?* for it was too late in the season for wolves to be this far south. Weiland shrugged.

"He can't see those parts of the future that involve him," Lylene explained.

Shile chewed on his lip. "But you could see us reaching Saldemar?"

Harkta started to nod, felt the knife against his skin, and whispered weakly: "Yes."

"And? Do we succeed in rescuing the Lady Lylene's sister from Theron?"

Harkta hesitated and Weiland, still holding onto the front of his shirt, twisted.

"No," Harkta answered. "You don't."

Lylene was sure her heart stopped beating. Weiland looked up, meeting her eyes. She turned her face, swallowed away the buzzing in her ears, felt the warmth of Shile's hand on her wrist. The moment passed.

"Liar," Weiland said. He let go of Harkta's shirt and jerked his head back by the hair.

"No." Lylene would have never guessed she'd say *no* to someone killing Harkta. "No, I don't think he can lie about the future." She shook her head for emphasis. "It's part of his magic."

"The future," Shile said thoughtfully, "can't be a stable thing?" He said it like a question. "It must be fluid, moving. Endless possibilities affected by endless possibilities."

"What?" Lylene asked testily. *Oh, Beryl*, she thought. All this for nothing?

"He's said we go to Saldemar and don't succeed. That's one possibility. Now that we know that, what if we don't go to Saldemar? That's another possibility, another future, and already different from the one he's foreseen. *What if we go to Saldemar forewarned?*"

Lylene swallowed hard again.

Weiland released Harkta's hair. "What exactly do you foresee, wizard?" he asked between clenched teeth.

"Ease off," Shile murmured. "You're scaring him so much he can't think."

Weiland shoved Harkta's head away from him and stepped back.

Harkta put his hand to his bloody shoulder and glowered. Then his lip curled back in a sneer. "You don't believe me? You want to help her? Go ahead. But *you*"—he pointed at Weiland—"if you go in there, you must be prepared to die."

Again the cold came up from the ground and seeped into Lylene.

Weiland never flinched or blanched. He stepped forward and put the knife to Harkta's throat again. "How are you at self-resurrections?"

"Leave him," Shile said. He, at least, looked properly shaken. He got a rope from his pack and bound Harkta to the tree. "Do you have a horse nearby?" he asked the wizard.

"Just over the hill."

"You alone? Or am I likely to meet anyone?"

"I told you: I went to Saldemar to warn Theron she was coming. Theron's not in the habit of providing me with escort. He even skimped on the payment. He wasn't terribly impressed with my news." He glanced at Lylene. "He didn't care. Said you were a pathetic *child* and you could come if you wanted. I wouldn't even be here except that I decided to stop for some herbs I'd been needing. Then I saw you."

"Then you saw us." Shile rubbed the back of his neck. "I'll get the horse," he told Lylene and Weiland. "If he gives you any trouble, go ahead and slice him up for the wolves."

Weiland gave a feral grin and got his sword from beside his bedroll. He unsheathed the blade, letting it scrape noisily along its great length, then he crouched down in front of Harkta, the naked blade across his knees.

"I'll bleed to death by the time he gets back," Harkta complained, trying to look pathetic.

Weiland shrugged.

"Half that blood is illusion," Lylene told Weiland. "The wound's not that bad at all."

Weiland didn't appear interested, one way or the other.

Lylene went to search for something to stanch the bleeding. The only thing she found was a red handkerchief in Shile's saddlebag, the original of the one Duncan had worn. She almost stuffed it back in.

After fixing the cloth about the wizard's shoulder, she crouched next to Weiland, resting her chin on her hands, watching, waiting.

Harkta's eyes darted from one to the other of them. "Damn it, I kept my part of the bargain. You got your magic, and I was willing to teach you how to use it. But you got all upset about the age thing. I explained that to you. If you kill me, you'll never learn. Lylene. Lylene, you know I've always had a soft spot in my heart for you."

"Shall we hug and make up?" she asked.

He licked his lips. "You don't know how to use your magic properly. Those human duplicates you made—"

Her breath caught.

"—I saw that. You went about it all wrong. It doesn't have to be like that. You put too much power in it, too much concentration. All you want is a . . . a likeness, a fetch, just a mindless, soulless—"

"Shut up."

Weiland was silently taking all this in.

"No harm," Harkta said. "Really. To you or your friends. I can show you how. You can go on making duplicates of them indefinitely, and it won't hurt anyone."

She covered her ears.

Weiland stood.

"No!" Harkta cried, cringing.

Weiland slammed the sword back into its sheath. "Damn," he muttered.

Beyond Harkta, Shile was approaching, leading Harkta's horse. He motioned Lylene and Weiland to leave Harkta under the tree and moved beyond his range of hearing. "Well," he said to them, "so what do you think?"

"About *what*?" Weiland asked, never a patient man.

"Plans for breaching Saldemar."

"Shile, weren't you listening—"

"I was listening. I have my doubts."

"You . . ." Weiland gave up without saying anything. He turned to Lylene. "I'm sorry," he said. "I am not willing to die for you. You or your sister."

She could understand that. But Shile cut her off before she could answer. "I can see how you feel that way," he told Weiland.

"And don't talk to me in that—"

"You keep a watch on the wizard. The Lady and I will rescue the sister."

Weiland shook his head in disbelief, but this time it was Lylene who got her voice to work first: "No. This isn't your affair."

"Of course it is," Shile said. "You hired us."

"Then I'm releasing you. It's too dangerous."

"You'd leave your sister to her fate?"

"I'll . . . come up with a new plan."

"My Lady—"

"He said the rescue wouldn't work. He said Weiland would die."

"I don't believe it, and anyway—"

"I do believe it. Shile, he's clever, he's treacherous, but he can't lie about what he Sees. I *did* learn something during my stay with him."

"Well, it's on that chance that we're leaving Weiland here."

"Shile—" Weiland started.

"Weiland," Shile said. "My Lady. I will go."

"Shile," Weiland pleaded. "Wizardry is too dangerous to—"

"Just wait here," Shile said. "This wizard . . . Weiland, this wizard can make us a fortune."

"Damn it, *listen to me*."

"No. No, I will not. For once would you just listen to me? With no arguing, no grumbling—"

"Shile, you're an idiot." Weiland hooked sword onto harness and stalked away. He grabbed up his saddle kit and headed for his horse. "You want the wizard, you watch him. I'm not waiting around."

Lylene looked from Weiland's retreating back to Shile to Weiland. "Weiland," she called, because Shile was going to let him go.

But Weiland didn't turn back. They had left the horses' equipment on loosely, and it took him only a moment to tighten and check, and then he swung on.

"You're not just going to let him go?" Lylene demanded of Shile. But he did.

16

Shile crouched by the dying embers of the campfire, trying to catch enough light to read the paper he held. The sun was just visible over the horizon, casting a pink glow over everything. Lylene stooped next to him.

"Map of Saldemar," he explained, though that wasn't what she wanted to talk about. "Weiland drew it yesterday evening while you were . . . resting."

"Oh, Shile, I'm so sorry—"

"Don't worry. He'll be back."

His confidence was reassuring. "He's . . . walked out before?"

Shile hesitated.

"Shile, I'm sorry. You're partners. I didn't mean to come between you." She didn't add that Weiland was the one who was more likely to keep his feet firmly on the ground.

"Shhh. It's all right. Probably safer this way. Though I'm still not convinced that wizard of yours is being honest with us. Weiland's real skittish when it comes to magic. We'll find him after we finish this job." He patted her hand and went back to studying the map.

"Speaking of that wizard . . ."

Shile looked up again.

"What are we going to do with him?"

"Take him with us, of course."

"You can't be serious. He'll turn on us the first chance he gets."

Shile shook his head.

"Shile, he's dangerous."

"But controllable."

Lylene couldn't believe they were even arguing about this. "How?"

"With a knife to his ribs."

Lylene rested her chin on her palm, watching Harkta. "I don't know: I kind of liked the plan with the wolves."

The wizard sat in a pathetic slump, pretending he couldn't hear.

Shile said: "Besides, with his ability to cast illusions he can disguise us."

"Why? Theron doesn't know either of us."

"Someone in his employ may have seen me before."

She sighed. Cheating at cards or picking purses, probably.

"Or—more likely—might recognize you as the aggrieved sister."

She suspected he just liked disguises. "We can be disguised without him," she pointed out. "Shile—"

"Tell you what . . ." He pulled a coin from his pocket.

"No, this isn't the kind of thing to be settled with a coin toss."

"It's exactly the kind of thing to be settled with a coin toss. A difference of opinion. Neither party able to convince the other. No compromise possible. Look," he showed her the ancient gold coin, worn almost to obliteration, "on this side, His Royal Highness King Something-or-other of Phoenicia. On this side . . . looks like a god who bears an uncanny resemblance to a fish-eyed falcon. Pick a side."

Being a devout Christian, she felt obliged to select the king.

"All right," Shile said: "God, we have Harkta get us inside Saldemar; king, you come up with another plan."

"But—"

It didn't make any difference: The coin landed god's face up.

Shile grinned, pocketing the coin.

Harkta. She hoped Shile knew what he was doing. "All right. What's he going to disguise us as?"

Shile thought about it for a moment. "Glaziers."

"Glaziers?"

"We'll say Theron has hired us to fit the windows with glass. It's the latest fashion. To please his pretty new wife." Shile caught himself. "My Lady, I'm sorry. Sometimes my mouth . . ."

She considered. "It might work. If Theron did want glass, it'd be in the living quarters. So we'd have an excuse to be wandering around there."

"The west tower. That's what Weiland said." He raised his voice for Harkta. "Can you do it, wizard?" He pulled a knife from his belt and flipped it in the air, catching it by the handle, a trick she'd be willing to bet Weiland had taught him. "Horses and all?"

Harkta nodded.

"Show us."

Shile's features shimmered, shifted. He was suddenly bald, with a round, florid face. Harkta had a gray beard and a bulbous nose. Lylene looked down and saw that her chest was flat, though broad, and her hands large and calloused: a man, a young laborer. Shile's horse was a dappled gray mare, and Harkta's a light brown one, working men's horses.

Maybe, she thought. *If*— She fought not to think of all the *ifs*, to hold on to the maybe. Maybe.

It was still early morning when they reached Saldemar. Just before cresting the last hill, Shile had to untie Harkta. For this they switched horses. Lylene got Harkta's, which was still a large, restive gelding, no matter what it looked like, and just about all she could handle. Shile sat behind Harkta on the horse that seemed to be a dappled mare. From the expression on the wizard's face, Shile had been serious about keeping a knife to his ribs.

Saldemar was no bigger than Delroy, but much better fortified. There were lookout towers in good repair, a gatehouse which probably included a portcullis, and the walls were heavily crenellated and looped for archers. The whole structure sat on a hill and was surrounded by a moat.

"Everyone," Shile said, "keep calm, act natural. Wizard, twitch and you die."

At the outer gate, Shile talked loud and fast, and the guards waved them into the barbican.

Lylene dismounted, bumping one of the guards, then the other, leaving each a year older. Anyone who worked for Theron, she reasoned, had probably done more than enough to deserve it. She caught Shile glancing upward, and she did likewise. She'd been right to worry about the portcullis. That would come down at the first hint of something amiss—locking those who were out, out, and those who were in—if they didn't belong in—would be in serious trouble.

At the stable, there was a dice game going on the floor.

Make your wager, hope for the best, and throw, she thought. She walked around the circle, studying several throws, leaning here, resting a hand there, accidentally stepping on toes. She began to get dirty looks.

Shile hissed in her ear: "You're affecting the illusion Harkta made for you. You're making your disguise younger." He motioned with his head for her to leave. He followed Harkta, close enough to step on his heels as they climbed the stairs to the entrance of the keep itself.

"Glaziers," Shile said, shoving Harkta in through the doorway, "come to measure."

The guard shoved them back out. "I don't know nothing about no glaziers."

"Nobody seems to," Shile complained. "We had trouble at the gate, too. Lord Theron hired us."

"Didn't tell me about it."

"Oh. Well then. Obviously. If he didn't discuss it with you . . . You can't be too careful about rogue craftsmen coming in and doing all sorts of work for free."

The guard scowled.

"Go on, go call Lord Theron away from whatever it is he's doing. He's a patient man, I understand. Just make sure you tell him it was *you* who wanted to know."

The guard sucked on his teeth. "Well, I think it'll be all right then."

"Are you sure? You might want to demand that Lord Theron come all the way over here to tell you it's all right."

Lylene kicked his heel.

"No," the guard said slowly. "I guess it'll be all right."

"I thank you," Shile said. "My assistants thank you. My poor dead father—"

Lylene pushed Shile, and Shile pushed Harkta, and they were inside the castle. "You don't know when to stop, do you?" she demanded in a harsh whisper. Weiland was right.

"We don't want him with any lingering doubts. Let's see, if I remember correctly—"

A squad of soldiers came around a corner, looking more sharp and alert than those with whom they had dealt so far. Shile tugged Harkta to the side to let them pass.

And Harkta burst into flame.

With a startled oath, Shile jumped back, letting go of him.

"No!" Lylene cried. No heat, no burning, but it happened so fast she couldn't blame Shile for reacting instinctively.

And by then they had all reverted back to their real forms, and Harkta was screaming, "Arrest them! Arrest them! Arrest them!"

In an instant, the men had their swords out.

Shile, just going for his, stopped and left his hands where the guards could see them.

The guard who'd been in the lead grabbed Harkta by the front of his shirt. "Don't you give orders to my men, wizard," he snarled.

"These are the ones!" Harkta insisted.

The man looked down at the wizard coolly until Harkta spoke more calmly.

"Sorry, Sir Owen. But these are the people I was telling Lord

Theron about, the ones who've been threatening him, that were going to break into Saldemar.''

"I see. That's why you led them in."

Harkta twitched a smile. "Into your capable hands, Owen, as captain of the guard."

"You always have an answer, wizard." The captain shoved him away. "Go," he said to one of his men. "Take him to see Theron." And to another: "Disarm them."

The man took Shile's sword and dagger, then patted his hands up and down Lylene's body. She got through it by telling herself that—bad as it was—at least he took no liberties. Apparently this Owen had his charges under strict control.

"Nothing, sir."

Owen looked at Shile. "So," he said. And grinned. "Weiland's friend."

"I was about to say the same."

"Then you would have said wrong. Where is he?"

Shile shook his head. "Didn't come."

"I don't blame him. Harkta said you were coming. Said why. I found it hard to believe Weiland'd be stupid enough to come back. Especially for a whore." He glanced at Lylene, and she felt her cheeks go red, that he would think that of her.

"Owen," Shile said, "I know Weiland always thought of you as a friend and was very sorry—"

"No," Owen interrupted, hand upraised. "Please. Don't. Let's have some respect for each other, shall we? I liked Weiland. I considered him a friend. He showed a lot of promise, and I recommended him for promotion. When he walked off with half the year's tax monies—during my watch . . . ." Owen shook his head. ". . . I don't think he was looking back and feeling sorry."

The guard who had taken Harkta to see Theron came back. "Says to put 'em down in the dungeon until he's got the time to question them."

At least he didn't order us killed out of hand, Lylene thought. But it was hard to find comfort in that.

Owen and his guards brought them down an incredibly steep set of stairs with a heavy oak door at the bottom.

Someone on the other side opened a tiny metal door set at eye level.

"Prisoners," Owen announced.

The metal peephole slammed shut, and the wooden door opened. There were two guards down here. One of them led their group down a corridor, passing through another locked door.

The cell, when they finally got to it, was small, the walls rough and crumbly, and it smelled damp. It was also dark, as she discovered when the door slammed shut on them.

The dungeon guard worked the metal window back and forth to ease the rusty hinge. "This is where you'll get your food," he said. "If anybody authorizes food for you." He slammed it shut again.

In the dark, something brushed against her hand. She snatched it away with a startled squeak.

"Just me," Shile said.

She felt for his hand, and he squeezed reassuringly. "My eyes haven't adjusted yet," she said.

"I don't think they will: It's too dark. I think we better sit. On the count of three: one, two, three."

They sat.

And he was right.

Their eyes didn't adjust.

17

Lylene *was disconcerted that her surroundings got no blacker* when she shut her eyes. She listened to the steady drip of water from somewhere behind their cell, and to the little rustling noises which came from every direction. She tried to convince herself that rats were the least of her worries.

Shile had nothing to say for the longest time.

Occasionally a far-off door slammed, bringing a snatch of conversation on an air current, the words indecipherable.

Hours passed. Lylene felt the stir of a draft around her ankles. She raised her head and swallowed hard. Shile squeezed her hand.

Voices approached, still indistinct. Laughter. The creak of hinges straining under a heavy weight. The dark lessened. Not brightness, but now there was a difference between eyes open and eyes closed.

Footsteps. The jangle of mail. A shaft of light appeared underneath the door of their cell. Tiny red eyes close to the floor were caught in that light, blinked in surprise, then disappeared into a crack in the wall.

"This them?" The voice was slurred and unsteady. "Are you the dangerous prisoners?"

Laughter. "You idiot. I haven't opened the peephole yet."

"Could of sworn I saw 'em. Two—s'cuse me—two big, hairy brutes."

Shadows danced under their door as the guards outside—three or four of them by the noise they made—stumbled around with their torches. It sounded as if they all had been drinking.

Shile slumped back down, his interest gone.

Muffled giggling, then a new voice said: "Damnation, that's some strong ale you brought. What's in it?"

"Wizards' blood and wolf piss," the first voice answered. "Want some more?"

Apparently he did. Apparently they all did.

Lylene rocked back and forth. Obviously these weren't sent by Theron to fetch them or question them. They probably weren't even supposed to be here. She just hoped they weren't so drunk they'd try anything on their own. She hadn't appreciated before how lucky they'd been with Owen.

She put her head down on her knees, so that only her hair would show. Hopefully the grayness of it would keep the men from being interested. She appeared in her forties now, and that wasn't so very old that it would protect her.

"So." It was the first man again. "So, where are they?"

The little door in front of the barred window was flung open, flooding the cell with torch-light.

"Hey. Hey, dangerous prisoners. Le'see your faces."

Lylene screwed her eyes shut and prayed they'd go away.

"They look—s'cuse me—they look like they're friends."

One of the others snorted.

"S'good to have friends," the first insisted. "Specially when one is indis . . . posed. Isen it? Isen it nice to have friends?"

The words were uncannily familiar. A tingle began at the base of Lylene's spine and went up all the way to the tips of her hair. Shile had said that, or something very like it, outside the Happy Wench. Playing the drunk. A disguise of sorts. Slowly, not daring to hope, she raised her head.

Four faces crowded together around a torch to peer into their barred window. Guards, all wearing helmets, their faces made similar by no hair showing, by the noseguards, and by the flickering torch.

She didn't have to look past the second one on the right.

"Well"—how could she not have recognized Weiland's voice, despite the drunken slur?—"you'ere right about one thing: She ain't no big hairy brute."

Lylene stole a glance at Shile, who sat in a disconsolate slump, staring at the tips of his boots, ignoring everything. She nudged him. He ignored that too.

The man on Weiland's left punched his shoulder amicably. "Not so dangerous, not so interesting. Come on, lad, let's go have some more of that ale you brung."

Weiland's blue eyes shifted back and forth between her and Shile.

She moved her foot, kicking Shile's leg, but that seemed to drive him even deeper into his own thoughts.

One of the others had already turned to go, and the man on Wei-land's left said again, "Come on."

Her arms were still wrapped around her knees. She reached her left hand under her right arm and, as hard as she could, pinched the inside of Shile's thigh.

That got his attention.

"Now that one," Weiland said, abandoning as much of the drunken slur as he dared, "*is* a big, hairy brute."

Shile looked up.

Weiland pushed himself away from the grate.

"Hey!" Shile bellowed. "You! Swine-breath!"

Trouble: The other three guards made appreciative noises and turned back.

Weiland pointed to himself, incredulous. "Me? Are you talking to me?"

Shile scrambled to his feet. "No, I'm talking to your mother. Of course, I'm talking to you, you stupid oaf."

Lylene got up also, to be ready for whatever was coming.

Weiland pulled his sword and staggered forward. "Just be thankful this door is between us."

Shile stepped closer. "Scare me some more."

"Back off," one of the guards warned him, the one who held the torch. "Keep away from the door."

"I'm going to volunteer for your execution," Weiland said, raising his sword. Then, turning to the others: "Let's drink to that."

"Good thinking, lad." Two of the guards started moving down the corridor to the guard-room. The last reached to close their window open-ing. Weiland swung the sword around, cutting deep into his back. The man dropped without uttering a sound, but the remaining guards heard the thud of metal on flesh. As if that weren't warning enough, the slain guard's torch fell to the floor, still burning, sending bizarre shadows dancing on the walls.

One swore.

The other didn't.

They both had their swords out faster than Lylene would have be-lieved.

Weiland moved fast too. Swords came together, scraped, came to-gether again. Weiland circled around, so that they had their backs to the cell door. He lunged, which seemed folly, but one of the guards took a step backward.

Weiland darted back, and Shile, waiting by the grate, grabbed the collar of the guard who had come too close. He slammed him into the door, then shoved him away, then slammed him again. He repeated the back and forth movement three more times before he let go, and the man slid down and out of sight.

The sounds of fighting in the corridor had stopped.

Shile turned to wink at Lylene. She stepped closer to the window grating. Three bodies on the floor and Weiland taking the keys off one of them. She concentrated on him, on his welcome face, and tried to avoid taking in the bloody bodies. It was her doing, all of this.

"I was sure you'd come," Shile said.

"*I* wasn't sure I'd come," Weiland objected. But then he said, "They were talking in town about an execution planned for tomorrow, and I figured that had to be you." He got the door open and Shile flung his arm around him, almost toppling him.

Lylene would have hugged him, too, if she could have been sure of his reaction.

"How'd you get in?" Shile asked.

"Asked if they were hiring men and walked in."

Shile, no doubt remembering their disguises, sighed.

Weiland looked at Lylene appraisingly. She had taken off eight years since last night. "This life suits you," he observed dryly.

Was "thank you" appropriate under the circumstances?

Shile's dark eyes went from one to the other. "We better talk about a new plan. Weiland, we've lost track of the time—is it night yet?"

"Not quite supper."

"All right, it'd probably be safest to wait here until everyone goes to bed—"

"Watch'll change before then."

Shile stooped to loosen the sword belt from one of the guards. "We appreciate the timely rescue," he said, "but maybe a few more hours—"

"I talked to the guards who were going to be coming on. Their captain didn't seem one to take any nonsense. I didn't think I could talk him into letting me in, free ale or not."

Lylene, about to ask how he had come by the ale, decided she probably didn't want to know.

Shile looked up from taking a helmet. "My Lady, I'm afraid we'll have to make a guard out of you." He put one of the sword belts in her hand.

"I can't . . . I'll never pass—"

"Try it."

"Shile—"

"Try it."

"Be reasonable."

He reached into his pocket. "King, we do it my way; god, you come up with a plan."

"Shile—" she started as Shile flipped the old coin into the air.

Weiland caught it mid-spin and broke into a stream of profanity.

"What?" Lylene asked. "What is it?"

"Has he tried this before?"

She glanced at Shile.

"He knows how to control it. Nine times out of ten he can make it land on the side he's called."

"That's not possible." But Shile's face told her it was. "Blackguard," she said. "Cheater."

"Well," Shile said, "yes."

Weiland handed her the coin. "If you need it to make decisions, *you* do the flipping."

She nodded.

"But for now . . ." Weiland took the belt and fastened it around her waist. "We won't get out of here otherwise."

Shile put one of the helmets on her head. It smelled of stale sweat and slipped down almost to her eyes, with the noseguard overlapping her upper lip.

"Put your hair up," Weiland suggested. "That'll hide it and make for a snugger fit."

He must have done something of the sort also, for his distinctive blond hair didn't show. She made a quick braid. The helmet still smelled, but the fit was better.

Shile said: "If anyone asks, we're heading for the west tower— sent to help in a matter of some particularly audacious rats which have been terrorizing the women." He turned suddenly. "We met that friend of yours."

"Owen," Lylene said.

No telling from Weiland's expression what he thought of that.

As they passed through the guardroom, he suddenly turned to Lylene. "Here"—he had pulled a sheathed dagger from who-knew-where and held it out to her—"the sword's just for show. You'll need a weapon you won't kill yourself trying to use."

She hesitated. "Thank you."

Weiland made a sound of contempt. "Take it out and see if the handle's comfortable."

She slipped the blade partially from its sheath. "It's fine. Thank you."

Weiland snatched the weapon out of her hand and hooked it onto

her belt before she had a chance to protest that she could manage herself.
"Lady, is this a game to you, or what?"

"Leave her alone, Weiland," Shile said.

"No," Lylene said to Weiland. "This is no game."

Shile made to move between them, but she just raised her voice. "I
don't know what you expect of me. I was raised—" She knew it'd be
better not to say it but couldn't help herself. "I was raised in polite
company." That was to hurt Weiland, who she suspected couldn't say
the same. But his expression never changed. "My parents didn't think
to teach us how to use daggers and swords. But when my sister was
stolen away, I vowed to fight back. I've lied and cheated people and
hurt them and done so many shameful things, I can't even remember
them all. And the thing is . . . the thing is I'm not used to all this. *You*
tell me what to do, you point me in the right direction, and when the
time comes I'll take this knife and slit Theron's throat with it."

Weiland looked openly skeptical.

"I'm not going to back down or hamper you: I shall kill Theron."

She could tell by Shile's face that she had said the wrong thing,
that she had touched on something Weiland wasn't going to let pass.

Weiland said, "You stubborn, arrogant—"

"*Me?*" Of all the people to accuse her of that—and just when she'd
been letting herself start to like him—

"—self-centered—"

"Weiland," Shile begged, "leave it."

Weiland shrugged out from under his hand. " 'I will, I shall, I can.'
Since when do you have the gift of prophecy? Things are *never* what
you presume. You *presume* you know how you'll handle some situation,
but it's never exactly the situation you're prepared for. You say, 'If
that'd been me' or 'I'd never have done that,' but then it happens so
fast, or someone's there with you, or nobody's there, or something's
different, and your *presumptions* about yourself are wrong, and there
you are with no one else to blame and all the rest of your life to regret
it." Weiland sat down heavily on the table and crossed his arms across
his chest, daring her to disagree.

Not Lylene. She had no idea what he was talking about, and at the
same time she knew exactly what he was talking about.

Shile finally said, "Let us know when you're through."

Weiland continued to look down his nose at both of them for another few moments before standing. "I'm through."

"I'll take the lead," Shile said.

"You don't know your way around."

"You can tell me from behind."

It was to protect Weiland: Harkta's prophecy preyed on Shile's mind, no matter how he denied it—Weiland was the one in the greatest danger.

Lylene slowed so that Weiland had to either drop further behind and lose sight of Shile or catch up to her.

"The thing about regrets," she said, and this was new to her, too, "is that they don't change anything, and they eat away at you from the inside out until there's nothing left at all."

Weiland regarded her coldly for a moment. He lengthened his stride to close the gap Shile was forming. "I regret nothing," he said.

18

They only made it as far as the top of the stairs.

Lylene was puffing from the exertion—her added years were felt most keenly with stairs—and it was a long, steep climb that curved dizzyingly. They had just stepped through the doorway when a deep voice yelled: "Hey!"

Weiland swore under his breath, then pushed in front of Shile, muttering, "Frazier." To the guard, he said: "Sir?"

The man scowled at him, thumbs hooked into his sword belt. "You're the new man."

"Tearle," Weiland said.

"Yeah, Tearle. What were you doing down there?"

"Looking. Getting a feel for the lay of the place."

"You were shown around this afternoon."

"It's a big place."

The man wasn't sure. He inched his hand closer to the sword hilt. His eyes shifted warily. "And who are these?"

Confidently, aggressively, Shile said: "Damn, Frazier, it's me—Garrett. Is your memory slipping, getting too old? And you've got to remember Dillon." He gave Lylene a good-natured punch on the arm.

The fact that they knew his name made Frazier hesitate, mistrust his instincts. His hand stayed by the sword, though. He returned his attention to Weiland. "So what is this: Your first day on the job, and they give you the night off? You all got the night off?"

"He's supposed to be on the western bartizan," Shile said, inclining his head toward Weiland, "but he never showed up. Captain Owen sent us to fetch him. We found him drinking and gaming with the downstairs crew. I don't think he's going to work out at all."

Frazier looked almost convinced. "They're hiring lackwits." He started toward the door. "I'd better check on the watch if they've been drinking."

"No," Shile said, too quickly. "*They* haven't. Just . . ." He had obviously forgotten the name Weiland had used and finished lamely, "him." Frazier took them all in at a glance. "Oh." He stepped backward. "Well. So long as everything's all right."

Weiland went for his sword first, then Shile did.

Shile's hadn't cleared the scabbard when Frazier hit him in the face with his elbow, knocking him backward down the stairs. Part of the same movement: Frazier's fist slammed into Lylene above her heart. She felt her left foot go over the edge, skidding first off one step, then the next. She threw her weight forward so her right knee scraped the edge of the landing, but at least she broke her fall. Frazier kicked at her, hitting the crown of the helmet. It flew off and she heard it bouncing down the steep stairs.

He had drawn his sword now but turned to fend off Weiland.

She grabbed Frazier's leg and dragged on it with all her weight, distracting, putting him off balance.

Weiland slashed across his throat. Blood splattered Lylene, and then Frazier toppled. Weiland threw himself down to catch her arm before she had time to realize she was in danger. She let go of Frazier's leg, and he slid about halfway down the curved stairs before coming to rest against the wall.

Weiland leapt first over her, then over Frazier, hurtling down the stairs after Shile.

Lylene came two steps behind him all the way. "Sweet Saint Marcelle," she breathed, for the right side of Shile's face was bloody and his limbs were all at impossible angles.

Weiland knelt beside him, and she sank to her knees on the other side.

"Shile." Weiland leaned close and Shile's eyelids fluttered. More urgently: "Shile."

"S'alright," Shile muttered thickly, giving up on opening his eyes. "Doesn' hurt."

Which didn't sound good at all.

Weiland looked up at her, as though waiting for her—*her*—to tell him what to do.

She found Shile's hand, squeezed it.

He didn't respond at all. "Don' feel anything," he muttered. "Jus' dizzy. Jus' . . ."

She had to lean close to make sure that his chest was still moving, that he was still breathing, though common sense said that after the exertion of the fight and the fall, he should have been breathing hard, his chest heaving, as were hers and Weiland's.

Weiland leaned back on his heels. "He's dying."

She made a shushing motion. Shile didn't need to hear that.

"He's dying." His voice was flat, emotionless. Only his paleness belied her impression that he felt nothing.

She nodded, hating him anyway.

"Can your magic help?"

"No," she whispered.

He took a deep breath. "Then do whatever it is you do to become younger."

She looked at him in horror.

"In a couple moments he'll be dead, and it'll be too late." He reached over his dying partner to grab her arm, and she twisted away.

"Damn you," she said.

He took hold of her again, hard enough to hurt. "It won't make any difference to him, and it might help us get out of here alive."

"Let go of me."

"You're too old, you're too slow."

"Let go—"

He lunged to grab her gray braid at the nape of her neck and forced her down closer to the unconscious Shile. "Do it!"

She tugged at his fingers. "I hate you!"

"I don't care. Do it."

She could have transferred those years to Weiland. Perhaps he didn't realize that. Perhaps he trusted her not to.

She did consider it.

Instead, she took Shile's face in her hands and leaned to kiss his lips. She closed her eyes and saw him at the Happy Wench, watching her. *I'll help you*, his eyes said. Dark, sparkling eyes in which she'd seen loyalty and kindness.

She'd betrayed that once before, by creating Jerel and Duncan and Newlin.

There was no tingle this time, or perhaps she just didn't feel it. She opened her eyes. It was still Shile's face. But now the hair, except where it was plastered to his cheek with blood, was shot through with gray. The crinkles he'd always had at the corners of his eyes and mouth were exaggerated, and the cheeks were sunken. She caressed the sticky hair away from his cheek, and he sighed once. Then he didn't move again.

After a long while she looked up.

Weiland had let go of her; she hadn't noticed that. He must have got up and walked away, which she hadn't noticed either, for he was sitting now at the far side of the landing. He had taken off his helmet, and he sat—with his back to the wall and his knees drawn up to his chest—leaning forward, his face hidden.

She stood, wishing he'd died instead of Shile. Shile wouldn't have betrayed him. Shile wouldn't have betrayed either of them. Her braid fell in front of her shoulder, copper orange. Her hands were young, her face, the rest of her body. She'd be able to keep up now.

She pushed the braid back, and it was only that motion which made her notice there was something different about Weiland. He had taken off his helmet, but now she saw he hadn't braided or twisted his long hair to hide it—he had cut it off. Of course he'd have had to. He wouldn't have been wearing a helmet when he came to Saldemar, and that long hair, reminiscent of the Vikings, was too distinctive, would have been remembered from when he'd worked here before.

He looked up, his grimy face streaked with tears, which she hadn't expected. The roughly shorn hair and the tears made him look very young. He put his face in his hands, and his shoulders, shook hard enough she could see it from here.

She knelt next to him and he threw his arms around her. "It was supposed to be me," he said.

Which was when she remembered Harkta's prophecy was yet to be fulfilled.

19

"It was Shile always had the plans," Weiland said.

Lylene could sympathize with that. But it didn't help. "We have to get out of here. Out of the castle." Try again, she thought. Some other plan, some other people. God help her: Beryl had waited eight months, she could wait a few days more. "If we can hide someplace until tomorrow, until they open the gate—"

Weiland shook his head. "We'll finish it."

"Harkta said you'd die." Fear made her blunt.

"I'm already here. I might die trying to get out. I may as well die rescuing your sister."

It was hard to think, faced with that logic. "We have no plan," she reminded him.

Weiland talked slowly, considering. "They'll all be at supper now in the Great Hall. We'll go to her room, hide there till everyone's asleep, and then break out, the three of us."

"We can't just leave Shile," she said.

"Yes, we can."

She saw how much that cost and didn't argue.

It cost her, too.

He tossed her helmet to her, and they went up the stairs, ignoring the lifeless lump that had been Frazier.

Through passages they went, up stairs, across more passages, up more stairs. There were few servants about, but Lylene kept her head ducked down, just in case. It was in this stance that they rounded a corner and she almost bumped into a guard.

Weiland saluted, kept on walking. Lylene copied the gesture. Took one step beyond. Two. Three.

"You."

She closed her eyes, thinking, *Not again.*

"They finished downstairs yet?"

It took several thumping heartbeats to realize he meant supper and nothing to do with them or the dungeon.

Weiland said, "Who knows? We don't get our meal until we've checked for rats in the ladies' quarters."

"Rats?" the man repeated incredulously. He was eying Lylene, her blood-speckled shirt.

Weiland shrugged. "So the ladies say."

"Where, exactly?"

Beside her, she felt Weiland tense, about to go for his sword. Not here, she thought. It was too close to Beryl's room. Blood and dead bodies up here would raise too much commotion.

A bell rang loudly, clamoring alarm.

"That's the signal for escaped prisoners," Weiland said. "You take these stairs. We'll circle round by the kitchens." He slapped Lylene's arm to get her moving, and the two of them sprinted toward the back stairs.

But they stopped as soon as they saw the guard had followed Weiland's instructions.

Lylene leaned against the wall, feeling weak.

Weiland grabbed her arm and pulled her back the way they had come. "Here," he whispered, stopping in front of one of the doors. He listened for movement within, then took a torch from its socket on the wall and cautiously eased open the door.

The room was empty, though lit already. It was a lady's dressing area, more ornate than she would have expected, with thick tapestries on the walls and furs strewn on the floor to protect dainty feet from morning chills. There was a table littered with glass jars of ointments and creams, tortiseshell combs, ivory trinkets. At least Theron knew what the apartments of a woman of gentle birth should be like.

Weiland looked at her with raised eyebrows, then moved silently toward the inner room, the sleeping bower. He eased the door open.

Three guards waited in the bedchamber, standing with armed crossbows pointed at them.

And Harkta lay sprawled on the bed. Grinning.

"Ah, the conjurer princess," he said. "And her consort. You certainly did take your time."

Weiland flung the torch.

It *whoosh*ed through the air, over the wizard's head and between and beyond two of the guards. All instinctively ducked. And the torch hit the tapestry-hung wall behind.

Lylene turned to flee.

Standing in front of her, a drawn sword not a fingerwidth from her bosom, was a fourth guard.

And Owen stood before Weiland, in similar pose.

Behind Lylene, Harkta swore. The guards tore down the tapestry. There was already the stench of burning—wool and the more acrid fur of the floor throwings. Lylene could hear the men stamping out the fire.

"Bells ringing," Owen said, "people shouting, alarms in the night, fire in the west tower: I would have known anywhere it was you, Weiland." Owen walked around him appraisingly, tapping the sword pensively on Weiland's shoulders.

Don't, Lylene prayed, *don't*.

"You see—" Harkta scrambled off the bed—"I was right. I told Lord Theron they'd come here. I told him."

"You told him," Owen acknowledged. "You almost botched the capture, but you told him."

Harkta glared at the captain's back, stung by his rebuke. He lashed out at Weiland: "Prepared to die, villein?"

"He's just a hireling," Lylene told Owen. He was the power here, no matter what Harkta thought. *Not Weiland, too*, she thought. Of all the deaths she had caused—at least three, of men far more innocent—she couldn't bear the thought of Weiland's blood on her hands. "He's not responsible. I am. Theron's quarrel is with me, not him."

"Interesting," Owen said. "Interesting development."

Weiland stared at the floor.

Harkta was still trying to act like the one in charge. "Tie his hands," he ordered. "Get her sword."

The men waited until Owen nodded assent.

"Look," Owen said, "wizard: I don't like you. Lord Theron doesn't like you. He tolerates you because . . . Actually I don't know why he tolerates you. You're a mealy-mouthed, treacherous little worm. So don't press your luck."

Harkta flushed with embarrassment. And again took it out on the prisoners. "Laugh," he told Lylene, though she hadn't. "Go ahead. You always were a stupid girl. Mistake after mistake after mistake. The first thing you did wrong—today—was you didn't even think to ask if both of your companions would die."

The breath she sucked in hurt all the way down.

"And second—second, you little ninny—you didn't even have the sense to use your hard-earned magical ability: You should have used fetches of them. Then it wouldn't have mattered if they had died."

Emotions fell over each other to get to the forefront. Guilt. Rage. Grief. Fear.

Rage won.

She gave a cry as of pain and covered her face with her hands. She made her shoulders shake and gave loud sobbing noises.

"Ninny," Harkta gloated, coming in closer. That was like him: He had to rub it in, especially after being humiliated by Owen. "You never learned to use your brain." He tapped his finger roughly against her head.

She grabbed his hand and wished.

The guard standing behind her swore and took a step away.

Even the normally steady Owen was startled. "What the hell is that?" He looked from one form of Harkta to the other.

"You . . . You . . . You . . ." said the one on the left, the original, pointing at her, his face turning purple.

"How dare you?" the other demanded, a similar shade.

Weiland, his arms tied behind his back, gave her a wary glance that asked why they needed two Harktas.

"I want you to kill them," she said, without letting her eyes rest long on either Harkta. "I want you to kill all the guards, and Theron, too. Quick, look like you don't know what I'm talking about." It was pure fabrication, of course. The fetch was an exact replication of Harkta, with all of Harkta's hopes and fears and desires, and no more likely to do her bidding than the wizard himself. Only she and Harkta and Weiland knew that.

But to Owen, both Harktas were doing exactly what she had ordered: They were looking like they didn't know what she was talking about.

"Back," Owen quietly ordered his men.

The men fell back, fingering their weapons.

"Now see here," Harkta said. "This creature does not take her orders."

The second Harkta said: "That's true."

"Which—?" one of the guards asked.

"Me." Harkta pointed to himself. "I'm the original. That one's perfectly harmless, but kill it if that'll make you feel better."

"No!" the other said, Harkta's instinct for self-preservation strong in it. No matter that it would fade away before dawn, it didn't want to die now. "*I'm* the original."

"See here." Harkta laughed nervously. "Owen. Friend. It's me.

Just this afternoon, we stood in Lord Theron's chamber and toasted to our success.'' He forced a confident grin.

'' 'Excelsior,' we said,'' the fetch finished.

Owen's eyes flicked from one to the other.

"Magic?" Harkta offered. "Shall I prove it's me by doing magic?''

"Kill them both,'' Owen ordered.

Harkta, his hands raised in the opening gesture of a spell, and the fetch, turning to flee the room, both cried, "It's me!"

Lylene heard the *twang* of two crossbows releasing, then two muffled thuds. Both Harktas dropped to the floor.

Pain slammed into her heart. She staggered, moaning, and for one instant Harkta's fetch's fear was her fear; she shared his surprise, his denial, his pain. The room whirled and blackened.

The guard behind jerked on her collar, forcing her upright, leaving her panting and drained. Hearing returned, then sight. She felt her hands being tied behind her back, never having heard Owen give the order, never having seen Owen approach the lifeless bodies, though he was there now, with an expression of mild distaste on his face.

"Well," he said, "that'll save Theron a fat fee, so he won't be complaining." He stopped in front of Weiland. "Now for you. Where is he?"

"Who?"

"Your companion."

"Dead." Weiland looked away. "He died in the dungeon."

"Don't"—Owen held a finger in Weiland's face—"think our friendship is going to save you. I just came from the dungeon. He's not there—only four of our guards and one old man who has yet to be accounted for."

That hurt, more than Lylene would have thought.

"The old man is Shile. He—"

Owen nodded, and the guard behind kicked the back of Weiland's knee.

Weiland dropped.

With his left hand Owen yanked Weiland's short-cropped hair at the neck, forcing his head down. His right hand raised the sword. "No time for this nonsense. Last chance."

Lylene saw Weiland brace himself for the blow.

Owen saw it too and took that for his answer.

"It's true!" she cried as Owen heaved the sword up another handspan. "I did it magically. Stop!"

Owen slammed the sword down. The blade whistled through the air hitting the floor with enough force to chip the wooden planking.

Barely its own width in front of Weiland's face.

Owen jerked on Weiland's hair again, this time forcing his head back, forcing him to look up. "Suicidal fool!" he screamed.

Weiland, for once, was scared, was breathing hard.

"I thought you had more sense than that. I thought you were smart enough not to get yourself killed over some stupid whore of a girl." Owen gave one last angry yank on his hair.

Weiland looked as though his nerves were strung as far as they could go. He wouldn't be able to go through that again. All Owen had to do was ask, she thought, and Weiland would tell him everything, switch sides, anything.

Owen didn't ask. Instead, he said to the guards, "I'd better get Lord Theron's approval before something that irrevocable. You"—he indicated one—"go down to Hall and explain the situation. The rest of you, bring the bodies, so he can judge the likeness for himself."

One of the guards hesitated. "Leaving you—" he started.

"With two bound prisoners," Owen finished. "I think I can handle that."

Owen waited till they were alone in the room. Then, shaking his head, he used his sword to cut Weiland's bonds. "I swear this is it," he said. "Never again. We ever meet on opposite sides again, and I swear I'll kill you."

Weiland's reactions were uncharacteristically sluggish.

Owen dragged him to his feet and flung him toward the door. He cut Lylene's ropes and pushed her after him. "What the hell you want—an armed escort? Go. Get out of here. Try to keep out of Theron's way because if he captures you and sends you to me, I *will* kill you."

Weiland stiffened his arms out, preventing Owen from pushing him through the doorway. "What about you?"

"God's teeth! Do I have the entire garrison out searching the castle for me? I'll be fine if you just get the hell out of here. I'll say you got loose and overpowered me." He shoved them both toward the door. "Forget the slut," he advised Weiland.

It hurt, even though she knew he had every reason to believe it.

"And kindly don't steal any of the castle silver on your way out."

"Our swords," Weiland said.

As Owen turned toward the bed where the guards had thrown their weapons, Weiland slammed his elbow into the side of Owen's head. Owen staggered and Weiland hit him again. Owen dropped to the floor.

Lylene looked at Weiland in horror as he went to fetch the swords himself. Seeing her expression, he said, "He'll survive. They'd have never believed we overpowered him if he didn't have a mark on him."

It was obvious, and she was chagrined with herself for not realizing that, for thinking . . . But Weiland seemed to encourage that kind of thinking.

He fastened his sword belt before things apparently all caught up to him at once. He leaned against the wall with his hands on his knees, having trouble catching his breath. He looked up at her and shook his head.

She put her back to the opposite wall, suddenly weak herself. "You were prepared to die."

He regarded her blankly.

"Harkta's prophecy." She spoke between great shuddering breaths. "He never said you *would* die. Just that you had to be prepared to die."

Weiland looked as though he were seriously considering strangling all wizards, starting with her.

"Let's get out of here," she said. "Before Owen's messengers come back."

20

They *traveled at a run, through corridors, up stairs and down,* outside the main building, then back in.

Weiland finally paused in front of a door, checking to make sure no one was watching, then pulled her in. The smoothness of the move was balanced by the fact that he had to go back out to get a torch so they could see.

She removed her helmet, which was heavy and overly warm. They were in a room that was obviously used for weapons storage.

Weiland pulled a crossbow from its hanging place on the wall. "Know how to use one of these?"

She shook her head.

"I'll show you."

"I'm not very strong."

He put the weapon in her hands. "You don't have to be strong to use a crossbow. You don't have to be clever or skilled. You're supposed to be gentry, but I never let that stop me." He positioned her hands, then moved behind her, supporting her arms.

Lylene stiffened against his touch. Relax, she told herself. It was only Weiland, who had no designs on her body but was innocently teaching her how to kill more efficiently. She let him reposition his hands beneath her elbows, taking some of the weight of the crossbow.

"Sight." He pointed. "Trigger. Crank. The arrow—the bolt—fits in here, like this." He reached around to show her.

He won't hurt me, she told herself; but she already knew that. Overall, the sensation was a pleasant one, and that was what scared her. How could Weiland have this effect on her? She wished, as she had used to

wish when she was a little girl—before she had seen it was useless—
that she could be pretty.

"Higher. If it slips, you'll release into your foot. See this? All right,
back. That's the way." He pointed out the window, to a target leaning
against the wall that surrounded the keep. "See that bullseye?"

"I can't—"

Weiland turned her around, his cheek almost touching hers, his arms
around her, supporting her. "Steady. It'll kick back a bit. *Don't* close
your eyes. Steady. Release."

The release did throw her back against him, but the bolt hit the
target, which was a surprise.

"Good. Try it again. Keep your eyes on the target, even after you
release." He stepped back for her to do it on her own.

She told herself she missed his touch because she wouldn't be able
to do it without him.

She hit the target, though not in the center this time.

He handed her another bolt.

This time she got it loaded more smoothly and it hit between the
first and second shots.

Weiland reached around her again. "Here," he said. "Pull it up
closer—"

She turned her face to look at him just as he turned to look at her.
"Pull it up closer," he repeated, softly, "like this." That shown, he
stepped away, his eyes downcast.

This arrow landed almost in the center.

"You're a born archer," he said. But he suddenly sounded as awkward, as self-conscious, as she felt. And he avoided her eyes, which he
had never done before.

Weiland selected a wooden bow for himself, and two quivers—one
of arrows, the other crossbow bolts. "You don't want to over-practice
and tire your arms out." He glanced at the door. "We better get going."

She took two deep breaths.

He tossed the torch in the corner by the wooden practice-shields.
The flame sputtered, caught, began to grow.

"You're becoming alarmingly fond of setting fires lately." It wasn't
what she wanted to say.

He stood by the door waiting, and she didn't say anything else.

Again they went running through the castle passageways.

A man, an unarmored knight or servant, opened a door. A moment
later and they would have run into it. "Hey!" the man called after them.
"Where—"

Weiland turned, raising his bow, and fired.

The man toppled behind the door, and Lylene had no idea whether he was injured and hiding or dead.

Weiland slowed long enough to ready another arrow, not long at all, then picked up the pace again.

They stopped short of the last door. Weiland whispered even though the noise from the room was loud enough that he probably could have shouted and gone unnoticed. "You fire to get their attention. I'll keep them covered."

They stepped through the open doorway.

There were several entrances to the Great Hall. Weiland had chosen one that opened above. Stairs followed the curve of the outside wall, leading down into the huge room. A strategic position, she recognized, easy to defend. The air was thick with smoke. Her eyes took a moment to adjust. Her ears were assailed by the din: many conversations going on at once while servants clearing off the tables clattered dishes. Someone strummed a stringed instrument. Two large dogs were fighting over something found under one of the tables, and in their struggles they pulled down the cloth and the platters still on it.

Owen's men had to have arrived before them. Apparently the death of the wizard hadn't been considered worth interrupting supper for.

She could see why Weiland had told her to get their attention. Nobody even noticed them.

She surveyed the crowd. There. There was Beryl. She appeared unharmed. She sat at the main table in a low-cut green gown, her pale blonde hair in a multitude of intricate braids that framed her flushed and pretty face.

And that, sitting next to her, his arm draped over her shoulder so that his hand came close to resting on her breast, that must be Theron. Skinny blond moustache, cold blue eyes.

Lylene concentrated on keeping her arms steady, and sighted.

Weiland leaned down to put his mouth by her ear. "We don't want Theron dead."

"We don't?"

"Kill him like this, and be prepared to be hunted for the rest of your short miserable life. Church and King and people who for years have wanted Theron dead will be after you."

She spared him a sidelong glance.

"*Not this way*," he insisted. "Not like some sneak assassin. Proclaim yourself."

"*Chivalry*, Weiland?"

"For our own protection."

"And then?"

"And then anything. But proclaim yourself first."

Weiland was always, she reminded herself, the one with both feet on the ground.

She found Theron's coat of arms hanging on the wall behind the table and sighted on that. Steady. Eyes on. She released.

The bolt cut through the thick smoky air with a hiss and thudded into the snout of the boar's head mounted to the right of the coat of arms.

No matter. It did get their attention.

Immediate silence. Broken only by the dogs, still snarling and circling each other, their nails clicking on the flagstones until someone reached down and cuffed one of them.

All those eyes, looking up, looking at her. And at Weiland with his bowstring drawn back, poised and ready while she reloaded.

Theron got to his feet and motioned his men not to try anything—at least for the moment.

Weiland stepped back, so that Lylene was in the forefront. She wanted Theron to know what was happening. And why. "Do you know who I am, *Lord* Theron?"

"The Lady Lylene Delroy of Dorstede." She thought she detected the slightest hint of a quaver in his voice. "My wife's sister."

"Just so you know." Lylene brought the crossbow up the way Weiland had shown her.

"Lylene! No!"

Lylene paused at the familiar voice. "Beryl?" She lowered the bow slightly. She was aware of Weiland still beside her, still with his bow drawn.

Her sister stepped forward from behind the table. Stepped forward to Theron's side. "Lylene, don't. You don't understand."

Lylene looked at the pretty, upturned face, at the golden hair. "Get away from him!" she warned, for he could easily grab Beryl and use her as a shield.

"Lylene, sister, listen. Theron's been kind to me—"

"He's responsible for Shile dying!" Lylene cried. This wasn't going at all the way it should have. "He killed Aunt Mathilde."

Beryl ignored the first part, as she always ignored what she didn't understand. "I heard about Mathilde, Lylene. But it was an accident."

"Accident?" Lylene cried. "How can you call what happened at Delroy an accident? Was the arrow they shot through your husband's heart an accident?"

Beryl looked close to putting on the pout she had worn whenever Lylene refused to play by her constantly changing rules. "Lylene, Randal is not the point. The point is Theron is a kind and gentle man who has treated me very well . . .''

She kept on talking, but Lylene stopped hearing. Theron had treated her well, Theron had treated her well: The words went round and round Lylene's head. She had seen the fine furnishings in her sister's room, the exquisite hangings in the Hall—all mirroring Beryl's tastes. Suddenly the gown of green silk embroidered with gold seemed to Lylene a more grown-up version of the kind of dresses Beryl had always favored.

Weiland moved closer, so that his arm was against hers, solid reassurance, steadying her.

Beryl stood below, her hand resting lightly on the front of her gown, her face chubby and content, her breasts full and rosy where the gown was cut low, and the gown . . . the gown . . .

Lylene noticed for the first time what should have been readily apparent: that Beryl was heavy with child; her time must be near. ''You're expecting a baby,'' she blurted out.

Beryl stopped what she was saying, closed her eyes and sighed. ''Yes, dear sister, I'm expecting a baby.''

''And you're protecting this man—*this man*—who killed the father of your child?''

''Lylene!'' Beryl stamped her foot, as Beryl was always wont to do. ''Lylene, Theron *is* the father.''

Lylene's hand shook on the bow. That seemed all the more reason . . . But she was obviously missing something. If Randal . . . If Theron . . . Beryl had only been gone eight months . . . She felt icy fingers stroke her soul. ''When is the baby due?''

''Lylene—''

''*When is the baby due?*''

Beryl turned pale. She stepped away from Theron, putting space between herself and trouble. ''Lylene,'' she said, tipping her head prettily to one side, as she had done since childhood.

''You planned it,'' Lylene said. ''The two of you planned it. You murdered Randal so you could get his lands and titles, and you didn't care how many other people got killed along the way.''

''That's not true,'' Theron said. ''Some of my men got out of control, and I had them properly disciplined.'' He moved closer to Beryl, who sidestepped away from him.

''*I* told him it wasn't a good plan,'' Beryl said. ''You can't believe *I*'d have anything to do with killing people.''

''You murderer!'' Lylene whispered, cutting off the protest Theron was about to start. She swung the bow up. ''I gave up everything for you! People have died for you!'' She realigned the arrow, aiming for Beryl's ivory throat. She found the trigger. She watched Beryl's hand scrabble for Theron's. "*People have died for you!*" She drew back the trigger and released.

Just as Weiland jostled her arm.

The arrow angled up and sideways, struck one of the banners, then dropped to the floor.

"Sorry," Weiland murmured, his bow still aimed and at the ready. "Shall I go down and hold her for you, do you think, to make sure you hit her this time?"

Lylene's shaking got out of control. "Damn you," she said to him. The crossbow fell from her numb fingers. She turned and ran.

"Back off!" she heard Weiland snarl at someone. And then he was in the corridor running beside her. "Lady, this way."

"Let go of me." She beat at his hands.

"Lady," he said between clenched teeth and shook her. "Do you want to die, or do you want to live?" It was just like Weiland to cut through to the basics.

"I want to live," she conceded.

21

He dragged her to a narrow archer's loop, and for a moment she feared he was going to try to get her to squeeze through and either jump or climb down. Instead, he only leaned out and shouted: "Fire! Fire in weapons storage! Sound the alarm!"

Without waiting for a reaction, he took off again.

Outside, a bell started ringing. "Why *up*?" she shouted as they started up a flight of stairs.

"Because they'll be guarding all the downstairs exits." He let go her arm and threw open a window shutter. "Go." He lifted her through the window and onto the rampart walk, a jump no higher than from a horse. Immediately she crouched below the level of the parapet, and in an instant he was beside her.

They peeked over the edge. The soldiers' quarters were almost directly beneath. Smoke poured into the night sky from the fire Weiland had set, and guards and servants had already begun to rush back and forth with water buckets.

Weiland tapped her shoulder, motioned for her to follow.

They ran at a half crouch because the wall was crenellated for defense: high, wide merlons to hide behind, spaced by narrow embrasures from which to shoot. All anybody below needed to do was look up at the wrong moment . . .

They rounded to the northern face of the keep, and here Weiland slowed.

"What's—"

He cut her off with a glare. He was studying the parapet. Counting, she realized, just as he stopped at one of the merlons. He reached up to the top and brought down a coil of rope, which he proceeded to tie around the merlon.

She looked through the opening. It was a long, long way down.

Weiland wrapped the other end of the rope around his waist, put his arm through the bowstring and slung the bow around his back. "I'll go first. You come down at the same time, so I can help support your weight."

She nodded, hoping he didn't notice she was shivering. "Lucky the excitement is away from where you hid the rope," she whispered. Then, as he tugged to make sure the rope was secure: "Or did you plan to set that fire all along?"

"No." Weiland went over the side, and the rope went taut. He braced his feet against the wall. "Take the rope. Spread your hands. Come on, swing over: I'll support you. *Don't close your eyes.*"

She tore her attention away from the ground and concentrated on the length of rope above Weiland's hands.

"Lady."

It all came down to whether she trusted him. She squeezed through the embrasure, felt her heart go in one direction, her stomach in another, and then Weiland had an arm around her waist and his shoulder under her rump.

"Get your feet against the wall. Hand under hand—if you slide, the rope will burn."

"I'm all right," she assured him. "How did you happen to choose here to hide your rope?"

"I didn't. I hid one on each face."

She started to look at him but caught a glimpse of treetops and far-off ground. "I thought you said Shile always did all the planning." They seemed to be plummeting down the sheer side. "You're moving too fast."

He didn't counter that she was moving too slow.

Just when she thought it couldn't get worse—with the rope biting into her hands, and her arms and shoulders straining—he said, "The rope isn't long enough. We'll have to jump."

"What?" She finally looked earthward and saw that they were only thirty or forty hands up.

"Hold on. Don't slide."

She had thought she was doing a good job of supporting her own weight, but as soon as he was gone, she felt the almost unbearable tug on her arms.

"All right, let go," he called. "I'll catch you."

There was the possibility that she could break both legs if he missed. She took a deep breath and let go.

He caught her.

She held onto him even after she caught her balance and her breath. "Owen meant her," she said. "I thought he was talking about me. When he said you shouldn't be risking your life for a whore."

"Lady . . ." He shook his head helplessly.

She finally let go of him. "What now?"

He sighed. "Try to scale the outer wall, I guess. Theron will have his men coming out the front, and the fire brigade's taken over the back."

"Scale the wall?" she asked. "If they don't pick us off while we're still trying to make it up there, then we'll walk home?"

He folded his arms, waiting.

"The people putting out the fire don't look very well organized. Shile . . . Shile would have gone up to them waving his arms, talking loud and fast, given them some orders, and circled around past to the stables."

"I'm . . . not Shile," he said.

"And I can't talk or they'll know I'm not a guard."

In the end they had no choice but to do it her way.

They came round into the inner bailey at a run, Weiland swearing loudly. "Who's in charge here?" he bellowed. "What is this? Can't you move any faster? Keep that line straight. Can't they get the water out here any faster?" The louder he shouted, the more the workers tried to stay out of his way. "You"—he pointed at Lylene—"come with me, and we'll see what can be done."

They dodged through the line of workers and headed off in the direction of the well, which was also the direction of the stables.

"Fire!" Weiland shouted, any stablemaster's nightmare. "Burning embers on the roof."

Only one man came out—apparently Theron hadn't gotten here to post guards yet. Lylene pointed to the roof, and the man stepped back to see. Weiland dropped the bow off his back and nocked an arrow.

"Where?" the guard was demanding. "I see no sm—"

The arrow hit him in the back, and he toppled without a sound.

"Why couldn't you just have knocked him out?" Lylene demanded as Weiland dragged him into the stable, out of view.

He counted out on his fingers: "One, too risky. Two, we'll be in here too long. Three, don't question my methods. *Don't*," he added as she opened her mouth—"say anything."

She didn't. Instead, while Weiland saddled the horses, she walked up and down the aisles making duplicates of Theron's horses.

Weiland finally looked up. *"What are you doing?"* he demanded.

"Hopefully, confusing Theron's men. I just put a little bit of power into those duplicates. Anybody that chooses a made horse to come after us will find himself on foot in a very short while."

He swore, softly, still distrustful of her sorcery.

She held up the knife he had given her. "I've also been slashing saddle girths."

This time he did flash a smile. "Good work. Get up."

She realized he'd saddled Shile's horse. She shook her head. "I can't ride him. Where's Harkta's?"

"This is the better horse."

"That makes no difference if I can't ride it."

"He's well trained, and he'll follow mine. All you have to do is hold on."

"Shall we flip a coin for it?"

"Will you get on the goddamn horse?"

She got on the horse.

They rode as fast as they thought they could without raising suspicion.

"Is there a postern gate?" she called to him.

"No."

That left the way they had come in, through the barbican. There had been two guards then, plus, presumably, one in the upper room which housed the mechanism for the drop-gate.

As they approached, Weiland shouted up to the guards: "Did they get out? Has anyone lowered the portcullis?"

Five guards stepped out of the shadows, three armed with crossbows, two with swords.

"Have you lowered the portcullis?" Weiland demanded again. "What's the matter with you? Give the order."

The guards hesitated, and by then Weiland and Lylene were too close. "The bowmen," Weiland told her, and she aimed her horse at one of those guards, praying that the man had the sense to get out of her way.

Weiland drew his sword, and he slashed at one of the bowmen, then rode down a second.

The last scrambled to get out of Lylene's path. He released the bolt too quickly, and it flew harmlessly against the barbican wall. Shile's horse reared, recognizing attack and flailing his hooves at it. Lylene held on with hands and knees and will. She thought the guardsman was hit, but didn't know for certain. Didn't want to know for certain.

Weiland had wheeled his horse around and was going after the two swordsmen.

There was still, Lylene knew, a guard in the upstairs room. She caught a glimpse of movement through the *meurtrière*, the hole in the ceiling: the guard positioning himself with a crossbow. She tugged on her horse's reins, causing it to sidestep toward the wall. She grabbed a torch from its bracket and flung it up into the hole. She heard the guard curse and knock the torch away. "Weiland!" she called and pointed up.

He had killed the remaining two guards and now leapt from his horse's back, swinging up on top of the barbican and scrambling into the windlass-control room through the window.

Lylene grabbed another torch, duplicating it even as she threw it up into the *meurtrière*. She made another, threw that one also, hoping that she was distracting the guard more than hampering Weiland.

Through the barbican, from the direction of the keep, she could hear men yelling and horses galloping. No sight of them yet. She made another torch.

"Lady. Enough. Keep one." Weiland reached down from the opening to take the other from her. "Ride out to the other side of the drawbridge."

"But—"

"Start duplicating that torch, and drop them onto the drawbridge."

"Guards are coming. What are you doing?"

"I'm trying to set this torch so that it'll burn the windlass ropes after we're out but before anybody else can pass through."

"Hurry." If Weiland mistimed, the portcullis would drop and trap him in the castle. She urged her mount through the barbican, gazing up, as she passed, to see the spiked ends of the gate. If Weiland mistimed badly enough, the portcullis would drop while he was passing under it.

She started doubling torches, letting them fall on the wooden drawbridge.

She heard the thud as Weiland dropped down from the upper room. Behind him, she could now see the approaching mounted guard, about fifteen men, with a second, larger, party behind.

Weiland swung onto his horse, keeping low. Two crossbow bolts flew past where his head would have been if he'd been sitting upright. "Go!" he shouted at her. But she stayed to see him make it past the deadly portcullis. His horse clattered over the drawbridge, disregarding the fires. "I said *go*—dammit, don't you ever listen?"

An arrow whistled between them.

She put heels to the horse's sides, but Weiland had been right: The horses knew they belonged together. Shile's horse had started even before she moved, as soon as Weiland passed, and quickly lengthened its stride until the ground flew precariously beneath them.

More arrows flew at them, the mounted archers' aim shaken by the speed they were traveling.

There was a crash and the unmistakable screaming of a horse in pain: Weiland's torch had eaten through the rope.

She saw Weiland check over his shoulder. She didn't dare—not at the speed they were traveling. Somebody must have made it through the gate and over the drawbridge, for he didn't slow down. They were passing through the outlying farms, and no cover in sight.

Another flurry of arrows, fewer this time, and almost spent. Weiland glanced back once, then a second time, then pulled his horse to a stop. Shile's horse stopped, either because she pulled up on the reins or because Weiland's had.

She turned.

Behind them, six knights were on foot—and, from the look of them, very suddenly on foot. Saddles and equipment were strewn on the ground with them—but no sign of any horses. A seventh knight was still mounted, but finding himself the lone pursuer, had decided to turn back.

Lylene leaned forward, exhausted but unable to keep the satisfied grin off her face as she turned to Weiland.

He saw her watching him, and wheeled his horse about. "That downed gate and burned drawbridge aren't going to hold them back forever," he said.

"You're welcome," she answered.

22

"**T**he trouble with relatives," Weiland said when they felt safe enough to let the horses—and themselves—rest, "is that nobody checks beforehand to see whether you want them."

"I don't have any relatives," Lylene said.

"Neither do I," Weiland said. "But Shile . . ." He didn't finish that thought. When he finally spoke again, it was only to ask, "What are your plans?"

She was unable to make anything of the tone. Or the expression either. She had never thought beyond Beryl before. "My aunt is . . . was . . . a friend of the abbess at the convent of Saint Marcelle sur la Mer." She probably would have ended up there anyway, once Beryl was settled. Now that she realized she owed the Bishop of Glastonbury an apology, now that she realized that the Church hadn't been plotting against her but had simply recognized the situation for what it was. . . . It wouldn't be a bad life—quiet, provided for. Not what she'd been used to the past several months. She'd learned a lot, and some of that she'd have to work very hard to forget.

Weiland said nothing, and she turned to face him. He was sitting on a downed tree, making aimless patterns in the dirt with a stick. There was a faint breeze, which played with his hair, whose shortness was a constant reminder of what they'd been through.

She rubbed her sweaty palm on her breeches. (Shile's breeches, Shile's horse, Shile's Phoenician coin.) "I don't have anyplace else to go." She could have kicked herself for admitting that. It sounded as though she wanted him to take her under his care, which was, of course, totally inappropriate, and anyway, he was bound to say no.

He didn't answer. What could he have said?

"How about you?" she asked.

"I don't know. Set off north, I guess."

"What's north?"

He shrugged. "I've never been there."

"Ahh," she said, trying to sound as though that was promising, trying to sound as though he'd said he was really a baron's son with inherited lands waiting for him.

They weren't good for each other, she told herself. They were too different, and neither would ever understand the other.

"Do you *want* to be a religious?" Weiland asked.

It was the safe thing to do, and would only cost her freedom. "No," she admitted. She had learned she didn't need anyone to take care of her. She had her magic, and surely people made their way in the world with less.

"We could ... If you wanted ... Maybe it might ..." Weiland closed his eyes, obviously unused to and frustrated by this inarticulation. "I thought, maybe ..."

Make your wager, she thought. *Hope for the best. And throw the dice.*

"Yes," she agreed.

He released a breath.

"Work together?" she supplied. "See how it goes? Nothing definite, nothing permanent, just until something better comes along for either of us?"

He nodded, slowly.

"Yes," she repeated.

He had a nice smile, actually, when he wasn't scowling.

She didn't let that distract her. "On condition."

"What," he said, "condition?"

"Well, for one thing, I will not use my magic power to make temporary money to pay our way."

He considered, then gave a terse nod.

"For another thing," she went on before he could say a word, "I would appreciate your not stabbing or shooting people in the back any more than absolutely necessary."

He folded his arms across his chest.

"And then there's your language."

"My what?"

"It's probably no worse than half the other men in the country, but you've got to consider my background: I find it offensive to hear the name of our Lord and Savior used casually or in anger."

She almost lost him there. He took a deep breath. Looked at her levelly. Then finally said, "I will try. Is there anything else you don't like?"

"Well, I'm not especially fond of that narrow-eyed look you're giving me right now, but I suppose I can live with it."

"Jes—" Weiland started, but bit it off. "I have a condition too."

It was Lylene's turn to hold her breath.

"That you refrain from questioning every move I make."

Lylene released her breath. "I will try," she agreed.

And she did.

Though it was easier some days than others.

Just Another Dragon-Slaying

Bad enough, Lylene thought, having the kind of dragon which demands young virgins at regular intervals: after all, only a small percent of the community is directly affected, commerce continues more or less as usual, and those most personally involved are prohibited by age and sex from sitting at council where policy is determined. It's quite another matter when a dragon goes on a general rampage, laying waste to valuable farmland on which all depend, devastating trade, scattering tax records and recorders alike.

Lylene thought about economic exigencies and evaluated the blackened fields, the scorched and/or flattened cottages, and decided she had seen worse. The citizens of Cheldenholme would not be relieved to hear that. They were no doubt in a state approaching panic despite the fact that, uncharacteristically, the most serious damage was to the outlying areas.

Lucky townspeople, Lylene thought.

Lylene didn't believe in luck.

Approaching the center of the town, she snapped the reins to get the draft horses moving faster and nudged Weiland with her foot. Then she glanced at him, slouched next to her, with his arms folded across his chest, and she saw that he was awake after all, and making his own silent appraisals.

They were used to getting more of a reaction. The expensive destriers tethered to the back of the wagon were unusual enough, as was her waist-length copper-colored hair. But then there was Weiland's hair—blond and shoulder-length, evidence of a Viking heritage—more noticeable even than his weapons, the swords and knives and daggers he wore ostentatiously tucked into belt and harness.

She slowed to avoid a barefooted child's gaggle of geese, then pulled the horses to a stop in front of the wealthiest-looking house: the one made of stone. Here, finally, was attention: a score of townspeople clustered, their faces pinched in disapproval.

Weiland looked at her with raised eyebrows.

Lylene scrambled from the wagon. Though she barely came to Weiland's shoulder, she was as tall as most of the men they faced—too tall, her mother had always complained. Weiland insisted her height was an advantage. She tried to bear this in mind as she addressed an elderly man in the forefront, a merchant by his dress, who was flanked by another merchant and a clergyman. "You sent for us?"

The man's eyes flicked from Weiland to Lylene back to Weiland. "You're the wizard?" he asked, as though unsure whether that should be a source of relief or concern.

"Yes," said Lylene, and nothing more until he faced her again and not Weiland. "I am the wizard."

The priest made the sign of the cross while the crowd muttered warily.

"You?" the second merchant sputtered. "But you . . . you're . . . you're . . ."

"You're a *woman*," the first finally got out, in a tone which could, conceivably, have been surprise.

"Yes," she said.

The three drew in, to confer in frantic whispers. The rest of the crowd, eager to voice their opinions also, swallowed them up.

Lylene played at nonchalance. She wasn't used to doing the talking; normally Weiland set things up. But their constant bickering of the last few weeks had escalated into a full-fledged argument that morning, an argument she had ended by declaring that, after all, *she* was the wizard and therefore *she* was in charge.

"You want me to leave?" he had asked.

"No!" That was instinctive—and came out sounding panicked. Then, "No," she'd said, "damn you. We're in this together. We agreed. The advance is spent, and you're not backing out now and leaving me to do this all by myself."

He'd said nothing, sitting beside her in the wagon, distractingly close.

"The dragon first. Then you can suit yourself. I don't care."

"All right." Weiland had been, as always, impenetrably cool.

And now he offered no help at all, but only watched with his infuriating bland but superior expression.

Annoyed all over again, she forced her attention to the countryside.

Cheldenholme was situated next to a small lake, dominated by a mountain which had a vast stretch of level ground almost at the top. Dragon country. It didn't take an expert to see that.

Weiland, she could tell, was focused in closer, gauging the townspeople.

"Our agents," the elder merchant said, breaking away from the priest—who, by his fluttery hands and sour expression, hadn't had all his say—"our agents were supposed to hire a wizard."

He was going to demand back the advance fee, she could tell.

"May I be so bold as to ask what sort of magic you specialize in?" the second merchant cut in.

"Multiplications," she said. "And divisions."

"I beg your pardon?"

Beside her, Weiland shifted position. Had it been anyone else, Lylene would have thought it idle fidgeting. But she knew Weiland never made idle moves, and the townspeople seemed to guess that too. Several backed away a pace or so.

She hoped nobody noticed her face flush with annoyed embarrassment at his unsolicited aid. "I will collect the balance of my fee when the dragon is gone," she said.

The elder glanced around for support, found it wasn't coming, and nodded.

"We will need a room—clean and well lit, either an inn or someone's home."

In a tone indicating his worst presumptions had been confirmed, the priest said, "One room?"

The two merchants tried to unobtrusively shoulder him back, into the anonymity of the crowd.

But she only said, "Yes." Let them think what they would: despite any disagreements, she and Weiland always closed ranks in times of danger. And this, she was convinced—despite the plain peasant faces and the innocuous words—surely qualified.

Evening. The door to the room—neither clean nor well lit—flew open, banging into the wall, and she jumped. But it was only Weiland, come back from scouting out the town. He unbuckled his sword belt and tossed it onto the bed beside her, then started removing his knives one by one.

"Well," said Lylene, as though he hadn't left fully six hours earlier, "so what do the townspeople have to say?"

"They wonder why a wizard needs a bodyguard."

Bodyguard. Lylene shrugged. Whatever Weiland was, he wasn't her bodyguard.

He rested his foot on the bed to take the long thin blade from his boot. "We're in the barony of Sir Tirrell de Montgrise."

She fought to pay attention. She had been startled, not only by the suddenness of his entrance but by the fact that he had returned at all. On the best of days, there was always the possibility that he would not. And this had certainly not been the best of days. She prepared herself for the inevitable by repeating each time they separated that this was the time, and that it made no difference. It never got easier.

If Weiland noticed her tendency to jump whenever he entered a room, he never mentioned it.

"So what has this Sir Tirrell of Montgrise done to try to kill the dragon?"

"Ah. Well." He glanced up and flashed his cold smile. "Nothing."

"Nothing?" She thought back to the man who had contracted them. What had originally seemed innocently vague now seemed dangerously elusive. "Who's paying us—Tirrell or the town?"

"Town." Weiland unfastened the leather harness that housed most of his weapons—or at least most of the ones he wanted seen.

"But that doesn't make any sense."

"No. It doesn't."

Angry with herself for being so desperate for companionship, she finally observed, "You were gone a long time."

It was his turn to shrug. He nodded toward her papers, papers she had bought, along with a certain package, from a Saracen trader just back from the Orient. "Figure out how to use that magic powder?"

"As a matter of fact, yes. Figure out how to use that bent sword?" If he thought she had thrown their money away buying the powder without a demonstration, she didn't see what he wanted with yet another weapon, particularly such an awkward-looking one.

"Curved," he corrected. "Scimitar. Someday." He pulled his shirt over his head, and she glanced away, unwilling to admit to the fluttery things he did to her resolve, even when she was angry. "Do you get the bed," he asked a bit too smoothly, "being the wizard, and in charge and all?"

She pulled out the old Phoenician coin they kept for such decisions. "King or god?" she asked, tossing it into the air. They had bedded together, she and Weiland, those nights it had been too cold to think of anything else, and that time he'd held her throughout the night when she'd been convulsed with fever, an arrowhead in her shoulder. But sex was one complication she knew they didn't need, and perhaps Weiland knew it too, for it was one of the few things about which he didn't give her an argument.

"King," he said as she caught the coin against her thigh.

Lylene checked, then dumped her things onto the floor. Normally she'd say something like, "I hope the bedding has fleas," but tonight that seemed to be pushing too far. "I'll take first watch," she said instead.

Wrapped in the spare blanket, watching the flickering shadows the undoused candle made on the rough plastered walls, she listened for the low rumble of talk and laughter and song which normally comes from an inn's common room, and heard none of it.

Dawn was hot and humid.

The two of them passed close enough to the abbey, halfway up the mountain, to hear the bells ring for the sunrise prayers of Prime. A little farther on, they rested, and that was when they saw the dragon. It circled the mountain summit lazily, and when its enormous shadow touched her skin, Lylene shivered. It was big. Much bigger than the townspeople had indicated. This was Lylene's third dragon, and they were always bigger than the townspeople indicated. But if she and Weiland worked fast enough, they'd be gone before it returned from its foraging.

By the time the brothers at the abbey would be singing Tierce, she and Weiland had reached the broad, flat expanse visible from the town of Cheldenholme below.

It was as though the peak had been split vertically, and one half removed. The level rock on which they stood was scored with grooves, which Lylene thought were probably from the dragon's talons, and spattered with dark stains that didn't bear thinking on at all. The remaining half of the peak was hollowed out, forming a huge cave.

Between them and that cave was a knight, sitting on horseback, watching them.

He lowered his lance, with the soft metal whisper of chain mail, and said: "I respectfully request you to leave."

Lylene's horse snorted, pawing at the hard ground. She patted its neck and told the knight, "Listen, it's all right. You don't understand. I'm a wizard. There's nothing to worry about. I—"

"I respectfully request you to leave," he repeated.

For a moment she felt light-headed. Nothing seemed to fit, and she had to start fresh. "Are you here to fight the dragon?"

He hesitated a moment too long before answering, "Yes."

"One of Baron Tirrell's men?"

He inclined his head.

"I see."

Despite the heat, he was wearing a helmet, and the noseguard gave his face the distorted, anonymous look of any other knight, in any other place. His chain-mail tunic sparkled in the sunlight, though the eastern half of the sky was filling with dark thunderclouds. Did dragons mind rain? On top of everything else, did she have to worry that the creature was even now heading back here? "We could stay," Lylene suggested, "in case—"

"No."

It was more than knightly arrogance could account for. Lylene believed the part about Baron Tirrell, but not that the man was here to fight the dragon. Which left that Tirrell wanted to stop them. But why? Why would anybody want to protect a dragon?

"Please get out of the way," she said. Then, when the man made no move, she said to Weiland: "Get rid of him."

She meant, *Scare him off*, but when she turned to him, she saw that he had been sitting with his hands crossed over the reins. And Lylene knew there was a small throwing knife hidden in the leather bracer that bound his left wrist, the wrist on which his right hand was resting.

Before either of them had time to do anything—Weiland to extract the knife or Lylene to protest (which she would have done, she assured herself)—Baron Tirrell's knight let drop the lance which gave him such an advantage and drew a sword. This he raised before his face, commending his soul to God.

"I am Sir Sherard, son of Volney," he declared, formality which startled them, "and I normally do not fight unarmored men, sir. But if you persist, I must challenge you for the right to be here. Should I win, you must depart, with no further questions; should you win, you shall, of course, do as you please."

"Chivalry," Weiland said, almost a purr, "how nice." His hand dropped from his wrist and went for his own sword.

Lylene fought back her horse, which—battle-trained—wanted to join the coming fracas. She dragged on the reins, but that only pulled him into a tight circle just as Weiland and the knight Sherard came at each other. She missed seeing the first blow, but whoever struck it, the other parried successfully.

In fact, in almost no time Lylene saw that the fight was just about evenly matched, certainly more even than Weiland was used to.

"Back!" she snapped at her horse. She thought to use sorcery to help Weiland, but realized she couldn't bring herself to it, and that was a surprise, to find at this stage of her life that there were some things, after all, which were beneath her.

Sherard moved in to parry what turned out to be a feint, left himself overextended and unbalanced as Weiland began the real slash. He tried to wheel about, but Weiland's mount kicked his on the shin, and horse and knight both went down. He hit the ground and rolled, just missed getting his head caved in as his horse struggled to regain its feet.

Weiland leapt off his horse to close in and finish the fight before the other could regain his orientation. But the knight was not so badly rattled as it had seemed he must be: his foot lashed out, hooking behind Weiland's leg, and Weiland came down hard, sitting, his sword skittering across the rocky ground. It was over that quickly.

Sherard, who had somehow held onto his own weapon, was already back on his feet, holding that weapon against the base of Weiland's throat.

"No!" Lylene cried, though logic said that had Sherard intended, Weiland would have been skewered already.

Weiland remained motionless, his arms extended behind for balance.

Without moving the sword, Sherard included her with an upward nod of the head. "I have successfully overcome you on the field of combat. Agree you to depart?"

"Yes," Lylene said even as he was still speaking.

The knight hesitated.

"Yes," Weiland said.

Sherard sheathed his sword and removed his helmet, revealing a chubby, well-scrubbed face. "It was a well-fought fight." He extended his hand to help his opponent to his feet.

Weiland winced, as though more than his pride had been hurt. Sherard took him by the arm, supporting his weight. Weiland let him do all the work, then drove his elbow into the side of the knight's head.

Sherard dropped, probably without knowing what had hit him.

Weiland rubbed his elbow and looked down at him. "Jackass," he said.

His action, Lylene complained as he bound and gagged Sir Sherard, had been unfair and reprehensible.

Weiland, never loud, let his voice drop practically to a whisper. "If you feel that bad about it, we could still do what he asked, and leave."

She turned her back on him. In the end, that was the only argument with which she was left: that she *had* no argument, but that at least she didn't like it. She turned her back on him and left him. There wasn't much time. The sky was ominously dark for the hour, and the papers she had purchased from the Saracen indicated the spell wouldn't work in the wet. There was also the danger that the threat of rain could bring the dragon back to its den.

She knelt before the cave. With her hands around, but not touching, the package for which she had paid the entire fee from their last job, she closed her eyes against the glare that always formed. A second package pressed against her hands, forcing them farther apart. Again she concentrated. Two more packages materialized; then those also doubled.

When they grew again to sixteen, she stacked the packages so that they would be less bulky. She was aware of Weiland, crouched just off to one side, watching with his usual dispassionate interest.

"Isn't that enough?" he asked. "How many do you need?"

"Better too much than too little."

Finally satisfied, she saved the original package for future use, since her duplicates had a tendency to fade after several hours, and were always gone within a day. She tied that one behind her saddle, then went to help Weiland arrange the others inside the cave.

Baron Tirrell's man, Sherard, had come to, and was watching with eyes grown large. Lylene glanced at the still-darkening sky and considered ordering him to help; but while she would have trusted him had Weiland won fairly, trust under these circumstances seemed risky.

Finished, Weiland stretched, pressing against the small of his back. "Use him, why don't you?" he suggested, with a nod toward Sherard.

She shook her head.

"I mean for your magic."

"I know what you mean," she snapped, angry with herself because she hadn't known, not for sure, and the clarification, by its very nature, chilled her. She looked away, shook her head again. "Get Sherard mounted, then I'll need you."

Weiland approached, gingerly as always, and now angry as well. She put a hand on either side of his shoulders and closed her eyes. This was her one advantage, the only thing no one could touch. In her darkest moods, she didn't care. She put less energy into this than she had with the powder, for she wanted a mere fetch, an image, not an exact duplicate which would have a life and feelings of its own. The first time she had used her sorcery like this, she had felt the death of the creature she had made, had felt it *know* its death, an anguish inside her head from which she had thought she would never recover. But, of course, she had.

She stepped back, unable to look this duplicate Weiland in the eye. "Go into the cave," she said. "When the dragon returns, let it see you."

The fetch nodded, expressionless. There was no telling at this point how much it knew or felt.

Weiland had never looked at it, was single-mindedly attending to his horse. They had discussed once whether she might be all unwittingly chipping away at his life, at his very soul: a double murder. Weiland insisted he felt nothing more than squeamishness at the sight of his own form on someone, something, else. Would he know?

No danger, the one who had given her the power had said, but that had been no friend—hers or Weiland's. She would have used Sherard, could she be certain his fetch would do what she commanded.

They took the same path down as they had used to come up, though Sherard's presence indicated there were others. They rode where they could, walked when necessary. During a rocky, narrow stretch that was easier on foot, she removed Sherard's gag, warning, "One wrong word, and it'll go right back on." She had seen the way his pale face had stolen glances at her, but still she waited for him to nod before unfastening the cloth.

"The hands stay tied," Weiland growled, tethering Sherard's mount to his own.

And Lylene, for the third or fourth time, said, "We're not going to harm you."

Again Sherard nodded, obviously forcing himself to believe.

The black clouds closed in, smelling of imminent rain, and she rubbed her chilled arms. "Now. What's going on with this dragon? Why doesn't Tirrell want it destroyed?"

Weiland, never interested in motivations, walked ahead, guiding the two horses.

Lylene held onto her own reins and fell in next to Sherard. "Why?" she repeated.

Sherard moistened his lips. "Money."

"How do you mean?"

"The Baron sold some land and rights to the townspeople, which he now regrets. He stands to get them back at a good price should the people be desperate enough."

"If the land is temporarily unusable," Lylene mused. Then, another thought: "Or the people dead."

Sir Sherard, the honorable knight, shrugged.

Up ahead, Weiland suddenly swore. A living black shadow swooped down to the heights they had just left. Even from this distance, she could feel the whoosh of air from its passing.

They all instinctively pressed against the side of the mountain, though if the dragon had looked their way, it would have seen them; and if it had seen them, they were beyond help already.

In the lead, Weiland picked up the pace.

Sherard held his hands out to her. "If you unbound my wrists, I could move faster."

Lylene stopped, but Weiland, without turning back, called: "No."

She hesitated, watching him broaden the distance between them. Sherard waited. "Come on," she told him, avoiding his eyes.

The path, a narrow shelf on the outside edge of the mountain, narrowed yet more so that Lylene and Sherard had to go single file, her horse between them. "Tirrell thinks he can control *that?*" she called back to him. No doubt but that he'd follow: protecting an absent dragon is one thing, going back to warn it is another.

"Now what?" he panted.

"Hopefully the dragon will become enraged when it sees what looks like a human challenger in its cave."

"It'll incinerate him."

"Yes." She was glad he couldn't see her face.

"Those packages you were making—what was in them?"

"Magic powder from Cathay, east of the Holy Land."

"Poison?"

"No. It—"

Above them, at the mountain's almost-summit, Weiland's fetch died.

Lylene fought for air. The repercussions of her creation's never-vocalized scream threatened to shatter her skull. She pressed her hands to her ears, shuddering convulsively, and sank to her knees even though she knew she was inches from the edge.

The top of the mountain blew off, and the ground beneath them shook.

Over the incredible crashing noise, she was aware of Weiland shouting her name, unable to get around the suddenly frantic horses which separated them. Her own horse shied and reared, missed trampling her by chance alone.

They were spattered by falling stones, and a huge boulder hit the shelf to which they clung, shattering the section they had crossed seconds earlier.

A loud *crack!* and an entire section of the mountain behind them seemed to just crumble away.

Sherard was trying to calm her horse which separated them, and Weiland was leaving, going on without them after all, pulling the two other horses with him.

"Look out!" Sherard cried, and Lylene pressed herself tighter against the mountain as another boulder bounced down the steep slope. It skipped over her, hit the shelf just beyond her knees, splintering it even narrower. Her horse made an almost human scream, then was gone in a flurry of sliding debris.

Lylene put her hands on the unsteady rock wall behind and grappled herself to her feet. Sherard ducked a smaller flying rock, was suddenly beside her, once more holding his bound wrists to her. "Cut the rope!"

She reached for the knife Weiland insisted she wear, and the mountain shuddered again.

Sherard, unable to fling his arms out for balance, tipped precariously. Then slowly, so slowly that it seemed Lylene had all of time to grab for him, he slid over the edge, and her hands closed on empty air.

She reached too far, teetered out of control, saw the ground tip up to catch her.

Then straighten again. At a safe distance again. Weiland was holding onto the back of her shirt, pulling her from the crumbling edge. "Sherard," she said, but he wasn't interested. He guided her, dragging her when she stumbled, to where the path widened—to where he had been able to maneuver his way around the horses.

"Overhang," he shouted over the noise, pointing. "Do we take our chances out here, or risk getting trapped?"

Nothing, she figured, could be worse than this. They crawled into the tight space, coughing from the dust of crushed rock, and huddled with their arms around each other, silently praying that it wouldn't collapse on them. Or at least Lylene prayed: there was never any telling with Weiland.

Eventually the ground stopped quaking. Their overhang had stood firm. They crawled out into a new landscape, a landscape where even the birds had been shocked into silence, and the mountain had taken on a new shape entirely.

Somehow Weiland had wrenched a knee. (She assumed he had wrenched it. The alternative—having to do with the dead fetch, with the progression of dead fetches—was too awful to consider.) He was able to walk, but only by leaning on her. Lylene kept waiting for him to say, "I told you that was enough powder," but he didn't, which was even worse.

For her part, she kept thinking that if she had untied Sherard's hands when he first asked, he would still be alive.

The surviving horses, Weiland's and Sherard's, they found grazing peacefully by the abbey. The avalanche had swept away at least one of the annex buildings and damaged several others, including the granary.

The monks were scurrying about trying to get the scattered wheat and barley under cover, out of the light drizzle which had started. They gave Lylene and Weiland baleful stares, but said nothing.

Silently, the two of them mounted the horses and continued toward Cheldenholme. Her horse, carrying the magical powder which had cost so much, was gone without a trace.

The drizzle turned to a fierce rain, and they were soaked by the time they reached the town. A good section of the town wall was crushed under a new arm of the mountain, which had moved on to flatten the adjoining houses.

Townspeople peered out of windows. Not a word was spoken. At the inn, their belongings had been removed from their room and placed in their wagon, which was standing, hitched to the workhorses, all unprotected in the rain.

Lylene clenched her teeth, and didn't look at Weiland.

They rode on to the house in front of which they had stopped the day before. Now there was nobody there, friendly or not, to greet them.

"Yo! Townsman!" Weiland called. When there was no answer, he dismounted stiffly and banged on the door, He sighed, then kicked in the door.

Lylene followed him in. She caught a glimpse of a badly aged twenty-year-old who clutched several children by the unlit hearth and who watched Weiland drip rainwater on her well-scrubbed floor. The older of the merchants to whom she had spoken the day before approached, brandishing a wooden stave. But Weiland stood there, with his arms crossed over his chest as though daring him, and the man let the weapon drop.

"We got rid of the dragon," Weiland said cooly.

The merchant tried twice before he got his voice to work. "It destroyed an entire warehouse this morning before you got around to it," he finally answered, angry enough to transcend his fear, "and *you*: you took down half the town wall, scattered rocks over two-thirds of the few fields the dragon had left us, destroyed seven shops—including my brother-in-law's—killed five people, injured a score more, caved in the public well, and pelted the whole community with barrel-sized pieces of roast dragon."

"Well," said Weiland, "those things happen."

Lylene stepped forward. "I'm sorry. The magic I used was stronger than I had thought. We'll settle for half the balance of the agreed-upon fee. The rest can go to the affected families."

"Half?" the merchant squeaked. "*If* that would pay for the damages—which it would not—"

Weiland grabbed him by the front of his shirt.

"We don't have it," the merchant whispered.

"You don't have what?"

"The rest of the fee."

Weiland turned to her, still holding onto the merchant. "Shall we burn down the town?"

"What do you mean, you don't have the fee?" Lylene asked. "What trickery is this?"

"No. No trickery. We *had* the money. But the town alderman . . ."

"What?" Weiland shook him.

"Made off with it. We're still looking for him."

"All this since morning?"

The man squirmed. "Two weeks ago."

"Let's burn the town down," Weiland repeated.

Lylene turned and pushed past him. She walked out of the house, past Sherard's horse, past the inn with their wagon parked in front, past the rubbled wall. She kept walking, through fields ruined that day and before, until she slipped in the wet and landed on her knees in the mud, with the rain beating down on her bowed back.

Eventually she heard the rattle of the wagon coming up behind her. She didn't look up, even when Weiland came round to stand before her. Absently, she noticed that his limp had gotten worse. "Did you burn down Cheldenholme?" she asked.

"It *is* raining," he pointed out, which she hoped, in a detached sort of way, meant no.

"I've been thinking about leaving." She finally looked at him. "This isn't working, you know, you and me together."

He stooped down in front of her, wincing at the movement, close enough to touch.

But never touching.

"Sometimes," she said, "sometimes your conduct is despicable."

"Mine?" he asked, his blue eyes wide with innocence and amazement that she could say such a thing. But she remembered too many things, and knew better. He flashed a smile. "Ah, but you've known that from the beginning."

She nodded, wouldn't look at him anymore.

"So you want to divide up the things, then? Go our separate ways?"

"I don't know what I want." She rested her face in her hands. "I'm too tired to think. You decide, Weiland."

When he didn't answer, she looked up. He shook his head, refusing the responsibility; and the cold rain continued to pelt them. Finally he reached forward, took her money purse.

At first she thought it was to count the money for dividing, but he took only the old Phoenician coin. With a questioning look, he held it in front of her. "King, we stay together; god, we separate," he suggested.

She nodded, thinking she was too tired to care, much less to make the decision. But by the time the coin reached the top of its arc, she found herself wishing which face would land up.

Which was a good thing, because that's the one that did.